Critical acclaim for THE PIANO TUNER

'Confidently weaving historical fact together with his own imaginative constructions, Mr. Mason creates a riveting narrative, spangled with fascinating asides . . . a seductive and lyrical novel that probes the brutalities and compromises of colonization, even as it celebrates the elusive powers of music and the imagination' – *New York Times*

'An extraordinary, finely crafted work of fiction . . . a lovingly reconstructed Victorian travelogue' – *Independent*

'An intriguing and alluring first novel . . . those strange images of Europe meeting the east, of the east engulfing Europe, linger like a haunting tune' – *Guardian*

'Mason is amazingly adept at creating the sense of place that novels of this ilk thrive on. It's as if the exotica that is Burma in the mid 19th century is a character in its own right' – *Denver Post*

'[An] accomplished first novel . . . an engrossing read . . . like the hapless Edgar himself, beguiled by Carroll's beautiful Burmese mistress into forgetting the wife he has left behind, the reader falls under the spell that the author is weaving, surrendering the considerations of mere realism to the story's exotic magic' – *The Times*

'A thrilling and atmospheric adventure story' – *Spectator*

'So cinematic you can almost hear the popcorn crunching . . . a haunting, passionate story of empire and individuality that couldn't be more timely' – *San Francisco Chronicle*

'Mason's writing achieves that kind of reverie in which every vision, tone, flavor and sensation is magnified. The scenes are rendered with resolute command, alive with lush metaphor' – *Los Angeles Times*

'Mason memorably evokes the Burmese landscape, at once exotically beautiful and menacing' – *Sunday Times*

'A virtuoso tale . . . a depth of quirky historical knowledge and a feel for the brutal politics of colonialism . . . a complex and subtly imagined adventure . . . a highly dexterous and involving performance'
– *Observer*

'This is an exquisite novel. It will captivate your heart and mind with its beautiful language and its evocative characterisation'
– *Good Book Guide*

'His powerful prose style and his ability to embrace history, politics, nature and medicine within a fully imagined 19th-century fictional world . . . are astonishing' – *New York Times*

'Daniel Mason has woven together an elegant and unusually engrossing story, one that offers the reader the best possible journey – into a world that no longer exists. Rich, atmospheric and evocative of the sights, smells and textures of nineteenth-century Burma, *The Piano Tuner* is an astonishingly accomplished first novel. I truly enjoyed it.' – Arthur Golden, author of *Memoirs of a Geisha*

'Mason's novel is a richly imagined, densely textured and technically assured debut . . . as an adventure story it is supreme'
– *Daily Mail*

'Daniel Mason's stylish debut brings poise, understatement and subtle evidence of intense research to the historical fiction genre . . . Mason's achievement lies in the evocation of a lush physical world of sunlight and shadows, myths and fears and the ongoing clash between cultures' – *Irish Times*

'Mason proves himself equally adept at scenes of wry humour and moments of rapture; most remarkable, he has written a profound adventure story with an unexpected climax' – *New Yorker*

'Bottom line: A first-rate concerto con brio' – *People*

The Piano Tuner

DANIEL MASON received his bachelor's degree in biology at Harvard in 1998 and spent a year studying malaria on the Thailand–Myanmar border, where much of *The Piano Tuner* was written. He is currently a medical student at the University of California, San Francisco.

DANIEL MASON

The Piano Tuner

PICADOR

First published 2002 by Alfred A. Knopf, Inc., New York

First published in Great Britain 2003 by Picador

This paperback edition published 2003 by Picador
an imprint of Pan Macmillan Ltd
Pan Macmillan, 20 New Wharf Road, London NI 9RR
Basingstoke and Oxford
Associated companies throughout the world
www.panmacmillan.com

ISBN 0 330 49266 7

A CIP catalogue record for this book is available from
the British Library.

Typeset by Intype London Ltd
Printed and bound in Great Britain by
Mackays of Chatham plc, Chatham, Kent

FOR MY GRANDMOTHER, HALINA

'Brothers,' I said, 'O you who, having crossed
a hundred thousand dangers, reach the west
to this brief waking time that is left
unto your senses, you must not deny
experience of that which lies beyond
the sun, and all the world that is unpeopled.'

Dante, *Inferno*, Canto XXVI

Music, to create harmony, must investigate discord.

Plutarch

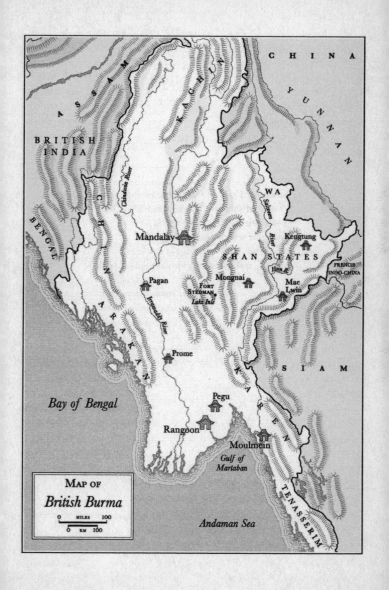

CHINA

ASSAM

YUNNAN

BRITISH
INDIA

Chindwin River

KACHIN

WA

Salween River

Mandalay

Kengtung

BENGAL

CHIN

SHAN STATES

FRENCH
INDO-CHINA

ARAKAN

Pagan

Irrawaddy River

Mongnai

Hun R.

Mae
Lwin

FORT
STEDMAN
Lake Inlé

SIAM

Prome

KAREN

Bay of Bengal

Pegu

Rangoon

Moulmein

*Gulf of
Martaban*

TENASSERIM

MAP OF
British Burma

0   MILES   100

0   KM   100

Andaman Sea

In the fleeting seconds of final memory the images that will become Burma are the sun and a woman's parasol. He has wondered which visions would remain — the Salween's coursing coffee flow after a storm, the pre-dawn palisades of fishing nets, the glow of ground turmeric, the weep of jungle vines. For months the images trembled in the back of his eyes, at times flaming and fading away like candles, at times fighting to be seen, thrust forward like the goods of jostling bazaar merchants. Or at times simply passing, blurred freight wagons in a travelling circus, each one a story that challenged credibility, not for any fault of plot, but because nature could not permit such a condensation of colour without theft and vacuum in the remaining parts of the world.

Yet above these visions the sun rises searing, pouring over them like gleaming white paint. The Bedin-saya, who interpret dreams in shaded, scented corners of the markets, told him a tale that the sun which rose in Burma was different from the sun which rose in the rest of the world. He only needed to look at the sky to know this. To see how it washed the roads, filling the cracks and shadows, destroying perspective and texture. To see how it burned, flickered, flamed, the edge of the horizon like a daguerreotype on fire, over-exposed and edges curling. How it turned liquid the sky, the banyan trees, the thick air, his breath, throat and his blood. How the mirages invaded from distant roads to twist his hands. How his skin peeled and cracked.

Now this sun hangs above a dry road. Beneath it a lone woman walks under a parasol, her thin cotton dress trembling in the breeze, her bare feet *carrying her away towards the edge of perception. He watches her, how she approaches the sun alone. He thinks of calling out to her, but he cannot speak.*

The woman walks into a mirage, into the ghost reflection of light and water that the Burmese call than hlat. *Around her the air wavers, splitting her body, separating, spinning. And then she too disappears. Now only the sun and the parasol remain.*

Dear Mr Drake,

I have been informed by our staff that you have received our Office's request for service in the name of Her Majesty, but have not yet been notified as to the nature of your mission. This letter serves to explain the specifics and urgency of a most serious matter, and requests that you report to the War Office, where you will be further briefed by Colonel Killian, Director of Operations for the Burma Division, as well as myself.

A brief history of this matter. As you are most likely aware, since our occupation of the coastal states of Burma sixty years ago, through the recent annexation of Mandalay and Upper Burma, Her Majesty has seen the occupation and pacification of the territory as central to the security of our Empire throughout Asia. Despite our military victories, several developments seriously endanger our Burmese possessions. Recent intelligence reports have confirmed the consolidation of French forces along the Mekong River in Indo-China, while within Burma local insurgence threatens our hold on the remoter regions of the country.

In 1869, during the reign of the Burmese King Mindon Min, we stationed in Burma a physician named Surgeon-Major Anthony Carroll, a graduate of University College Hospital in London, who, in 1873, was appointed to a remote post in the Shan States, in the eastern reaches of the colony. Since his arrival, Surgeon-Major Carroll has been indispensable to the army, well beyond his immediate medical duties. He has made remarkable progress in forming alliances with native princes and, although distant from our command, his site provides critical access to the southern Shan Plateau, and rapid deployment of troops to the Siamese border. The details of Carroll's success are rather unusual, and you will be duly briefed when you report to the War Office. Of concern to the Crown now is a most peculiar note received from the Surgeon-Major last month, the latest in a series of somewhat vexing communications regarding his interest in a piano.

The source of our concern is as follows: although we are accustomed to receiving unusual requests from the Surgeon-Major with regard to his medical investigations, we were perplexed by a letter which arrived last December, requesting the immediate purchase and delivery of one Erard grand piano. At first, our officers in Mandalay were sceptical about the enquiry, until a second message arrived by courier two days later insisting on the seriousness of the demand, as if Carroll had correctly anticipated the incredulity of our staff. Our reply, that the delivery of a grand piano was logistically impossible, was answered by the arrival of yet another breathless messenger one week later. He brought a simple note, whose contents merit reprinting in full:

> Gentlemen, With all due respect to your Office, I hereby resubmit my request for a piano. I know the importance of my post to the security of this region. Lest the urgency of my request again be misunderstood, be

assured that I will resign my post if the piano is not delivered to me within three months. I am well aware that my rank and years of service entitle me to honourable discharge and full benefits, *should I return to England.*

Surgeon-Major Anthony J. Carroll,
Mae Lwin, Shan States

As you might imagine, this letter precipitated serious consternation among our staff. The Surgeon-Major had been a flawless servant of the Crown; his record was exemplary, yet he understood well our dependence on him and his alliances with the local princes, as well as how critical such alliances are for any European power. After some debate, we approved his request and an 1840 Erard grand piano was shipped from England in January, arriving in Mandalay in early February, and being transported to the site by elephant and on foot by Carroll himself. Although the entire escapade was the source of considerable frustration for some of our staff in Burma, nevertheless it was a successful mission. In the following months, Carroll continued his fine service, making excellent progress in surveying supply routes through the Shan Plateau. Then last month we received another request. The humidity, it appears, has stretched the body of the Erard such that it is no longer in tune, and all local attempts to mend the instrument have failed.

And thus we arrive at the intent of this correspondence. In his letter Carroll specifically requested a tuner who specializes in Erard grands. While at first we replied that perhaps there was some easier means by which the piano could be repaired, the Surgeon-Major remained adamant. At last we agreed, and a survey of London piano tuners has produced a list of several fine craftsmen. As you must know, most of the practitioners of your craft are quite advanced in age and not fit for difficult travel. A more detailed enquiry led us to the names of yourself and Mr Claude Hastings of Poultry, in the City. As you are listed as an expert in Erard pianos, we felt it appropriate to solicit your services. Should you refuse our request, we will proceed to contact Mr Hastings. The Crown is prepared to reimburse you with a fee equivalent to one year's work for service of three months.

Mr Drake, your skills and experience commend you for this mission of extreme importance. We would request that you contact our office as soon as possible to discuss this matter.

Respectfully yours,

Colonel George Fitzgerald,
Assistant Director of Military Operations,
Burma and East India Division

It was late afternoon. Sunlight streaked through a small window to light a room filled with the frames of pianos. Edgar Drake, Piano Tuner, Erards-a-Speciality, put the letter down on his desk. An 1840 grand is beautiful, he thought, and he folded the letter gently and slid it into his coat pocket. And Burma is far.

BOOK ONE

fugue [from French *fugue*, an adaptation of the Italian *fuga*, literally 'flight'; from the Latin *fuga*, related to *fugere* to flee.]

1. A polyphonic composition constructed on one or more short subjects or themes, which are harmonized according to the laws of counterpoint, and introduced from time to time with various contrapuntal devices.

2. *Psychiatry.* A flight from one's own identity . . .

The Oxford English Dictionary, 2nd edn (1989)

ONE

IT WAS AFTERNOON in the office of Colonel Killian, Director of Operations for the Burma Division of the British army. Edgar Drake sat by a pair of dark, rattling heating pipes and stared out of the window, watching the sweep of rain. Across the room sat the Colonel, a broad, sunburnt man with a shock of red hair and a thick moustache, which fanned out in combed symmetry, underlining a fierce pair of green eyes. Behind his desk hung a long Bantu lance and a painted shield, which still bore the scars of battle. He wore a scarlet uniform, edged with braid of black mohair. Edgar Drake would remember this, for the braid reminded him of a tiger's stripes, and the scarlet made the green eyes greener.

Several minutes had passed since the Colonel had entered the room, drawn up a chair behind a deeply polished mahogany desk and begun to thumb through a stack of papers. At last he looked up. From behind the moustache came a stentorian baritone. 'Thank you for waiting, Mr Drake. I had a matter of urgency to attend to.'

The piano tuner turned from the window. 'Of course, Colonel.' He fingered the hat in his lap.

'If you don't mind, we will begin at once with the matter at hand.' The Colonel leaned forward. 'Again, welcome to the War Office. I imagine this is your first visit here.' He did not leave time for the piano tuner to respond. 'On behalf of my staff and superiors, I appreciate your attention to what we consider a most serious matter. We have prepared a briefing regarding the background to this affair. If you agree, I think it would be most expedient if I summarize it for you first. We can discuss any questions you may have when you know the details.' He rested his hand on a stack of papers.

'Thank you, Colonel,' replied the tuner quietly. 'I must admit that I was intrigued by your request. It is most unusual.'

Across the table the moustache wavered. 'Most unusual indeed, Mr Drake. We do have much to discuss of this matter. If you haven't recognized it by now, this commission is as much about a man as it is about a piano. So I will begin with Surgeon-Major Carroll himself.'

The piano tuner nodded.

The moustache wavered again. 'Mr Drake, I will not bother you with the details of Carroll's youth. Actually, his background is somewhat mysterious, and we know little. He was born in 1833, of Irish stock, the son of Mr Thomas Carroll, a teacher of Greek poetry and prose at a boarding school in Oxfordshire. Although his family was never wealthy, his father's interest in education must have been passed on to his son, who excelled at school, and left home to pursue medicine at University College Hospital in London. Upon graduation, rather than open a private surgery as most were inclined to do, he applied for a position at a provincial hospital for the poor. As earlier, we have few records for Carroll at this time, we only know that he remained in the provinces for five years. During this time he married a local girl. The marriage was short-lived. His wife died in childbirth, along with their child, and Carroll never remarried.'

The Colonel cleared his throat, picked up another document, and continued. 'Following his wife's death, Carroll returned to London, where he applied for a position as a physician at the Asylum for the Ragged Poor in the East End during the cholera outbreaks. He held this post for only two years. In 1863 he secured a commission as a surgeon on the army medical staff.

'It is here, Mr Drake, that our history becomes more complete. Carroll was appointed as a doctor to the 28th Foot in Bristol, but applied for a transfer to serve in the colonies only four months after his enlistment. The application was accepted immediately and he was appointed deputy director of the military hospital in Saharanpur in India. There he gained an early reputation not only as a fine physician but also as somewhat of an adventurer. He frequently accompanied expeditions into the Punjab and Kashmir, missions which put him in danger from local tribes as well as Russian agents, a problem which persists as the Tsar tries to match our territorial gains. There he also earned a reputation as a man of letters, although nothing that would suggest the, well, let us say, fervour that led him to request a piano. Several superiors reported him shirking rounds and observed him reading poetry in the hospital gardens. This practice was tolerated, albeit grudgingly, after Carroll apparently recited a poem by Shelley – "Ozymandias", I believe – to a local chieftain who was being treated at the hospital. The man, who had already signed a treaty of cooperation, but had refused to commit any troops, returned to the hospital a week after his convalescence, and asked to see Carroll, not the military officer. He brought with him a force of three hundred, "to serve the 'Poet-Soldier'" – his words, not ours, Mr Drake.'

The Colonel looked up. He thought he saw a slight smile on the piano tuner's face. 'Remarkable story, I know.'

'It is a powerful poem.'

'It is, although I admit the episode was perhaps somewhat unfortunate.'

'Unfortunate?'

'We are getting ahead of ourselves, Mr Drake, but I am of the mind that this matter with the Erard has something to do with the "soldier" attempting to become more of a "poet". The piano – and, granted, this is just my opinion – represents a – how best to put this? – an illogical extension of such a strategy. If Doctor Carroll truly believes that bringing music to such a place will hasten peace, I only hope he brings enough riflemen to defend it.' The piano tuner said nothing and the Colonel shifted slightly in his seat. 'You would agree, Mr Drake, that to impress a local noble with recitation and rhyme is one thing, to request a grand piano be sent to the most remote of our forts is quite another?'

'I know little of military matters,' said Edgar Drake.

The Colonel looked at him briefly before returning to the papers. This was not the kind of person ready for the climate and challenges of Burma, he thought. A tall, thin man with thick, greying hair which hung loosely above a pair of wire-rimmed glasses, the piano tuner looked more like a schoolteacher than someone capable of bearing any military responsibility. He seemed old for his forty-one years; his eyebrows were dark, his cheeks lined with soft whiskers. His light-coloured eyes wrinkled at their corners, although not, the Colonel noted, in the manner of someone who had spent a lifetime smiling. He was wearing a corduroy jacket, a bow tie and worn wool trousers. It all would have conveyed a feeling of sadness, the Colonel thought, were it not for his lips, unusually full for an Englishman, which rested in a position between bemusement and faint surprise and lent him a softness which unnerved the Colonel. He also noticed the piano tuner's hands, which he massaged incessantly, their wrists lost in the cavities of his sleeves. They were not the type of hands to which the Colonel was accustomed, too delicate for a man's, yet when they had greeted each other, the Colonel had felt a roughness and strength, as if they were moved by wires beneath the callused skin.

He looked back to the papers and continued. 'So Carroll remained in Saharanpur for five years. During this time he served on no fewer than seventeen missions, passing more time in the field than at his post.' He began to thumb through the reports on the missions the Doctor had accompanied, reading out their names. September 1866 – Survey for a Rail Route along the

Upper Sutlej River. December – Mapping Expedition of the Corps of Water Engineers in the Punjab. February 1867 – Report on Childbirth and Obstetric Diseases in Eastern Afghanistan. May – Veterinary Infections of Herd Animals in the Mountains of Kashmir and Their Risk to Humans. September – the Royal Society's Highland Survey of Flora in Sikkim. He seemed compelled to name them all, and did so without taking breath, so that the veins on his neck swelled to resemble the very mountains of Kashmir – or so thought Edgar Drake, who had never been there or studied its geography, but who, by this point, was growing impatient with the notable absence of a piano from the story.

'In late 1868,' the Colonel continued, 'the deputy director of our military hospital in Rangoon, then the only major hospital in Burma, died suddenly of dysentery. To replace him the Medical Director in Calcutta recommended Carroll, who arrived in Rangoon in February 1869. He served there for three years, and since his work was mainly medical we have few reports on his activities. All the evidence suggests he was occupied with his responsibilities at the hospital.'

The Colonel slid a folder forward on the desk. 'This is a photograph of Carroll in Bengal.' Edgar waited briefly, and then, realizing he should rise to accept it, leaned forward, dropping his hat on the floor in the process. 'Sorry,' he muttered, grabbing the hat, then the folder, and returning to his chair. He opened the folder on his lap. Inside was a photo, upside-down. He rotated it gingerly. It showed a tall, confident man with a dark moustache and finely combed hair, dressed in khaki, standing over the bed of a patient, a darker man, perhaps an Indian. In the background there were other beds, other patients. A hospital, thought the tuner, and returned his eyes to the face of the Doctor. He could read little from the man's expression. His face was blurred, although strangely all the patients were in focus, as if the Doctor was in a state of constant animation. He stared, trying to match the man to the story he was hearing, but the photo revealed little. He rose and returned it to the Colonel's desk.

'In 1871 Carroll requested to be moved to a more remote station in central Burma. The request was approved, as this was a period of intensifying Burmese activity in the Irrawaddy River valley south of Mandalay. In his new post, as in India, Carroll busied himself with frequent surveying expeditions, often into the southern Shan Hills. Although it is not known exactly how – given his many responsibilities – Carroll apparently found the time to acquire near fluency in the Shan language. Some have suggested that he studied with a local monk, others that he learned from a mistress.

'Monks or mistresses, in 1873 we received the disastrous news that the Burmese, after decades of flirtation, had signed a commercial treaty with France. You may know this history; it was covered quite extensively in the newspapers. Although French troops were still in Indo-China, and had not advanced past the Mekong, this was obviously an extremely dangerous precedent for further Franco-Burmese cooperation and an open threat to India. We immediately began rapid preparations to occupy the states of Upper Burma. Many of the Shan princes had shown long-standing antagonism to the Burmese throne, and . . .'. The Colonel trailed off, out of breath from the soliloquy, and saw the piano tuner staring out the window. 'Mr Drake, are you listening?'

Edgar turned back, embarrassed. 'Yes . . . yes, of course.'

'Well, then, I will continue.' The Colonel looked back at his papers.

Across the desk, the tuner spoke tentatively. 'Actually, with due respect, Colonel, it is a most complex and interesting story, but I must confess that I don't yet understand exactly why you need my expertise . . . I know that you are accustomed to give briefings in this manner, but may I trouble you with a question?'

'Yes, Mr Drake?'

'Well . . . to be honest, I am waiting to hear what is wrong with the piano.'

'I'm sorry?'

'The piano. I was contacted because I am being hired to tune a piano. This meeting is comprehensive with regards to the man, but I don't believe that he is my commission.'

The Colonel's face grew red. 'As I stated at the beginning, Mr Drake, I do believe that this background is important.'

'I agree, sir, but I don't know what is wrong with the piano or even whether or not I can mend it. I hope you understand.'

'Yes, yes. Of course I understand.' The muscles in his jaw tensed. He was ready to talk about the withdrawal of the Resident from Mandalay in 1879, and the Battle of Myingyan, and the siege of the Maymyo garrison, one of his favourite stories. He waited.

Edgar stared down at his hands. 'I apologize, please, please, do continue,' he said. 'But I must leave soon, since it is quite a long walk to my home, and my interest is mostly in the Erard grand.' Despite feeling intimidated by the Colonel, he secretly savoured this brief interruption. He had always disliked military men, and had begun to like this Carroll character more and more. In truth, he did want to hear the details of the story, but it was almost night, and the Colonel showed no sign of stopping.

The Colonel turned back to the papers, 'Very well, Mr Drake, I will make this brief. By 1874 we had begun to establish a handful of secret outposts in the Shan territories, one near Hsipaw, another near Taunggyi, and another – this the most remote – in a small village called Mae Lwin, on the bank of the Salween River. You won't find Mae Lwin on any maps, and until you accept the commission, I can't tell you where it is. There we sent Carroll.'

The room was getting dark and the Colonel lit a small lamp on the desk. The light flickered, casting the shadow of his moustache across his cheekbones. He studied the piano tuner again. He looks impatient, he thought, and took a deep breath. 'Mr Drake, so as not to detain you much further, I will spare you the details of Carroll's twelve years in Mae Lwin. Should you accept the commission, we can talk further, and I can provide you with military reports. Unless, of course, you would like to hear them now.'

'I would like to hear about the piano, if you don't mind.'

'Yes, yes, of course, the piano.' He sighed. 'What would you like to know? I believe you have been informed of most of the details of this matter in the letter from Colonel Fitzgerald.'

'Yes, Carroll requested a piano. The army purchased an 1840 Erard grand and shipped it to him. Would you mind telling me more of that story?'

'I can't really. Other than hoping to repeat the success he found in reciting Shelley, we can't understand why he would want a piano.'

'Why?' The piano tuner laughed, a deep sound that came unexpectedly from the thin frame. 'How many times I have asked myself the same question about my other clients. Why would a society matron who doesn't know Handel from Haydn purchase an 1820 Broadwood, and request that it be tuned weekly, even though it has never been played? Or how to explain the County Justice who has his instrument revoiced once every two months – which I might add, although entirely unnecessary, is wonderful for my affairs – yet this same man refuses an entertainment licence for the annual public piano competition? You will excuse me, but Doctor Carroll doesn't seem so bizarre. Have you ever heard, sir, Bach's Inventions?'

The Colonel stuttered, 'I think so . . . I'm certain I must have, but – no offence is intended, Mr Drake – I do not see how that has anything to do with . . .'

'The thought of living for eight years in the jungle without Bach's music is horrid to me.' Edgar paused and then added, 'It sounds most beautiful on an 1840 Erard.'

'That may be, but our soldiers are still fighting.'

Edgar took a deep breath. He could suddenly feel his heart

beating faster. 'I apologize. I do not intend my remarks to seem presumptuous. In fact, every minute of your history makes me more interested. But I am confused. If you so disapprove of our pianist, Colonel, then why am I here? You are a very important person; it is rare for someone of your rank to spend several hours interviewing a civilian, even I know this. I also know that the War Office must have invested a tremendous sum in shipping the piano to Burma, let alone purchasing it. And you have offered to pay me generously, well, *fairly* in my opinion, but, from an objective perspective, generously. Yet you seem to disapprove of my commission.'

The Colonel leaned back in his chair and crossed his arms over his chest. 'Very well. It is important that we discuss this. I am open in my disapproval, but please do not confuse that with disrespect. The Surgeon-Major is an extremely effective soldier, an unusual person perhaps, but he is irreplaceable. There are some, very high within this office, who have a great interest in his work.'

'But not yourself.'

'Let's just say that there are men who lose themselves in the rhetoric of our imperial destiny, that we conquer not to gain land and wealth, but to spread culture and civilization. I will not deny them this, but it is not the duty of the War Office.'

'And yet you support him?'

The Colonel paused. 'If I speak bluntly, Mr Drake, it is because it is important that you understand the position of the War Office. The Shan States are lawless. Except Mae Lwin. Carroll has accomplished more than several battalions. He is indispensable and he commands one of the most dangerous and important posts in our colonies. The Shan States are essential to securing our eastern frontier; without them we risk invasion, French or even Siamese. If a piano is the concession we must make to keep him at his post, then it is a small cost. But his post is a military post, not a music salon. It is our hope that when the piano is tuned he will return to his work. It is important that you understand this, that you understand that *we*, not the Surgeon-Major, are hiring you. His ideas can be . . . seductive.'

You don't trust him, thought Edgar. 'Just a concession, then, like cigarettes,' he said.

'No, this is different. I think you understand.'

'So I should not try to argue that it is *because* of the piano that he is indispensable?'

'We will know when it is tuned, won't we, Mr Drake?'

And at his words the piano tuner smiled. 'Perhaps we will.'

The Colonel sat forward. 'Do you have any other questions?'

'Only one.'

'Yes, what is it?'

Edgar looked down at his hands. 'I am sorry, Colonel, but what exactly is *wrong* with the piano?'

The Colonel stared. 'I think we have discussed this.'

The tuner took a deep breath. 'With all due respect, sir, we discussed what you thought wrong with *a* piano. But I need to know what is wrong with this piano, with the 1840 Erard that sits somewhere in a jungle far away, where you are asking me to go. Your office has told me little about the piano besides the fact that it is out of tune, which, I might add, is due to the swelling of the soundboard, not the body as you mentioned in your letter. Of course, I am amazed that you did not anticipate this, the piano going out of tune. Humidity works horrors.'

'Again, Mr Drake, we were doing this for Carroll. You will have to make such philosophical enquiries of the man himself.'

'Well, then may I ask what it is that I need to mend?'

The Colonel coughed. 'Such details were not provided to us.'

'He must have written about the piano somewhere.'

'We have only one note, strange and uncharacteristically short for the Doctor, usually a man of eloquence, which made us somewhat sceptical about the request until it was followed by his threat to resign.'

'May I read it?'

The Colonel hesitated and then passed a small brown piece of paper to the piano tuner. 'It is Shan paper,' the Colonel said. 'Supposedly the tribe is famous for it. This is odd because the Surgeon-Major has never used it for any other correspondence.' The paper was soft, a handmade matte with visible fibres, now stained with a dark ink.

Gentlemen, the Erard Grand can no longer be played, and must be tuned and repaired, a task which I have attempted but failed in. A piano tuner who specializes in Erards is needed urgently in Mae Lwin. I trust that this should not be difficult. It is much easier to deliver a man than a piano.

Surgeon-Major Anthony J. Carroll, Mae Lwin, Shan States

Edgar looked up. 'These are spare words to justify sending a man to the other side of the world.'

'Mr Drake,' said the Colonel, 'your reputation as a tuner of Erard grands is well known by those in London who concern themselves with music. We anticipate the duration of the trip to be no longer than three months from when you leave to when you return to England. As you know, you will be rewarded well.'

'And I must go alone.'

'Your wife will be well provided for here.'

The piano tuner sat back in his chair.

'Do you have any more questions?'

'No, I think I understand,' he said softly, as if speaking only to himself.

The Colonel set the papers down and leaned forward in his seat. 'Will you go to Mae Lwin?'

Edgar Drake turned back to the window. It was dusk, and wind played with the falling water, intricate crescendos and diminuendos of rain. I decided long before I came here, he thought.

He turned to the Colonel and nodded.

o

They shook hands. Killian insisted on taking the piano tuner to Colonel Fitzgerald's office, where he reported the news. Then more words, but Edgar was no longer listening. He felt as if he were in a dream, the reality of the decision still floating above him. He felt himself repeating the nod, as if doing so would make real his decision, would reconcile the insignificance of that movement with the significance of what it meant.

There were papers to sign and dates to be set and copies of documents to be ordered for his 'further perusal'. Doctor Carroll, explained Killian, had requested that the War Office provide a long list of background reading for the tuner: histories, studies of anthropology, geology, natural history. 'I wouldn't worry yourself too much with all of this, but the Doctor did ask that we provide it for you,' he said. 'I think I have told you all you really need to know.'

As he left, a line from Carroll's letter followed him, like a faint trail of cigarette smoke from a salon performance. *It is much easier to deliver a man than a piano.* He thought he would like this Doctor, it was not often that one found such poetic words in the letters of military men. And Edgar Drake had great respect for those who find song in responsibility.

TWO

HEAVY FOG DRIFTED along Pall Mall as Edgar left the War Office. He followed a pair of torch boys through mist so thick that the children, swathed in heavy rags, seemed disembodied from the hands that held the dancing lights. 'Do you want a cab, sir?' one of the boys asked. 'Yes, to Fitzroy Square, please,' he said, but then changed his mind. 'Take me to the Embankment.'

They walked through the crowds, through the stern and marbled corridors of Whitehall and then out again, through a jumble of carriages filled with black coats and top hats, and sprinkled with patrician accents and the smoke of cigars. 'There is a dinner at one of the clubs tonight, sir,' confided one of the boys and Edgar nodded. In the buildings around them tall windows gave onto walls of oil paintings, lit by high-ceilinged chandeliers. He knew some of the clubs, he had tuned a Pleyel at Boodle's three years ago, and an Erard at Brooks's, a beautiful, inlaid piece from the Paris workshop.

They passed a crowd of well-dressed men and women, their faces ruddy from the cold and brandy, the men laughing beneath dark moustaches, the women squeezed in the embrace of whalebone corsets, lifting the hems of their dresses above a road glistening with rain and horse dung. An empty carriage waited for them on the other side of the street, an elderly turbaned Indian already at the door. Edgar turned. *Perhaps he has seen what I* will, he thought, and had to suppress the desire to speak to him. Around him, the crowd of men and women parted, and losing the light of the torch boys he stumbled. 'Watch where you are going, my dear chap!' roared one of the men, and one of the women, 'These drunks.' The crowd laughed and Edgar could see the old Indian's eyes light up, only modesty keeping him from sharing this joke with his fares.

The boys were waiting by the low wall that ran along the Embankment. 'Where to, sir?' 'This is fine, thank you,' and he flipped them a coin. Both boys jumped for it, dropped it, and it bounced on the irregularity of the road and down a grating. The boys fell to their knees. 'Here you, hold the torches, No, then you will take it, you never share, *You* never share, this is mine, I talked to him . . .' Embarrassed, Edgar fished two new coins from his pockets, 'Here. I am sorry, take these.' He walked off. The boys remained arguing by the grating. Soon only the light of their torches was visible. He stopped and looked out at the Thames.

Below, sounds of movement came from the river. Watermen maybe, he thought, and he wondered where they were going to or coming from. He thought of another river, distant, even its name new, pronounced as if a third syllable lay between the 'l' and the 'w', soft and hidden. Salween. He whispered it, and then, embarrassed, turned quickly to see if he was alone. He listened to the sound of the men and the splash of waves against the Embankment. The fog thinned over the river. There was no moon, and it was only by the light of lanterns swinging from the tugboats that he could see the vague line of the shore, the vast, heavy architecture that crowded the river. Like animals at a waterhole, he thought, and he liked the comparison, I must tell Katherine. He then thought, I am late.

He walked along the Embankment, past a group of tramps, three men in rags huddled around a small fire. They watched him as he went by, and he nodded at them, awkwardly. One of the men looked up and smiled, a broad mouth full of broken teeth.

He muttered to himself, a Cockney voice heavy with whisky. The other men were silent and turned back to the fire.

He crossed the street and left the river, squeezing through swarms of people gathered outside the Metropole, following Northumberland Avenue to Trafalgar Square, where masses shifted around carriages and omnibuses, where policemen tried to move the crowds in vain, where conductors hollered for fares, where whips snapped and horses shat, where signs rose shouting

SWANBILL CORSETS FOR THE THIRD TYPE OF FIGURE

CIGARS DE JOY

One of these cigarettes gives immediate relief in the worst attack of
ASTHMA, COUGH, BRONCHITIS and SHORTNESS OF BREATH

HOP BITTERS HOP BITTERS

This Christmas Day, when church bells chime,
Give yourself the gift of time
ROBINSON's Quality Watches

Beneath the glow of the fountains around Nelson's Column, he stopped to watch an organ grinder, an Italian with a screeching monkey in a Napoleon hat, which hopped around the barrel organ, waving its arms while its master turned the crank. Around it, a group of children were clapping, torch boys and chimney sweeps, rag collectors and the children of costermongers. A policeman approached, his baton swinging. 'Get home now, all of you, get that filthy animal out of here. Play your music in Lambeth, this is a place for gentlemen.' The group moved away slowly, protesting. Edgar turned. Another monkey, giant and grinning, groomed itself in a jewelled mirror, BROOKE's SOAP MONKEY BRAND: THE MISSING LINK IN HOUSEHOLD CLEANLINESS. The billboard rolled past on the side of an omnibus. The busboy hollered for fares, Fitzroy Square, Hurry for Fitzroy Square. That is home, thought Edgar Drake and he watched the omnibus pass.

He left Trafalgar Square and pushed his way through the darkening swirl of merchants and carriages, following Cockspur Street as it funnelled into the din of Haymarket, hands deep in his jacket now, regretting he hadn't taken the omnibus. At the top of the street the buildings drew closer and darker as he entered the Narrows.

He walked, not knowing exactly where he was, but only the general direction of his movement, past dark brick houses and fading painted terraces, past scattered bundled figures hurrying home, past shadow and shade and glints of light in the thin puddles that ran in veins between the cobbles, past weeping mansard rooftops and then the rare scattered lantern, perched and flickering, casting shadows of cobwebs in distorted magnification. He walked and then it was dark again and the streets narrowed, and he brought his shoulders closer. He did this because it was cold and because the buildings did the same.

The Narrows opened onto Oxford Street and the walk became lit and familiar. He passed the Oxford Music Hall, and turned onto Newman, Cleveland, Howland Streets, one, two blocks, then right, into a smaller lane, so small that it had been missed, much to the chagrin of its residents, by London's most recent map.

Number 14 Franklin Mews was the fourth in the terrace, a brick house virtually identical to those of Mr Lillypenny, the flowerseller, who lived at Number 12, and Mr Bennett-Edwards, the upholsterer, at Number 16, each home sharing a common wall and brick facade. The entrance to the house was at street level. Beyond an iron gate, a short path spanned an open space between pavement and the front door, down which a set of iron stairs descended to the basement, where Edgar kept his workshop. Flowerpots hung from the fence and outside the windows. Some held fading chrysanthemums, still blooming in the cold of autumn. Others were empty, half filled with soil, now dusted with mist that reflected the flicker of the lantern outside the door. Katherine must have left it burning, he thought.

At the door he fumbled with the keys, deliberate now in his attempt to delay his entry. He looked back out at the street. It was dark. The conversation at the War Office seemed distant, like a dream, and for a brief moment he thought that maybe it too would fade like a dream, that he couldn't tell Katherine, not yet, while he doubted its reality. He felt his head jerk involuntarily, the nod again, The nod is all I have brought from the meeting.

He opened the door and found Katherine waiting in the parlour, reading a newspaper by the soft glow of a single lamp. It was cold in the room and she wore a thin shawl of embroidered white wool over her shoulders. He closed the door softly, and stopped and hung his hat and jacket on the coatstand, saying nothing. There was no need to announce his late arrival with a fanfare, he thought, Better to slip in silently, Maybe then I can convince her I have been here some time already, although he knew he couldn't, just as he knew that she was no longer reading.

Across the room Katherine continued to stare at the newspaper in her hands. It was the *Illustrated London News*, and later she would tell him that she was reading 'Reception at the Metropole', where the music of a new piano was described, although not its make and certainly not its tuner. For another minute she continued to flip through the journal. She said nothing, she was a woman of impeccable composure and this was how best to deal with tardy husbands. Many of her friends were different. You are too easy with him, they often told her, but she shrugged them off, The day he comes home smelling of gin or cheap perfume, then I will be angry. Edgar is late because he is absorbed in his work, or because he gets lost walking home from a new assignment.

'Good evening, Katherine,' he said.

'Good evening, Edgar. You are almost two hours late.'

He was used to the ritual, the innocent excuses, the explainings away: I know, dear, dearest, I am sorry, I had to finish all the strings so I can retune them tomorrow, or This is a rushed commission, or I am being paid extra, or I got lost on the way home, the house is near Westminster, and I took the wrong tram, or I just wanted to play it, it was a rare, 1835 model, Erard, beautiful of course, it belongs to the family of Mr Vincento, the Italian tenor, or It belongs to Lady Neville, unique, 1827, I wish you could come and play it too. If he ever lied, it was only in exchanging one excuse for another. That it was a rushed contract, when really he had stopped to watch street players. That he took the wrong tram, when actually he had stayed late to play the piano of the Italian tenor. 'I know, I am sorry, still working on the Farrell contract,' and this was enough, he saw her close the *News*, and he slid across the room to sit next to her, his heart racing, She knows something is different. He tried to kiss her, but she pushed him away, trying to hide a smile, 'Edgar, you're late, I overcooked the meat, stop that, don't think you can keep me waiting and make it up to me with endearments.' She turned from him and he slipped his arms around her waist.

'I thought you would have finished that contract by now,' she said.

'No, the piano is in lamentable shape, and Mrs Farrell insists that I tune it to "Concert Pitch".' He raised his voice an octave to imitate the matron. Katherine laughed and he kissed her neck.

'She says her little Roland will be the next Mozart.'

'I know, she told me again today, even made me listen to the rascal play.'

Katherine turned towards her husband. 'You poor dear. I can't be angry at you for long.' Edgar smiled, relaxing slightly. He looked at her as she tried to summon an expression of mock sternness. She is still lovely, he thought. The golden curls that had entranced him so when he had first met her had faded somewhat, but she still wore her hair loose, and they became the same colour again whenever she went in the sun. They had met when, as an apprentice tuner, he had repaired her family's Broadwood upright. The piano hadn't impressed him – it had been rebuilt with rather cheap parts – but the delicate hands which played it had, as had the softness of the figure that had sat beside him at the keyboard, the presence that stirred him even now. He leaned towards her to kiss her again. 'Stop it,' she giggled, 'not now, and be careful of the sofa. This is new damask.'

Edgar sat back. She is in a good mood, he thought, Perhaps I should tell her now. 'I have a new contract,' he said.

'You must read this report, Edgar,' said Katherine, smoothing out her dress and reaching for the *News*.

'An 1840 Erard. It sounds as if it is in dreadful shape. It should pay wonderfully.'

'Oh, really,' standing and walking to the dining table. She didn't enquire who owned the piano, nor where it was, these were not questions often asked, as for the last eighteen years the only answers had been Old Mrs So-and-So and London's Such-and-Such Street. Edgar was glad she didn't ask, the rest would soon come, he was a man of patience and not one to press his fortune, a practice which he knew led only to over-tightened piano strings and angry wives. Also, he had just looked down at the copy of the *Illustrated London News*, where, below the story on the reception at the Metropole, was an article on 'The Atrocities of the Dacoits', written by an officer in the '3rd Ghoorka Regiment'. It was a short piece, detailing a skirmish with bandits who had looted a friendly village, the usual fare about efforts of pacification in the colonies, and he wouldn't have noticed it, were it not for its title 'Sketches of Burmah'. He was familiar with the column – it ran almost every week – but he had paid it little attention until now. He tore the article from the page and tucked the newspaper under a pile of magazines on the small table. She shouldn't see this. From the dining room came the clink of silverware and the smell of boiled potatoes.

o

The following morning Edgar sat at a small table set for two, as Katherine made tea and toast and set out jars of butter and jam. He was quiet, and as she moved through the kitchen, she filled the silence with talk of the endless autumn rain, of politics, news. 'Did you hear, Edgar, of the omnibus accident yesterday? Of the reception for the German baron? Of the young mother in the East End who has been arrested for the murder of her children?'

'No,' he answered. His mind wandered, distracted. 'No, tell me.'

'Horrible, absolutely horrible. Her husband, a coal haulier I think, found the children, two little boys and a little girl, curled together in their bed, and he told a constable, and they arrested the wife. The poor thing. The poor husband, he didn't think she had done it – think of that, losing both your wife and children. And she says she only gave them a patent medicine to help them sleep. *I* think they should arrest the patent-medicine maker. I believe her, wouldn't you?'

'Of course, dear.' He held his cup to his mouth and breathed in the steam.

'You are not listening,' Katherine said.

'Of course I am; it is terrible.' And he was; he thought of the image of the three children, pale, like baby mice with unopened eyes.

'Alas, I know I shouldn't read such stories,' she said. 'They bother me so. Let's talk of something else. Will you finish the Farrells' contract today?'

'No, I think I will go later this week. At ten I have an appointment at the Mayfair house of some MP. A Broadwood grand, I don't know what is wrong with it. And I have some work to finish in the shop before I leave.'

'Do try to get home on time tonight. You know I hate waiting.'

'I know.' He reached over and took her hand in his. An exaggerated effort, she thought, but dismissed it.

o

Their servant, a young girl from Whitechapel, had returned home to tend to her mother, who was sick with consumption, so Katherine left the table and went upstairs to arrange the bedroom. She usually stayed at home during the day, to help with the chores, to receive house calls from Edgar's clients, to arrange commissions, and to organize their social life, a task which her husband, who had always found himself more comfortable among musical instruments, was more than happy to let her manage. They had no children, although not for want of trying. Indeed, their marriage had stayed quite amorous, a fact which sometimes surprised even Katherine when she watched her husband wander absentmindedly through the house. While at first this notable Absence-of-Child, as Katherine's mother described it, had saddened the two of them, they had become accustomed to it, and Katherine often wondered if it had made them closer. Besides, Katherine at times admitted to her friends a certain relief, Edgar is enough to look after.

When she had left the table, he finished his tea and descended the steep stairs to his basement workshop. He rarely worked at home. Transporting an instrument through the London streets could be disastrous, and it was much easier to take all his tools to his work. He kept the space primarily for his own projects. The few times he had actually brought a piano home, it had had to be lowered by ropes down the open space between the street and his house. The shop itself was a small space with a low ceiling, a warren of dusty piano skeletons, tools that hung from the walls and ceilings like joints in a butcher's shop, fading schematics of pianos and portraits of pianists nailed to the walls. The room was dimly lit by a half-window tucked beneath the ceiling. Discarded keys lined the shelves like rows of dentures. Katherine had once called it 'the elephants' graveyard', and he had to ask if this was for the hulking ribcages of eviscerated grands or the rolls of felt like hide, and she had answered, You are too poetic, I meant only for the ivory.

Coming down the stairs, he almost tripped over a discarded

action leaning against the wall. Beyond the difficulty of moving a piano, this was another reason he didn't bring customers to his shop. For those accustomed to the shine of polished cases set in flowery parlours, it was always somewhat disconcerting to see an opened piano, to realize that something so clearly mechanical could produce such a heavenly sound.

Edgar made his way to a small desk and lit the lamp. The night before he had hidden the packet given to him at the War Office beneath a musty stack of printed tuning specifications. He opened the envelope. There was a copy of the original letter sent by Colonel Fitzgerald, a map and a contract specifying his commission. There was also a printed briefing, given to him at the request of Doctor Carroll, titled in bold capitals, THE GENERAL HISTORY OF BURMA, WITH SPECIAL ATTENTION TO THE ANGLO-BURMESE WARS AND BRITISH ANNEXATIONS. He sat down and began to read.

The history was familiar. He had known of the Anglo-Burmese wars, conflicts notable both for their brevity and for the considerable territorial gains wrested from the Burmese kings following each victory: the coastal states of Arakan and Tenasserim following the first war, Rangoon and Lower Burma following the second, Upper Burma and the Shan States following the third. And while the first two wars, which ended in 1826 and 1853, he had learned about at school, the third had been reported in the newspapers last year, and the final annexation announced only in January. But, beyond the general histories, most of the details were unfamiliar: that the second war began ostensibly over the kidnapping of two British sea captains, that the third stemmed in part from tension following the refusal of British emissaries to remove their shoes on entering an audience with the Burmese King. There were other sections, including histories of the kings, a dizzying genealogy complicated by multiple wives and what appeared to be the common practice of murdering any relatives who might be pretenders to the throne. He was confused by new words, names with strange syllables he couldn't pronounce, and he focused his attention mainly on the history of the most recent king, named Thibaw, who had been deposed and exiled to India after British troops seized Mandalay. He was, by the army's account, a weak and ineffective leader, manipulated by his wife and mother-in-law, and his reign had been marred by increasing lawlessness in the remoter districts, evidenced by a plague of attacks by armed bands of dacoits, a word for brigands that Edgar recognized from the article he had torn from the *Illustrated London News*.

Above, he heard Katherine's footsteps and paused, ready to slip the papers back into their envelope. The steps stopped at the top of the stairs.

'Edgar, it's nearly ten,' she called.

'Really? I must go!' He blew out the lamp and stuffed the papers back into the envelope, surprised at his own precautions. At the top of the stairs Katherine met him with his coat and his toolbag.

'I will be on time tonight, I promise,' he said, slipping his arms into the sleeves. He kissed her on her cheek and stepped out into the cold.

o

He spent the remainder of the day tuning the Broadwood grand of the Member of Parliament, who thundered in the next room about the building of a new Hospital for the Genteel Insane. He finished early, he could have spent more time fine-tuning, but he had a feeling that it was rarely played. Besides, the acoustics in the drawing room were poor and the politics of the MP distasteful.

It was early afternoon when he left. The streets were full of people. Heavy clouds hung low in the sky, threatening rain. He elbowed his way through the crowds and crossed the street to skirt a team of labourers who tore at the cobblestones with picks, stalling traffic. Around the waiting carriages, newspaper hawkers and petty merchants clamoured, and a pair of boys kicked a ball back and forth through the crowds, scattering when it hit the side of a carriage. It began to drizzle.

Edgar walked for several minutes, hoping to see an omnibus, but the drizzle turned to heavier rain. He took shelter in the doorway of a public house, its name etched in the frosted glass, the backs of suited gentlemen and pink-powdered women pressed up against its windows, wiping silhouettes in the condensation. He tucked his collar higher around his neck and stared out at the rain. A pair of drivers left their carts across the street, half-running with their jackets raised above their heads. Edgar stepped aside to let them pass, and as they entered the public house the door swung open with the steaming smell of perfume and sweat and spilled gin. He could hear drunken singing. The door swung to and he waited and watched the street. And thought again of the briefing.

In school, he had never been very interested in history or politics, preferring the arts and, of course, music. If he had any, his political leanings tended to be towards Gladstone and the Liberals' support for Home Rule, although this was hardly a conviction born out of serious contemplation. His distrust of military men was more visceral; he disliked the arrogance they carried forth to the colonies and back again. Moreover, he was uncomfortable with the popular portrayal of the Oriental as lazy and ineffectual, one only had to know the history of pianos, he would tell Katherine, to know this wasn't true. The mathematics of equal temperament tuning had engaged thinkers from Galileo Galilei to Father Marin Mersenne, the author of the classic *Harmonie universelle*. And yet Edgar had learned that the correct figures were actually first published by a Chinese prince named Tsaiyu, a puzzling fact as, from what he knew about Eastern music, the music of China, which lacked harmonic emphasis, technically had no need for temperament. Of course, he rarely mentioned this in public. He didn't like arguments and he had enough experience to know that few could appreciate the technical beauty of such an innovation.

The rain relented slightly and he left the shelter of the doorway. Soon he reached a larger road, where buses and cabs passed. It is still early, he thought, Katherine will be pleased.

He boards an omnibus, wedging himself between a portly gentleman in a thick coat and a young ashen faced woman who coughs incessantly. The bus lurches forward. He looks for the window but the bus is crowded, he cannot see the streets pass.

o

This moment will remain.

He is home. He opens the door, and she is sitting on the sofa, in the corner, at the edge of a half-circle of damask that falls over the cushions. Just as yesterday, but the lamp is not burning, its wick is black, it should be trimmed, but the servant is in Whitechapel. The only light slants through curtains of Nottingham lace and catches itself on particles of suspended dust. She is sitting and staring at the window, she must have seen his silhouette pass in the street. She holds a handkerchief, her cheeks have been hastily wiped. Edgar can see tears, their tracks cut short by the handkerchief.

A pile of papers is scattered across the mahogany table, and an opened brown wrapping, still in the form of the papers it once held, still tied with twine, carefully unfolded at one end, as if its contents have been examined surreptitiously. Or were intended to be, for the strewn papers are anything but surreptitious. Nor are the tears, the swollen eyes.

Neither of them moves or says anything. His jacket is still in his hand, she sits on the edge of the sofa, her fingers nervously entwined in her handkerchief. He knows immediately why she is crying, he knows that she *knows*, that even if she doesn't, this is how it would be, the news needs to be shared. Perhaps he should have told her last night, he should have known that they would come to his house, now he remembers that before he left the War

Office the Colonel even told him so. Had he not been so lost in the magnitude of his decision, he wouldn't have forgotten. He should have planned this, the news could have been broken more delicately. Edgar keeps so few secrets that those he does become lies.

His hands tremble as he hangs up the jacket. He turns. Katherine, he says. What is wrong, he wants to ask, a question of habit, but he knows the answer. He looks at her. There are questions whose answers he doesn't yet know, Who brought the papers, When did they come, What do they say, Are you angry.

You were crying, he says.

She is quiet, now she begins to sob softly. Her hair is loose over her shoulders.

He doesn't move, doesn't know whether to go to her, this is different from before, this is not a time for embraces, Katherine, I meant to tell you, I tried to last night, only I didn't think it was right then—

He crosses the room now, he slides between the sofa and the table, he sits next to her.

Dear—. He touches her arm, gently, trying to turn her towards him, Katherine, dear, I wanted to tell you, please look at me, and she turns slowly, looks at him, her eyes are red, she has been crying for a long time. He waits for her to speak, he doesn't know how much she knows. What happened? She doesn't reply. Please, Katherine. Edgar, you know what happened. I know and I don't know. Who brought these? Is it important? Katherine dear, don't be angry with me, I wanted to talk to you about this, Please, Katherine—

I am not angry, Edgar, she says.

He reaches into his pocket and pulls out a handkerchief, Look at me. He touches the handkerchief to her cheek.

I was angry this morning when he came. Who? A soldier, from the War Office, He came asking for you, with these. She motioned to the papers. And what did he say? Very little, only that these papers were for your preparation, that I should be proud, that you are doing something very important, and when he said that, I still didn't know what he was talking about. What do you mean? That is all he said, Mrs Drake, do you know that your husband is a brave man, and I had to ask him, Why, I felt like a fool, Edgar, He seemed surprised when I asked, he laughed and said only that Burma is far away, I almost asked what that meant, I almost told him that he had the wrong house, the wrong husband, but I only thanked him and he left. And you read them. Some, only some, Enough. She was silent. When did he come? This morning, I know I shouldn't read your mail, I left the package on the table, it wasn't mine, I went upstairs, to try to finish the needlework for our bedcover, I was distracted, I kept poking myself with the needle, I was thinking about what he said, and I went downstairs, I sat here for almost an hour, wondering if I should open it, telling myself it was nothing, but I knew it wasn't, and I thought about last night. Last night. Last night you were different. You knew. Not then, but this morning I knew, I think I know you too well.

He takes her hands.

They sit for a long time like that, their knees touching, her hands in his. She says again, I am not angry. You can be angry. I *was* angry, the anger came and went, I only wish you had told me, I don't care about Burma, no that is wrong, I *do* care about Burma, I just . . . I wondered why you didn't tell me, if maybe you thought that I would stop you from doing this, That hurt the most, I am proud of you, Edgar.

The words stay before them, suspended. He releases her hands, and she begins to cry again. She wipes her eyes, Look at me, I am behaving like a child. I can still change my mind, he says.

It isn't that, I don't *want* you to change your mind. You want me to go. I don't want you to go, but at the same time, I know you *should* go, I have been expecting this. You have been expecting an out-of-tune Erard in Burma? Not Burma, *this*, something different, It is a lovely idea, to use music to bring about peace, I wonder what songs you will play there. I am only going to tune, I am not a pianist, I am going because it is a commission. No, this one is different, and not only because you are going away. I don't understand. Different, something different from your other projects, a cause, something worthy.

You don't believe that my work is worthy already. I didn't say that. You said as much. I watch you, Edgar, sometimes it is as if you are my child, I am proud of you, you have abilities that others don't, you have ways of hearing sounds that other people can't, you are skilled in the mechanics of things, you make music beautiful, that is enough. Except now it sounds like it isn't.

Edgar, please, now *you* are angry. No, I am only asking you for your reasons, You have never told me this before, This is still just another assignment, I am still a mechanic, let us be careful before we give credit for Turner's paintings to the man who makes his brushes.

Now you sound as if you don't know if you should go. Of course I don't know, only now my wife is telling me I should do it to prove something. You know that is not what I am saying. I have had other strange commissions, Katherine. But this is different, This is the only one you have kept hidden.

Outside the sun dips finally behind the rooftops and the room grows suddenly darker.

Katherine, I didn't expect this from you. What then did you expect? I don't know, I have never done this before. You expected me to cry as I am now, to implore you not to go because that is how women behave when they lose their husbands, you expected that I will be afraid if you are gone because you will not be here to take care of me, that I will be afraid I will lose you. Katherine, that isn't true, that isn't why I didn't tell you. You thought I would be scared, You tore a page from the *Illustrated London News* because it had an article on Burma.

There was a long silence. I am sorry, you know this is new for me. I know, this is new for me too.

I think you should go, Edgar, I wish *I* could go, It must be beautiful to see the world. You must return to me with stories.

It is only another commission.

You keep saying that, You know it isn't.

The ship doesn't leave for another month, That is a lot of time.

There is a lot to get ready.

It is very far, Katherine.

I know.

o

The following days passed swiftly. Edgar finished the Farrell contract, and refused a new commission to voice a beautiful 1870 Streicher grand with an old Viennese action.

Officers from the War Office visited frequently, arriving each time with more documents: briefings, schedules, lists of items to take with him to Burma. After the tears of the first day, Katherine seemed to embrace the mission enthusiastically. Edgar was grateful for this; he had thought she might still be upset. Moreover, he had never been organized. She had always teased him that the precise ordering of piano strings seemed to necessitate a chaotic disorganization in every other aspect of his life. On a typical day a soldier would come to their house to drop off paperwork while Edgar was away. Katherine would take the papers, read them and then organize them on his desk into three piles: forms which required completion and return to the army, general histories, and papers specific to his mission. Then he would come home and within minutes the stack of papers would be in disarray, as if he had merely sifted through the piles looking for something. That something, Katherine knew, was information about the piano, but none came, and after about three or four days, she would greet him with, 'More papers arrived today, lots of military information, nothing about a piano,' which left him looking disappointed, but helped considerably in keeping the table neater. He would then collect whatever was sitting on top of the pile and retire to his chair.

Later she would find him asleep with the folder open on his lap.

She was astonished by the amount of documentation they supplied, apparently all at Carroll's request, and she read the papers avidly, even copying out sections of a history of the Shan written by the Doctor himself, a piece she had expected to be dull, but which thrilled her with its stories, and gave her confidence in the man whom she felt she had entrusted to watch over her husband. She had recommended it to Edgar, but he told her he would wait, I will need things to distract me when I am alone. Otherwise, she rarely mentioned her readings to him. The stories and descriptions of the people fascinated her; she had loved tales of far-off places since she was a young girl. But while she caught herself daydreaming, she was glad she wasn't going. It seemed, she confided to a friend, like one big silly game for boys who haven't grown up, like stories from *Boys' Own* or the penny cowboy serials imported from America. 'Yet you let Edgar go,' her friend had responded. 'Edgar never played those games,' she said. 'Perhaps it is not too late. Besides, I have never seen him so excited, so filled with purpose. He is like a young man again.'

After several days other packages arrived, these marked from Colonel Fitzgerald, to be delivered to Surgeon-Major Carroll. They looked as if they contained sheets of music and Edgar started to open them, but Katherine scolded him. They were packed neatly in brown paper, and he would surely leave them disorganized. Fortunately, the names of the composers had been written on the outside of the paper, and Edgar contented himself with the knowledge that, should he be stranded, he would at least have Liszt to keep him company. Such taste, he said, gave him confidence in his mission.

The departure date was set for 26 November, one month to

the day following Edgar's acceptance of his commission. It approached like a cyclone, if not for the mad preparations that preceded it, then for the calm that Katherine knew would follow. While he spent his days finishing his work and tidying up the workshop, she packed his trunks, modifying the recommendations of the army with knowledge unique to the wife of a tuner of Erards. Thus to the army's list of items such as water-repellent rotproof clothes, dinnerware, and an assortment of pills and powders to 'better enjoy the tropical climate', she added ointment for fingers chapped from tuning and an extra pair of spectacles, as Edgar invariably sat on a pair about once every three months. She packed a dress coat with tails as well, 'In case you are asked to play,' she said, but Edgar kissed her on the forehead and unpacked it. 'You flatter me, dear, but I am not a pianist. Please don't encourage such ideas.'

She packed it anyway. She was used to such protestations. Since he was a boy Edgar had noticed in himself an aptitude for *sound*, although not, he had also sadly learned, an aptitude for *composition*. His father, a carpenter, had been an avid amateur musician, collecting and constructing instruments of all shapes and sounds, scavenging even the immigrant bazaars for strange folk instruments brought from the Continent. When he realized that his son was too shy to play for visiting friends, he had invested his energies in Edgar's sister, a delicate little girl who had later married a singer with the D'Oyly Carte Company, now quite well known for his starring roles in the operettas of Mr Gilbert and Mr Sullivan. So while his sister sat through hours of lessons, Edgar spent the days with his father, a man whom he remembered primarily for his large hands, Too large, he would say, for finery. And so it had become Edgar's job to tend to his father's growing collection of instruments, most of which, to the boy's delight, were in manifest disrepair. Later, as a young man, when he had met and fallen in love with Katherine, he had been equally delighted to hear her play, and had told her this when he proposed. You dare not be asking me to marry you simply so you may have someone to test the instruments you tune, she had said, her hand lightly resting on his arm, and he had replied, a young man flushed by the feeling of her fingers, Don't worry, if you wish you may never play, Your voice is music enough.

Edgar packed his own tools. Because the army had still not given him details about the piano, he visited the shop where it had been purchased, and spoke at length with the owner about the instrument's specifics, how extensively it had been rebuilt, which of the original parts remained. With limited space, he could afford only to bring tools and replacement parts specific to the piano. Even so, the tools filled half of one of his trunks.

o

A week before he was due to leave, Katherine held a small goodbye tea party for her husband. He had few friends and most of them were also tuners: Mr Wiggers, who specialized in Broadwoods, Mr d'Argences, the Frenchman whose passion was Viennese uprights, and Mr Poffy, who wasn't actually a piano tuner since he repaired organs mostly – It is nice, Edgar once explained to Katherine, to have variety in one's friends. Of course, this hardly spanned the full array of Those Associated with Pianos. The *London Directory* alone, between Physicians and Pickle and Sauce Manufacturers, listed Pianoforte makers, Pianoforte action-makers, Pianoforte fret-cutters, hammer coverers, hammer- and damper-felt manu- facturers, hammer rail-makers, ivory bleachers, ivory cutters, key makers, pin makers, silkers, small-work Manufacturers, Pianoforte string makers, Pianoforte tuners. Notably absent from the party was Mr Hastings, who also specialized in Erards, and who had snubbed Edgar ever since he had put up a sign in his workshop reading 'Gone to Burma to tune in the service of Her Majesty; please consult Mr George Hastings for minor tunings that cannot await my return'.

Everyone at the party was thrilled about the Erard commission, and speculation ran late into the evening about what could be wrong with the piano. Eventually, bored with the discussion, Katherine left the men and retired to bed, where she read from *The Burman*, a wonderful ethnography by a newspaperman recently appointed to the Burma Commission. The author, one Mr Scott, had taken the Burmese name Shway Yoe, meaning Golden Truth, as a *nom de plume*, a fact that Katherine dismissed as further proof that the war was but a 'boys' game'. Nevertheless, it made her uneasy, and she reminded herself before falling asleep to tell Edgar not to return with a ridiculous new name as well.

And the days passed. Katherine expected a last-minute flurry of preparation, but three days before the set departure, she and Edgar awoke that morning to find nothing left to prepare. His bags were packed, his tools cleaned and ordered, his shop closed.

They walked down to the Thames, where they sat on the Embankment and watched the boat traffic. There was a clarity to the sky, Edgar thought, to the feeling of Katherine's hand in his, All that is lacking to complete the moment is music. Since he was a boy, he had had the habit of attaching not only sentiment to song but song to sentiment. Katherine learned this in a letter he wrote to her after he visited her home for the first time, in which he described feeling 'like the "Allegro con brio" of Haydn's Sonata No. 50 in D major'. She had laughed and wondered whether he was serious or if it was only the sort of joke that piano tuners enjoyed. She showed it to her friends, and they decided together that surely it was a joke, if a strange one, until later she bought the sheets for the sonata and played them, and from the piano, newly tuned, came a song of giddy anticipation that made her think of butterflies, not the kind that follow spring, but rather the pale flittering shadows that live in the stomach of those who are young and in love.

As they sat together, fragments of melodies played in Edgar's head, like an orchestra warming up, until one tune slowly began to dominate and the others fell in line. He hummed. 'Clementi, Sonata in F sharp minor,' Katherine said, and he nodded. He had once told her it reminded him of a sailor lost at sea. His love awaiting him on shore. In the notes hid the sound of the waves, gulls.

They sat and listened.

'Does he return?'

'In this version he does.'

Below them men unloaded crates from the smaller boats used for river traffic. Seagulls cried, waiting for discarded food, calling to each other as they circled. Edgar and Katherine walked along the shore. As they turned away from the river and began their return, Edgar's fingers wrapped around those of his wife. A tuner makes a good husband, she had told her friends after they had returned from their honeymoon. He knows how to listen, and his touch is more delicate than that of the pianist: only the tuner knows the inside of the piano. The young women had giggled at the scandalous implications of these words. Now, eighteen years later, she knew where the calluses on his hands lay and what they were from. Once he had explained them to her, like a tattooed man explaining the stories of his illustrations, This one which runs along the inside of my thumb is from a screwdriver, The scratches on my wrist are from the body itself, I often rest my arm like this when I am sounding, The calluses on the inside of my first and third fingers on the right are from tightening pins before using regulating pliers, I spare my second finger, I don't know why, a habit from youth. Broken nails are from strings, it is a sign of impatience.

They walk home, now they speak of inconsequentials like how many pairs of stockings he has packed, how often he will write, gifts he should bring home, how not to become ill. The conversation rests uneasily; one doesn't expect goodbyes to be burdened by such trivialities. This is not how it is in the books, he thinks, or in the theatre, and feels the need to speak of mission, of duty, of love. They reach home and close the door and he doesn't drop her hand. Where speech fails, touch compensates.

o

There are three days and then two and he cannot sleep. He leaves home early to walk, while it is still dark, shifting out from the warm pocket of scented sheets. She turns, sleeping, dreaming perhaps, Edgar? And he, Sleep, love, and she does, burrowing back into the blankets, murmuring sounds of comfort. He lowers his feet to the floor, to the cold kiss of wood on soles, and crosses the room. Dressing quickly. He carries his boots so as not to wake her, and slips quietly out the door, down the staircase layered with a wave of carpet.

It is cold outside, and the street is dark save for a gathering of leaves, which twirl, trapped in a wind which has taken a wrong turn down Franklin Mews, which tumbles over itself, backing out of the narrow row. There are no stars. He tucks his coat around his neck and pulls his hat down tightly over his head. He follows the wind's retreat and he walks. Along streets empty and cobbled, past terraced houses, curtains drawn like eyes shut and sleeping. He walks past movement, alley cats perhaps, perhaps men. It is dark, and they have not yet electrified these streets so he notices the lamps and candles, hidden in the depths of the houses. He tucks himself deeper into his coat and walks, and the night turns imperceptibly to dawn.

o

There are two days and then one. She joins him, anticipates his early morning waking, and together they walk through the vastness of Regent's Park. They are mostly alone. They hold hands as the wind races along the broad paths, skimming the surface of puddles and tugging at the wet leaves that mat the grass. They stop and sit in the shelter of a gazebo, and watch the few who have ventured out into the rain, hidden beneath umbrellas that tremble in the gale: old men who walk alone, couples, mothers leading children through the gardens, perhaps to the zoo, skipping, Mummy, what will we see? 'Shhhh! Behave yourself, there are Bengal tigers and Burmese pythons and they eat naughty children.'

They walk. Through the darkened gardens, flowers dripping with rain. The sky is low, the leaves yellow. She takes his hand and leads him away from the long avenues and across the vast emerald lawns, two tiny figures moving through the green. He doesn't ask where they are going, but listens to the mud suck at his boots, foul sounds. The sky hangs low and grey and there is no sun.

She takes him to a small arbour and it is dry there, and he brushes her wet hair from her face. Her nose is cold. He will remember this.

Day turns to night.

o

And it is 26 November 1886.

A carriage pulls up to the Royal Albert Dock. Two men in pressed army uniforms emerge and open the doors for a middle-aged man and woman. They step tentatively to the ground, as if it is the first time they have ridden in a military vehicle, its steps are higher and its threshold thicker to support the carriage over rough terrain. One of the soldiers points to the ship and the man looks at it and then turns back to the woman. They stand by each other and he kisses her lightly. Then he turns and follows the two soldiers towards the boat. Each carries a trunk, he a smaller bag.

There is little fanfare, no bottles are broken over the bow – this custom being reserved for the christeners of maiden voyages and the drunks who sleep at the dock and occasionally wash up at the fairgrounds downstream. From the deck, the passengers stand and wave to the crowd. They wave back.

The engines start to rumble.

As they begin to move, the fog closes in over the river. Like a curtain, it covers the buildings and the piers and those who have come to bid goodbye to the steamship. Midstream, the fog grows thicker and creeps over the deck, erasing even the passengers from one another.

Slowly, one by one, the passengers return inside, and Edgar remains alone. Mist beads on his glasses and he removes them to wipe them on his waistcoat. He tries to peer through the fog, but it reveals nothing of the passing shoreline. Behind him, it obliterates the ship's smoke stack, and he feels as if he is floating in emptiness. He holds his hand out before him and watches as the swirls of white wrap around it in currents of tiny droplets.

White. Like a clean piece of paper, like uncarved ivory, all is white when the story begins.

THREE

Dear Katherine,

It has now been five days since I left London. I am sorry I have not written to you sooner, but Alexandria is our first mail stop since Marseilles, so I have decided to wait to write rather than send you letters that bear only old thoughts.

My dear, beloved Katherine, how can I describe the last few days to you? And how I wish that you were here on this journey to see everything that I am seeing! Just yesterday morning a new coastline appeared on the starboard side of the ship and I asked one of the sailors where it was. He answered, 'Africa', and seemed surprised by my question. Of course I felt foolish, but I could hardly control my excitement. This world seems both so small and so vast.

I have much to write, but before all else let me tell you about the voyage thus far, beginning from when we said goodbye. The journey from London to Calais was uneventful. The fog was thick and rarely parted long enough to give us a glimpse of anything more than the waves. The trip takes but a few hours. When we arrived in Calais it was night, and we were taken by carriage to the station, where we boarded a train for Paris. As you know, I have always dreamed of visiting the adopted home of Sebastien Erard. But no sooner had we arrived than I was on another train heading south. France really is a beautiful country, and our route took us past golden pastures, and vineyards, and even fields of lavender (famous for their perfumes – which I promise to bring you when I return). As for the French people, I have less positive words, as none of the Frenchmen I happened to meet had ever heard of Erard or the *mécanisme à étrier*, Erard's great innovation. They only stared at my enquiries as if I were mad.

In Marseilles, we boarded another ship, owned by the same line, and soon we were steaming across the Mediterranean. How I wish you could see the beauty of these waters! They are a blue like none that I have ever seen before. The closest colour I can think of is the early night-time sky, or perhaps sapphires. The camera is a wonderful invention indeed, but how I wish we could take photographs in true colour so you could see for yourself what I mean. You must go to the National Gallery, and look for Turner's *Fighting Temeraire*, it is the closest to this that I can imagine. It is very warm and I have already forgotten the cold English winters. I spent much of the first day on deck, and ended up with quite a sunburn. I must remember to wear my hat.

After the first day we passed through the Strait of Bonifacio, which runs between the islands of Sardinia and Corsica. From the ship we could see the Italian coastline. It looks very still and peaceful, and it is hard to imagine the tumultuous history that was born deep in those hills, that this is the country that gave birth to Verdi, Vivaldi, Rossini and, most of all, Cristofori.

How to describe my days to you? Apart from simply sitting on the deck and staring at the sea, I have spent many hours reading reports sent by Anthony Carroll. It is strange to think that this man, who has occupied my thoughts for weeks now, does not yet even know my name. Regardless, he does have extraordinary tastes. I opened one of the packages of sheet music that I was given to deliver to him, and found it to contain Liszt's Piano Concerto No. 1, Schumann's Toccata in C major, and others. There are some sheets whose music I don't recognize, and when I try humming them out I can't decipher any melody. I will have to ask him about these when I reach his camp.

Tomorrow we stop in Alexandria. The coast is very close now, and in the distance I can see minarets. This morning we passed a small fishing boat, and a local fisherman stood and watched us steam by, a net hanging loosely from his hands, so close that I could see the dried salt which dusted his skin. And less than a week ago I was still in London! Alas, we will stay only a short time in port and I will have no time to visit the pyramids.

There is so much more I want to tell you . . . the moon is almost full now, and at night I often go on deck to stare at it. I have heard that the Orientals believe there is a rabbit in the moon, but I still cannot see this – only a man winking, mouth wide open in surprise and wonder. And now I think I understand why he looks so, for if all is wondrous from the deck of a ship, imagine what it must be like from the moon. Two nights ago I couldn't sleep for all the heat and excitement, and I went on deck. I was looking out at the ocean when slowly, not a hundred yards from the ship, the water began to shimmer. At first I thought it was the reflection of the stars, but it appeared to take form, glowing, like thousands of tiny fires, like the streets of London at night. By its brightening, I expected to see a bizarre sea animal, but it stayed amorphous, floating on the water. It stretched for nearly a mile and then, after we had passed it and I turned back to look for it in the sea, it was gone. Last night the beast of light came again, and I learned from a travelling naturalist, who had come to the deck to look at the sky, that the light was not the light of one monster, but millions of microscopic creatures which the man called 'diatoms', and that similar creatures dye the Red Sea its famous colour. Katherine, what a strange world this is where the invisible can illuminate the waters and colour the very sea red!

My dear, I must go now. It is late, and I miss you terribly, and I hope you are not lonely. Please do not worry about me. In truth, I was a little frightened when I left and sometimes, when I lie in bed, I question why I am going. I still don't have an answer. I remember what you told me in London, that it is such noble work, that it is my duty to my country, but this cannot be: I never enlisted in the army when I was young and have little interest in our foreign affairs. I know it made you angry when I suggested that it was my duty to the piano and not the Crown, but I still feel very strongly that Dr Carroll is doing the proper thing, and that if I can help in the cause of music, perhaps *that* is my duty. Part of my decision certainly rests in my confidence in Dr Carroll, and a sense of shared mission with him and his desire to bring the music I find beautiful to places where others have only thought of bringing guns. I know that such sentiments often pale when faced with reality. I do miss you dearly and I hope that I am not on some hopeless mission. But you know that I am not one to take unnecessary risks. I might be more frightened than you by stories I hear about the war and the jungle.

Why am I wasting words on my fears and insecurities when I have so much that is beautiful to tell you? I suppose it is because I have no one else to share these thoughts with. In truth, I am already happy in ways that I have never known. I only wish you could be here with me to share this journey.

I will write again soon, my love.

Your devoted husband,

Edgar

He posted the letter in Alexandria, a short stop, where the ship took on new passengers, men in flowing robes who spoke a language that seemed to come from deep within their throats. They stayed in port for several hours, time only to wander briefly through the docks amid the smells of drying octopus and the scented bags of the spice traders. Soon they were moving again, through the Suez Canal and into another sea.

FOUR

THAT NIGHT, as the boat steamed slowly through the waters of the Red Sea, Edgar couldn't sleep. At first he tried to read a document provided for him by the War Office, a turgid piece about military campaigns during the Third Anglo-Burmese War, but gave up in boredom. The cabin was stifling, and the small porthole did little to welcome the sea air. At last he dressed and walked down the long corridor to the companionway leading onto the deck.

Outside it was cool, the sky was clear and the moon full. Weeks from now, after he has heard the myths, he will understand why this was important. Although the English call the thin, anaemic slivers of light 'new moons', this is only one way to understand them. Ask any child of the Shan, or the Wa, or the Pa-O, and they will tell you that it is the full moon which is new, for it is fresh and sparkling like the sun, and it is the thin moon which is old and frail and soon to die. And thus full moons mark beginnings, eras when change begins and one must pay close attention to portent.

Yet there remain many days before Edgar arrives in Burma, and he does not yet know the divinations of the Shan. That there are four classes of auguries: those being the omens from the sky, the omens of flying birds, the omens of feeding fowl, and the omens of the movement of four-footed beasts. He doesn't know the meanings of comets or haloes or showers of meteorites, that divination can be found in the direction of a crane's flight, that one must look for augury in the eggs of hens, in the swarming of bees, and not only if, but also where, a lizard, rat, or spider drops on one's body. That if water in a pond or river turns red, the country will be laid waste by a devastating war; such a portent foretold the destruction of Ayutthaya, the old capital of Siam. That if a man takes anything in his hand and it breaks without apparent cause, or if his turban falls off of its own accord, he will die.

Such auguries need not be invoked for Edgar Drake, not yet. He does not wear a turban and rarely breaks strings when he tunes and repairs, and as he stood on the deck the sea reflected the light of the moon with a glittering of silver on blue.

The outline of the coast could still be seen, and even the distant wink of a lighthouse. The sky was clear and sprayed with thousands of stars. He looked out at the sea, where waves flashed with their reflections.

o

The following evening Edgar sat in the saloon at the end of a long table laid with clean white cloth. Above him a chandelier betrayed the motion of the ship. An elegant affair, he had written to Katherine, They have spared no luxury. He sat alone and listened to an animated conversation between two officers about a battle in India. His thoughts wandered away to Burma, to Carroll, to tuning, to pianos, to home.

A voice from behind brought him back to the steamship. 'The piano tuner?'

Edgar turned to see a tall man in uniform, 'Yes,' he said, swallowing his food and rising to extend his hand. 'Drake. And you, sir?'

'Tideworth,' said the man, with a handsome smile. 'I am the ship's Captain from Marseilles to Bombay.'

'Of course, Captain, I recognize your name. It is an honour to meet you.'

'No, Mr Drake. The honour is mine. I am sorry that I could not introduce myself sooner. I have looked forward to making your acquaintance for several weeks now.'

'*My* acquaintance, really!' said Edgar. 'Whatever for?'

'I should have told you when I introduced myself. I am a friend of Anthony Carroll. He wrote and told me to expect your passage. He is eagerly looking forward to meeting you.'

'And I him. He is, indeed, my commission.' He laughed.

The Captain motioned to the chairs. 'Please, let's sit,' he said. 'I didn't mean to interrupt your meal.'

'Of course not, Captain, I have eaten enough already. You serve us too well.' They sat down at the table. 'So, Doctor Carroll wrote about me? I am curious as to what he said.'

'Not much. I think they haven't even informed him of your name. He did tell me you were a fine tuner of pianos and that your safe passage is extremely important to him. He also said that you may be out of sorts on this journey and that I should watch over you.'

'That is too kind. But I seem to be managing. Although, without an Indian war under my belt,' he tilted his head towards the men beside him, 'I am not much for conversation here.'

'Oh, they are usually bores,' answered the Captain, lowering his voice, an unnecessary precaution for the officers were fairly drunk and hadn't even noticed his presence.

'Regardless, I hope I am not taking you away from your duties.'

'Not at all, Mr Drake. The sailing is smooth, as they say. We should be in Aden in six days, if we don't have any problems. They will call if they need me. Tell me, have you enjoyed the journey?'

'Enchanting. This is my first trip away from England and everything is beautiful beyond my imagination. I know the Continent mostly through its music, or its pianos.' When the Captain didn't respond, Edgar added awkwardly, 'I am a specialist in Erard pianos. It is a French model.'

The Captain looked at him with curiosity. 'And the journey to Alexandria? No pianos there, I imagine.'

'No, no pianos,' he laughed. 'But quite a view, nonetheless. I have spent hours on deck. It is as though I am a young man again, you must understand.'

'Of course. I still remember the first time I sailed this route. I even wrote poems about it, silly odes about sailing at the cusp of two continents, each vast and barren, stretching through hundreds of miles of sands and fabled cities, each rising to sky, to the Levant, to the Congo. You can imagine, I am sure. Being at sea has lost none of its thrill, although thankfully I long ago abandoned poetry. Tell me, have you made the acquaintance of any of the other passengers?'

'Not really. I am not the outgoing sort. The passage is thrilling enough. It is all quite new for me.'

'Well, it's a pity you haven't met more of the others. They are always an extraordinary lot. Without them, I might even tire of this view.'

'Extraordinary. How so?'

'Oh, if only I had the hours to tell you all the tales of my passengers. Where they embark is exotic enough. Not only from Europe or Asia, but any of the thousands of ports of call along the Mediterranean, the North African coast, Arabia. They call this route the "axis of the world". The stories, though! I need only to look around the room . . .' He leaned closer. 'For example, over there at the back table, do you see the old gentleman dining with that white-haired woman?'

'I do. He is probably the oldest fellow on the ship.'

'His name is William Penfield. Former officer with the East India Company. Bloody Bill, they called him. Perhaps the most decorated and violent soldier to serve in the colonies.'

'That old man?'

'The same. Next time you are near him look at his left hand. He is missing two fingers from a skirmish during his first tour. His men used to joke that he took a thousand lives for each of his fingers.'

'Terrible.'

'That's not the least of it, but I will spare you the details. Now look to his left. That young fellow, with dark hair, they call *him* "Teak Harry". I don't know his real name. An Armenian from Baku. His father was a timber man, who licensed steamers to carry Siberian wood from the northern shore of the Caspian Sea to its southern coast. For a time, they say, he controlled the entire market into Persia, until he was assassinated ten years ago. The whole family fled, some to Turkey, others to Europe. Teak Harry headed east, for the Indo-Chinese market. Reputation as a swashbuckler and adventurer. There are rumours that say he even funded Garnier's journey up the Mekong to find its source, although there is no proof of this, and if it is true Harry has been discreet, to preserve his British shipping contracts. Harry will probably be with you all the way to Rangoon, although he will take one of his company steamships to Mandalay. He has a mansion, no, a court, lavish enough to make the kings of Ava jealous which, apparently, it did. They say Thibaw twice tried to have Harry killed, but the Armenian escaped. You may pass his quarters in Mandalay. He lives and breathes teak. Difficult to talk to unless you are in the business.' The Captain scarcely stopped to breathe. 'Behind him, the portly fellow, a Frenchman, Jean-Baptiste Valerie, professor of linguistics at the Sorbonne. They say he speaks twenty-seven languages, three of which aren't spoken by any other white men, not even the missionaries.'

'And the man beside him, the man with the rings? A striking fellow.'

'Ah, the rug dealer Nader Modarress, a Persian who specializes in Bakhtiari rugs. He made this journey with two mistresses – unusual, because he keeps enough wives in Bombay to keep him too busy to sell rugs. He is staying in the royal cabin. He can always afford the fare. As you saw, he has gold rings on each finger – you must try to look at them, each ring is set with extraordinary jewels.'

'He boarded with another gentleman, a large blond fellow.'

'Bodyguard. A Norwegian, I think. Although I doubt he is much good. He spends half his time smoking opium with the stokers – nasty habit, but it keeps them from complaining much. Modarress has another character in his hire, a spectacled fellow, a poet from Kiev whom Modarress hired to compose odes to his wives – the Persian fashions himself a romantic, but has trouble with his adjectives. Ah – forgive me – I am gossiping like a schoolgirl. Come, let's take some air before I have to return to work.'

They rose and walked outside on deck. In the bow stood a lone figure wrapped in a long white robe, which fluttered about his body.

Edgar watched him. 'I don't think he has moved from that spot since we left Alexandria.'

'Perhaps our strangest passenger of all. We call him the Man with One Story. He has travelled this route for as long as I can remember. He is always alone. I do not know who pays his fare or what his business is. He travels in the lower berths, boards in Alexandria and disembarks at Aden. I have never seen him make the return journey.'

'And why do you call him the Man with One Story?'

The Captain chuckled. 'An old name. On the rare voyages that he chooses to speak, he tells only one tale. I have heard it once, and I have never forgotten it. He doesn't make conversation. He only begins the story and doesn't stop until it is finished. It is eerie, as if one is listening to a phonograph. Mostly he's silent, but for those who hear the story . . . they are rarely the same again.'

'He speaks English?'

'A deliberate English, almost as if he is reading.'

'And the subject of this story?'

'Ah, Mr Drake, that I will leave for you to discover, if you are meant to. Really only he can tell it.'

And, as if rehearsed, there was a call from the galley. Edgar had other questions, about Anthony Carroll, about the Man with One Story, but the Captain quickly bid him goodnight and disappeared into the dining hall, leaving him alone, breathing the scent of the sea air, loaded with salt and premonition.

o

The next morning Edgar awoke early to the heat pounding at the porthole. He dressed and walked down the long corridor and up to the deck. It was bright and he could feel the sun even as it barely hovered over the eastern hills. The sea was wide and both shores could still be faintly seen. Further aft he saw the man in white robes standing at the rail.

He had become accustomed to taking this stroll every morning, circling the ship's deck until it became too warm. It was on one of these walks that he had first seen the man unroll his prayer mat to pray with the others. He had often seen him since then, but he said nothing.

Yet on this warm morning, as he followed the same route of his usual morning stroll, aft along the railing, towards the man in the white robes, he felt his legs weakening, I am afraid, he thought, and he tried to tell himself that this morning's walk was no different from the previous day's, but he knew it wasn't true. The Captain had spoken with a seriousness that seemed oddly out of character for the tall, light-hearted sailor and, for a moment, Edgar thought that perhaps he had imagined the conversation, that the Captain had left him in the dining hall, that he had gone on deck alone. Or, he thought several steps later, the Captain knew they would meet, a new traveller and a storyteller, Perhaps this is what is meant by the gravity of stories.

He found himself standing near the man. 'Fine morning, sir,' he said.

The old man nodded. His face was dark, his beard the colour of his robes. Edgar didn't know what to say, but he forced himself to remain at the railing. The man was silent. Waves washed against the bow of the ship, their sound lost in the roar of the steam engines.

'This is your first time in the Red Sea,' said the man, his voice deep with an unfamiliar accent.

'Yes, it is, this is my first time away from England, actually—'

The old man interrupted him. 'You must show me your lips when you speak,' he said. 'I am deaf.'

Edgar turned. 'I am sorry. I didn't know . . .'

'Your name?' asked the old man.

'Drake . . . here . . .'. He reached into his pocket and pulled out a card which he had had printed especially for the journey.

Edgar Drake
Piano Tuner – Erards-a-Speciality
14 Franklin Mews
London

The sight of the tiny card with curlicue lettering in the wrinkled hands of the old man suddenly embarrassed him. But the old man puzzled over the card. 'An English piano tuner. A man who knows sound. Would you like to hear a story, Mr Edgar Drake? An old deaf man's story?'

o

Thirty years ago, when I was much younger and not crippled by the pains of old age, I worked as deckhand, travelling this very route from Suez to the Straits of Bab al Mandab. Unlike today's steamers that plough directly through the sea without stopping, we rode by sail and criss-crossed the Red Sea, dropping anchor at dozens of tiny ports on both the African and Arabian shores, towns with names like Fareez and Gomaina, Tektozu and Weevineev, many of which have been lost to the sands, where we stopped to trade with nomads who sold rugs and pots scavenged from abandoned desert cities. I was travelling this same route when our boat was caught in a storm. She was old and should have been banned from sailing. We reefed the sails, but the hull sprung a leak, and the rush of the water split the boat. I fell and struck my head, and entered blackness.

When I awoke I was lying on a sandy shore, alone amidst some wreckage of the hull, which I must have clung to by good fortune. At first I found myself immobile and feared I had been paralysed, but found only that I was wrapped tightly in my headdress, which must have unravelled from my head and clung to my body like a child's swaddling, like the mummies they pull out of the Egyptian sands. It took me a long time to regain my wits. My body was badly bruised, and when I tried to breathe pain shot through my ribs. The sun was already high in the sky and my body was caked with the salt of the sea, my throat and tongue parched and swollen. Pale blue water lapped at my feet and at the piece of broken hull, which still bore the first three scrawled Arabic figures from what was once the ship's name.

At long last I unravelled my headdress and retied it loosely. I rose to my feet. The land around me was flat, but in the distance I could see mountains, dry and barren. Like any man who has grown up in the desert, I could only think of one thing: water. I knew from our travels that the coastline is marked by many small estuaries, most brackish, but some of which, according to the nomads, merge with sweet-water streams draining aquifers or the snows that have fallen on the peaks of distant mountains. So I decided to follow the coast, in the hope of finding such a river. At least the sea would keep me oriented and perhaps, perhaps, I might sight a passing ship.

As I walked, the sun rose over the hills, which I knew meant that I was in Africa. This realization was simple but frightening. We have all been lost, but it is rare that we do not know on which continent's sandy shore we wander. I did not speak the language, nor did I know the land as I did Arabia. Yet something emboldened me, perhaps youth, perhaps the delirium of the sun.

I had not walked one hour, when I reached a turn in the coastline, where a sliver of the sea sliced into the shore. I tasted the water. It was still salty, yet beside me lay a single thin branch which had been washed downstream, and on it a single leaf, dry and shaking in the wind. My travels and trading had taught me a little about plants, for when we anchored in Fareez and Gomaina, we traded for herbs with the nomads there. And this little leaf I recognized as the plant we call *belaidour*, and Berbers call *adil-ououchchn*, whose tea brings the drinker dreams of the future, and whose berries make women's eyes wide and dark. Yet at that moment I thought little of the preparation of tea and much of botany. For *belaidour* is expensive because it does not grow along the Red Sea, but in wooded mountains many miles west. This gave me the faint hope that man had once been here, and if man then perhaps water.

So with this hope alone I turned inland, following the sliver of sea south, with the prayer that I would find the source of the *belaidour*, and with it the water that nourished those who traded it.

I walked for the remainder of the day and into the night. I still remember the arc of the moon as it passed through the sky. It wasn't half full, but the cloudless sky gave no shelter from the light that cast itself over the water and sand. What I don't remember is that sometime during the night I lay down to rest, and I fell asleep.

I awoke to the gentle prodding of a goatherd's staff and opened my eyes to see two young boys, wearing only loincloths and necklaces. One of them crouched in front of me, staring with a quizzical gaze. The other, who looked younger, stood behind him, watching over his shoulder. We stayed like this for the duration of many breaths, neither of us moving, watching only, he squatting, holding his knees, looking curiously, defiantly into my eyes. Slowly I rose to a sitting position, never dropping my gaze. I raised my hand and greeted him in my own tongue.

The boy didn't move. Briefly his eyes left my face and jumped to my hand, stared at it and looked back at my face. The boy behind him said something in a language that I didn't understand and the older one nodded, still not dropping his gaze. He raised his free hand behind him, and the younger boy unstrapped a leather canteen from his shoulders and placed it in the raised hand. The older boy untied a thin lace that had closed the mouth of the bag and handed it to me. As I raised the bag to my lips, I closed my eyes and began to drink.

I was so thirsty I could have emptied the bag ten times over. But the heat bid temperance; I did not know where the water had come from, nor how much remained. Finished drinking, I lowered the bag and handed it back to the older boy, who tied it without looking, his fingers winding the leather lace. He stood up and spoke to me in a loud voice, and although the language was foreign, the commanding tone of a child faced with responsibility is universal. I waited. He spoke again, louder this time. I pointed to my mouth and shook my head, as I do today to my ears. For then I was not yet deaf. That story is yet to come.

Beside me, the boy spoke again, loud and sharply, as if frustrated. He banged his staff on the ground. I waited a moment and then rose slowly, to show I did so out of my own will and not for all his shouting. I would not let myself be commanded by a boy.

Once I had risen, I had my first chance to examine the landscape around us. I had fallen asleep by water and no further than thirty paces ahead I could see where a little brook bubbled into the estuary, casting reflected currents across the pebbles. At its mouth a scattering of pale plants clung to the rocks. I stopped at the brook to drink. The boys waited and said nothing, and soon we continued up a bluff, where a pair of goats gnawed at the grasses. The boys prodded them along, and we followed a dry streambed that must have fed the river in the rains.

It was morning but already hot, and steep walls rose on either side of the sandy path, intensifying both the heat and the sound of our steps. The boys' voices echoed as they chattered to the goats, strange sounds that I recall vividly. Now that I am old, I wonder if this was due to any physical property of the ravine, or because in less than two days I would no longer hear.

We followed the ravine for several miles, until, at a bend identical to hundreds we had passed in our route, the goats scampered instinctively up a steep track. The boys followed nimbly, their sandals finding impossible toeholds in the sandy wall. I tried my best to keep up, but slipped, skinning my knee before finding a solid grip and pulling myself up the track they had trodden so delicately. At the top, I remember stopping to inspect my leg. It was a small, superficial wound and would dry immediately in the heat. And yet I remember this action, not for itself, but for what followed. For when I looked up the boys were running down a broad slope, chasing the goats. Below them stretched one of the most stunning visions I have ever seen. Indeed, had I been struck with blindness rather than deafness, I think I would have been content. For nothing, not even the pounding surf of Bab al Mandab could match the scene that stretched out before me, the slope descending, flattening into a vast desert plain that stretched into a horizon blurred with sandstorms. And out of the thick dust, whose silence belied the rage known to anyone who has ever been caught in the terror of one of the storms, marched legions of caravans, from every point on the compass, long, dark trails of horses and camels, all emerging from the blur which swept across the valley, and all converging on a tent encampment that lay at the base of the hill.

There must have been hundreds of tents already, perhaps thousands if approaching caravans could be counted. From my perch on top of the mountain I gazed out over the tents. A number of the styles I recognized. The peaked white tents of the Borobodo people, who often came to the ports at which we called to trade camel skins. The broad flat tents of the Yus, a warrior tribe who haunted the southern reaches of the Sinai, famous among the Egyptians for raids on traders, so fierce that ships would often not drop anchor if the tents were sighted on shore. The Rebez, an Arabian race, who dug holes in the sand before laying skins as a roof and setting a long pole at the thresholds of their homes, which serves as a beacon should shifting sands bury a home and its inhabitants. Beyond these, however, most of the structures were foreign to me, suggesting perhaps that their people came from deeper in the African interior.

I heard a piercing whistle from down the hill. Halfway between me and the tent city the older boy was shouting and waving his staff. I ran and soon I reached the boys, and we descended the remainder of the hill together. We passed another group of boys playing with rocks and sticks, and my friends called out to them in greeting. I noticed they held their heads high and pointed frequently to me. I was, I imagine, an impressive find. We passed the first tents, where camels were tethered to stakes outside. I could see firelight through their entrances, but no one came out to greet us. Then more tents, and as I followed my guides to a mysterious end, the paths between them began to bustle with more activity. I passed hooded nomads, whose faces I couldn't discern, dark Africans bedecked with fine furs, veiled women who stared at me and dropped their eyes quickly when our gazes met. In such a gathering, I caused little sensation. Twice I passed men I heard speaking Arabic, but both shame at my dishevelment and the haste of the boys kept me from stopping. We passed several camp-fires, where silhouetted musicians played songs I did not recognize. The boys stopped briefly at one, and I could hear the older one whisper the words as they watched the singers. Then we turned and plunged back into alleyways of tent and sand. At last we reached a large circular tent with a flat, slightly pointed roof and an open hole in the centre, from which wisps of smoke followed the glow of the fire into the night sky. The boys tied the goats to a post outside the tent, next to a pair of camels. They lifted the tent flap and motioned me inside.

Before I saw the people sitting beside the fire, I was struck by the rich smell coming from the central spit. It was testament to my hunger that I should notice the roasting flank of meat before I noticed my new hosts. It was a single leg of goat, and drops of blood swelled on the simmering meat until they dropped to the fire. At my side the boys spoke rapidly, gesturing at me. They were addressing a withered old woman, who lay on a thin camel-skin rug on a raised bed near the edge of the tent. Her hair was wrapped tightly in a thin, translucent shawl, lending her head the illusion of a desert tortoise. She held a long pipe to her mouth and puffed at it in contemplation. The boys finished talking and for some time the woman said nothing. Finally she nodded to them and they bowed and scampered to the other edge of the tent, where they threw themselves onto a rug, pulled their knees to their chests and stared at me. There were others in the tent as well, perhaps ten silent faces.

'You have come from far away,' said the old turtle woman.

I was shocked. 'You speak Arabic?' I asked.

'Enough to trade. Please, sit.' She nodded at a young girl who sat near the door. The girl jumped to her feet and brought a small rug, which she laid on the sand for me. I sat.

'My grandchildren said that they found you near the coast of the Red Sea.'

'They did. They gave me water and, by doing so, saved my life.'

'How did you get there?' Her voice was stern.

'An accident. I was on a ship travelling from Suez to Bab al Mandab when there was a storm. The ship was wrecked. I do not know what happened to my shipmates, but I fear them dead.'

The turtle woman turned to the room and spoke to them. There was nodding and hasty chatter.

When she stopped speaking, I spoke again. 'Where am I?'

The old woman shook her head. One eye, I noticed, deviated from the other, giving her an eerie sense of watchfulness, as if while she scrutinized me, she was also carefully watching the room. 'That is a dangerous question,' she said. 'Already there are those who feel that the fame of the appearance has spread too far, that if too many people come She will not return. You are fortunate to have found me, for there are those here who would have killed you.'

With those words, the relief of finding civilization was washed over with the nausea of fear. 'I don't understand,' I said.

'Do not ask too much. You have come at an auspicious time. The Bantu astrologers say that tomorrow She may appear to sing. And then your questions will be answered.' And with those words she raised her pipe to her mouth once again and turned first one eye, and then the other, back to the fire. No one spoke to me for the remainder of the evening. I feasted on the roasted leg and drank a sweet nectar until I fell asleep before the fire.

I awoke the next morning to find the tent empty. I prayed and then lifted the flap of the tent, emerging into the heat. The sun hung in the centre of the sky; in my exhaustion, I had slept nearly to noon. The camels were still tethered, but both goats were gone. I went back inside the tent. I had no water to wash myself, but I tried my best to fold and smooth my headdress with my hands. I returned outside.

The paths were relatively empty; everyone must have been hiding from the sun. I saw a group of men saddling camels in preparation for hunting, and nearby a group of young girls, dressed in a vivid blue, grinding grain. Towards the outer edge of the encampment I saw the new arrivals, some of whom must have arrived at dawn and who still worked to unroll tents from the backs of stoical camels. I walked to the edge of the camp, where the tent city ended suddenly, where a line had been etched, drawn by many tribes as a ritual barrier between their camp and the desert. The sands stretched out unbroken. I thought back on the old woman's words. Long ago, when I was a child, I had accompanied my brother to Aden, where we had spent the night with a tribe of Bedouin. The Bedouin speak their own dialect, but I understood some as much of my youth had been passed in trading bazaars, where the young achieve a great collection of tongues. I remembered we had joined the family by their fire and listened to their grandfather tell a story of a congress of tribes. In the light of the fire he had described in exquisite detail each tribe, the robes they wore, their customs, their beasts, even the colour of their eyes. I had been spellbound and sometime during the night fell asleep before the story was finished, to awake only when my brother prodded me and we crawled back into the tent. Now, standing at the edge of the desert, something in that old man's story returned to me, a sensation only, like a memory of a dream.

In the distance, beyond a small dune, I saw a flutter of red fabric, tickled by the wind. It was brief, like the short flight of a bird, but such visions are rare in the desert and beg inspection. I stepped across the line – at the time I thought this a superstition of infidels, although now I am not so certain. I climbed the dune and descended into a plain of sand. There was no one. I felt a presence behind me and turned. It was a woman. She stood nearly one hand shorter than me and stared up from behind a red veil. I thought by the darkness of her skin that she must be from one of the Ethiopian tribes, but when I kept staring at her, she greeted me.

'Salaam aleikum.'

'Wa aleikum al-salaam,' I answered. 'Where are you from?'

'From the same land as you,' she said, but her accent was strange.

'Then you are far from home,' I said.

'And you as well.'

I stood speechless, entranced by the softness of her words, by her eyes. 'What are you doing alone in the sands?' I asked.

For a long time she didn't speak. My eyes followed her veil down to her body, which was covered in thick red robes that gave no clue to the form that lay beneath. The fabric fell and pooled on the ground, where the wind had already dusted it with a layer of sand, giving the impression that she had risen from the dunes. Then she spoke again. 'I must fetch water,' she said and looked down at an earthen pot she was balancing on her hip. 'I am afraid I will get lost in the sand. Will you come with me?'

'But I don't know where to find any,' I protested, shaken by the boldness of her proposition, how close she stood to me.

'I do,' she said.

But neither of us moved. I had never seen eyes the colour of hers – not dark brown like the women from my home, but softer, lighter, the colour of sand. A breeze danced about us and her veil shook, and I had a fleeting glimpse of her face, strange in ways I couldn't understand for I blinked and again she was hidden.

'Come,' she said, and began to walk. A wind whipped up around us, firing sand against our skin, stinging, like a thousand pins.

'Perhaps we should turn back,' I said, 'or we will be lost in the storm.'

She kept walking.

I caught up with her. The storm was getting worse. 'Let's turn back. It is too dangerous to be caught out here alone.'

'We cannot go back,' she said. 'We are not from here.'

'But the storm—'

'Stay with me.'

'But—'

She turned. 'You are frightened.'

'Not frightened. I know the desert. We can return later.'

'Ibrahim,' she said.

'My name.'

'Ibrahim,' she said again and stepped towards me.

My hands hung limply at my side. 'You know my name.'

'Quiet,' she said. 'The sand will stop.'

And suddenly the wind disappeared. Fine particles of sand froze in the air, like tiny planets. They stayed suspended in space, unmovable, whitening the sky, the horizon, erasing everything but her.

She stepped towards me once more and set the pot on the ground. 'Ibrahim,' she repeated and lifted her veil from her face.

I have never seen a vision so beautiful and yet so hideous. With woman's eyes she stared at me, but her mouth wavered, like a mirage, not the mouth and nose of a woman, but of a deer, its skin covered with a soft fur. I couldn't speak, and there was a howling, and the sand took motion once again, spinning about us, blurring her. I raised my hands to my eyes.

And then again the sand stopped.

I lowered my hands tentatively. I was alone, suspended in the sand. My eyes knew not what to focus on, nor what direction lay the sky or the earth. '*Salaam*,' I whispered.

And then from somewhere hidden came the sound of a woman singing.

It began softly and at first I didn't recognize it as song. It was low and sweet, a song like wine, forbidden and intoxicating, like nothing I have ever heard. I could not understand its words and its melody was utterly foreign. And yet in it there was something so intimate that I felt naked, ashamed.

The wailing crescendoed, the sand began again to spin about me. Through its whirling I caught glimpses of images. Of circling birds, of the camp, the cities of tents, the sun setting quickly, splintering, igniting the desert into a giant flame that stretched out across the dunes, enveloping all and then receding, leaving only scattered campfires. Then it was suddenly night and around the campfires gathered travellers, dancers, musicians, drummers, a thousand instruments that wailed like shifting sand, rising, louder and piercing, and before me a snake charmer came and played an oud, and his snakes climbed out of their basket and over his legs. Girls danced, their bodies buttered and scented, glistening in the campfires, and I found myself staring at a giant with scars on his skin like stars, a flesh tattooed with stories, and the scars became men clothed in the skins of lizards and children made of clay, and they danced and the children shattered away. And then it was day again and the visions vanished. I was left only with the sand and the scream, and suddenly this stopped. I lifted my hand before my face, and called out, 'Who are you?' But I could no longer hear my voice.

I felt a hand on my shoulder, and opened my eyes to find myself lying by the sea, my legs half-submerged in the water. There was a man squatting beside me. I saw his mouth move, but I couldn't hear him. Several others stood along the shore, watching me. The man started to speak again, but I heard nothing, not his voice, not the wash of the waves as they lapped over my legs. I pointed to my ears and shook my head. 'I cannot hear you,' I said. 'I am deaf.'

Another man approached me and the two raised me to my feet. There was a small boat, its bow wedged into the sand, its stern shifting in the waves. They walked me to the boat and we boarded. If they spoke, I could not hear them. They paddled into the Red Sea and towards a waiting ship, whose marks I knew as a merchant ship from Alexandria.

○

For the entire narration the old man's eyes had not left Edgar's face. Now he turned to the sea. 'I have told this story to many,' he said. 'For I want to find another soul who has heard the song that made me deaf.'

Edgar touched his arm lightly, so he would turn and see his

lips. 'How do you know it wasn't a dream? That you didn't hit your head in the accident? Songs cannot make men deaf.'

'Oh, I would wish it was a dream. But it couldn't have been. The moon had changed and by the ship's calendar, which I saw the next morning at breakfast, it was twenty days after my boat had capsized. But by then I already knew this, for that night when I undressed for bed I remarked at how worn my sandals were. And in Rewesh, our last port of call before the accident, I had bought a new pair.

'Besides,' he said, 'I don't believe it was the song that made me deaf. I think that after I had heard something so beautiful my ears simply stopped sensing sound because they knew that they would never hear such perfection again. I don't know if this makes sense to a tuner of strings.'

The sun was now high in the sky. Edgar felt its heat against his face. The old man spoke. 'My One Story is over, and I have no more stories to tell, for just as there can be no sound after that song, for me there can be no stories after that one. And now we must go inside, for the sun has ways of making even the sane delirious.'

o

They steamed through the Red Sea. The waters lightened and they crossed the Straits of Bab al Mandab, the shore washed by waves from the Indian Ocean. They dropped anchor in the port of Aden, where the harbour was full with steamers destined for all over the world, in whose shadows tiny Arab dhows darted beneath lateen sails. Edgar Drake stood on the deck and watched the port and the robed men who clambered to and from the ship's hull. He didn't see the Man with One Story leave, but when he looked at the spot on the deck where the man always sat he was gone.

FIVE

THE JOURNEY IS faster now. In two days the coast appears
tentatively, as tiny wooded islands that dot the shore like
shattered fragments of the mainland. They are dark and green;
Edgar can see nothing through the deep foliage and wonders if
they are inhabited. He asks a fellow traveller, a retired civil administrator, who tells him that one of the islands is home to a temple
that he calls Elephanta, where the Hindus worship an 'Elephant
with Many Arms'.

'It is a strange place, full of superstitions,' says the man, but
Edgar says nothing. Once, in London, he tuned the Erard of a
wealthy Indian banker, the son of a Maharaja, who showed him
a shrine to an elephant with many arms, which he kept on a shelf
above the piano. He listens to the songs, the man had said, and
Edgar liked this religion, where gods enjoyed music, and a piano
could be used to pray.

Faster. Hundreds of tiny fishing boats, lorchas, ferries, rafts,
junks, dhows, swarm at the mouth of Bombay harbour, parting
before the towering hull of the steamer. The steamer slows into
port, squeezing between two smaller merchant ships. The passengers disembark, to be met on the dock by carriages belonging
to the shipping company, which take them to the railway station.
There is no time to walk the streets, a uniformed representative
from the ship's line says, The train is waiting, Your steamship is a

day late, The wind was strong. They go through the back gate of the station. Edgar waits as his trunks are unloaded and loaded again. He watches closely; if his tools are lost, they cannot be replaced. At the far end of the station, where the third-class carriages wait, he sees a mass of bodies pushing forward on the platform. A hand takes his arm and leads him onto the train and to his berth and soon they are moving again.

Faster now, they move past the platforms, and Edgar Drake looks out over crowds such as he has never seen, not even on the poorest streets of London. The train picks up speed, passing shanty towns built to the edge of the track, children scattering only feet before the engine. Edgar presses his face to the glass to watch the jumbled houses, the peeling tenements stained with mildew, balconies decorated with hanging plants, and every street filled with thousands of people, pushing forward, watching the train pass.

o

The train hurtled into the interior of India. Nashik, Bhusawal, Jabalpur, the names of the towns growing stranger and, thought Edgar, more melodic. They crossed a vast plateau, where the sun rose and set and they didn't see a soul moving.

Occasionally they stopped, the engine slowing, screeching into wind-beaten, lonely stations. There, from the shadows, vendors would descend on the train, pushing up against the windows, thrusting in pungent plates of curried meat, the sour smell of lime and betel, jewellery, fans, picture postcards of castles and camels and Hindu gods, fruits and dusted sweets, beggars' bowls, cracked pots filled with dirty coins. Through the windows would come the wares and the voices, Buy sir, please buy sir, for you sir, special for you, and the train would start to move again, and some of the vendors, young men usually, would hang on, laughing, until they were prised off by a policeman's baton. Sometimes they made it further, jumping off only when the train started moving too fast.

One night Edgar awoke as the train pulled into a small, dark station, somewhere south of Allahabad. Bodies huddled in the crevices of the buildings lining the tracks. The platform was empty except for a few vendors who marched along the windows, peeking in to see if anyone was awake. One by one they stopped at Edgar's window, Mangoes, sir, for you, Do you want your shoes polished, sir, just pass them through the window, Samosas, they are delicious, sir. This is a lonely place for a shoeblack, thought Edgar, and a young man walked up to the window and stopped. He said nothing, but looked in and waited. At last, Edgar began to feel uncomfortable beneath the boy's gaze. What are you selling? he asked. I am a Poet-Wallah, sir. A Poet-Wallah. Yes, sir, give me an anna, and I will recite for you a poem. What poem? Any poem, sir, I know them all, but for you I have a special poem, the poem is old and it is from Burma, where they call it 'The Tale of the Journey of the *Leip-bya*', but I only call it 'The Butterfly-Spirit', for I have adapted it myself, It is only one anna. You knew I am going to Burma, How? I know, for I know the direction of stories, my poems are daughters of prophecy. Here is an anna, quick now, for the train is moving. And it was, groaning as the wheels turned. Tell me quickly, said Edgar, suddenly feeling a swell of panic, There is a reason you chose my carriage. The train was moving faster, the young man's hair began to whip with the wind. It is a tale of dreams, he yelled, They are all tales of dreams. Faster now, and Edgar could hear the sounds of other voices, Hey, boy, get off the train, You, stowaway, get off, and Edgar wanted to shout back, when briefly there appeared at the window the form of a turbaned policeman, also running, and the flash of a baton, and the boy broke off and fell into the night.

o

The land fell and became forested, and their route approached that of the Ganges, passing the holy city of Benares, where, as the passengers slept, men rose at dawn to sink themselves into the water of the river and pray. They reached Calcutta after three days and once again climbed into carriages, that pushed through the swarms of people to the docks. There Edgar boarded a new ship, smaller now, for there were fewer people travelling to Rangoon.

Once again the steam engines rumbled. They followed the muddy outflow of the Ganges into the Bay of Bengal.

Gulls circled overhead and the air was heavy and humid. Edgar peeled his shirt from his body and fanned himself with his hat. To the south storm clouds hovered, waiting. Calcutta soon disappeared from the horizon. The brown waters of the Ganges faded, spinning off into the sea in spirals of sediment.

He knew from his itinerary that only three days remained before they would reach Rangoon. He began to read again. His bag was packed with papers, with equal contributions from Katherine and the War Office. He read military briefings and newspaper clippings, personal reports and chapters of gazetteers. He pored over maps, and he tried to study some phrases of Burmese. There was an envelope addressed 'To the Piano Tuner, to be opened only upon arriving in Mae Lwin, A.C.'. He had been tempted to read it since leaving England, but had resisted only out of respect for the Doctor; surely Carroll had good reason to ask him to wait. There were two longer pieces, histories of Burma and the Shan. The first he had read in his workshop back in London, and he continued to return to it. It was intimidating, he thought, there were so many unfamiliar names. Now he remembered the second history as the one Katherine had recommended, written by Anthony Carroll himself. He was surprised he hadn't recalled this earlier, and carried the report to his bunk to read. Within the first few lines, he saw how different it was from the others.

A GENERAL HISTORY OF THE SHAN PEOPLES,
WITH SPECIAL ATTENTION TO THE POLITICAL SITUATION
OF THE REVOLT IN THE SHAN STATES
Submitted by Surgeon-Major Anthony Carroll,
Mae Lwin, Southern Shan States

(From the War Office: Please be advised that the content of
this report is subject to change. It is recommended that all
concerned parties follow closely updates of these reports,
available upon request from the War Office.)

I General History of the Shan

If one were to ask a Burman about the geography of his
land, perhaps he would first answer with a description of the
nga-hlyin, the four giants who live beneath the earth. Sadly,
official memoranda afford no space for such complexities. Yet,
it is impossible to understand the history of the Shan without
considering briefly the physiognomy of their home. The area
currently referred to as 'the Shan States' consists of a large
plateau that floats to the east above the dusty central valley
of the Irrawaddy River. It is a vast and green Elysian plain,
which extends north to the border of Yunnan and east to
Siam. Through this plateau cut powerful rivers, twisting south
like tails of the Himalayan dragon. The largest of these is the
Salween River. The importance of this geography to history
(and thus to the current political situation) lies in the affinity
of the Shan to other races of the plateau, as well as their
isolation from the lowland Burmans. Here, a sometimes
confusing terminology merits explanation: I use 'Burman' to
refer to an ethnic group, while I use 'Burmese' to describe
the kingdom and government of Burma, as well as the language. Although these words are often used interchangeably,
here I have chosen to stress this distinction: not all Burmese
kings were Burman; all Burmese kings had non-Burman subjects, including, among many others, the Kachin, the Karen,

and the Shan, each of whom once had their own kingdoms within the present borders of 'Burma'. Today, although these tribes are racked by internal divisions, they still resent the rule of others. As will become clear from the remainder of this report, the Shan revolt against British rule finds its beginnings in an incipient revolt against a Burman king.

The Shan, who refer to themselves as the Tai or Thai, share a common historical heritage with their eastern neighbours, the Siamese, the Lao and the Yunnanese. The Shan believe their ancestral home was in southern China. Although some scholars question this, there is ample evidence that by the late twelfth century, at the time of the Mongol invasions, the Tai-Thai people had established a number of kingdoms. These included the fabled Yunnanese kingdom of Xipsongbanna, whose name means 'Kingdom of ten thousand rice fields', the ancient Siamese capital at Sukhothai, and – more importantly for the subject of this briefing – two kingdoms within the present borders of Burma: the kingdom of Tai Mao in the north and the kingdom of Ava in the vicinity of present-day Mandalay. The power of these kingdoms was substantial indeed; the Shan ruled much of Burma for over three centuries, from the fall of the great Burman capital of Pagan (whose vast wind-worn temples still sit in lonely vigil on the banks of the Irrawaddy River) at the turn of the thirteenth century, until 1555, when the Burman state of Pegu eclipsed the Shan empire at Ava, beginning three centuries of rule that grew into the recent kingdom of Burma.

Following the fall of the Shan kingdom of Ava in 1555 and the destruction of the Tai Mao kingdom by Chinese invaders in 1604, the Shan splintered into small principalities, like shards of a once-beautiful porcelain vase. This fragmentation continues to mark the Shan States to this day. Despite this general disunity, however, the Shan were occasionally able to mobilize against their common Burman enemy, notably in a popular Shan revolt in Hanthawaddy in 1564 or, more recently, in a rebellion following the execution of a popular leader in the northern Shan city of Hsenwi. While these events may seem of distant memory, their importance cannot be underestimated, for at times of war these legends spread out over the plateau like flames through a drought-stricken land, rising on the smoke of campfire tales, whispered on the lips of elders to circles of wide-eyed children.

The result of this fragmentation was the development of unique political structures, which are important to consider because they play a great role in our current situation. Shan principalities (of which there were forty-one by the 1870s) were the highest order of political organization in a highly hierarchical system of local rule. Such principalities, termed *muang* by the Shan, were ruled by a *sawbwa* (Burmese transliteration, which I will adopt in the remainder of this report). Immediately below the *sawbwa* were other divisions, from districts to groups of villages to individual hamlets, each ultimately subservient to the rule of the *sawbwa*. This fragmentation of rule resulted in frequent internecine wars on the Shan Plateau and a failure to unite to throw off the yoke of Burman rule. Here the analogy of the shattered vase grows useful: just as fragments of porcelain cannot hold water, so the fragments of governments could do little to control a growing anarchy. As a result, much of the Shan countryside is plagued by bands of dacoits (a Hindustani word meaning bandits), a great challenge to the administration of this region, although distinct from the organized resistance known as the Limbin Confederacy, which is the subject of the remainder of this report.

II The Limbin Confederacy, Twet Nga Lu and the Current Situation

In 1880 an organized Shan movement against Burmese rule emerged, which still persists today. (Note that at this time England only controlled Lower Burma. Upper Burma and

Mandalay were still ruled by the Burmese King.) In that year the *sawbwa*s of the states of Mongnai, Lawksawk, Mongpawn and Mongnawng refused to appear before the Burmese King Thibaw in an annual act of New Year's obeisance. A column sent by Thibaw failed to capture the upstart *sawbwa*s. Then, in 1882, this defiance became violent. In that year, the *sawbwa* of Kengtung attacked and killed the Burmese Resident in Kengtung. Inspired by the boldness of the Kengtung *sawbwa*, the *sawbwa* of Mongnai and his allies broke into open revolt. In November 1883 they attacked the Burmese garrison at Mongnai, killing four hundred. But their success was short-lived. The Burmese counter-attacked, forcing the rebellious Shan chiefs to flee to Kengtung, across the Salween River, whose steep defiles and dense jungles gave them shelter against further incursions.

Although the rebellion was directed against the Burmese government, the goal of the resistance was not Shan independence, a fact of history which is frequently misunderstood. Indeed, the Shan *sawbwa*s recognized that without a strong central power the Shan States would always be plagued by war. Their chief goal was the overthrow of Thibaw, and the crowning of a suzerain who would repeal the *thathameda* tax, a land tax they deemed unjust. Thus, as their candidate, they selected a Burman known as the Limbin Prince, a disenfranchised member of the House of Alaungpaya, the ruling dynasty. This rebellion became known as the Limbin Confederacy. In December 1885 the Limbin Prince arrived in Kengtung. Although the movement carries his name, evidence suggests he is only a figurehead, with true power being wielded by the Shan *sawbwa*s.

Meanwhile, as the Limbin Prince followed the lonely trails into the highlands, war had broken out once again between Upper Burma and Britain: the Third and final Anglo-Burmese War. The defeat of the Burmese at Mandalay by our forces was completed two weeks before the Limbin Prince arrived in Kengtung, but because of the vast and difficult terrain separating Kengtung from Mandalay, the news failed to reach the Confederacy until after he arrived. While we had hoped that the Limbin Confederacy would drop its resistance and submit to our rule, instead it switched its original aims and declared war on the British Crown in the name of Shan independence.

It is said that nature abhors a vacuum and this can also be said of politics. Indeed, the retreat of the Limbin Confederacy to Kengtung in 1883 had left vacant thrones in many of the powerful Shan *muang*, thrones which were rapidly filled by local warlords. Notable among these usurpers was a warrior named Twet Nga Lu, who became the de facto ruler of Mongnai. A native of Kengtawng (not to be confused with Kengtung – at times one wonders if the Shan have named their cities to confuse the English tongue), a sub-state of Mongnai, Twet Nga Lu was a defrocked monk turned local brigand whose violence was notorious throughout the region, earning him the nickname 'the Bandit Chief'. Before the *sawbwa* of Mongnai had retreated to Kengtung, Twet Nga Lu had led several attacks on Mongnai. These were for the most part unsuccessful, and Twet Nga Lu changed his tactics from the battlefield to the bed, at last gaining power by marrying the widow of the *sawbwa*'s brother. When the *sawbwa* fled to Kengtung, Twet Nga Lu, with the support of Burmese officials, seized control of Mongnai.

Twet Nga Lu, along with the other de facto usurpers, ruled until earlier this year, 1886, when Limbin forces launched an offensive and reclaimed much of their land. Twet Nga Lu fled back to his native town, from where he continues a campaign of violence, leaving swathes of burnt villages in the wake of his armies. The feud between him and the Mongnai *sawbwa* represents one of the greatest challenges to the establishment of peace. While the *sawbwa* commands the respect of his subjects, Twet Nga Lu is renowned not only for his ferocity but for his reputation as a master of tattoos and charms; his flesh is said to be embedded with hundreds of amulets which lend him invincibility and for which he is feared and revered. (A short note: such charms are an important aspect of both Burman and Shan culture. They can be anything from small gems to shells to sculptures of the Buddha and are placed under the skin through a shallow incision. A particularly shocking variant is found mainly among fishermen: the implantation of stones and bells beneath the skin of male genitalia, a practice whose purpose and function continues to elude enquiries by this author.)

At the time of this report, the Limbin Confederacy continues to grow in power, and Twet Nga Lu remains at large, with the evidence of his reign of terror visible in the embers of burnt towns and slaughtered villagers. All efforts at negotiation have proved futile. From my command at the fort at Mae Lwin, I have been unable to make contact with the Limbin Confederacy and my attempts to contact Twet Nga Lu have also failed. To date, there have been few confirmed British sightings of the warlord, and questions have even been raised as to whether the man truly exists, or whether he is just a legend, grown out of the summation of terror from hundreds of unassociated dacoit attacks. Nevertheless, a ransom has been placed on the Bandit Chief, dead or alive, one of many continuing efforts to bring peace to the Shan Plateau.

Edgar read the entire report without stopping. There were some other short notes by Carroll, and they were all similar, filled with digressions into ethnography and natural history. On the first page of one, a survey of trade routes, the Doctor had scrawled at the top of the page, 'Please include to educate the piano tuner as to the geography of the land'. Inside there were two appendices, one on the accessibility of certain mountain tracks to the passage of artillery, the second a compendium of edible plants 'in case a party is lost without food', with sketches of flower dissections and the name of each plant in five different tribal languages.

The contrast of the Doctor's reports with the other official military notes he had read was striking. Edgar wondered if perhaps this was the source of some of the military's enmity. Most of the officers were landed gentry, he knew, educated at public school. He could imagine their resentment of a man such as the Doctor, who came from a more modest background, but who seemed vastly more cultured. Perhaps this too is why I like him already, he thought. When Edgar had finished school, he had left home to live and work with a piano tuner in the City, an eccentric old man who believed that a good piano tuner must have knowledge not only of his instrument, but of 'Physics, Philosophy, and Poetics', so that Edgar, although he did not attend university, reached his twentieth birthday with more education than many who had.

There were other similarities as well, he thought. In many ways our professions are alike, rare in that they can transcend class distinction – everyone becomes ill, and concert grands as well as gin-palace uprights get out of tune. Edgar wondered what this meant for the Doctor, for he had learned early that being needed was not the same as being accepted. Although he was a frequent visitor to upper-class homes, where the owners of expensive pianos often engaged him in talk about music, he never felt welcome. And this distinct sense of estrangement extended in the other direction as well, as he often felt awkwardly refined in the presence of the carpenters or metalsmiths or porters whom he frequently contacted for his work. He remembered telling Katherine about this feeling of not belonging soon after they were married, one morning while they walked beside the Thames. She had only laughed and kissed him, her cheeks reddened by the cold, her lips warm and moist. He remembered this almost as well as he remembered what she had said, Believe what you may about where you belong, all I care is that you are *mine*. As for other acquaintances, he found friendship in common interest, of the kind that now, steaming towards Rangoon, he felt towards the Doctor.

It is unfortunate that the Doctor has not written about the piano itself, he thought, for *it* is the hero of this endeavour, its absence an obvious omission in the narrative thus far. He was amused by this thought: Carroll made the army read his natural histories, so it would only be fair that they be forced to learn about the piano as well. In the midst of his creative rapture, and growing sense of united mission with the Doctor, he rose, took out an inkwell, pen and paper, lit a new candle, for the first one had burned low, and began to write.

Gentlemen,

I write to you from on board our steamer bound for Rangoon. It is now the fourteenth day of our journey and I have been very much entertained by the view afforded by our route, and by the most informative briefings provided to me by your office. It has come to my attention, however, that little has been written about the very purpose of our endeavour, namely, the piano. Thus for the purpose of history, as well as the general education of those in the War Office, I feel it necessary to record this story myself. Please feel free to share it with anyone you wish. Should you care for any further information, gentlemen, I would be more than happy to provide it.

The History of the Erard Piano

The history of the Erard piano could naturally be told with two beginnings, that of the history of the piano, and that of the history of Sebastien Erard. But the former is long and involved – fascinating naturally, but too much a challenge for my pen, for I am a tuner with a love of history, not a historian with a love of tuning. Suffice it to say that following its invention by Cristofori in the early eighteenth century, the piano underwent great modifications, and the Erard, the subject of this letter, is indebted, as all modern pianos are, to this tremendous tradition.

Sebastien Erard was from Strasbourg, a German, but he went to Paris in 1768 when he was sixteen and apprenticed himself to a harpsichord maker. The boy – to put it simply – was a prodigy and soon he quit his apprenticeship and opened his own shop. The other Parisian craftsmen felt so threatened by the boy's gift that they launched a campaign to have him close his shop after he designed a *clavecin mécanique*, a harpsichord with multiple registers, with quill and cowhide plectra, all operated by an ingenious pedal mechanism which had never been thought of before. But, despite the boycott, the design was so impressive that the Duchess of Villeroi gave the young Erard her sponsorship. Erard started to make pianofortes, and the Duchess's noble friends started to buy them. This time he aroused the ire of importers who resented the competition with their imported English pianos. They tried to raid his house, only to be blocked by none other than soldiers of Louis XVI; Erard was so renowned that the King gave him full licence to trade.

The sponsorship of the King notwithstanding, Erard eventually looked abroad and in the mid-1780s he travelled to London, where he set up another shop on Great Marlborough Street. He was there on 14 July 1789 when the Bastille was stormed, and when, three years later, the purges of the Reign of Terror shook France. This history I am certain you know well. Thousands of the bourgeoisie fled the country or were condemned to die by the guillotine. But one fact few people know: those who fled or were executed left thousands of works of art, including musical instruments. Whatever can be said about French taste, it is worth noting perhaps that even in the throes of revolution, when scholars and musicians were losing their heads, someone decided that music must be protected. A Temporary Commission of Arts was set up and Antonio Bartolomeo Bruni, a mediocre violinist at the Comédie Italienne was named Director of the Inventory. For fourteen months he collected the instruments of the condemned. In all, over three hundred were gathered, and each carries its own tragic tale. Antoine Lavoisier, the great chemist, lost his life and his French-made Zimmerman grand to the Terror, and countless other pianos still played today have similar pedigrees. Of these, sixty-four were pianofortes, and of the French makes the majority seized were Erards, twelve in number. Whether this was evidence of the taste of Bruni or of the victims, this dark distinction perhaps most permanently established Erard's reputation as the finest of piano makers. It is significant that neither Sebastien nor his brother Jean-Baptiste, who remained in Paris, was ever brought before the Terror, despite their sponsorship by the throne. Of the twelve pianofortes, the whereabouts of eleven are known, and I have tuned all those that now reside in England.

Sebastien Erard is dead now, of course, but his manufacturing shop is still in London. The remainder of his story is one of technical beauty, and if you cannot understand the mechanics of what I describe, you must at least appreciate them, as I appreciate the function of your cannons without understanding the chemical nature of the gases which make them fire. His innovations revolutionized piano construction. The double-escapement repetition action, the *mécanisme à étrier*, attaching hammers singly to the rail instead of in groups of six as in the Broadwood pianos, the agraffe and the harmonic bar – all these are Erard's innovations. Napoleon played on an Erard; Erard sent a grand to Haydn as a gift; Beethoven played one for seven years.

I hope this information will be found useful to your staff in furthering the understanding and appreciation of the fine instrument now located in the distant borders of our empire. Such a creation merits not only respect and attention. It should be cared for as one would protect an objet d'art in a museum. The service of a tuner is worthy of the instrument's quality and, I hope, just the first step in the continuing care of the instrument.

Your humble servant,

Edgar Drake
Piano Tuner and Voicer
Erards-a-Speciality

When he finished he sat looking at the letter, twirling his pen. He thought for a minute, crossed out 'cared for' and wrote above it 'defended'. They were military men, after all. He folded it into an envelope and put it in his bag, to be posted in Rangoon. At long last he grew sleepy.

I hope they read the letter, he thought, smiling to himself as he fell asleep. Of course, at the time he couldn't know just how many times it would be read, inspected, sent to cryptographers, held to lights, even examined under magnifying lenses. For when a man disappears, we cling to anything he left behind.

SIX

IT WAS MORNING when they first sighted land, three days from Calcutta, a lighthouse perched on a tall red stone tower. 'The Alguada reef', Edgar heard an elderly Scotsman beside him tell a companion. 'Bloody hard to navigate. She's a graveyard for passing ships.' Edgar knew from the maps that they were only twenty miles south of Cape Negrais and that soon they would reach Rangoon.

In less than an hour the ship passed buoys marking the shallow sandbanks that spilled out from the mouth of the Rangoon River, one of hundreds of rivers which drained the Irrawaddy delta. They passed several anchored ships, which the old man explained were trading ships trying to evade port dues. The steamer turned north and the sandbars rose above the land to become low wooded shores. Here the channel was deeper, but still almost two miles wide and, were it not for the large red obelisks on either side of the mouth, Edgar wouldn't have known they were navigating inland.

They steamed upriver for several hours. It was low, level, mostly unremarkable country, yet Edgar felt a sudden excitement when they passed a series of small pagodas, their coats of white-wash peeling. Further inland, a collection of shacks clustered at the water's edge, where children played. The river narrowed and both shores came into closer focus, the sandy banks fringed with thickening vegetation. The ship followed a tortuous course, hindered by sandbanks and sharp bends. At last, at one of these bends, boats appeared in the distance. On deck there was a murmur and several passengers filed towards the stairs to return to their rooms.

'Are we there?' Edgar asked the old man.

'Yes, soon. Look over there.' The man raised his arm and pointed to a pagoda that capped a distant hill. 'That's the Shwedagon Pagoda. You must have heard of it.'

Edgar nodded. Actually, he had known of the temple before he had been given the Erard commission, reading of its splendours in a magazine article written by the wife of a judge from Rangoon. Her descriptions were loaded with adjectives: gilded, golden, glittering. He had scanned the article, wondering if he'd find mention of an organ or a Buddhist equivalent, conjecturing that such an important house of worship needed music. But there were only descriptions of 'shimmering, golden jewels' and the 'quaint ways of Burmans', and he tired of the article and had forgotten about it until now. In the distance the temple looked like a small, shiny trinket.

The steamer slowed. The dwellings that dotted the shore now began to break through the foliage with regularity. Further along the bank, he was startled to see timber elephants working, their drivers sitting across their necks as they hauled giant logs from the water and stacked them on the shore. He stared, incredulous at the strength of the animals, at how they whipped the logs out of the water as if they were weightless. As the boat approached the bank, they came into clearer view, rivulets of brown water spinning down their hides as they splashed along the shore.

They met other vessels on the river now with increasing frequency, double-decked steamers, worn fishing boats painted with swirling Burmese script, tiny rowboats and thin skiffs, fragile and scarcely large enough for a man. There were others, vessels of unfamiliar shape and sail. Close to the shore, they were passed by a strange ship with a vast sail fluttering over two smaller ones.

They were approaching the docks quickly now, and a series

of European-style government buildings came into view, stately structures of brick and gleaming columns.

The steamer approached a covered landing attached to the bank by a long, hinged platform, where a crowd of porters waited. The steamer hesitated, its engines churning in reverse to slow its course. One of the deckhands threw a rope to the quay, where it was caught and tied around a pair of bollards. The porters, naked except for loincloths tied around their waists and tucked between their legs, clamoured to lower a plank. It slapped loudly against the deck, and they crossed it to help the passengers with their luggage. Edgar stood in the shade of the awning and watched the men. They were small and wore towels wrapped around their heads to guard against the sun. Their skin was patterned with tattoos, stretching over their torsos, emerging on their thighs to twist and twine and end above their knees.

Edgar looked at the other passengers: most stood idly on the deck, talking to each other, some pointing and remarking at the buildings. He turned back to the porters, to watch them move, the shape of their tattoos changing as the sinewy arms tensed under the leather trunks and portmanteaus. On the shore, in the shade of the trees, a crowd waited by the growing pile of bags. Beyond them Edgar could see the khaki uniforms of British soldiers standing by a low gate. And beyond the soldiers, in the shade of a line of sprawling banyan trees that followed the shore, hints of movement, shifting patterns of darkness.

At last the tattooed men finished unloading the luggage, and the passengers walked across the gangplank to waiting carriages, the women emerging under parasols, the men beneath top hats or sola topis. Edgar followed the old man he had spoken to earlier that morning, checking his balance as he crossed the rickety gangplank. He stepped onto the quay. His itinerary said that he would be met at the port by military personnel, but little more. For a brief moment he felt a sudden surge of panic, *Perhaps they don't know I have arrived.*

Beyond the guards the shadows stirred, like an animal awakening. Edgar was sweating profusely and he took out his handkerchief to wipe his forehead.

'Mr Drake!' someone shouted from the crowd. Edgar looked for the voice. There was a crowd of soldiers standing in the shade. He saw a raised arm. 'Mr Drake, over here.'

Edgar pushed his way through the crowd of passengers and servants milling about their bags. A young soldier stepped forward. 'Welcome to Rangoon, Mr Drake. It is good you saw me, sir. I would not have known how to recognize you.' He held out his hand. 'Captain Dalton, Herefordshire Regiment.'

'How do you do? My mother's family is from Hereford.'

The soldier beamed. 'Fine luck!' He was young and tanned, with broad shoulders and blond hair combed back diagonally across his head.

'Yes, fine luck,' said the piano tuner and expected the young man to say something else. But the soldier just laughed, if not for the small coincidence, then because he had recently been promoted to Captain and he was proud to state his rank. And Edgar returned the smile, for the journey, after five thousand miles, suddenly seemed to have brought him back home.

'I trust you had a pleasant trip?'

'Pleasant indeed.'

'I hope you won't mind waiting for one moment. We have some other luggage to carry to headquarters.' When everything had been gathered together one of the soldiers called to the porters, who loaded the trunks onto their shoulders. They walked past the guards at the gate and crossed the street to where the carriages waited.

Later Edgar would write to Katherine that in the fifteen paces that carried him from the gate to the waiting carriages, Burma appeared as a curtain lifted from a stage. As he stepped into the street, the crowd swelled around him. He turned. Hands struggled to thrust baskets of food forward. Women stared at him, their faces painted white, their fists grasping garlands of flowers. At his feet, a beggar pressed up against his leg, a mournful boy covered with scabs and weeping sores, and he turned again and tripped over a group of men carrying crates of spices suspended between long poles. Ahead, the soldiers pushed through the crowds and, had it not been for the branches of the giant banyan trees, those looking out from the office buildings would have seen a line of khaki passing through the mosaic and a single man moving slowly, as if lost, turning at the sound of a cough, now staring at a betel vendor who spat near his feet, trying to discern if this was a threat or perhaps merely an advertisement, until he heard one of the soldiers say, 'After you, Mr Drake,' for they had arrived at the carriage. And as quickly as he had entered the world, he escaped, ducking his head inside the carriage. The street seemed to recede immediately.

Three of the soldiers followed, taking seats facing him and at his side. There was a scuffling on the roof as the baggage was loaded. The driver mounted the box, and Edgar heard shouting and the sound of a whip. The carriage began to move.

He was seated facing forward, and the position of the window made it difficult to see outside, so that images passed in quick succession, like the flipping pages of penny picture-books, each vision unexpected, framed. The soldiers sat across from him, the young Captain still smiling.

They moved slowly through the crowd, picking up speed as the vendors cleared, past rows of more government buildings. Outside one a group of moustachioed Englishmen in dark suits stood talking, while a pair of Sikhs waited behind them. The road was macadamized and surprisingly smooth. They turned up a small cross street. The wide facades of the government offices gave way to smaller houses, still in European style, but with terraces festooned with languid tropical plants and walls stained with the dark, musty patina he had seen on so many houses in India. They passed a crowded shop, where dozens of younger men sat on small stools around low tables laden with pots of fried food. The acrid smoke of cooking oil wafted into the carriage and stung his eyes. He blinked and the tea shop disappeared, to be replaced by a woman holding a plate of betel nuts and tiny leaves. She pressed close to the carriage and stared inside from beneath the shade of a wide straw hat. Like some of the vendors by the shore, her face was painted with white circles, moon-like against her dark skin.

Edgar turned to the soldier. 'What's that on her face?'

'The paint?'

'Yes. I saw it on some of the women by the docks. But different patterns. Peculiar.'

'They call it *thanaka*. It is made from ground sandalwood. Almost all the women wear it and many of the men. They cover the babies with it too.'

'Whatever for?'

'Protects against the sun, they say, makes them beautiful. We call it "Burmese face powder". Why do English women wear face powder?'

Just then the carriage jolted to a halt. Outside they could hear voices.

'Are we here?'

'No, still quite far. I don't know why we have stopped. Wait a moment while I look outside.' The soldier opened the door and leaned out. He pulled himself back into the carriage.

'What's happening?'

'Accident. Look for yourself. This is always the problem of taking the small streets, but today they are repaving Sule Pagoda Road, so we had to go this way. This could take several minutes. You may get out and watch, if you like.'

Edgar poked his head out of the window. In the street in front of them, a bicycle lay sprawled amidst scattered mounds of green lentils, spilled from a pair of overturned baskets. One man, apparently the rider, nursed a bloodied knee while the lentil wallah, a thin Indian man dressed in white, frantically tried to salvage the few lentils which had not soaked up the muck of the street. Neither man seemed particularly angry, and a large crowd had gathered, ostensibly to help, but mostly to stare.

Edgar stepped down from the confines of the carriage.

The street was narrow, flanked by a continuous facade of houses. In front of each one steep steps climbed three or four feet to a narrow patio, now filled with onlookers. The men were wearing loosely tied turbans and skirt-like lengths of fabric around their waists, which were brought between their legs and tucked in the back. The turbans were distinct from those of the Sikh soldiers, and, remembering a traveller's account of Burma, Edgar guessed they must be *gaung-baung*s, the skirts *paso*s. He recalled that on women the skirts carried a different name, *hta main*, strange syllables that seemed breathed, not spoken. The women all wore the sandalwood paint, some covering the cheeks in thin parallel stripes, others with the same circles as the woman they had just seen from the carriage, others yet with swirls, with lines descending the crest of their noses. To the darker-skinned women it gave an eerie, ghost-like appearance, and Edgar noticed that some of the women also wore a red lipstick, giving the *thanaka* an aura of the burlesque. There was something disturbing about it that he couldn't identify, but once his surprise wore off, he would admit in his next letter to Katherine that it wasn't unattractive. Perhaps not fitting for an English complexion, he wrote, but beautiful, and he added, with emphasis, *in the same way that one appreciates art*. There is no need for any misunderstanding.

His eyes followed the faces of the buildings up to balconies draped with hanging gardens of ferns and flowers. These too were filled with spectators, mostly children, their skinny arms interlaced in the wrought-iron banisters. Several called down to him and giggled, waving. Edgar waved back.

In the road, the bicyclist had righted his machine and was straightening the bent handlebars, while the porter had given up on salvaging lentils, and had set about repairing one of the baskets in the middle of the road. The driver shouted something at him, and the crowd laughed. The porter scurried to the side of the street. Edgar waved at the children once again and climbed back into the carriage. And again they were moving, the thin street opening onto a wider road that circled around a vast gilded structure bedecked with golden umbrellas, and the Captain said, 'Sule Pagoda'. They passed a church, then the minarets of a mosque, and then, by the Town Hall, another market that was set up on the promenade before a statue of Mercury, the Roman god of merchants, which the British had erected as a symbol of their commerce, but who watched over the street merchants instead.

The lane widened and the carriage picked up speed. Soon the images spun past the window too fast to be seen.

o

They drove for half an hour and then stopped on a cobbled road outside a two-storey house. Ducking their heads, the soldiers climbed out of the carriage one by one, while the porters scrambled onto the roof to pass the trunks down from above. Edgar stood and took a deep breath. Despite the intensity of the sun, which had now begun its descent, the air was cool compared to the stuffiness of the carriage.

The Captain beckoned Edgar towards the house. At the entrance they passed two stone-faced guards, swords hanging at their sides. Edgar nodded to them in greeting and hurried inside. The Captain disappeared down a hallway and reappeared with a stack of papers.

'Mr Drake,' he said, 'it seems we have several changes in our plans. It was our original intention that you would be met here in Rangoon by Captain Nash-Burnham, from Mandalay, who is familiar with Doctor Carroll's projects. Nash-Burnham was here only yesterday for a meeting on efforts to control dacoits in the Shan States, but I am afraid the boat you were scheduled to take up the river is under repair, and he was in a hurry to return to Mandalay. So he left on an earlier ship.' Dalton paused to look through the papers. 'Don't worry. You will have plenty of time to be briefed in Mandalay. But it does mean that you will be departing later than expected, as the first steamer we could find you a berth on was with the Irrawaddy Flotilla Company, leaving at the end of the week. I trust this is not too much of an inconvenience?'

'No, that shouldn't be a problem. I wouldn't mind a few days to wander about.'

'Of course. In fact, I was going to invite you myself to join us on a tiger hunt tomorrow. I mentioned the idea to Captain Nash-Burnham, who said it might be a fine way to pass the time as well as become familiar with the surrounding countryside.'

Edgar protested, 'But I've never hunted.'

'Then this is an excellent way to start. Always a jolly good time. Anyway, you must be tired now. I will call on you later this evening.'

'Is there anything else planned now?'

'No schedule for this afternoon. Again, Captain Nash-Burnham had hoped to be here with you. I would recommend that you rest in your quarters. The porter can show you where they are.' He nodded to an Indian who was waiting.

Edgar thanked the captain and followed the porter out of the door. They collected his trunks and walked to the end of the lane, where they reached a larger road. A large group of young monks walked past in saffron robes. The porter seemed not to notice.

'Where are they coming from?' Edgar asked, entranced by the beauty of the shifting cloth.

'Who, sir?' asked the porter.

'The monks.'

They were standing at the corner of the road, and the porter turned and pointed in the direction from which the monks had come. 'Why, the Shwedagon, sir. Anyone who is not a soldier in these quarters has come to see the Shwedagon.'

Edgar found himself standing at the base of a slope lined with dozens of small pagodas, rising to the golden pyramid that had winked at him from the river, now massive, towering. A row of pilgrims milled about the foot of the stairs. Edgar had read that the British army had established itself around the pagoda, but he had never imagined it was this close. Reluctantly, he hurried after the porter, who had already crossed the road and was continuing along the small street. They reached a room at the end of a long barracks. The porter set down the trunks and opened the door.

It was a simple space used by visiting officers and the porter told him that the surrounding buildings were also living quarters for the garrison, 'So should you need anything, sir, you can just knock on any door.' He bowed and took his leave. Edgar waited only long enough for the sound of the man's steps to disappear, before he opened the door and walked back down the lane, and stood at the base of the long flight of stairs leading to the temple. A sign read 'No shoes or umbrella carrying', and he recalled what he had read of the beginnings of the Third Anglo-Burmese War, when the British emissaries had refused to remove their shoes in the presence of Burmese royalty. He knelt and untied his boots and, carrying them in his hand, began the long walk up the steps.

The tiles were moist and cool on his feet. The climb was lined with vendors selling a riot of religious goods: paintings and statues of the Buddha, garlands of jasmine, books and fans, baskets filled with offerings of food, stacks of scented joss sticks, gold leaf and lotus flowers made of fine silver foil. The merchants languished in the shade. Everywhere pilgrims climbed the steps – monks and beggars and elegant Burmese women dressed in their finery. At the top he passed beneath an intricate portico, and onto a vast platform of white marble and gilded domes of smaller pagodas. The crowd of supplicants swirled in clockwise fashion, staring at the tall Englishman as they passed. He stepped into the current of bodies, following it past rows of smaller shrines and kneeling worshippers, who fingered rosaries of large seeds. As he walked, he stared up at the pagoda, its bell-like swell tapering to a fine tip capped with a cylindrical umbrella. He was blinded by the glint of gold, the reflection of the sun on the white tiles, the pulsing mass of worshippers. Halfway around the pagoda, he stopped to rest in the shade and was wiping his face with his handkerchief when the faint chime of music caught his attention.

At first he couldn't tell where it came from, the notes reflecting off the corridors of shrines and mixing with the chants. He followed a small path behind a vast platform, where a monk led a group in prayer, hypnotic words he would later learn were not Burmese but Pali. The music became louder. Beneath the hanging branches of a banyan tree he saw the musicians.

There were four of them and they looked up to acknowledge his presence. He smiled and studied the instruments: a drum and a xylophone-like board, a long goose-necked horn and a harp. The last was the instrument that most caught his attention, for he knew the harpsichord well, of course, as the grandfather of the piano. This was a beautiful harp, curved in a form that looked like both a ship and a swan; the strings were strung close together, which he noted was possible because of the harp's unique shape. It was a clever design, he thought. The man's fingers worked slowly over it. The melody was eerily discordant and Edgar found it difficult to pick out a pattern. He noted the haphazard way it danced along the scale. He listened more closely, yet still the melody eluded him.

Soon another observer came, an elegantly dressed Burmese man holding the hand of a child. Edgar nodded to the man and the boy and they listened to the song together. The presence of the other man reminded him that Captain Dalton would be calling on him that evening and that he had to bathe and dress. Reluctantly he left the musicians. He finished circling the pagoda, joining the crowd once again where it pooled up against the entrance and poured over the stairs. He followed it back down to the street and sat on the bottom steps to tie his shoes. Around him, men and women slipped easily in and out of sandals. Fumbling with his laces, he began to whistle, trying to recapture the piece he had just heard. He rose to his feet. It was then he saw her.

She was standing about five feet away, a baby perched on her hip, her clothes in rags, her hand outstretched, her body painted a deep yellow. At first he blinked, thinking she was an apparition, the colour of her skin a ghostly image of the gold of the pagoda, like the floating illusion one gets from staring too long at the sun. She caught his eye and stepped closer, and he saw that she was gold not from paint but from a yellow dust, which covered her face and arms and her bare feet. As he stared, she extended the baby towards him, her yellow hands clasped tightly around the tiny sleeping person. He looked at her face and the dark pleading eyes outlined with yellow; only later would he learn that the dust was turmeric, which the Burmese call *sa-nwin*, and which women spread over their bodies after childbirth to protect against spirits, but which this woman wore to beg, for by tradition a woman who still wears the *sa-nwin* should not leave her home for days after childbirth, and if she did, it could only mean that the child was sick. But, standing at the base of the Shwedagon, he did not know this, he could only stare at the gilded woman, until she took a step closer, and he could see flies at the mouth of the child and a widening sore on its tiny head. He stepped back, horrified, and rummaged through his pocket for coins and without counting, dropped them into her hands.

He backed away, his heart racing. Around him, the pilgrims continued their procession, oblivious to the gilded girl counting the coins in surprise and to the tall, lanky Englishman, who looked one last time at the temple and the girl beneath its soaring spire, thrust his hands into his pockets and hurried down the street.

o

Later that evening, he received a visit from Captain Dalton, who invited him to join some of the officers for billiards at the Pegu Club. He declined, feigning fatigue. It had been several days since he had written to his wife, he said. He did not tell Dalton of the image that still stayed with him, that it felt wrong to drink sherry over war gossip while he thought of the girl and her child.

'Well, there will be plenty of time for billiards,' said Dalton, 'but I do insist that you join us for the hunt tomorrow. Only last week an infantryman reported seeing a tiger near Dabein. I have made plans to travel there with Captain Witherspoon and Captain Fogg, both of whom arrived recently from Bengal. Would you care to join us?' He stood silhouetted in the doorway.

'But I have never hunted before, and I don't think I'm—'

'Please! I will not hear of it. This is a matter of duty. This tiger has been terrorizing the local villagers. We leave early tomorrow. Meet us at the cavalry stables, Do you know where they are? No, you do not need to bring anything. Your hat, perhaps, We have plenty of riding boots, and of course, rifles. A man with such skilled fingers as yourself will be a fine shot.' And at this flattery, and because he had already turned down one invitation, Edgar accepted.

SEVEN

THE FOLLOWING MORNING Edgar found the Captain outside the stables. Five other men were gathered around him, two Englishmen and three Burmans. Seeing the piano tuner approach, Dalton came out from under the horse, where he had been cinching the saddle. He wiped his hand on his breeches and extended it. 'Mr Drake, beautiful morning, isn't it? Wonderful when a breeze comes this far inland. So refreshing. It means the rains may be earlier this year.' He stood and looked up at the sky, as if to confirm his meteorology. Edgar was struck by how handsome and athletic he looked: his face ruddy and tanned, his hair combed back, his shirt sleeves rolled up over his dusty forearms.

'Mr Drake, let me introduce you to Captains Witherspoon and Fogg. Gentlemen, this is Mr Drake, London's finest piano tuner.' He pounded Edgar on the back. 'A good man, family's from Hereford.'

The two men extended their hands amiably. 'Good to meet you, Mr Drake,' said Witherspoon. Fogg nodded.

'I will be finished saddling this horse in a moment,' said Dalton, ducking back under its belly. 'She can be very naughty, this one, and I don't want to fall off when a tiger is in my sights.' He looked up and winked at the tuner. The men laughed. Ten feet away the Burmans squatted on their heels in loose *paso*s.

They mounted the horses. Edgar struggled to get his leg over the saddle and had to be helped by the Captain. Outside the stables one of the Burmans rode ahead and soon disappeared. Dalton led their small group, chatting with the two other captains. Edgar followed them. Behind the other two Burmans rode together on the same horse.

It was still early and the sun hadn't yet burnt the mist off the lagoons. Edgar was surprised at how quickly Rangoon became farmland. They passed several ox-carts travelling into the city, whose drivers pulled over to the side of the road to let them pass, but otherwise scarcely acknowledged their presence. Fishermen poled thin boats through the marshes, materializing out of the mist. Egrets hunted in the marsh close to the road, lifting and placing their feet with precision. Ahead, Witherspoon asked if they could stop to shoot them.

'Not here,' answered Dalton. 'Last time we shot birds the villagers made a huge fuss. The egrets are part of the founding myths of Pegu. Bad luck to shoot them, my friend.'

'Superstitious nonsense,' huffed Witherspoon. 'I thought we were educating them to abandon such beliefs.'

'Indeed, indeed. But I, for one, would rather hunt a tiger than spend my morning quarrelling with some local chieftain.'

'Humph,' said Witherspoon, enunciating the noise as though it were a word. But this answer seemed to satisfy him. They rode on. In the distance, the men threw spirals of fishing nets, blurs of rope that spun out water droplets in illuminated cascades.

They rode for an hour. The marshes began to give way to thin brush. The sun was already quite warm and Edgar felt sweat trickling down his chest. He was relieved when the track turned and entered a thick forest. The dry burn of the sun was replaced by a sticky humidity. They had ridden only a few minutes into the forest when they were met by the lead Burman. While the man conferred with the others, Edgar looked around him. As a boy, he had read many tales of jungle explorers, and spent hours imagining the chaos of dripping flowers, the teeming legions of ferocious animals. This must be a different type of jungle, he thought. It is too quiet and too dark. He peered into the depths of the forest, but could only see five yards into the tangle of hanging vines.

At last the men ceased talking among themselves, and one of them rode up to Dalton and began to speak. Edgar was too distracted to watch the conversation. His glasses steamed over and he took them from his nose and wiped them on his shirt. He put them back on his face and they fogged again. He took them off. After the third time he let them sit on his face, looking at the forest through the thin layer of condensation.

Up ahead, Dalton had finished conferring with the Burman. 'All right then,' he shouted and turned his horse around, the animal's hooves trampling the tangle of underbrush. 'I spoke to our guide. He says that he rode to the nearest village and asked the villagers about the tiger. Apparently, it was sighted only yesterday tearing the throat from the breeding sow of a local swineherd. The whole village is distraught, one of the soothsayers said that this same tiger is the one that killed an infant two years ago. So they are organizing their own tiger hunt, trying to flush it out of the jungle. They said that we can try to hunt it. It was last sighted three miles north of here. Or he said we could try heading south to a series of swamps where there are many wild boars.'

'I didn't come all the way out here to shoot pigs,' Fogg interjected.

'Nor did I,' said Witherspoon.

'And Mr Drake,' asked Dalton. 'Your vote?'

'Oh, I won't even be firing a shot, I couldn't hit a stuffed, glazed pig if it lay on the table in front of me, let alone a boar. You decide.'

'Well, I haven't hunted a tiger in months,' said Dalton.

'It's decided then,' said Witherspoon.

'Just watch where you fire,' said Dalton. 'Not everything that moves is a tiger. And, Mr Drake, be careful of snakes. Don't grab anything that looks like a stick unless you are certain that it doesn't have fangs.' He kicked his horse's flank and the other men followed, winding on through the forest.

The vegetation grew thicker, and they stopped frequently for the first rider to cut at vines that hung over the trail. More plants seemed to grow from the trees than from the ground, twisting creepers that climbed vines towards the sunlight. Jagged epiphytes, orchids, pitcher plants, clung from the larger trees, losing their roots in the confusion of shoots that criss-crossed the sky. Edgar had always enjoyed gardens and he prided himself on his knowledge of Latin plant names, but he searched in vain for a plant he could recognize. Even the trees were foreign, massive, borne by elephantine trunks that stretched across the ground with fin-like buttress roots, tall enough to hide a tiger behind their walls.

They rode for another half-hour and then passed the ruins of a small structure, wrapped in the tangled roots of the trees. The Englishmen rode past it without stopping. Edgar wanted to call out to ask what it was, but his companions were too far ahead. He turned to look at the stones, hidden in moss. Behind him, the Burmans also seemed to notice. One of the men, who had been carrying a small wreath of flowers, quickly dismounted and laid it at the base of the ruins. Edgar turned as his horse walked on. Through the tesselations of hanging vines he saw the man bow and then the vision was lost, the vines closed in, and his horse pushed forward.

The others had ridden ahead and he almost collided with them at a turn in the track. They were all gathered at the base of a large tree. Dalton and Witherspoon were arguing in a whisper.

'Just one shot,' Witherspoon was saying. 'You can't let a pelt like that pass. I promise I could get it in one shot.'

'I told you, for all we know the tiger could be watching us. Fire now and you will scare it away for certain.'

'Nonsense,' said Witherspoon. 'The tiger is scared already. Three years and I don't have a good monkey pelt. They are always so old, and the only fine pelt I could have had was ruined by an inept skinner.'

Edgar followed the direction of their argument up the tall tree. At first he saw nothing, only a tangle of leaves and vines. But then something moved, and the small head of a young monkey poked out over an epiphyte. Edgar heard a rifle being loaded next to him and Dalton's voice again, 'I am telling you, leave it alone,' and then, above, the monkey seemed to sense something was wrong, lifted itself up and began to leap. Witherspoon raised the rifle and Dalton said again, 'Hold your fire, damn it,' and then above, the monkey's jump was matched by the flick of Witherspoon's finger, the flash from the gun barrel, the explosion of the shot. For a brief second there was a pause, silence, as a scattering of debris from where the monkey had jumped drifted down through the clearing. And then Edgar heard another sound, directly above, a soft chirping, and he looked up to see a figure silhouetted against the backdrop of trees and fragments of sky, falling. It seemed so slow, the body rotating in space, tail streaming up, fluttering, avian in its descent. He stared transfixed as the monkey fell past him, not three feet from his horse, and crashed into the brush. There was a long pause and then Dalton cursed and kicked his horse forward, as one of the Burmans jumped down from his saddle, picked up the monkey and held it out to Witherspoon, who briefly inspected the coat, now bloody and matted with dirt. He nodded at the Burman, who threw the monkey into a canvas sack. Then Witherspoon kicked and the group moved on. Following behind, Edgar watched the tiny figure in the bag swing against the side of the horse, shifting shadows of the forest playing over the stain of red that spread across the canvas.

They marched forward. Near a small stream they passed through a swarm of mosquitoes, which Edgar tried to wave away from his face. One landed on his hand and he watched it with fascination as it probed his skin, looking for a place to bite. It was much larger than those he had seen in England, with tiger-striped legs. Today, I am the first to slay the tiger, Edgar thought, and he crushed it with a slap of his hand. Another landed and he let it bite, watching it drink, its belly swelling, and then this one he crushed as well, smearing his own blood over his arm.

The forest thinned and opened into rice fields. They passed several women bent over in the mud, planting seeds. The road widened and they could see a village in the distance, a scrambled mass of bamboo houses. As they approached, a man came out and greeted them. He was wearing nothing but a worn red *paso*, and spoke with animation to the head rider, who translated.

'This man is one of the village leaders. He says that they sighted the tiger this morning. Men from this village have joined in the hunt. He begged us to join them too. They have very few guns. He will send a boy with us as a guide.'

'Excellent,' said Dalton, unable to control his excitement. 'And I thought that after Witherspoon's hastiness we had lost our chance.'

'And I will have a fine tiger pelt in addition to the monkey,' exclaimed Witherspoon. 'What an excellent day!'

Even Edgar felt his blood surge. The tiger was close, and dangerous. The only other time he had seen a tiger was at London Zoo, a thin, pathetic animal losing its hair to a disease which puzzled even London's best veterinary surgeons. His discomfort at having to kill something – amplified by the shooting of the baby monkey – vanished. Indeed, Dalton was right, this village needs us, he thought. He looked behind the villager, to where a group of women had gathered, each of whom held a baby against her hip. He felt a tugging at his boot and looked down to see a naked little boy touching the stirrups. 'Hello,' he said, and the boy stared upwards. His face was smeared with dust and mucus. 'You are a handsome little fellow, but quite in need of a bath.'

Fogg heard him talking and turned. 'Made a friend I see, Mr Drake.'

'Seems to be the case,' Edgar said. 'Here.' He rummaged in his pocket until he found an anna. He tossed it down. The boy reached out but missed it, and the coin bounced into a small puddle by the side of the road. The boy dropped to his knees and thrust his hands into the water, searching for the coin, a frightened look on his face. Suddenly, his hand grasped something and he pulled the coin from the water and looked at it triumphantly. He spat on his hand and wiped off the coin, then scampered back to show his friends. Within seconds they were gathered around Edgar's horse. 'No,' said Edgar. 'No more coins.' He looked forward and tried to ignore the little outstretched hands.

The villager who had spoken to them left the group and returned minutes later with an older boy, who climbed onto the horse of the first rider. They followed a trail that led out of the village and ran between the rice fields and the uncleared jungle. Behind them the group of boys ran in gleeful pursuit, their bare feet pattering across the road. At the base of the slope they turned away from the fields, following a rough clearing which skirted the forest. Soon they passed two men standing at the edge of the jungle. Naked to the waist, one of the men wore a poor imitation of a British helmet and held a rusty old rifle.

'A soldier,' Witherspoon joked. 'I hope he didn't get that from someone he shot.'

Edgar frowned. Fogg chuckled. 'I wouldn't worry. Defects from our factories in Calcutta have an astonishing way of finding their way into places where even our soldiers are afraid to travel.'

Dalton rode up with their guide. 'Have they seen the tiger?' Fogg asked.

'Not today, but it was last seen near here. We should load our rifles. Drake, you too.'

'Oh, really, I don't think . . .'

'We are going to need all the firepower possible if the beast rushes us. Now where did all those little children go?'

'I don't know. I saw them chasing a bird into the forest.'

'Good. Let's not play Father Christmas here. The last thing we want is an entourage of noisy children.'

'Sorry, I didn't think . . .'

Suddenly Witherspoon raised his hand. 'Shhh!'

Dalton and Edgar looked to him. 'What is it?'

'I don't know. Something in the bushes at the far end of the clearing.'

'Come on. Move carefully,' Dalton said, kicking at his horse. The party advanced slowly.

'There, now I see it!' This time it came from their guide. He raised his arm and pointed to thick bushes. The horses stopped. They were less than twenty yards from the edge of the clearing.

Edgar felt his heart pound as he followed the man's arm out towards the forest. There was stillness, a slowing, and he gripped his rifle and felt the tension of his finger against the trigger. At his side Witherspoon raised his rifle.

They waited. The bushes trembled.

'Blast it, I can't see a thing. It could be anywhere in there.'

'Don't fire unless you know it is the tiger. You took enough chances in the forest with that monkey. We have one chance and we all need to fire at once.'

'It's there, Captain.'

'Easy now.'

'Damn it, get your rifles ready. It's moving again.' Witherspoon cocked his rifle and peered through the sights. There was movement in the bushes, slinking steadily, the shaking growing stronger. 'It's coming. Get your rifles up.'

'All right, rifles up. Mr Drake, you too. We only have one shot at this, Fogg.'

'Locked and loaded. You call the shot, Captain.'

Edgar felt cold sweat break out over his body. His arms were shaking. He could barely raise the rifle stock to his shoulder.

Above them a vulture flew, looking down on the scene, a group of eight men, six horses, standing in the dry grass of the clearing, hedged on either side by dense jungle which stretched out over the hills. Behind, in the rice fields, a group of women was advancing towards them, walking faster, now running.

Edgar's horse stood in the back of the group, and so he saw the women first. They seemed to be shouting. He turned and yelled, 'Captain!'

'Quiet, Drake, it's coming.'

'Captain, wait—'

'Shut up, Drake,' Witherspoon snarled, not dropping his eyes from the sights.

But then they heard the shouts too and Dalton turned. 'What's going on?'

The Burman said something. Edgar turned back to look at the bushes. They were shaking harder now. He could hear the crash of feet in the underbrush.

The women were screaming.

'What the hell is going on?'

'Someone shut them up. They are going to scare it away.'

'Witherspoon, drop your rifle.'

'Don't ruin this, Dalton.'

'Witherspoon, I told you, drop the rifle. Something is wrong.'

The women were closer. Their cries rose up above the men's voices.

'Damn! Someone get them to shut up. Fogg, do something!'

Edgar could see Witherspoon staring down his rifle. Fogg, who had been silent until now, swung around on his horse and faced the women. 'Halt!' he yelled. The women kept running, crying, lifting the edge of their *hta mains* as they came.

'Halt! Damn you!'

All was a blur, the running, the shouts, the incessant sun.

Edgar whirled to look back at the forest.

'There it is!' Fogg yelled.

'Captain! Drop your weapon!' Dalton shouted and kicked his

horse towards Witherspoon, who tightened his grip on his rifle and fired.

o

The rest remains frozen, a set, a sun-washed memory, a slanting. There are cries and screams, but it is the slanting that will haunt Edgar Drake most, the impossible angle of grief, mother to child, the arms outstretched, reaching, pulling at those who try to restrain. A slanting he has never seen, but still recognizes, from pietàs, Greek urns with tiny figures waiting *oi moi*.

He stands and watches for a long time, but it will be days before the horror of what happened comes to him, slamming into his chest, entering him as if he is suddenly possessed. It will happen at an officers' function at the Administrator's residence, when he will see a servant girl walk by, carrying her child on her hip. Then it will come, he will feel himself drowning, choking, mumbling half-excuses to puzzled officers who ask him if he is feeling well, and he, Yes, don't worry, I am just a little faint, that's all, and now stumbling, outside and down the steps, into the garden, where he will fall vomiting into the roses, tears welling up behind his eyes, and he will begin to cry, sobbing, shaking, a grief beyond all proportion, so that later he will think back and wonder for what else he mourned.

But in that moment, in the stillness of the day, as he stands before the scene he doesn't move. The boy, the mother, the quiet hush of branches, swayed by a sweet wind that sweeps over the stillness and the screams. They stand, he and the other pale men. They watch the scene below them, the mother shaking the little body, kissing it, running her bloodied hands over his face, over her face, wailing in an unearthly tone which is both so foreign and so familiar. Until at his side there is a rustling, flashes of other women who rush in, falling by the mother, pulling her back from the boy. Her body tenses forward, against gravity, a cancelling of forces.

A man at his side, his face washed out in the sun, takes a step backward, staggers briefly, balances against the ground with the butt of his rifle.

That night he awakes many times, disorientated. It will be two days before he collapses in the rose garden, but he feels already that a tear has begun, irreparable, like bits of paint lost as dust to the wind in the ripping of a canvas. It has changed everything, he thinks, This is not part of my plan, my contract, my commission. He remembers writing to Katherine when he first reached Burma that he couldn't believe that he had arrived, that he was really away. A letter that now probably sits on a mail train speeding towards home. And I am alone in Rangoon.

EIGHT

Two days later Edgar received a message from the War Office. They had secured an extra berth on a teak ship with the Irrawaddy Flotilla Company. The boat would depart from the docks at Prome in two days. He would leave for Prome on the train; the trip to Mandalay would take seven days.

In his four days in Rangoon he had hardly unpacked. Since the hunt he had stayed in his room, leaving only when called upon by various officials or occasionally to wander the streets. The bureaucracy of the colonial operation astounded him. Following the shooting, he had been subpoenaed to sign statements at the Departments of Civil and Criminal Justice, the Police Station, at the Department for Village Administration, the Medical Department, even the Department of Forests (because, as the subpoena stated, 'the accident occurred in the act of wild game control'). At first he was surprised that the event was even reported. He knew that if all the men had agreed, it could easily have been covered up; the villagers would never have found a way to complain, and even if they did, it was unlikely that they would have been believed, and even if they had been, it was unlikely that the officers would be disciplined.

Yet everyone, including Witherspoon, insisted on reporting the incident. Witherspoon paid a minor fine to be distributed to the victim's family, along with army funds set aside for compensation.

It all *seems* remarkably civil, Edgar wrote to Katherine, Perhaps this is evidence of the positive influence of British institutions, despite the occasional aberrance of hasty British soldiers. Or perhaps, he wrote a day later after signing his seventh statement, this is all merely a salve, a tried and effective method of dealing with such terror, to absolve something deeper, The afternoon is already blurring behind the screen of bureaucracy.

Witherspoon and Fogg left for Pegu as soon as the paperwork was completed, arriving on time to relieve a pair of officers who were returning to Calcutta with their regiments. Edgar didn't say goodbye. Although he had wanted to place the blame for the incident on Witherspoon, he couldn't. For if Witherspoon had been hasty, he had only been two seconds hastier than the rest of them, all of whom shared the bloodlust of the hunt. Yet each time Edgar saw him after the accident, whether at meals or in government offices, he couldn't suppress the memory of the rifle raised against the heavy jowl, the beads of sweat running down the back of the sunburnt neck.

As he had avoided Witherspoon, Edgar avoided Captain Dalton as well. On the night before his departure a messenger brought an invitation from Dalton, once again inviting him to the Pegu Club. He declined politely, excusing himself as too tired. In truth, he wanted to see Dalton, to thank him for his hospitality, to tell him that he held no anger towards him. Yet the thought of reliving the incident terrified him, and he realized that all that he shared with the Captain now was that moment of horror, and to see him would be to relive it. So he refused the invitation and the Captain didn't call again, and although Edgar told himself that he could always visit the Captain when he came back to Rangoon, he knew that he wouldn't.

On the morning of his departure he was met at his door by a carriage, which took him to the railway station, where he boarded a train for Prome. While the train was being loaded, he stared out over the bustle on the platform. Down below he saw a group of small boys kicking a coconut husk. His fingers reflexively fingered a single coin that he held in his pocket, which he had kept since the hunt: a symbol of responsibility, of misplaced munificence, a reminder of mistakes, and so a talisman.

In the chaos of mourning, when all had left carrying the boy, Edgar had seen the coin lying on the ground, tipped in the dusty imprint of the boy's body. He had assumed that it had been overlooked and he picked it up simply because it was the boy's and it didn't seem right for it to be lost at the edge of the forest. He didn't know that this was a mistake, that it had been neither forgotten nor missed: in the sunlight it glinted like gold and every child eyed it and wanted it. But what the children knew, and he didn't understand, he could have learned from any porter who loaded crates onto the train below. The most powerful talismans, they would have told him, are those that are inherited, and with such talismans the fortune is inherited as well.

o

In Prome he was met by the staff of a district army officer, who took him to the docks. There he boarded a small steamer of the Irrawaddy Flotilla Company, whose engines had already begun to turn by the time he boarded. He was shown to his berth, with a view of the left bank of the river. It was small but clean and his apprehension about the trip was assuaged. As he unpacked, he felt the steamer push away from the shore and he walked to the window to watch the banks disappear. Still thinking of the tiger hunt, he had noticed little in Prome, only some crumbling ruins and a bustling market by the port. Now, on the river, he felt a lightening, a separation from the hot, crowded streets of Rangoon, of the delta, from the boy's death. He climbed to the deck. There were several other passengers, some soldiers, an older couple from Italy who told him they had come sightseeing. All new faces, none of whom knew of the accident, and he vowed to put the experience behind him and leave it on the muddy banks.

There was little to the view from the centre of the river, so he joined the soldiers in a game of cards. At first he had been hesitant to meet them, remembering the haughtiness of many of the officers he had met on the ship from Marseilles. But these were enlisted men, and when they saw he was alone they invited him to play, and in exchange he entertained them with news about the football league; even month-old news was fresh in Burma. He knew little about the sport, really, but he had tuned the piano of a London club owner and been given free tickets to some matches. On Katherine's suggestion, before he had left he had memorized some scores, in her words to 'facilitate conversation and meeting people'. He revelled in the attention, and in the soldiers' enthusiasm for the news. They drank gin together and laughed and proclaimed Edgar Drake a fine chap, and he thought how happy these young men were. And yet they too must have seen terror, but here are content with stories of two-month-old football matches. And he drank more gin laced with tonic water, which the soldiers joked was 'prescribed by the doctor', for the quinine in the tonic fought the ague.

That night he had his first good sleep in days, heavy and dreamless, and he awoke long after the sun had risen, with a heavy headache from the gin. The banks were still distant, with little relief from the wooded shore other than scattered pagodas. And so he joined another card game and treated the soldiers to several more rounds of gin.

They drank and played for three days, and when he had repeated the football scores so many times that even the drunkest soldier could recite them, he sat back and listened to them tell stories of Burma. One of the soldiers had been at the battle for Minhla Fort during the Third War, and he recounted the advance through the mist and the fierce resistance of the Burmese. Another had served on a mission in the Shan States in the territory of the warlord Twet Nga Lu and he told his story, and to this Edgar listened carefully, for he had heard the name of the brigand many times. And he asked the soldier, Have you ever seen Twet Nga Lu? He hadn't, they had marched days through the jungle and everywhere found evidence they were being followed – dead fires, shapes shifting in the trees. But they were never attacked and returned with neither defeat nor conquest; land claimed without witnesses is never land truly claimed.

And Edgar asked the soldier more questions: had *anyone* ever seen Twet Nga Lu? How far did his territory extend? Were rumours of his ferocity true? To these the soldier answered that the warlord remained elusive, and sent only messengers, and that few had ever seen him, not even Mr Scott, the Political Administrator to the Shan States, whose success at forming friendships with tribes such as the Kachins was legendary. And, yes, rumours of his ferocity were true, the soldier had seen with his very own eyes men crucified on mountaintops, nailed side by side to rows of timber Xs. As to the extent of his territory, no one knew. There were reports that he had been driven deep into the hills, beaten back by the *sawbwa* of Mongnai, whose throne he had usurped. But many felt this loss of territory was insignificant; he was so feared for his supernatural powers, for his tattoos and charms, for the talismans he wore beneath his skin.

Finally, when the bottle of gin drew near empty, the soldier stopped speaking and asked why the good man wanted to know so much about Twet Nga Lu. The heady feeling of camaraderie and acceptance overrode concerns of confidentiality, and Edgar told them that he had come to tune the piano of a certain Surgeon-Major Anthony Carroll.

At the sound of the Doctor's name, the other men, who had been playing cards, stopped and stared at the piano tuner.

'Carroll?' shouted one in a rough Scottish accent. 'Bloody hell, did I just hear the name Carroll?'

'Yes, why?' asked Edgar, surprised by the outburst.

'Why?' the Scotsman laughed and turned to his comrades. 'You hear this, we have been on this boat for three bloody days, begging this chap for football scores and today he tells us he is friends with the Doctor himself.' They all laughed and exchanged a clinking of glasses.

'Well, not a friend, well . . . yet . . .', corrected Edgar. 'But, I don't understand. Why all the excitement? Do you know him?'

'Know him?' guffawed the soldier. 'The man is as legendary as Twet Nga Lu. Hell, the man's as legendary as the Queen.' More clinking of glasses, more gin.

'Really?' asked Edgar, leaning forward. 'I didn't think he was so . . . notorious. Maybe some of the officers knew of him, but I perceive many of them aren't so fond of him.'

'Because he is so bloody competent compared to them. A true man of action. Of course they don't like him.' Laughter.

'But you like him.'

'Like him? Any soldier who has had to serve in the Shan States loves the bastard. If it wasn't for Carroll, I would be stuck in some bloody stink of a jungle covered in mud and fighting a bloodthirsty band of Shan. God knows how he does it, but he has saved my pale arse, I'm certain of that. If we have a full-scale war in the Shan States, each one of us will be strung up within days.'

Another soldier raised a glass. 'To Carroll. Damn his poetry, damn his stethoscope, but God bless the bloody bastard, because he saved me for my dear mum!' The men roared.

Edgar could hardly believe what he was hearing. 'God bless the bastard,' he cried and raised his glass, and when they had drunk, and then drunk again, the stories began.

●

You want to know about Carroll? I haven't met the man, Me neither, No, nor I. Nor I, just stories, well, none of us have met the man, hell, raise your glasses to that, the man is but a fairy tale. That's right, a fairy tale, They say he stands seven feet tall and breathes fire, Really, I haven't heard that one, Well I've heard that your mum stands seven feet tall and breathes fire, Come on, Jackson, be serious you bastard, this fine gentlemen wants True stories about Carroll, Truth, raise your glass to Truth then, hell, I would be less in awe if the man did stand seven feet tall and breathed fire, Have you heard the story of the building of the fort? That's a wild one, You tell it, Jackson, you tell it, Well then, I'll tell it, Quiet, you bastards, Mr Drake, pardon my French, bit tipsy you know, Get on with the story, Jackson, Fair enough, the story, I'll get fast to it, where does it start? No, you know what? What? I am going to tell the story of the journey, that's a better one, Tell it then, All right I will, The *Story*, ready, boys? Carroll arrives in Burma, he's been here a couple of years, medical stuff, couple of trips into the jungle, but still this fellow's pretty fresh, I mean, I don't think he has ever fired a gun or anything, but still he volunteers to set up camp in Mae Lwin, secret stuff at the time, God knows why he wants to go, but he goes anyway. Not only is the country overrun with armed bands, but this is long before we annexed Upper Burma, so if he needs reinforcements we may not even be able to get there to help him, but still he goes, why, no one knows, every man has his own theory, me, I think the chap was maybe running away from something, wanted to get away, you know, far away, but that's just my opinion, I don't know, What do you boys think? Glory maybe, Girls! the bastard likes Shan girls, Thanks, Stephens, I should have expected as much from your mind, this is a fellow who will skip church to sneak down to the Mandalay bazaar to chase the painted *mingale*s, How about you, Murphy? Me, hell, maybe the chap just believes in the cause, you know, civilize the uncivilized, make peace, bring law and order to an untamed land, not like us drunken bastards, Poetic, Murphy, real poetic, Listen you wanted my opinion, All right, how long is this story going to take? Where was I? Carroll heads into the bloody jungle, Yeah, Carroll heads into the jungle, under escort, maybe ten soldiers, that's it, that's all he will allow, says it isn't a military expedition, Well, military expedition or not, before they even reach the site they are attacked, they are crossing a clearing and suddenly an arrow whizzes past and hits a tree above his head, The soldiers, they take cover in the trees and ready their rifles, but Carroll just stands in the clearing, not moving, mad as a hatter I tell you, all alone, but calm, real calm, calm that would make a card dealer jealous, and another arrow flies by him, faster this time, nicking his helmet, Crazy bastard! Crazy all right, and what does Carroll do? Tell us, Jackson, Yeah, tell us, you bastard, All right, all right, I'll tell it, all right, what does he do? The crazy bastard takes off his helmet, where he had tied a little flute that he likes to play on the marches, and he puts the damn thing to his mouth and begins to play, He's mad I tell you! Bloody nuts if you ask me! You going to let me finish the story? Yeah, go on, go on, finish the bloody story! So Carroll begins to play, and what does he play? 'God bless the Queen?' Wrong, Murphy, 'The Wood-cutter's Daughter?' Damn it, Stephens, nothing dirty, please, Sorry for my friend, Mr Drake, and sorry, boys, but Carroll starts to play some crazy song that none of the soldiers has ever heard, weird little ditty, and I met a soldier once who had served in the escort, and he told me about it, says he never heard the song in his life, nothing fancy, maybe twenty notes, and then Carroll stops and looks around, and the troops are all kneeling, rifles to their cheeks, ready to fire if a bird chirps, but nothing happens, everything's still, and Carroll plays the tune again, and when he finishes he waits, and then plays it again, and he stares into the forest around the clearing, Nothing, not a peep, no more arrows, and Carroll plays again, and from the bushes comes a whistling, the same damn tune, and this time when the song finishes Carroll doesn't stop but repeats it, and now there's more whistling and he plays three more times, and then they are bloody singing together, Carroll and their attackers, and the men can hear laughter and cheering from the forest, but it is dense and dark and no one can be seen, At last Carroll stops and motions his men to stand, and they do so slowly, they are scared, you can imagine, and they climb back onto their mounts, and they continue their march, and never see the attackers again, although the soldier who told me the story said he could hear them the entire way, they were there, guarding the party, guarding Carroll, and this way Carroll passes through some of the most dangerous territory in the empire without firing a shot, and they reach Mae Lwin, where the local chief is waiting, expecting them, and takes the men's ponies and offers them warm rice and curries, and gives them shelter, and after three days of conferring, Carroll announces to the party that the chief has granted them permission to build a fort at Mae Lwin, in exchange for protection from dacoits, and the promise of a clinic. And more music.

o

The soldier stopped. There was silence. Even the rowdiest of the soldiers had quieted, awed by the story.

'What was the song?' asked Edgar, finally.

'Sorry?'

'The song. What was the song that he played on his flute?'

'The song . . . a Shan love ditty. When a Shan boy courts his sweetheart, he always plays the same song. It's nothing, rather simple, but it worked like a miracle. Carroll later told the soldier who told me the story that no man could kill one who played a song that reminded him of the first time he had fallen in love.'

'Bloody amazing.' There was soft chuckling, the men having drifted into contemplation.

'Any more stories?' asked Edgar.

'About Carroll? Oh, Mr Drake, so many stories. So many stories.' He looked down into his glass, now nearly empty. 'But tomorrow maybe, I'm tired now. The journey is long and our destination's days away. We have nothing but stories until bloody Mandalay.'

o

They steamed up the river steadily, passing towns, their names streaming together like an incantation. Sitsayan. Kama. Pato. Thayet. Allanmyo. Yahaing. Nyaungywagyi. As they moved further north, the land grew dry, the vegetation sparse. The green Pegu Hills soon tapered down to a flat plain, the dense foliage changed to thorn trees and toddy palms. They stopped at many of the towns, dusty ports with little more than a few huts and a fading monastery. There they picked up or unloaded cargo, and occasionally passengers, soldiers usually, ruddy-faced boys who joined the nightly conversations and brought their own stories.

And they all knew of Carroll. A trooper from Kyaukchet told them that he met a soldier who had been to Mae Lwin once, who said that it reminded him of stories of the Hanging Gardens of Babylon, a fort like none other, festooned with the rarest of orchids, where one could hear music playing at all hours and there was no need to take up arms, for there were no dacoits for miles. Where men could sit in the shade by the Salween and eat sweet fruit. Where the girls laughed and tossed their hair and had eyes like those you see in dreams. A Pegu rifleman told them that he had heard that Shan storytellers sang ballads about Anthony Carroll, and an infantryman from Danubyu told them that there was no sickness in Mae Lwin, for cool fresh winds followed the course of the Salween, and one could sleep outside under moonlit skies, and awake without a mosquito bite, and there was none of the fever or dysentery that had killed so many of his friends as they waded through steaming jungles and pulled leeches from their ankles. A private travelling with his battalion to Hlaingdet had heard that Anthony Carroll had dismantled his cannons and used them as pots for flowers, and the guns of the soldiers who were lucky enough to pass through Mae Lwin grew rusty as the men spent their days writing letters and growing fat, and listening to the laughter of children.

More men joined in the stories and, as the steamer groaned northwards, Edgar began to realize that the tales were less what each soldier knew was true than what he needed to believe. That, although the Commissioner proclaimed there was peace, for the soldiers there was only maintaining peace, which was very different, and with this came fear and the need for something to keep the fear away. And with this realization came another: that he was surprised how unimportant truth had begun to be for himself. Perhaps more than any lonely soldier he needed to believe in the Surgeon-Major he had never met.

o

Sinbaungwe. Migyaungye. Minhla. One night he awoke to hear an eerie song drifting in from the riverbank. He sat up in his bed. The sound was distant, a murmur, disappearing beneath the sound of his breath. He listened, barely moving. The boat moved on.

Magwe, Yenangyaung. And then, in Kyaukye, the long slow pace of the journey upstream was broken by the arrival of three new passengers in chains.

Dacoits. Edgar had heard the word many times since he read his first brief back in London. Thieves. Warlords. Highwaymen. When Thibaw, the last King of Upper Burma, had ascended the throne almost ten years ago the country had fallen into chaos. The new King was weak and the Burmese hold on their land began to crumble, not to any armed resistance but to an epidemic of lawlessness. Throughout Upper Burma bands of marauders attacked lone travellers and caravans alike, raided villages, demanded protection money from lonely farmers. Their capacity for violence was well known, testimony lay in the hundreds of razed villages, in the bodies of those who resisted nailed up along the roads. When the British inherited the rice fields of Upper Burma along with the annexation, they also inherited the dacoits.

The captives were brought on deck, where they squatted, three dusty men with three parallel lines of chain from neck to neck, wrist to wrist, ankle to ankle. Before the boat pushed off from the rickety docks, a crowd of passengers had already gathered in a semi-circle around the prisoners, who let their hands dangle between their knees and stared back, emotionless, defiant of the crowd of soldiers and travellers. They were watched over by three Indian soldiers, and Edgar was terrified to think what the dacoits must have done to deserve such a guard. He didn't have to wait long for an answer, for as the crowd of passengers stared down at the prisoners the Italian woman traveller asked one of the soldiers what the men had done, and the soldier in turn asked one of the guards.

The three men, explained the guard, were the leaders of one of the fiercest bands of dacoits, who had terrorized the foothills east of Hlaingdet, near the British fort established during the early military expeditions into the Shan States. Edgar knew the name Hlaingdet, for this was where he was to receive an escort on the road to Mae Lwin. The dacoits had been bold enough to attack villages in the vicinity of the fort, where villagers had thought that by moving close to army headquarters they would be safe from the marauders. They had burned rice fields and robbed caravans, and finally had attacked and burned one village and raped women and girls by holding knives to the throats of their children. It had been a large band, perhaps twenty men. When tortured, they had pointed out these three as their leaders. Now they were being taken to Mandalay for questioning.

'And the other men?' the Italian woman had asked.

'Killed in the encounter,' said the soldier stoically.

'All seventeen?' asked the woman, 'I thought you said they

were captured and confessed . . .' but she let the sentence trail off into silence as her face flushed red. 'Oh,' she said, weakly.

Edgar stood and stared at the prisoners, trying to see in their expressions evidence of their terrible deeds, but they revealed nothing. They sat in the heavy irons, their faces covered with thick dust that coloured their dark hair a lighter brown. One of them looked very young, with a thin moustache, and his long hair tied up in a bun on his head. His tattoos were blurred by the dirt, but Edgar thought he could make out the deep stain of a tiger across the boy's chest. Like the others, his face was set and defiant. For one brief moment, his eyes met Edgar's, and held there before the piano tuner was able to look away.

Slowly the passengers lost interest in the captives and filed away to their rooms. Edgar followed, still shaken by the story. He would not write to Katherine about this, he decided; he didn't wish to frighten her. As he tried to sleep, he imagined the attack and thought of the women villagers, of how they must have carried their children, wondering if they were merchants or if they worked in the fields, wondering if they wore *thanaka* too. He lay down and tried to sleep. The images of painted girls came to haunt him, the swirls of the white paint over skin blackened by the sun.

On the deck the dacoits crouched in their shackles.

The steamer pushed on. The night passed, and the day, and the towns.

Sinbyugyun. Sale. Seikpyu. Singu. Like a chant. Milaungbya. Pagan.

o

It was nearly sunset when the first of the temples appeared on the vast plain. A lone building, fallen into ruins and covered with vines. Below its crumbling walls an old man sat on the back of an ox-cart pulled by a pair of humpbacked Brahmin cows. The steamship was moving close to the shore to avoid sandbanks in the centre of the river, and the old man turned to watch them pass. The dust turned up by the cart reflected the rays of the sun, casting the temple in a golden haze.

A woman walked alone under a parasol, heading somewhere unseen.

The soldiers had told Edgar that the ship would stop 'for sightseeing' at the ruins of Pagan, the ancient capital of a kingdom that had ruled Burma for centuries. At last, after nearly an hour of steaming past rows of fallen monuments, as the river began its slow turn to the west, they stopped at a nondescript quay and a number of passengers disembarked. Edgar followed the Italian couple over a narrow plank.

They walked with a soldier, who led them up a dusty road. More pagodas soon became visible, structures that had been obscured by the scattered foliage or the rise of the bank. The sun was setting rapidly. A pair of bats flapped through the air. Soon they reached the base of a large pyramid. 'Let's climb here,' said the soldier. 'The finest view in all of Pagan.'

The steps were steep. At the top of the stairs, a wide platform circled the central spire. If they had arrived ten minutes later, they would have missed the sun as it cast its rays over the vast field of pagodas that stretched away from the river to the distant mountains, floating in the dust and smoke of burning rice fields.

'What are those mountains?' Edgar asked the soldier.

'The Shan Hills, Mr Drake. Finally we can see them.'

'The Shan Hills,' Edgar repeated and stared past the temples that stood like soldiers in formation to the mountains, which rose abruptly from the plain and seemed to hover in the sky. He thought of a river which ran through those hills, and how somewhere, hidden in the darkness, a man waited, who perhaps stared out at the same sky, but who had yet to know his name.

The sun set. The mantle of night crept across the plain,

enveloping each pagoda one by one, until at last the soldier turned and the travellers followed him back to the ship.

o

Nyaung-U, Pakokku, and then it was day again. Kanma, and the confluence of the Chindwin River, Myingyan, and Yandabo, and then it was night, and as the Sagaing Hills rose to the west, the passengers went to sleep knowing that during the night, the steamship, ploughing upstream, would pass the old capital of Amarapura, which means 'City of the Immortals'. Before the sun rose, they would arrive in Mandalay.

NINE

THE FOLLOWING MORNING Edgar was awakened by the sudden arrival of silence. The steamboat, after groaning relentlessly for seven days, cut her engines, and drifted on the current. New sounds slipped into the cabin: a faint sloshing, the whispered shriek of metal on metal as a kerosene lamp swung on its chain, the shouts of men, and the distant yet unmistakable clamour of a bazaar. Edgar rose and dressed without washing, left his room, and walked the length of the corridor towards the spiral stairs that climbed to the deck, conscious of the creaking of the floorboards beneath his bare feet. At the top of the stairs, he almost collided with one of the young deckhands, who swung down the banister like a langur. Mandalay, said the boy, grinning, and swept his arm towards the shore.

They were floating past a market. Or into it: the boat seemed to be descending, the bank and its inhabitants swirling to overflow from the quayside and onto the deck. The market pressed in on either side, hustling shapes and voices shouting, the floating outlines of *thanaka* in the shade of broad bamboo hats, the silhouettes of traders rising from the backs of elephants. A group of children laughed and leaped over the rail and onto the boat, chasing each other, weaving through the piles of coiled rope, the stacks of chain, and now bags of spices, carried forward by a row of vendors who swept over the deck of the ship. Edgar heard singing behind him and turned. A roti-wallah stood on the deck, grinning a toothless smile, his dough spinning on his fist. The sun, he sang, and raised his lips to point at the sky, The sun. His dough spun faster and he hurled it skywards.

Edgar looked back to the steamer, but he could no longer see the ship, it was all the bazaar. Spices spilled from the bags onto the deck. A line of monks wound past, chanting for alms, circling him as he watched their bare feet track patterns in scattered dust the colour of their robes. A woman shouted at him in Burmese, chewing betel, her tongue the colour of plums, her laughter turning into the pattering of footsteps. The children again ran past. Edgar turned to look back to the roti-wallah, and then up at the spinning dough. The man sang and reached up and picked the sun from the sky. It was dark and Edgar stared into the darkness of his cabin.

The engines had indeed stopped. For a brief moment he wondered if he was still dreaming, but his window was open and no light poured in. Outside he heard voices, and at first he dismissed them as those of the crew. But the sounds seemed to be coming from further away. He climbed on deck. The moon was nearly full, casting blue shadows on the men who swiftly rolled barrels towards the gangplank. The bank was lined with shacks. For the second time that night Edgar Drake arrived in Mandalay.

o

They were met on shore by Captain Trevor Nash-Burnham, who had originally intended to meet Edgar in Rangoon, and whom Edgar knew as the author of several of the reports he had read on Surgeon-Major Carroll. The reports were rich with descriptions of Mandalay, of the river, of the winding trails to Carroll's camp. Edgar had secretly longed to meet Nash-Burnham, as he had been unimpressed by most of the bureaucrats he had met after the hunt, whose dullness in the presence of such colour astounded him.

Standing on the bank, he now recalled how in Rangoon, in the administrative frenzy following the shooting, he had been walking home from a briefing with a member of the Department of Village Administration. They had passed a crowd of people trying to move the body of an opium addict who had fallen asleep under a wagon and been crushed when the horses pulled the cart forward. The man was crying, a low, stuporous wail, as a group of merchants alternately tried to coax the horses forward or back the wagon up. Edgar had been sickened, but the functionary hadn't even stopped talking about the teak tallies collected from the various districts of the colony. When Edgar asked where they could find help, the man shocked him not by answering 'Why?' – which would have been predictably insensitive – but 'For whom?' And this answer he could scarcely hear over the man's screams.

Standing on the banks of the city, he shifted awkwardly. As the Captain read a letter from the War Office, a detailed notice about supplies and timetables, Edgar scrutinized his face for the man who had written of the Irrawaddy as 'this shimmering serpent who carries off our dreams, only to bring fresh ones from the jewelled hills'. He was a squat man, with a broad forehead, who wheezed when he talked too fast, a striking contrast to the youth and fitness of Captain Dalton. It was an odd moment for an official briefing. Edgar looked at his pocket watch, a gift from Katherine before his departure. It was four, and only then did he remember that the watch had rusted to a halt three days after he had arrived in Rangoon, and now, as he had jokingly written to Katherine, was correct only twice a day, although he kept it 'to preserve appearances'. He now thought with some amusement of the London advertisement, This Christmas Day when church bells chime, give yourself the gift of time – Robinson's quality watches . . .

The river was beginning to come to life, and a stream of vendors could be seen making their way down the road to the water. The men boarded a carriage and drove into town. The centre of Mandalay, as Edgar would note in his next letter home, was about two miles from the Irrawaddy; when the capital had been moved from Amarapura, on the river, the kings wanted a site far from the noise of the foreigners' steamships.

The road was dark and rutted. Edgar watched shapes pass outside the window, until it became opaque with condensation. Nash-Burnham reached up and wiped it clean with a handkerchief.

o

By the time the carriage entered the town, the sun had begun to rise. Outside, the roads were filling with people. They approached a bazaar. Hands pressed against the window, faces peered in. A porter carrying two bags of spices on a pole dodged out of the path of the carriage, swinging his bags so that one of them touched lightly against the window, dusting it with curry powder, which caught the rising sunlight and stained the glass gold.

As they moved through the street Edgar tried to picture himself on one of the maps of Mandalay he had studied on the steamship. But he was lost and allowed himself to be caught up in the momentum of his arrival, the wonder and speculation that accompanies a new home. They passed seamstresses, their tables set out in the middle of the road, betel vendors, with trays of cracked betel-nut shells and cups of lime, knife sharpeners, sellers of false teeth and religious icons, of sandals, mirrors, dried fish and crab, rice, *pasos*, parasols. Occasionally, the Captain would point something out on the road, a famous shrine, a government office. And Edgar would answer, Yes I have read of it, or, It is even more beautiful than in the illustrations, or, Perhaps I will visit it soon.

At last the carriage pulled to a halt in front of a small, unremarkable cottage. 'Your temporary lodgings, Mr Drake,' said the Captain. 'Usually we put up guests in the barracks inside Mandalay Palace, but it is better if you stay here now. Please make yourself at home. We lunch today at the residence of the Commissioner of the Northern Division – a special reception in honour of the annexation of Mandalay. I will call for you at noon.'

Edgar thanked Nash-Burnham and slid out of the carriage. The driver carried his trunks to the door. He knocked and a woman answered. The driver led Edgar inside and left his luggage. From the anteroom Edgar followed the woman to a raised wooden floor, and into a room furnished sparsely with a table and two chairs. The woman pointed at his feet, and Edgar, seeing she had abandoned her sandals at the door, sat on the step and clumsily pulled off his shoes. She led him through a door to the right and into a room dominated by a large bed covered with a mosquito net. She set the luggage on the floor.

Off the bedroom was a bathing room, with a water basin and pressed towels. A second door led into a yard, where a small table sat beneath a pair of papaya trees. It all felt very quaint, thought Edgar, and very English, except for the papaya trees and the woman who stood beside him.

He turned to her. 'Edgar naa meh. Naa meh be lo . . . lo . . . kaw dha le?' A question mark as much for the correctness of his Burmese, as for the question itself. What is your name?

The woman smiled. 'Kyamma naa meh Khin Myo.' She pronounced it softly, the 'm' and 'y' melting together like a single letter.

Edgar Drake extended his hand and she smiled again and took it in hers.

o

His watch still read four. Now, by the reckoning of the sun, it was three hours off; he was free until it was eight hours off, when he would meet the Captain for lunch. Khin Myo had begun to heat water for the bath, but Edgar interrupted her. 'I go . . . out, walking. I go walking.' He made a motion with his fingers and she nodded. She seems to understand, he thought. He took out his hat from his bag and walked out to the anteroom, where he had to sit down again to tie his shoes.

Khin Myo was waiting at the door with a parasol. He stopped by her, unsure what he should say. He liked her immediately. She held herself gracefully and smiled and looked at him directly, unlike so many of the other servants, who seemed to sneak away shyly when their tasks were finished. Her eyes were dark brown, set beneath thick lashes, and she wore even lines of *thanaka* on both cheeks. She had placed a hibiscus flower in her hair, and when he walked in front of her he could smell a sweet perfume, like the mixed essences of cinnamon and coconut. She wore a bleached lace blouse, which hung down to her waist and a purple silk *hta main* folded with careful pleats.

To his surprise she walked with him. In the street he tried again to piece together some Burmese. 'Don't worry about me, *ma . . . thwa . . . um*, you don't need to um, um . . . *ma* walk.' This was only polite, I shouldn't burden her with taking care of me.

Khin Myo laughed. 'You speak good Burmese. And they said you have only been here two weeks.'

'You speak English?'

'Oh, not so well, my accent is rough.'

'No, your accent is very nice.' There was a softness to her voice that struck him immediately, like whispering, but deeper, like the sound of wind playing over the open end of a glass bottle.

She smiled, and this time dropped her gaze. 'Thank you. Please, continue. I don't want to interrupt your walk. I can accompany you if you wish.'

'But really, I don't want to bother you . . .'

'It is no bother at all. I love my city in the early morning. And I couldn't let you go alone. Captain Nash-Burnham said that you might get lost.'

'Well, thank you, thank you. I am surprised, really.'

'At my English, or that a Burmese woman is not ashamed to speak to you?' When Edgar couldn't find the words to reply, she added, 'Don't worry, they see me often with visitors.'

They walked down the street, past more houses with carefully swept dirt paths. Outside one house a woman hung clothes on a line. Khin Myo stopped to speak to her. 'Good morning, Mr Drake,' said the woman. 'Good morning,' he answered.

'Do all the . . .' he paused, awkward with the words.

'Do all the servants speak English?'

'Yes . . . yes.'

'Not all. I am teaching Mrs Zin Nwe when her master is away.' Khin Myo checked herself. 'Actually, please don't tell anyone that; perhaps I am a little too open with you already.'

'I won't tell a soul. You teach English?'

'I used to. It is a long story. And I don't want to bore you.'

'I doubt you would. But may I ask then how you learned?'

'You have a lot of questions, Mr Drake. Are you so surprised?'

'No, no. Not at all, I am sorry. I didn't mean to offend you.'

She was silent. As they walked on she still remained slightly behind him.

She spoke again, softly. 'I am sorry. Here you are kind and I am rude.'

'No,' Edgar answered. 'I *do* have too many questions. I haven't met many Burmese. And you know how most of the officers are.'

Khin Myo smiled. 'I know.'

They turned at the end of the street. To Edgar it seemed as if they were roughly following the road he had arrived on.

'Where would you like to go, Mr Drake?'

'Take me to your favourite place,' he answered, startled by the sudden intimacy implied in his answer. If she too was surprised, she kept it hidden.

o

They followed a wide road west, the sun rising behind them, and Edgar watched their shadows advance headfirst, snake-like over the ground. They spoke little and walked for nearly an hour. At a small canal, they stopped to watch a floating market. 'I think this is the most beautiful place in Mandalay,' Khin Myo said. And Edgar, who had been in the city less than four hours, said he agreed. Below them, the boats shifted by the banks.

'They look like floating lotus flowers,' he said.

'And the merchants like croaking frogs upon them.'

They were standing on a small bridge, watching boats move through the canal. Khin Myo said, 'I hear that you are here to repair a piano?'

Edgar hesitated, surprised by the question, 'Yes, yes I am. How did you know?'

'One learns a lot if others assume you are deaf to their tongue.'

Edgar looked at her. 'Yes . . . I imagine so . . . do you think that is strange? It is quite a distance to travel to repair a piano, I suppose.' He turned back to the canal. Two boats had stopped for a woman to measure out a yellow spice into a small bag. Some of the spice dusted the black water like pollen.

'Not so strange. I am confident that Anthony Carroll knows what he is doing.'

'Do you know of Anthony Carroll?'

Again she was silent, and he turned to see her staring out across the water. On the canal the merchants poled through ink and islands of hyacinth, calling out the price of spices.

●

They walked back to the house. The sun was higher now, and Edgar worried that he might not have enough time to bathe before Nash-Burnham came to take him to the reception. Inside, Khin Myo filled the basin in his bathroom with water and brought him soap and a towel. He bathed and shaved and dressed in a new shirt and new trousers, which she had pressed while he was bathing.

When he came outside, he found her kneeling by a washbasin, already washing his clothes. 'Oh, Miss Khin Myo, you don't need to do that.'

'What?'

'Wash my clothes.'

'Who will wash your clothes if I don't?'

'I don't know, it's just that—'

She interrupted him. 'Look! Captain Nash-Burnham is here.'

He turned to see the Captain rounding the corner. 'Hello!' he shouted. He was wearing mess dress: a scarlet shell jacket, a mess waistcoat, blue trousers. A sword hung from his waist.

'Hello, Mr Drake! Hope you don't mind a stroll. The carriage was needed for some of the less vigorous guests!' He walked into the yard and looked at Khin Myo. 'Ma Khin Myo,' he said, bowing with a flourish. 'Aaah, you smell lovely.'

'I smell like cleaning soap.'

'If only roses could bathe in such a soap.'

Here at last, thought Edgar, is the man who called the Irra-waddy a shimmering serpent.

o

The Commissioner's residence was twenty minutes on foot from the house. As they walked, the Captain tapped his fingers on his scabbard. 'How did you enjoy your morning, Mr Drake?'

'Well, Captain, very well. I went on a most charming walk with Miss Khin Myo. She is unusual for a Burmese woman, isn't she? They are all so shy. And she speaks beautiful English.'

'She is very impressive. Did she tell you how she learned English?'

'No, I didn't ask. I didn't want to pry.'

'That is kind of you, Mr Drake, although I don't think she

would mind telling you. But I appreciate your discretion. You wouldn't believe all the problems I have had with other guests. She is very beautiful.'

'She is. Many of the women are. If only I were a young man again.'

'Well, be careful. You wouldn't be the first Englishman to fall in love and never go home. Sometimes I think that the only reason we seek new colonies is for their girls. Let me be the one to warn you to stay away from matters of love.'

'Oh, I wouldn't worry,' Edgar protested. 'I have a dear wife in London.' The Captain looked at him askance. Edgar laughed, But I am telling the truth, I do miss Katherine even now.

They followed a fence that enclosed a broad lawn surrounding a stately Victorian building. At the entrance to the driveway an Indian in a police uniform stood guard. Captain Nash-Burnham nodded at him and he opened the gate. They walked up a long path, where several horses stood harnessed to carriages.

'Welcome, Mr Drake,' said Nash-Burnham. 'It should be a bearable afternoon if we survive lunch and the requisite poetry reading. We will be able to play cards once the ladies retire. We are all a bit jaundiced with one another, but we manage to get along. Just pretend that you are back in England.' He paused. 'But first some advice: don't talk to Mrs Hemmington about anything Burmese. She has some unpleasant views on what she calls the "Nature of Brown Races", which are embarrassing to many of us. Seems as if only mentioning a temple or Burmese food gets her talking and she won't stop. Talk to her about London gossip, or crochet, but nothing Burmese.'

'But I know nothing about crochet.'

'Don't worry. She does.'

They were near the top of the stairs. 'And be careful if Colonel Simmons drinks too much. And don't ask military questions – remember you are a civilian. And one last thing . . . perhaps I should have told you this first: most of them know why you are here, and they will extend the hospitality due a fellow countryman. But you are not among friends. Please try not to mention Anthony Carroll.'

o

They were met at the door by a tall Sikh butler. The Captain greeted him. 'Pavninder Singh, my good man, how are you today?'

'Fine, sahib, fine,' he smiled.

Nash-Burnham handed him his sword. 'Pavninder, this is Mr Drake.' He motioned to Edgar.

'The piano tuner?'

The Captain laughed, his hand on his belly. 'Pavninder is an accomplished musician himself. He is a wonderful tabla player.'

'Oh, sahib, you are too generous!'

'Quiet, and stop calling me sahib, you know I hate that. I know music. There are thousands of Indians in Her Majesty's service in Upper Burma, and you play the finest tabla of any of them. You should see the local girls swoon over him, Mr Drake. Perhaps the two of you can play a duet if Mr Drake is in town long enough.'

Now it was Edgar's turn to protest. 'Actually, Captain, I am quite unskilled on the piano, at playing, that is. I only tune and repair.'

'Nonsense, you are both too modest. Regardless, pianos seem to be quite a sore subject at the present time, so you have been spared. Pavninder, have they started lunch yet?'

'Soon, sir. You are just in time.'

He led them into a room crowded with officers and their wives, with gin and gossip. He was right, I am back in London, thought Edgar, They have even imported the Atmosphere.

Nash-Burnham was forging a path between two rather large and tipsy women in flowing muslin, each decorated with a cascade of sashes which perched like butterflies on the slopes of their dresses. He placed his hand on a large and dimpled elbow, Mrs Winterbottom, how are you? Introductions, Mr Drake?

They moved slowly about the party, the Captain leading Edgar through the eddies of chatter with the intensity of a boatman, his face shifting rapidly between a look of caution as he scanned the room and a wide, engaging grin when he pulled one powdered matron or another from their circle to introduce the tuner with a soliloquy, Lady Aston, my dear, I haven't seen you since the Commissioner's party in March, My dear you do look so lovely tonight, Was it the month in Maymyo, Yes? See, I knew! Well, I must bring myself to travel there again soon, Not much fun for a bachelor, though, Too peaceful! But soon, soon, I must visit. Wait, let me introduce you to a visitor, Mr Drake from London. A pleasure to meet you, Lady Aston. And you too, I *do* miss London dreadfully. Myself as well, madam, and I have only been away one month. Really? You have just arrived, well, welcome, I must introduce you to my husband, Alistair? Alistair, meet Mr Drick, recently arrived from London. A tall man with Dundreary whiskers held out his hand, My pleasure, Mr Drick . . . Mr Drake, actually, Lord Aston, It is a pleasure. Even I know Dundreary whiskers are long out of fashion in London, he thought.

Moving. I would like you to meet Mr Edgar Drake, recently arrived from London. Mr Drake, this is Miss Hoffnung, perhaps one of the craftiest whist hands in Upper Burma. Oh, Captain, you flatter me, Don't believe anything he tells you, Mr Drake. Mrs Sandilands, Mr Drake. Mrs Partridge, this is Edgar Drake from London. Mr Drake, this is Mrs Partridge, this is Mrs Pepper.

'What part of London are you from, Mr Drake?'

'Do you play lawn tennis?'

'What is your business in London, Mr Drake?'

'Franklin Mews, near Fitzroy Square. And, no I don't know how to play lawn tennis, Mrs Partridge.'

'Pepper.'

'My apologies, I *still* don't know how to play lawn tennis, Mrs Pepper.'

Laughing. 'Fitzroy Square, that is near the Oxford Music Hall, right, Mr Drake?'

'Indeed it is.'

'You sound as if you know it. You're not a musician, are you, Mr Drake?'

'No, not really, peripherally associated, you might say . . .'

'Ladies, enough questions for Mr Drake. I think he is quite tired.'

They stopped in the corner of the room, sheltered from the crowd by the broad back of a tall officer dressed in tartan. The Captain took a swift sip of gin.

'I hope you are not exhausted by the conversation.'

'No, I will manage. I am amazed though, it is all so . . . *reproduced*.'

'I hope you enjoy it. It should be a fine afternoon. The cook is a chap from Calcutta, they say one of the finest in India. I don't come to these functions regularly, but it is a special day. I expect you will feel at home.'

'At home . . .' and Edgar almost added, As much as I feel at home, at home. But a gong sounded in the hall and the crowd moved into the dining room.

o

After grace, lunch began. Edgar was seated across from Major Dougherty, an obese man who laughed and wheezed and asked Edgar about his journey, and made jokes about the state of river steamships. At his left, Mrs Dougherty, powdered and spindly, asked him if he followed British politics, and Edgar answered obliquely by recounting some news about ongoing preparations for the Queen's Jubilee. When she persisted, the Major interrupted her after several minutes, chuckling, 'Oh, my dear, I imagine one reason Mr Drake came to Burma was to escape British politics! Right, Mr Drake?' Everyone laughed, even Mrs Dougherty, who settled back into her soup, content with what little she had prised from the visitor, and Edgar tensed briefly because the conversation, like a tightrope walker, had tottered somewhat close to the real reason he had come to Burma. On his right, Mrs Remington jumped in to scold the Major for laughing about such matters, 'It *wasn't* idle talk, no, as British subjects, we must know such things, for the mail here comes so late, and how is the Queen now, and I heard that Lady Hutchings had contracted consumption; was that before or after the London Fancy Dress Ball?' 'After.' 'Well, that is fortunate, not for Lady Hutchings, but for the Ball, after all, it is so lovely, and how I wish I had been there,' and the other ladies twittered and then began a conversation about the last society ball each had attended, and Edgar sat back and began to eat.

They are polite, he thought, To think that in England I would never have been invited to such an affair. Yet he was rather comforted by the direction of the conversation, for what could be further from potentially flammable subjects such as pianos and unusual Doctors than the Fancy Dress Ball, when Mrs Remington asked, innocuously enough, 'Did you attend the Ball, Mr Drake?' and he answered, 'No, I didn't,' and she, 'You know so much about it, you must have gone,' and he, 'No,' and politely, 'I only tuned the Erard Grand that was played at the event,' and he realized right away that he shouldn't have said this, and she, 'Pardon, the what-ard Grand?' and he couldn't help himself, 'Erard, it's a type of piano, one of the finest in London, they had an 1854 Erard, quite a beautiful instrument, I had done the voicing on it myself a year before, it just needed tuning for the ball,' and she seemed quite content with this, and was silent, one of those silences that played prelude to a change in topic, except Mrs Remington said innocently, 'Erard . . . why, that's the piano Doctor Carroll plays.'

Even then the conversation could have been salvaged, for example, had Mrs Dougherty spoken quickly enough, for she had wanted to ask the visitor what he thought of the Burmese weather and hear him say how horrid it was, or had Major Dougherty spoken about a recent attack by dacoits outside Taunggyi, or had Mrs Remington pursued the subject of the Ball, which was far from being exhausted as she still wanted to know if her friend Mrs Bissy had attended. But Colonel West, sitting to Major Dougherty's left, who had been silent throughout the meal, muttered suddenly and quite audibly, 'We should have dumped that piece of rubbish in the water.'

Edgar turned from Mrs Remington. 'I am sorry, Colonel. What did you say?'

'Only that I wish that for the benefit of Her Majesty that infernal instrument had been dumped into the Irrawaddy or used for firewood.' There was silence around the table and Captain Nash-Burnham, who had been engaged in another conversation said, 'Please, Colonel, we have been through this before.'

'Don't tell me what to talk about, Captain, I lost five men to dacoits because of that piano.'

The Captain put down his silverware. 'Colonel, with all due respect, we are all very sorry about the attack. I knew one of the men. But I think the issue of the piano is separate, and Mr Drake here is our guest.'

'Are you telling me what happened, Captain?'

'Of course not, sir. I was only hoping that there was another time when we could discuss this.'

The Colonel turned to Edgar. 'Reinforcements to my post were delayed two days because they had to escort the piano. Did the War Office tell you that story, Mr Drake?'

'No.' Edgar's pulse raced; he felt dizzy. In his mind flashed images of the hunt in Rangoon, They didn't tell me about that either.

'Please, Colonel, Mr Drake has been briefed adequately.'

'He shouldn't even be in Burma. It is all nonsense.'

Silence had spread down the table. Faces turned towards the men. Captain Nash-Burnham clenched his jaw, his face reddening. He pulled his napkin from his lap and set it gently on the table.

'Thank you Colonel, for the lunch,' he said, standing. 'If you don't mind, Mr Drake, I think we'd best be going. We have . . . business to attend to.'

Edgar looked at the staring faces. 'Yes, yes, of course, Captain.' He pushed himself away from the table. He heard murmurs of disappointment. There are questions to ask about the Ball, murmur the ladies, He really was a pleasant fellow, Trust the men to bring war and politics to these functions. Nash-Burnham walked the length of the table and put his hand on the tuner's shoulder, 'Mr Drake.'

'Thank . . . thank you for the lunch, everyone.' He stood and held his hand in the air in an awkward goodbye.

At the door, the finest tabla player in Upper Burma handed a sword to Captain Nash-Burnham, who scowled.

o

Outside a woman walked past with a large basket balanced on her head. Captain Nash-Burnham dug his toe angrily into the ground. 'Mr Drake, I am sorry for that. I knew he would be here. I should not have brought you. It was a mistake.'

'Please, Captain, it was nothing of the sort.' They began to walk. 'I didn't know about his men.'

'I know you didn't know. It has nothing to do with this.'

'But he said—'

'I know what he said, but the reinforcements weren't due to travel to the Ruby Mines to join his patrol for a week. It had nothing to do with the piano. Doctor Carroll brought it to Mae Lwin himself. But I couldn't argue with him. He is my superior. Leaving early was insubordination enough.'

Edgar was silent.

'I am sorry I am angry, Mr Drake,' said the Captain. 'I often take remarks about Doctor Carroll quite personally. By now I should have grown used to such comments from some of the officers. They are jealous, or they want war. A balanced peace is a poor fertilizer for promotion. The Doctor . . .' he turned and looked steadily at Edgar. 'The Doctor and his music keep them from invading. Nevertheless, I shouldn't have brought you into this.'

It seems I am already, thought the piano tuner, but he was silent. They began to walk again, and said nothing until they reached his lodgings.

TEN

CAPTAIN NASH-BURNHAM returned that evening, whistling as Khin Myo led him through the house. He found Edgar in the small yard, eating a bitter salad of crushed tea leaves and dried pulses that Khin Myo had made for him.

'Ah ha, Mr Drake! Discovering the local cuisine, I see.' He held his hands over his belly, which strained at a white waistcoat.

'Indeed, Captain. I am glad to see you again. I must apologize. I have been regretting all afternoon what happened at the reception today. I think I should—'

'Think nothing of it, Mr Drake,' the Captain interrupted. He had removed his sword and now carried a cane, which he banged on the ground. His face fell easily into a smile. 'I told you already this afternoon, it was my responsibility. The others will soon forget this. Please, you should too.' His smile was reassuring.

'Are you certain? Perhaps I should send a note of apology.'

'For what? If anyone is in trouble it is myself, and I'm not worried. We often argue, but we must not let it ruin the evening. Ma Khin Myo, I thought that we could take Mr Drake to see a *pwè* tonight.'

'That would be lovely,' said Khin Myo. 'And Mr Drake,' she turned to look at him, 'is very lucky, as this is the perfect season for the *pwè*. I think there must be at least twenty in Mandalay tonight.'

'Excellent,' said the Captain, slapping his leg and standing up. 'Let's go then! Ready, Mr Drake?'

'Certainly, Captain,' said Edgar, relieved to see the Captain's good spirits. 'Dare I ask what a *pwè* is?'

'Oh, a *pwè*!' laughed Nash-Burnham. 'What's a *pwè*? You are in for a wonderful treat. Burmese street theatre, but that doesn't begin to explain it. You must see it really. Can you go now?'

'Of course. But it is night. Won't these plays have ended?'

'On the contrary, most have not yet begun.'

○

'A *pwè*,' began the Captain, before they were out the door, 'is uniquely Burmese and I might even say Mandalayan, for here the art is at its finest. There are many reasons to hold a *pwè*, for births or for deaths, for namings, when Burmese girls have their first ear piercing, when young men become monks, when they stop being monks, when pagodas are dedicated. Or even non-religious reasons: if one wins a lucky bet, builds a house or even digs a well, when there is a good harvest, a boxing match, when a fire balloon is released. Anything else you can think of. A propitious event and a man holds a *pwè*.'

They were walking down the road in the direction of the canal Edgar had visited that morning with Khin Myo. 'Actually,' said the Captain, 'I am surprised that we didn't see a *pwè* when we drove through town this morning. The driver probably knew about them and tried to avoid them. People will sometimes set them up in the middle of the road, completely halting traffic. It's one of the administrative problems we've inherited from the Burmese. During the dry season there may be dozens of *pwè*s throughout the city. And on nights like tonight, when the sky is clear, they are especially popular.'

They turned a corner. Down the street they could see lights, movement. 'There is one!' exclaimed Khin Myo, and Nash-

Burnham, 'Yes, we are lucky, lucky indeed. We have a saying that there are but two types of Englishmen in Burma, those who love the *pwè* and those who can't bear it. Since the first evening of my arrival when, sleepless with excitement, I took to the streets to explore and found myself at the edge of a *yôkthe pwè*, a puppet drama, I have fallen in love with the art.'

They were approaching the lights, and Edgar could see a wide crowd of people seated on mats in the middle of the road. These were arranged around an empty patch of earth and a thatched structure. In the centre of the empty plot stood a pole. Around the pole flames flickered in concentrically arranged earthenware pots, lighting the faces of the first row of spectators.

They stood at the edge of a crowd of seated families who looked up at the new arrivals. There was much chattering, and one man shouted something towards a large house behind the shack. Khin Myo answered him. 'They want us to stay,' she said.

'Ask him what is being performed,' said Nash-Burnham.

Khin Myo spoke again and the man answered at length.

'It is the story of the Nemi Zat,' she said.

'Wonderful!' The Captain thumped his cane on the ground with pleasure. 'Tell him we will stay for a moment, but that we wish to take our visitor to a *yôkthe pwè*, so we cannot stay here till the end.'

Khin Myo spoke again. 'He understands,' she said.

A servant emerged with two chairs and set them down on the outskirts of the crowd. Nash-Burnham spoke to her directly. When she brought another chair, he offered it to Khin Myo. They sat.

'It looks as though they haven't begun,' said the Captain. 'In fact, you can see the dancers still putting on their make-up.' He pointed to a group of women who stood by a mango tree applying *thanaka* to their faces. A little boy ran out into the centre of the circle and lit a cheroot from one of the flames in the earthenware pots.

'That circular space is the stage,' said Nash-Burnham. 'The Burmese call it the *pwè-wang* . . .'

'*Pwè-waing*,' corrected Khin Myo.

'Sorry, *pwè-waing*, and the branch in the centre is the *pan-bin*. Am I correct, Ma Khin Myo?' She smiled. He continued. 'The Burmese sometimes say it represents a forest, but I have a feeling that it sometimes only serves to keep the audience back. In any case, most of the dancing will take place within the *pwè-waing*.'

'And the earthenware pots?' asked Edgar. 'Is there any significance to them?'

'Not as far as I know. They light the stage if the moon is not enough and provide a constant fire for cheroot lighting.' He laughed.

'What is the subject of the play?'

'Oh, it varies widely. There are many types of *pwè*. There is the *ahlu pwè*, a *pwè* sponsored by a rich man to commemorate a religious festival or the entry of his son into the monastery. They are usually the best as he can afford to hire the finest actors. Then there are the subscription *pwè*, when a member of a neighbourhood will collect money from others and pool it to hire a *pwè* company, then an *a-yein pwè*, a dance performance, then the *kyigyin pwè*, a free performance offered by an actor or company trying to make their name famous. And then of course, the *yôkthe pwè*, puppets, which I promise you we will find this evening. If that is not enough to confuse you – please correct me if I make any errors, Ma Khin Myo,' 'You are doing very well, Captain,' ' – there is the *zat pwè*, or real story, a religious play that tells one of the stories of the Buddha's lives. There are many of these as the Buddha had five hundred and ten incarnations, although, only ten are usually performed, the so-called *Zatgyi Sèbwè*, dramas about how the Buddha overcame each of the deadly sins. That is what is playing tonight: the *Nemi zat* is the fifth,' 'Fourth,' 'Thank you, Khin Myo, the fourth *Zatgyi Sèbwè*. Khin Myo, would you like to explain the plot?' 'No, Captain, I am very much entertained listening to you speak,'

'Well, then I see I must be careful in what I say ... I hope you are not bored, Mr Drake?'

'No, not at all.'

'Well, we won't stay for more than an hour and the *pwè* will go on until dawn. It can take up to four days to complete ... In any case, you must know the plot. Everyone here does already, these are only retellings of the same story.' The Captain paused to think. 'This one is about Prince Nemi, one of the Buddha's incarnations, who is born into a long line of Burmese kings. As a young man, Prince Nemi is so pious that the spirits decide to invite him to see heaven. One moonlit night, perhaps very much like tonight, they send a chariot down to earth. I can only imagine the awe of Prince Nemi and his people as they watch the chariot descend, and fall before it, trembling with fear. The Prince boards it, and it disappears, leaving only the moon. The chariot takes Nemi first to the heavens, where the *nat*s live – *nat*s are Burmese folk spirits, even good Buddhists believe they are everywhere – and then to Nga-yè, the underworld where the serpents called *naga*s dwell. At last he returns reluctantly to his world to share the wonders he has seen. The finale is quite sad: it was the tradition of the kings that when they grew old and sensed that death was near they left their homes and travelled into the desert to die as hermits. And so one day Nemi, like his forefathers before him, wanders into the mountains to die.'

There was a long silence. Edgar could see the dancers packing away the *thanaka* and straightening their *hta main*s.

'It is perhaps my favourite story,' said Nash-Burnham. 'Sometimes I wonder if I love it so because it reminds me of myself, of what I have seen ... though there is a difference.'

'What is that?' asked Edgar.

'When I return from the plains of heaven and Nga-yè no one will believe my words.'

The night was hot, but Edgar felt a shiver through his body. Around them the crowd had grown silent, as if they too were listening to the Captain. But one of the dancers had arrived on stage.

It was a young girl and Edgar was immediately taken by her beauty, her dark eyes exaggerated by the heavy *thanaka* on her face. She was thin and looked perhaps fourteen, and she stood in the centre of the *pwè-waing*, waiting. Although Edgar hadn't seen them when he arrived, a group of musicians was seated on the opposite side of the *pwè*, a small ensemble: drums, cymbals, a horn, a bamboo instrument he couldn't identify, and the stringed instrument he had seen in Rangoon – it was called a *saung* Khin Myo told him, twelve strings strung on a boat-like frame. They began softly at first, like a tentative slip into water, until the man with the bamboo instrument began to play, and a song rose up over the *pwè-waing*.

'My God,' whispered Edgar. 'That sound. What is it?'

'Aaah,' said Captain Nash-Burnham. 'I should have realized you would love the music.'

'No, not that . . . sorry, I mean yes I do, but I have never heard *that* sound, the wailing.' And even though all instruments were playing, the Captain knew exactly which one the piano tuner was referring to. 'It is called a *hneh*, a sort of Burmese oboe.'

'Its song sounds like a dirge.'

On the stage the girl began to dance, slowly at first, bending at the knees, shifting her torso to each side, raising her arms higher with each pass until she began to wave them. Or better: until they began to wave themselves, for in the glow of the candles they seemed to float from her shoulders, defying the surgeons who would have one believe the arm is tethered to the body through an intricate rope of bone and tendon, muscle and vein. Such men have never seen an *a-yein pwè*.

The music still moved softly, out from the darkness at the edge of the *pwè-waing*, into the clearing and into the dancing girl.

The girl danced for nearly half an hour and only when she

stopped was Edgar shaken out of his trance. He turned to the Captain, but words eluded him.

'Beautiful, Mr Drake, no?'

'I . . . I am speechless, really. It is hypnotic.'

'It is. Often the dancers are not as good. You can see by her elbow movements that she has been trained for dancing since she was very young.'

'How?'

'The joint is very loose. When a girl's parents decide she will be a *meimma yein*, a female dance performer, they place her arm in a special brace to stretch and hyperextend the elbow.'

'That's horrid.'

'Not really,' Khin Myo spoke at his left. She held out her arm; at the elbow it bent back gracefully, curved like the body of the *saung*.

'You dance?' asked Edgar.

'Only when I was young.' Laughing. 'Now, I stay flexible by washing Englishmen's clothes.'

The girl had been replaced on stage by a harlequin-like character. 'The *lubyet*, the jester,' whispered Nash-Burnham. The crowd was watching the painted man, his clothes festooned with bells and flowers. He spoke excitedly, gesticulated, and made tooting sounds as if in imitation of the band, danced, somersaulted.

At his side Khin Myo giggled, covering her mouth. 'What is he saying?' Edgar asked her.

'He is making a joke about the host of the *pwè*. I do not know if you would understand. Can you explain it, Captain?'

'No, I hardly understand it – he is using quite a bit of slang, no, Khin Myo? Plus, the humour of the Burmese . . . twelve years here and it still eludes me. Khin Myo doesn't want to explain it because it is probably naughty.' At this she looked away and Edgar saw her touch her hand to a smile.

They watched the *lubyet* for some time and Edgar began to get restless. Many in the crowd had also stopped paying attention.

Some brought out meals from baskets and began to eat. Others curled up and even went to sleep. The *lubyet* wandered occasionally into the audience, plucking out cheroots from people's mouths, stealing food. Once he even approached Edgar, played with his hair and yelled out to the crowd. Khin Myo laughed. 'And now what is he saying?' asked Edgar. At his question, Khin Myo giggled again, 'Oh, I am too ashamed to say, Mr Drake.' Her eyes shone in the dance of the earthenware lanterns.

The *lubyet* returned to centre stage and continued to talk. Finally, Nash-Burnham turned to Khin Myo. 'Ma Khin Myo, should we try to find the *yôkthe pwè*?' She nodded and said something to the now drunk host, who jumped sloppily to his feet and waddled over to shake the hands of the two Englishmen. 'He says come back tomorrow night,' said Khin Myo.

They left the *pwè* and walked through the streets. There were no streetlights. Were it not for the moon, they would have been in complete darkness.

'Did he tell you where we could find *yôkthe pwè*?' asked Captain Nash-Burnham.

'He said there is one near the market, in its third night. They are playing *Wethandaya zat*.'

'Hmmm,' murmured the Captain approvingly.

o

They walked in silence through the night. Compared to the raucous scene of the *pwè*, the streets were quiet, empty except for the stray mongrels that the Captain chased away with his cane. Lighted cheroots bobbed on darkened doorsteps like fireflies. Once Edgar thought he could hear Khin Myo singing. He looked down at her. Her white blouse trembled lightly in the wind and sensing his stare she turned to him. 'What are you singing?' he asked.

'Sorry?' A small smile flickered over her mouth.

'Nothing, nothing,' he said. 'It must have been the wind.'

The moon was high in the sky when they reached the *yôkthe pwè*, their shadows had retreated beneath their feet. The play was well under way; beyond a raised bamboo platform, nearly thirty feet long, a pair of marionettes danced. Behind them a song rose up from a hidden singer. The audience sat in various states of attention, many children were curled up asleep, some of the adults talked among themselves. They were greeted by a fat man who motioned for a pair of chairs to be brought out, as before. And, as before, the Captain requested a third.

The man and Khin Myo talked at length, and Edgar's attention shifted to the play. At one end of the stage stood a model of a city, an elegant palace, a pagoda. It was there that the two elaborately dressed puppets danced. At the other end of the stage, where there were no lights, he could make out a small collection of twigs and branches, like a miniature forest. By his side the Captain was nodding approvingly. Finally, Khin Myo stopped speaking to the host and they sat down.

'You are very lucky tonight, Mr Drake, Maung Tha Zan is playing the Princess. He is perhaps the most famous Princess puppeteer in all of Mandalay and has played alongside the great Maung Tha Byaw, the greatest puppeteer ever – one sometimes even hears men from Mergui say "Tha Byaw Hé", whenever something wonderful happens . . . Oh, Maung Tha Zan is not as skilled as Maung Tha Byaw, but he sings wonderfully. Listen, soon he will start to sing the *ngo-gyin*.'

Edgar didn't have time to ask what this was, for at that instant from behind the stage rose a plaintive wail. He caught his breath. It was the same tune he had heard that night when the steamer had stopped on the river. He had forgotten it until now. 'The *ngo-gyin*, the song of mourning,' said Nash-Burnham at his side. 'Her Prince is soon to abandon her, and she sings of her sad fortunes. I can never believe that a man can sing like this.'

But it wasn't a woman's voice either. Soprano, yes, but not

feminine, not even, Edgar thought, human. He could not understand the Burmese words, but he knew of what the man sang. Songs of loss are universal, he thought, and with the man's voice something else rose into the night air, twisted, danced with the smoke from the fire, and drifted into the sky. The sequins on the body of the Princess marionette shimmered, star-like, and he thought that the song must be coming from her, the puppet, and not the puppeteer. At the base of the stage, a little boy, who had been holding the candles to light the puppets, moved them away from the Princess and her city, walking slowly to the other end of the stage until the forest emerged from the darkness.

It was a long time after the song finished before any of them spoke. Another scene began, but Edgar was no longer watching. He looked up at the sky.

'In Gautama's final incarnation before Siddhartha,' said Captain Nash-Burnham, 'he gives up everything he possesses, even his wife and his children, and leaves for the forest.'

'Do you find yourself in that story as well, Captain?' Edgar asked, turning towards him.

The Captain shook his head. 'No, I have not abandoned everything,' he said, and paused. 'But there are those who have.'

'Anthony Carroll,' said the piano tuner softly.

'Or others, perhaps,' said Khin Myo.

ELEVEN

I N THE DRY season the quickest route to Mae Lwin would have been by elephant, along a trail that had been cut by Shan troops during the Second Anglo-Burmese War and was now used sporadically by opium smugglers. But recently the road had fallen under attack, and Captain Nash-Burnham suggested that they travel by elephant to a small tributary of the Salween east of Loilem and from there by dugout to Carroll's camp. Nash-Burnham couldn't accompany them, he had work to attend to in Mandalay. 'But please give my regards to the Doctor,' he said. 'Tell him that we miss him in Mandalay.' It seemed an odd moment for such simple pleasantries, and Edgar expected him to say something else, but the Captain only touched his helmet in farewell.

On the morning of his departure Edgar was awakened by Khin Myo, who told him through his bedroom door that there was a man to see him. When he went to the entrance, he was disappointed not to see any elephants as planned, but only a young Burman whom he recognized as from the staff at the Administrator's residence. The man was breathless. 'On behalf of the Administrator, I apologetically announce that your departure will be subject to a certain delay.' Edgar tried to hide his smile at the stilted English, afraid it would convey approval of the news. 'When does the Administrator expect that I may leave?' he asked.

'Oh, sir! I have no knowledge of that! You may enquire of His Respectfulness yourself.'

'Can you at least tell me if we will be leaving later today?'

'Oh no! Not today, sir!'

The emphasis of the reply silenced Edgar, who meant to say something, but only nodded and closed the door. He shrugged to Khin Myo, who said 'British efficiency?' and he went back to sleep. Later in the afternoon he finished a long letter to Katherine which he had been writing for several days, describing his visit to the puppet theatre. He had begun to grow accustomed to the bureaucratic delays. The following day he wrote more letters, one about the much-discussed looting of Mandalay Palace by British soldiers, the second describing the current craze over the 'Hairy Lady of Mandalay', a distant relative of the royal family whose entire body was covered with long smooth hair. And the day after that he took a long walk through the bazaar. And waited.

Yet, by the fourth day after the scheduled departure, restlessness overcame the natural sense of respect and patience of a man who had spent his career repairing strings and tiny hammers, and he walked to the Administrator's residence to enquire when they would be departing. He was greeted at the door by the same Burman who had visited his quarters. 'Oh, Mr Drake!' he exclaimed. 'But the Administrator is in Rangoon!'

At army headquarters, he enquired about Captain Nash-Burnham. The young subaltern at the entrance looked puzzled. 'I thought you had been informed. Captain Nash-Burnham is in Rangoon with the Administrator.'

'May I ask what his business is? I was supposed to leave for Mae Lwin four days ago. I have come a long way and so much effort has been devoted to bringing me here. It would be a shame were I to waste any more time.'

The subaltern's face turned red. 'I thought they had told you. It . . . excuse me, wait one moment.' He rose quickly and entered a back office. Edgar could hear hushed whispering. The man returned. 'Please follow me, Mr Drake.'

The subaltern showed him into a small room, empty except for a desk piled high with stacks of papers held down by roughly carved figurines used locally to weigh opium. The weights were unnecessary; there was no breeze. The subaltern closed the door behind him. 'Please sit down.

'Mae Lwin has been attacked,' he said.

o

The details of the story were unclear, as was the identity of the attackers. The night before Edgar was due to depart a messenger on horseback had arrived at the Administrator's residence. He reported that, two days before, Mae Lwin had been raided by a group of masked riders, who had set fire to one of the storage depots and killed a guard. In the confusion that followed, a brief battle had broken out and another Shan sentry had been shot. Carroll was safe, but concerned. It was suspected that Twet Nga Lu, the bandit chief who was fighting his own war for the state of Mongnai was behind the attack. Most of the supplies in the storage depot had been rescued, but several of the Surgeon-Major's jars of elixir had been damaged, which had seemed to upset the Doctor deeply. 'Apparently a stray bullet also struck . . .', but then the subaltern stopped himself, and chose his words carefully, '. . . other supplies important to the Doctor's current work.'

'Not the Erard?'

The subaltern leaned back in his chair. 'Mr Drake, I understand the importance of your mission, and I understand the severe conditions you have endured to arrive here in a most impressive show of respect for and dedication to the Crown.' He let the final word hang. 'This attack comes at a very precarious time. As you may know, we have been directly engaged in military activities in the Shan States since November last year. A column led by Colonel Stedman left Mandalay earlier this month. Then, only six days ago, we received reports that they had been attacked. Because of the concentration of Limbin Confederacy forces in that region, the attack on our troops was not a surprise. The attack on Mae Lwin, however, *was* a surprise, and it is unclear who the masked riders were or where they obtained their rifles. There is speculation that they may even be supplied by French forces, whose whereabouts are unknown. However, for security reasons unfortunately I cannot tell you much more.'

Edgar stared at the subaltern.

'I don't mean to disappoint you, Mr Drake. Indeed, I am speaking without authorization, as ultimately these decisions will be made in Rangoon. But I do want you to understand the reality of our situation. When Captain Nash-Burnham returns, he will be able to discuss if you are to remain in Mandalay or return by steamship to Rangoon. Until then, I suggest you enjoy the amenities here and not worry yourself too much.' The subaltern leaned forward on the desk. 'Mr Drake?'

The piano tuner said nothing.

'Mae Lwin is a foul place, Mr Drake, despite whatever they have told you to bring you here. It is swampy and malarial, hardly a climate befitting an Englishman. And to add to that, the danger of these most recent attacks . . . perhaps it will be best to abandon the site entirely. I would not be disappointed. Indeed, I think you are fortunate to have seen already the finest cities of Burma.'

Edgar waited. The room was stiflingly hot. Finally he stood. 'Well, thank you, then. I will be on my way.'

The subaltern extended his hand. 'And, Mr Drake, please do not share this conversation with our superiors. Although your mission is minor, generally it is Captain Nash-Burnham who deals with civilian affairs.'

'It is minor, isn't it? Don't worry, I won't tell anyone. Thank you.'

The subaltern smiled. 'Think nothing of it.'

o

Dear Katherine,

I do not know which will reach you first, this letter or myself. One week has passed since the scheduled date of my departure and still I remain in Mandalay. I have already written many descriptions of this city to you, but I apologize that I no longer have the enthusiasm for more. Indeed, all this has become very confusing, and developments now cast doubt over whether I will ever even meet Dr Carroll or his Erard.

Mae Lwin has been attacked. I learned this from a subaltern at army headquarters. But I have learned little else. Whenever I ask anyone what is happening, I am answered only by blank stares or evasion. 'A major strategy meeting is being held in Rangoon,' they say. Or 'This incident can not be taken lightly.' Yet it puzzles me that Dr Carroll has not been summoned to the meeting; by all accounts he is still in Mae Lwin. They say this is because of the military importance of maintaining the fort, a good enough explanation it seems, except something about the way they say it bothers me. At first I was somewhat thrilled by the possibility of intrigue or scandal – after all, what would be more fitting in a country where everything else is so elusive? But even this has begun to exhaust me. The most scandalous option I can think of, that Dr Carroll is being kept from a critical decision, doesn't seem so scandalous any longer. They say a man with an obsession for a piano could hardly be immune to other eccentricities, that this man should not be trusted with such an important post. What is most painful for me is that, in some ways, I find myself agreeing. A piano means nothing if the French are planning to invade across the Mekong. What makes this so difficult to accept is that if I question the Doctor I question myself.

My darling Katherine, when I first left England, part of me doubted that I would ever reach Mae Lwin. It seemed too distant, its path beset with too many contingencies. Yet now, now that the cancellation of my mission seems more likely, I cannot believe I will not go there. For the past six weeks I have thought about little but Mae Lwin. I have resketched the fort in my mind from maps and others' accounts. I have made lists of things I will do when I arrive, of the mountains and streams described in Dr Carroll's reports which I wish to see. It is strange, Katherine, but I had already begun to think of the stories I would tell you when I return home. Of what it was like to meet the famous Doctor. Of how I mended and tuned the Erard, rescuing such a precious instrument. Of fulfilling my 'duty' to England. Indeed it is perhaps this idea of 'duty' that has become the most elusive goal of all. I know we spoke often of this at home, and I still don't doubt a piano's role. But I have come to think that 'bringing music and culture here' is more subtle – there are art and music here already – their own art, their own music. This is not to say that we should not bring such things to Burma; perhaps only that it should be done with more humility. Indeed, if we *are* to make these people our subjects, must we not present the *best* of European civilization? No one was ever harmed by Bach; songs are not like armies.

My dear, I digress. Or perhaps not, for I wrote to you of my hopes, and now, slowly, my hopes have begun to vanish, obscured by war and pragmatism and by my own suspicions. This entire trip has already coated itself in a veneer of seeming, a dream-likeness. So much of what I have done is tied to what I will do that at times the truth I have already experienced threatens to vanish with that which I have yet to see. How to express this to you? Whereas my journey until now has been one of potential, of imagination, now its loss seems to question everything I have seen. I have allowed dreams to melt into my realities, now realities threaten to melt to dreams, to disappear. I don't know if anything I am writing makes sense, but in the face of such beauty around me I only see myself standing outside our door in Franklin Mews, trunks at my feet, unchanged from the day I left.

What more can I write? I spend hours looking out at the Shan Hills, trying to decide how to describe them for you, for I feel that only by doing so can I take some of what I have seen home with me. I wander the markets, following the flow of ox-carts and parasols along the rutted roads, or I sit by the river watching the fishermen, waiting for the steamer from Rangoon that would bring news of my departure, or bring me home. The waiting has begun to grow unbearable, as has the oppressive heat and dust that smother the city. Any decision would be better than none.

My dear, I realize now that in all the frightening possibilities we discussed before I left, we never considered what now seems most likely: that I will return home with nothing. Perhaps these words are only the ramblings of boredom or loneliness, but when I write 'nothing', I mean not only that the Erard remains untuned, but that I have seen a world that is very different, yet I have not begun to understand it. Coming here has created a strange feeling of emptiness in me that I didn't know I had, and I don't know whether heading into the jungle will fill it, or tear it open further. I wonder about why I came here, about how you said I needed this, about how I am now set to return home, how I will have to face this as a failure.

Katherine, words were never my medium, and now I cannot think of music for what I feel. But it is growing dark and I am by the river, so I must go. My only solace is that I will see you soon and that we will be together again. I remain,

Your loving husband,

Edgar

He folded the letter, and rose from the benches by the Irrawaddy. He walked home slowly through the city streets. At the small house, he opened the door to find Khin Myo waiting.

She held an envelope and handed it to him without speaking. There was no address, only his name scrawled in bold letters. He looked at her and she stared back, expressionless. For a brief moment, he held it together with his letter to Katherine. As soon as he opened it, he recognized the elegant hand,

Dear Mr Drake,

It is my deep regret that our first personal correspondence must be burdened by such urgency, but I believe that you are well aware of the circumstances that have jeopardized your visit to Mae Lwin. My impatience must only be equalled by yours. In the attack on our camp, the strings belonging to the fourth octave A key were snapped by a musket ball. As you know, it is impossible to play any meaningful piece without this note, a tragedy that those in the War Office cannot fathom. Please proceed to Mae Lwin immediately. I have sent a messenger to Mandalay to convey you and Ma Khin Myo to our Fort. Please meet him tomorrow on the road to Mahamuni Pagoda. I take full responsibility for your decision and your safety. If you stay in Mandalay, you will be on a ship to England before the end of the week.

AJC

Edgar lowered his head. He knows my name, he thought. He looked up at Khin Myo.

'You are going too?'

'I will tell you more soon,' she said.

o

The following morning, they rose before dawn and boarded an ox-cart of pilgrims bound for Mahamuni Pagoda on the southern outskirts of Mandalay. The pilgrims stared at him and talked merrily. Khin Myo leaned close to Edgar. 'They are saying they are pleased that there are some British Buddhists.'

In the sky, dark clouds moved slowly over the Shan Hills. The ox-cart rattled along the road. Edgar clutched his bag to his chest. At Khin Myo's suggestion, he had left most of his belongings in Mandalay, taking with him only a spare change of clothes and important papers and tools to mend the piano. Now he could hear the faint chink of the metal as the cart struggled over ruts in the road. At Mahamuni Pagoda they disembarked, and Khin Myo led him along a small path to where a boy stood waiting. He was dressed in flowing blue trousers and a blue shirt, with a check cloth tied about his waist. Edgar had read that many of the Shan men, like the Burmans, kept their hair long and noticed that the boy wore his hair wrapped in a colourful turban, which looked like something between the Burmese *gaung-baung* and those of the Sikh soldiers. He held the reins of two small ponies.

'*Mingala ba,*' he said to them, bowing slightly. 'Hello, Mr Drake.'

Khin Myo smiled at him. 'Mr Drake, this is Nok Lek, he will take us to Mae Lwin. His name means "little bird".' She paused, then added, 'Don't let this mislead you. He is one of Anthony Carroll's best fighters.'

Edgar looked at the boy. He seemed scarcely fifteen years old. 'Do you speak English?' he asked.

'A little,' said the boy with a proud grin, and reached down to take their bags.

'You are being modest,' said Khin Myo. 'You are learning very fast.'

Nok Lek began to secure the bags to the saddles. 'I hope you know how to ride, Mr Drake,' he said when he had finished. 'These are Shan ponies. Smaller than English horses, but very good in mountains.'

'I'll try my best to hold on,' said Edgar.

'Ma Khin Myo will ride with me,' said Nok Lek. He put both hands on the pony's back and leaped lightly into its saddle. He was barefoot, and he slipped his feet into a pair of rope stirrups, holding the hemp between his first and second toes. Edgar noticed the boy's calves, muscles like knotted ropes. Nervously, he looked at his own pony: English metal stirrups. Khin Myo climbed on behind Nok Lek and sat sideways with both feet together. Edgar was surprised that the little animal could walk under such a load. He mounted his own pony. Without speaking, they began to move east.

Above the Shan Hills a smudge of light was spreading up the sky. Edgar expected to see the sun rise, to mark the day as the start of the final leg of a journey he had begun to think he would never make. But it was hidden in the clouds and the land brightened gradually. Ahead, Khin Myo opened a small parasol.

They rode east for several hours at a slow pace, along a road that ran past dry rice fields and empty granaries. Along the way they passed processions into town, men leading oxen to market, women with heavy loads balanced on their heads. Soon the crowds thinned and they found themselves alone. They crossed a small stream and turned south on a smaller, dustier road between two wide, fallow rice fields.

Nok Lek turned back. 'Mr Drake, we go faster now. It is days to Mae Lwin, and the roads here are good, not like in the Shan States.'

Edgar nodded and gripped his reins. Nok Lek hissed at his pony; it began to trot. Edgar kicked at the flank of his. Nothing happened. He kicked harder. The pony didn't move. Nok Lek and Khin Myo were getting smaller in the distance. He closed his eyes and took a deep breath. He hissed.

They galloped south along a small road that paralleled the Shan Hills to the east and the Irrawaddy to the west. Edgar stood in the saddle with one hand on the reins, the other holding his hat. As they rode, he found himself laughing, thrilled by the speed. On the hunt, they had only walked the ponies, and he tried to remember when he had last ridden a horse this fast. It must have been nearly twenty years ago when he and Katherine had spent a holiday with a cousin of hers who had a small farm in the country. He had almost forgotten the pounding thrill of the speed.

They stopped in the late morning at a rest station for pilgrims and travellers, and Nok Lek bought food from a nearby house: curries and scented rices and salads of mashed tea wrapped in the leaves of a banana plant. As they ate, Nok Lek and Khin Myo spoke in rapid Burmese. At one point Khin Myo apologized to Edgar for not speaking in English, 'There is much we need to talk about. And I think you would be bored by our conversation.'

'Please, don't mind me,' said Edgar, who was quite content with their spot in the shade, from which he could see the blackened rice fields. He knew they were burnt by farmers in preparation for the rains, but it was difficult to convince himself that it wasn't the sun's doing. They stretched for miles, from the river to the abrupt rise of the Shan Hills. Like the walls of a fortress, he thought as he stared at the mountains, Or maybe they are falling, like fabric over the edge of the table, pooling on the floor in small hills and valleys. His eyes searched vainly for a road that broke the facade, but found none.

They rested briefly after lunch and then remounted the ponies. They rode all evening and into the night, when they stopped in a village and Nok Lek knocked on the door of a small house. A shirtless man came out and the two spoke for several minutes. The man led them to the back, where there was another, smaller, raised structure. Here they tied the ponies, rolled out the mats on the bamboo floor, and hung mosquito nets from the ceiling. The entrance to the hut was to the south, and Edgar arranged his mattress so that his feet rested by the door, a precaution against any creatures that might visit during the night. Immediately Nok Lek grabbed the mat and turned it. 'Don't point your head to the north,' he said sternly. 'Very bad. That is the direction we bury the dead.'

Edgar lay down next to the boy. Khin Myo went to bathe, and

later slipped back quietly through the door. She lifted her mosquito net and climbed under it. Her mat lay inches from Edgar's and he pretended he was sleeping and watched her arrange her bed beside him. She lay down and soon her breathing changed, and in sleep she shifted so that her face rested close to his. Through the thin cotton of the two mosquito nets he could feel her breath, soft and warm, imperceptible were it not for the stillness and the heat.

o

Nok Lek woke them early. Without speaking, they packed the thin mattresses and mosquito nets. Khin Myo left and returned with her face freshly painted with *thanaka*. They loaded the ponies and rejoined the road. It was still dark. As he rode, Edgar felt a tremendous stiffness in his legs, his arms, his abdomen. He winced, but said nothing; Khin Myo and the boy moved gracefully and unencumbered. He laughed to himself, I am not young.

Instead of continuing south, they took another small road east, towards the lightening sky. The path was narrow and occasionally the ponies were forced to slow to a trot. Edgar was surprised at how Khin Myo managed to balance herself, let alone hold on to the parasol. He was also surprised that, when they stopped and he collapsed in exhaustion, covered with dust and sweat, she still had the same flower in her hair that she had plucked from a bush that morning. He told her this and she laughed. 'Do you too wish to ride with a flower in your hair, Mr Drake?'

At last, by late afternoon on the second day, they reached a set of small dry hills covered with brush and scattered boulders. The ponies slowed and followed a narrow track. They passed a crumbling pagoda with peeling white paint and stopped. Khin Myo and Nok Lek dismounted without speaking and Edgar followed. They left their shoes at the door and went through a small portal and into a dark and musty room. A gilded statue of Buddha sat on a raised platform, surrounded by candles and flowers. Its eyes were dark and mournful and it sat with its legs crossed, its hands cupped in its lap. There was no sign of anyone else. Nok Lek had brought a small wreath of flowers from his bag and set this on the altar. He knelt, and Khin Myo did the same, and both bowed low, so that their foreheads touched the cool tiles. Edgar watched Khin Myo, the tied bun of her hair shifting, baring the back of her neck. Catching himself staring, he quickly bowed in imitation.

Outside the pagoda, he asked, 'Who maintains this place?'

'It is part of a larger temple,' said Khin Myo. 'The monks come here to take care of the Buddha.'

'But I don't see anyone,' Edgar said.

'Don't worry, Mr Drake,' she said. 'They are here.'

There was something about the loneliness of the place that unsettled him, and he wished to ask her more, about what she was saying, what she was praying for, why she had stopped here and not at any of the other countless pagodas. But she and Nok Lek had begun to talk to each other again.

They mounted their ponies and began to walk. At the top of the hill they stopped to look back over the plain. Despite the low altitude, the flatness of the valley afforded them a view of their journey, a lonely country of empty fields and twisting streams. Small hamlets clasped rivers and roads, all of the same brown earth colour. In the far distance they could discern the grid of Mandalay and, further off, the snaking course of the Irrawaddy.

The track descended over the other side of the hill, and they followed a small rise to a group of houses which lay at the base of a larger mountain. There they stopped and Nok Lek dismounted. 'I will buy food. Maybe we won't see anyone for a long time.' Edgar sat on the pony and waited. The boy disappeared into one of the houses.

Some chickens wandered along the track, pecking at the dust.

A man lounging on a platform in the shade of a tree called out to Khin Myo and she answered him.

'What did he say?' Edgar asked.

'He asked where were we going.'

'And what did you say?'

'I said we are riding south, to Meiktila, but we came this way for surveying.'

'Why lie?'

'The fewer people who know we are going into the mountains the better. This is a lonely place. Usually we travel with an escort. But because of circumstances, this is somewhat . . . unofficial. If anyone wished to attack, we have no help.'

'Are you worried?'

'Worried? No. Are you?'

'Me? A bit. On the ship from Prome, there were some, prisoners, dacoits. Fierce-looking fellows.'

Khin Myo studied him for a moment, as if weighing what she should say. 'It is safe. Nok Lek is a very good fighter.'

'I don't know how reassuring that is. He is a child. And I hear they travel in bands of twenty.'

'You shouldn't think of such things. I have made this trip many times.'

Nok Lek returned with a basket, which he fastened to the back of Edgar's saddle. He bid goodbye to the man in the shade and hissed his pony forward. Edgar followed and raised his hand in greeting. The man said nothing as the Englishman passed.

From the basket rose the pungent scent of fermented tea and spices.

o

The track rose steeply, and as it did the vegetation changed, the low scrub giving way to taller plants, nourished by mists that thickened as they ascended. They climbed a spur coated in low forest, humid like the plains near Rangoon. Birds flitted through the trees, chirping loudly, and around them the movement of larger animals could be heard through fallen leaves.

A sudden crash, and Edgar turned quickly. Another, this time louder, and then the distinct sounds of breaking branches, something moving fast through the underbrush. 'Nok Lek, Khin Myo! Watch out, something is coming.' Edgar pulled his pony to a stop. Nok Lek heard it too and slowed his mount. Louder. Edgar looked around him for something, a knife, a gun, but he knew he had nothing.

Louder. 'What is it?' he whispered and suddenly, in front of them, a wild boar bolted across the trail and into the bushes on the other side.

'A bloody pig,' cursed Edgar. Nok Lek and Khin Myo laughed and their pony began walking again. Edgar tried to force a chuckle, but his heart was beating wildly. He hissed at his pony.

As the slope steepened, the path broke off along the flank of the mountain and emerged from the trees, affording the first view in several hours. Edgar was struck by how the scenery had changed. The opposite hillside rose so steeply that he felt that, with a running leap, he could touch the moss-coated branches on the facing slope, yet to walk there would involve a precipitous descent and ascent through impenetrable jungle. In the valley below, thicker vegetation hid any signs of a river or habitation, yet as the path rose the mountains opened onto another valley, where the floor flattened in a series of narrow, terraced fields. Far below, in the staircases of paddy, a pair of figures worked knee-deep in water that reflected the sky, transferring iridescent seedlings to the clouds.

Khin Myo saw him watching the farmers. 'The first time I travelled into the Shan Hills,' she said, 'I was surprised to see rice growing, while around Mandalay the land lay barren. The hills catch the rain clouds that pass up the Irrawaddy River basin, and even in the dry season they take enough water for a second planting.'

'I thought there was a drought.'

'On the plateau there is. There has been a terrible drought for several years now. Whole villages are starving and moving into the lowlands. The hills may catch the clouds, but they also keep them. If the monsoon rain doesn't move onto the plateau, it stays dry.'

'And the farmers below, are they Shan?'

'No, another group.' She spoke to Nok Lek in Burmese. 'Palaung, he says. They live in these valleys. They have their own language, dress, music. It is quite confusing, actually, even for me. The hills are like islands, each has its own tribe. The longer they have been separated, the more different they become. Palaung, Paduang, Danu, Shan, Pa-O, Wa, Kachin, Karen, Karenni. And those are just some of the biggest tribes.'

'I never . . .' said Edgar. 'Fancy that, hill islands.'

'That is what Anthony Carroll calls them, he says they are like Mr Darwin's islands, only here it is culture that changes, not the beaks of birds. He wrote a letter about that to your Royal Society.'

'I didn't know . . .'

'They haven't told you everything,' she said. 'That is not the least of it.' She told him then of the Doctor's studies, of his collections and correspondences, of the letters that he collected each month from Mandalay, letters from distant biologists, physicians, even chemists – chemistry was an old passion. 'Half the mail that comes to Upper Burma is scientific correspondence for Anthony Carroll. And the other half is music for him.'

'And do you help him with these projects, then?'

'Perhaps, a little. But he knows so much more. I only listen.' And Edgar waited for her to explain further, but she turned back to the path.

They rode on. It grew dark. New, unfamiliar sounds shifted in the darkness, the burrowing of scavengers, the howls of wild dogs, the rough voices of barking deer.

Finally, in a small clearing, they stopped and dismounted, unloading a military tent, which Nok Lek had brought. They pitched it in the centre of the clearing and Nok Lek disappeared inside to arrange the bags. Edgar remained outside near Khin Myo. Neither spoke. They were tired and the song of the forest was deafening. At last Nok Lek emerged from the tent and told them to enter. Edgar slipped under a mosquito net and arranged his mattress. Only then did he notice the pair of double-barrelled shotguns propped up against the inside of the tent, their cocked hammers reflecting the ray of moonlight that trickled in through a hole in the canvas.

o

It took two days to climb through the steep jungle and over a mountain pass. In front of them the descent was brief and steep, and softened into the plateau, a vast patchwork of field and forest. In the distance, at the edge of the plain, another set of hills rose, grey and undefined.

They descended a narrow, stony path, the ponies' hooves searching for footholds. Edgar let his body rock loosely in the saddle, relishing the stretching of muscles tightened by days of riding and sleeping on the ground. It was late. The sun cast their shadows long into the valley. Edgar looked back at the mountains, at the crest of mist that capped the peaks and spilled over the slopes. In the fading light of dusk, Shan farmers worked in the fields, wearing wide hats and trousers that flowed about their feet. The rocking of the pony was slow and rhythmic, and Edgar felt his eyes close, the fantasy world of crags and temples disappearing briefly, and he thought, Perhaps I am dreaming, It is all just like a child's fairy tale. Soon it was dark, and they galloped through the night, and he felt himself slumping forward on his pony.

He dreamed. He dreamed that he was riding a Shan pony, that

they were galloping, that in the pony's hair were twisted flowers that spun in the air like pinwheels as they moved through the paddy, past costumed ghosts, choreographed flashes of colour against an infinite green. And he awoke. He awoke and saw the land was barren, and burnt rice stalks swayed in a slight breeze, and out of the earth grew mountains of karst, crag towers that hid golden statues of the Buddha, rising from the floors of caves like stalagmites, so old that even the earth had begun to dust them with deposits of carbonate. And he dreamed again, and as they passed he could see into the caves, for they were lit by the lights of pilgrims, who turned to watch the strange foreigner, and behind them the Buddhas trembled and brushed off their lime cloaks and hovered, also watching, for the trail was lonely and few Englishmen ever passed this way. And he awoke, and before him on a pony's back rode a young boy and a woman, strangers, she sleeping too, and her hair broke loose and streamed back to him, and flowers drifted out, and he dreamed he caught one and he awoke and they were crossing a bridge and it was dawn and, beneath them, a man and boy paddled a dugout in the brown churning water, themselves the colour of the boat and the current, and so it was only by the shifting shadows of the water that he could see them, and they were not alone, for no sooner had they passed beneath the bridge than came another boat, drifting, a man and a boy, and he looked up and a thousand bodies paddled for they were the stream and he dreamed, and it was still night, and from the crags and valleys came not men nor the blossoming of flowers, but something else, like light, a chanting, and those who chanted told him that the light was made of myths and it lived in the caves with the white-clad hermits, and he awoke and they told him the myths, that the universe was created as a giant river, and in this river floated four islands and humans lived on one, but the others were inhabited by other creatures who existed here only in tales and he dreamed that they stopped by a river to rest and the woman awoke and unwrapped her hair from where the wind had tied it about her body, and the boy and she and he knelt and drank from the river, and in it catfish churned, and he awoke and they were riding, riding, and it was morning.

They climbed the hills on the opposite side of the valley. The land became mountainous and soon again it was night. Then Nok Lek said, 'Tonight we rest. In the dark we are safe.'

At their side there was a loud crash. Edgar Drake thought, 'Another pig,' and turned to catch a pistol butt in his face.

o

And now only trajectory, falling. A crack of wood on bone and a spray of spit and then a bending, slipping, slowed by boots in metal stirrups, fingers still in reins, releasing, down, now the crash of the bushes, the body against the ground. Later he will wonder how long he was unconscious, he will try to recollect memories but cannot, for only movement seems to matter, not only his but others, the descent of the men from the trees, the glinting arch of cutlasses, the sweep of shotgun barrels, the bolting of ponies. So that when he stands again in the crushed branches he sees a scene that could have composed itself in seconds or, if measured by heartbeats or breaths, much longer.

They are still on the pony. She holds the shotgun and the boy a sword, high above his head. They both face a band of four, three with knives drawn, flanking a tall man with his arm extended, a fist, a pistol. The weapons glint as the men crouch and dance, it is so dark that the glinting is the only clue that tells him they are moving. And for this moment they are all still, they bob only slightly, perhaps this movement is just from the deep breaths of their exertion.

The blades float imperceptibly, winking like starlight, and then a snap, and with a flash of light they move, it is dark, but somehow he can see the tall man's finger tense, and she must see it too, for she fires the shotgun first, and the tall man shouts and grabs his hand, the pistol is thrown across the forest floor, the others spring on the pony, grab the shotgun barrel before she can discharge the other chamber, pull her, and she doesn't scream, all he hears is a small cry of surprise as she hits the ground, one man whips the shotgun from her hands and points it towards the boy, now the other two are on top of her, one grabs her wrists, the other tears at her *hta main*, she cries out now, he sees a flash of her thigh pale in the thin light, he sees that the flower has fallen from her hair, he sees its petals and sepals and stamens still dusted with pollen, later he will wonder if this was his imagination, it is too dark, but he doesn't think now, he is moving, he springs out of the brambles, towards the flower and the fallen pistol which lies beside it.

It is not until he raises his hand, shaking, saying let her go let her go let her go, that he thinks he has never fired a gun.

Freeze, and now it is his finger that flickers.

o

He awoke to the coolness of a wet cloth against his face. He opened his eyes. He was still lying on the ground, but his head was resting on Khin Myo's lap. She gently cleaned his face with the cloth. Out of the corner of his eye he could see Nok Lek standing in the clearing, shotgun at his side.

'What happened?' he asked.

'You saved us.' She said it in a whisper.

'I don't remember, I passed out, I didn't . . . did I shoot . . . them . . .?' the words came out jumbled, incredulous.

'You missed.'

'I'm—'

'You almost hit the pony. It bolted. But it was enough.'

Edgar looked up at her. Somehow, in the midst of everything, she had thought to fasten the flower in her hair once again.

'Enough?'

She looked up at Nok Lek, who watched the forest nervously. 'I told you, one of Anthony Carroll's best men.'

'Where did they go?'

'They fled. Dacoits are fierce, but can be cowards when confronted. But we must go. They may return with others, especially now they have seen an English face. It is much more lucrative than robbing poor farmers.'

Dacoits. Edgar thought of the men on the steamship from Rangoon. He felt her run the cloth over his forehead. 'Have I been shot?'

'No, I think perhaps you fell after you fired, because you were still hurt from your fall from the horse. How do you say, you fainted?' She tried to appear concerned, but couldn't suppress a smile. Her fingers rested on his forehead.

Nok Lek spoke in Burmese. Khin Myo folded the cloth. 'Mr Drake, we should go. They may come back with others. Your pony came back. Can you ride?'

'I think so.' He struggled to his feet, the warmth of her thigh still on the back of his neck. He took several steps. He found himself shaking, but he didn't know if it was from fear or his fall. He climbed back on the pony. Ahead of him Khin Myo sat with a shotgun across her lap. She seemed strangely comfortable with it, the gleam of its barrel resting against the silk of her *hta main*. Nok Lek pulled another from his saddle and handed it to Edgar, and tucked the pistol into his belt.

Hiss. The ponies moved into the darkness.

o

They rode through an interminable night, moving slowly down a steep slope and then across empty rice fields. At last, when Edgar was certain it would never arrive, the sun's light spread out over the hill in front of him. They stopped to sleep at the house of a farmer and when Edgar awoke it was afternoon. Beside him, Khin

Myo slept peacefully. Her hair had fallen over her cheek. He watched it move with her breath.

He touched the wound on his forehead. In daylight the ambush seemed but a bad dream and he rose quietly so as not to wake Khin Myo. Outside he joined Nok Lek, who sat drinking green tea with the farmer. The tea was bitter and hot, and Edgar felt beads of sweat form on his face, cool in the light breeze. Soon there was stirring inside the hut, and Khin Myo came out and walked to the back of the house to wash. She returned with her hair wet and combed and her face freshly painted.

They thanked the man and returned to their ponies.

From the farmer's lonely house, they climbed a steep hillside. Edgar understood the geography better now. The course of the rivers descending from the Himalayas cut parallel north–south gorges in the plateau, so that any track they followed was cursed with a long succession of ascents and descents. Over the hillside lay another range of mountains, and these too they climbed, its valleys unpeopled, and over the next range they passed a small market, where villagers clustered around mounds of fruit. They ascended again and reached the ridge just as the sun was setting behind them.

Before them the mountain slope fell once again, but not to rise in another set of hills. Instead, the slope was long and steep and below it a river roared, cast in the darkness of the hills.

'Salween,' said Nok Lek triumphantly and hissed.

o

They rode down the steep path, the ponies bucking with each uncertain step. At the banks of the river, they saw a boat and a lantern and a sleeping man. Nok Lek whistled. The man jumped up, startled. He wore only a pair of loose trousers. His left arm hung limply at his side, twisted as if waiting to accept a bribe. He jumped to the shore.

They dismounted and passed the ponies' bridles to the man with the paralysed arm. Nok Lek unloaded the packs and stowed them in the boats. 'The boatman will bring the ponies by land to Mae Lwin. But we go by boat, it's faster. Please, Ma Khin Myo.' He held out his hand and she took it and jumped into the boat. 'Now you, Mr Drake.'

Edgar stepped towards the boat, but his boot slipped and caught in the mud. With one foot in the boat, he tugged, but the mud only made fierce sucking sounds. He grunted, cursed. The boat swung outwards into the water and he fell. Behind him the two men laughed, and he looked up to see Khin Myo, her hand covering a smile. Edgar cursed again, first at them, then at the mud. He tried to push himself up, but his arm sunk deeper. He tried and failed again. The men were laughing harder, and Khin Myo couldn't hide a soft giggle. And then Edgar too began to laugh, doubled over in that impossible position, one leg thigh-deep in the mud, the other held above the water, both arms soaked and dripping. I haven't laughed like this in months, he thought, and tears began to stream from his eyes. He stopped struggling with the mud and lay back, looking up at a dark sky through branches illuminated by the lantern. Finally, with an effort, he pulled himself up and then into the boat, dripping. He didn't even bother to clean the mud from his body; it was too dark to see, and Nok Lek had already boarded and was trying to push them off with a pole.

Once into the current, they floated quickly downstream. They left the lantern with the boatman, but the moon shone brightly through the trees. Still Nok Lek kept close to the riverbank. 'Not enough light for friends to see, but enemies can,' he whispered.

The river twisted through tree branches and past fallen trunks. The boy negotiated the current skilfully. The roar of insects was not as deafening as it had been in the jungle, as if hushed now by the susurration of the river as it ran its fingers through the shivering tree branches.

The banks were thick with foliage, and occasionally Edgar thought he saw something, but each time he convinced himself that they were only shifting shadows. An hour into their journey they passed a clearing and a house on stilts. 'Don't worry,' the boy said. 'Only a fisherman's hut. Now there is no one there.' The moon shimmered above the trees.

They floated for many hours, and the river dropped swiftly through steep defiles, past overhanging crags and cliffs. Finally, at a wide bend, Edgar saw a collection of flickering lights. The river carried them towards it. He could discern buildings, then movement on the bank. They pulled up next to a small jetty. There three men stood watching them, all in *pasos*, all shirtless. One was taller than the rest, his skin pale, a thin cigar hanging from the edge of his mouth. As the boat slowed, the man took the cigar and flicked it into the water. He reached down and extended a hand to Khin Myo, who gathered up her *hta main* and climbed onto the jetty. There she bowed slightly and moved forward, slipping into the brush with the ease of one who had been there before.

Edgar climbed out of the boat.

The man looked at him without speaking. The piano tuner's clothes were still soaked with mud, his hair matted against his forehead. He could feel the dried mud on his face crack as he smiled. There was a long silence and then he slowly raised his hand.

He had thought about this moment for weeks and about what he would say. The moment called for words fit for History, to be remembered and recorded once the Shan States were finally won and the empire secured.

'I am Edgar Drake,' he said. 'I am here to repair a piano.'

BOOK TWO

> I am become a name;
> For always roaming with a hungry heart
> Much have I seen and known – cities of men
> And manners, climates, councils, governments,
> Myself not least, but honoured of them all, –
> And drunk delight of battle with my peers
> Far on the ringing plains of windy Troy.
> I am a part of all that I have met;
> Yet all experience is an arch wherethrough
> Gleams that untravelled world whose margin fades
> For ever and for ever when I move.

Alfred, Lord Tennyson, 'Ulysses'

Some say that seven suns, and some that nine were created, and the world became like whirlwinds; there was no solid part remaining.

Shan creation myth, from Mrs Leslie Milne,
Shans at Home (1910)

TWELVE

EDGAR DRAKE WAS led by a porter along a short path, past a sentry and through dense brush. Ahead lights danced, framed in the branches of scattered trees. The track was narrow and the brush scraped his arms. It must be difficult to move a column of troops through here, he thought. As if to answer him, Doctor Carroll spoke from behind, his voice loud and confident, with an accent Edgar couldn't place. 'Excuse the difficulty of the path. It's our first line of defence from the river – with the brush there's no need to build ramparts. You would probably appreciate how hellish it was to carry an Erard through here.'

'It is trouble enough in the streets of London.'

'I can imagine. The brush is beautiful too. We had a little rain last week, rare for this time of drought, and it came alive with flowers. Tomorrow you will see the colour.' Edgar stopped to peer more closely, but realizing that the porter was far ahead, he began to walk again, quickening his gait. He did not look up again until the brush ended abruptly and they entered a clearing.

Later he would try to remember what he had dreamed Mae Lwin would look like, but the first vision overwhelmed all past imaginings. The moonlight swept over his shoulder to a cluster of bamboo structures that clung to the hillside. The fort had been built below a steep mountain, cresting about a hundred yards beneath its precipitous face. Many of the buildings were connected by stairs or hanging bridges. Lanterns swung from roof beams, although with the light of the moon, they seemed almost superfluous. There were perhaps twenty huts altogether. It was smaller than he had expected, flanked on either side by thick forest. He knew from the reports that there was a Shan village of several hundred people behind the mountain.

Doctor Carroll was standing at his side with the moon at his back, the details of his face dark. 'Impressive, isn't it, Mr Drake?'

'They told me so, but I hadn't thought it would be like this . . . Captain Dalton tried to describe it to me once, but—'

'Captain Dalton is a military man. The army has yet to send a poet to Mae Lwin.'

Only a piano tuner, Edgar thought and turned back to look at the camp. A pair of birds flew across the clearing, cooing. As if to answer their song, the porter who had carried Edgar's bags from the river called from the balcony on the second tier of houses. The Doctor answered in a strange language, which sounded different from Burmese, less nasal, with a different tonal quality. The man left the balcony.

'You should go to bed,' said Carroll. 'We have much to discuss, but we can wait until morning.'

Edgar started to say something, but the Doctor seemed intent on leaving. Instead he bowed slightly and bid the Doctor goodnight. He walked across the clearing and climbed the steps to the porter. On the balcony he paused to catch his breath. It must be the altitude, he thought, It is high on the plateau. He looked out and caught his breath again.

Before him the land sloped to the river, a gentle descent through scattered trees and brush. On the sandy bank, a cluster of dugouts rested side by side. The moonlight was almost blinding, and Edgar looked for the rabbit, as he had on many nights since they had passed through the Mediterranean. Now, for the first time, he saw it, running at the side of the moon, as if half in dance, half in a scurried attempt to escape. Below the rabbit the forest was thick and dark, and the Salween slipped by silently, the sky swimming almost imperceptibly through its currents. The camp was quiet. He had not seen Khin Myo since they arrived. Everyone must have left to sleep, he thought.

The air was cool, almost cold, and he stood for several silent minutes until he caught his breath, then he turned and ducked inside the doorway. He closed the door. There was a small mattress draped in a mosquito net. The porter had gone. Kicking off his boots, he climbed beneath the net.

He had forgotten to lock the door. A small gust of wind blew it open. Moonlight danced in on the wings of tiny moths.

o

The following morning Edgar awoke to the sensation of closeness, a rustling at the mosquito net, hot breath near his cheek, the muffled giggling of children. He opened his eyes to meet half a dozen other whites, irises, pupils, before their little owners shrieked and ran squealing out of the room.

It was light already and much cooler than in the lowlands. In the night he had pulled the thin sheet over him and he was still in his clothes from the journey, still filthy. In his fatigue he had forgotten to wash. The sheets were soiled with mud. He cursed and then smiled and shook his head, thinking, It is hard to be angry when one has been awakened by the laughter of children. Points of light shone through the cross-weave of the bamboo wall, speckling the room. They have brought the stars inside, he thought, and climbed out from under the mosquito net. As he walked to the door, the percussion of his footsteps on the wooden floor was echoed by a scurrying outside the door and more squeals. The door still hung open. He poked his head out.

A small head at the end of the landing ducked back behind the corner. More giggling. Smiling, he closed the door and slid a rough bolt of wood through a socket across the door jamb. He peeled off his shirt. Dried, matted pieces of mud flaked off and broke on the floor. He looked for a washbasin, but there was none. Not knowing what to do with the clothes, he folded them roughly and set them by the door. He dressed in fresh clothes, khaki trousers, a light cotton shirt and dark waistcoat. He combed his hair hastily and collected the package he had brought for the Doctor from the War Office.

The children were waiting by the door when he opened it. Seeing him, they fled down the walkway. In their hurry one boy tripped and the others fell on top of him. Edgar reached down, picked up one of the boys, and, tickling him, threw him over his shoulder, now surprised by his own sudden playfulness. The other children stayed at his side, emboldened by the realization that the tall foreigner had only enough arms for one package and one squirming child.

On the steps Edgar nearly collided with an older Shan boy. 'Mr Drake, Doctor Carroll want you. He eat breakfast.' He shifted his eyes to the child, who stared at him upside-down from Edgar's shoulder. He scolded him in Shan. All the children laughed.

'Don't be angry,' said Edgar. 'It is my fault entirely. We were wrestling . . .'

'Wrestling?'

'Never mind,' said Edgar, now slightly embarrassed. He put the boy down and the group scattered like birds released from a cage. Straightening his shirt and brushing his hair to the side with his fingers, he followed the boy down the stairs.

When they reached the clearing, he stopped. The dark blue shadows of last night's memory had become blossoming flowers, hanging orchids, roses, hibiscus. Butterflies flew everywhere, flitterings, tiny pieces of colour that filled the air like confetti. In the open space children played with a ball made of woven cane, shouting as it bounced whimsically over the rough ground.

They walked through the brush and onto the sandy bank, where Doctor Carroll sat at a small table set for two. He was dressed in a crisp white linen shirt, rolled up at the cuffs. His hair was combed neatly and he smiled as the piano tuner approached. In the sunlight Edgar was immediately reminded of the photo of the Doctor that he had seen back in London. It must have been taken twenty years earlier, but he recognized instantly the broad shoulders, the strong nose and jaw, the neatly combed hair and the dark moustache, now speckled with grey. Something else was familiar from the photo as well, a movement, an elusiveness, a sense of animation in the blue eyes. The Doctor held out his hand, 'Good morning, Mr Drake.' His grip was strong and his hands rough. 'I trust you have slept well.'

'Like a baby, Doctor. Until some of the children found my room.'

The Doctor laughed. 'Oh, you will get used to that.'

'I do hope so. It has been a long time since I woke to the sound of children.'

'Do you have children yourself?'

'No, sadly, never. I do have nieces and nephews.'

One of the boys pulled out a chair for him. The river flowed by swiftly, brown and spotted with foam. Edgar had expected to see Khin Myo, but the Doctor was alone. At first her absence struck him as somewhat odd since she also had been summoned from Mandalay. He thought to ask the Doctor about this, but the question made him uncomfortable. She had said nothing to him on their journey about why she was coming and she had disappeared quickly when they arrived.

The Doctor motioned to the package in Edgar's hands. 'Have you brought something?'

'Of course. I am sorry. Music sheets. You have admirable taste.'

'You opened the package?' The Doctor arched an eyebrow.

Edgar blushed. 'Yes, I'm sorry, I suppose I shouldn't have. But . . . well, I admit I was curious about what sort of music you had requested.' The Doctor said nothing, so Edgar added, 'Impressive choices . . . but then some others, unlabelled, which I didn't recognize, notes that didn't seem to make much musical sense . . .'

The Doctor laughed. 'It is Shan music. I am trying to put it to the piano. I transcribe it and send it home, where a friend, a composer, makes some adaptations and sends it back. I always wondered what someone who read them would think . . . Cheroot?' He unwrapped a sardine tin from a handkerchief to reveal a line of rolled cigars of the kind he was smoking the night before.

'No, thank you. I don't smoke.'

'Pity. There is nothing better. A woman in the village rolls these for me. She boils the tobacco in palm sugar and lines it with vanilla and cinnamon and Lord knows what other nepenthe. They dry in the sun. There is a Burmese story of a girl who dried the cheroots she made for her sweetheart by keeping them warm against her body . . . Alas, I am not so lucky.' He smiled. 'Tea, perhaps?'

Edgar thanked him and Caroll nodded to one of the boys, who brought a silver teapot and filled his cup. Another boy set plates of food on the table: small cakes, rice, a bowl of crushed peppers, toast and butter, and an unopened jar of marmalade, which Edgar suspected had been brought out only for him.

The Doctor took a cheroot from the tin and lit it. He took several puffs. Even outside, the incense was thick and pungent.

Edgar was tempted to ask the Doctor more about the music, but decorum told him it might be improper to discuss this before they became better acquainted. 'Your fort is impressive,' he said.

'Thank you. We tried to build it in Shan style – it is more beautiful, and I could use local craftsmen. Some of it – the double storeys, the bridges – are my own innovations, necessities of the site. I needed to stay close to the river and hidden below the ridge.'

Edgar looked out over the water. 'The river is much larger than I had thought.'

'It surprised me as well when I first came here. It is one of the largest rivers in Asia, fed by the Himalayas – you must know this already.'

'I read your letter. I was curious what the name meant.'

'Salween? Actually, the Burmese pronounce the word as "Thanlwin", whose meaning I have yet to ascertain. *Than-lwin* are small Burmese cymbals. Although my friends here insist that the river is not named for the instrument – perhaps the tone of the words is different – I think it is rather poetic. The cymbals make a light sound, like water over pebbles. "River of light sound" – a fitting name, even if it is incorrect.'

'And the village . . . Mae Lwin?'

'Mae is a Shan word for river. It is the same in Siamese.'

'Was that Shan you spoke last night?' Edgar asked.

'You recognized it?'

'No . . . no, of course not. Only that it sounded different from Burmese.'

'I am impressed, Mr Drake. Of course, I should have expected as much from a man who studies sound . . . wait . . . quiet . . .' The Doctor stared at the opposite bank.

'What is it?'

'Shhh!' The Doctor raised his hand. He furrowed his brow in concentration.

There was a faint rustling in the bushes. Edgar sat up straight in his chair. 'Is someone there?' he whispered.

'Shhh. No sudden moves.' The Doctor spoke quietly to the boy, who brought him a small telescope.

'Doctor, is something wrong?'

Peering through the telescope, the Doctor lifted his hand to ask for silence. 'No . . . nothing . . . don't worry, wait, there . . . Ah ha! Just as I thought!' He turned and looked at Edgar, the telescope still raised.

'What's the matter?' Edgar whispered. 'Are we . . . are we being attacked?'

'Attacked?' The Doctor handed him the telescope. 'Hardly . . .

this is even better, Mr Drake. Only one day here, and already you get to see *Upupa epops*, the hoopoe. It is a lucky day, indeed. I must record this – it is the first time I have ever seen one here at the river. We have them in Europe, but they usually prefer open, drier country. It must have come here because of the drought. Wonderful! Look at the beautiful crest on its head, it flies like a butterfly.'

'Yes.' Edgar tried to match the Doctor's enthusiasm. He peered through the telescope at the bird across the river. It was small and grey, but otherwise unremarkable from this distance, he thought. It flew away.

'Lu,' Doctor Carroll called, 'bring me my journal!' The boy brought a brown book, bound with a string. Doctor Carroll untied it, put on a pair of pince-nez and scribbled briefly. He handed the book back to the boy and looked over his glasses at Edgar. 'A lucky day indeed,' he said again. 'The Shan would say that your arrival is propitious.'

The sun finally broke over the trees that lined the bank. The Doctor looked up at the sky. 'It's so late already,' he said. 'We must get going soon. We have quite a long way to go today.'

'I didn't know we were going anywhere.'

'Oh! I must apologize, Mr Drake. I should have told you last night. It is Wednesday and every Wednesday I go hunting. I would be honoured by your company. And I think you would enjoy it.'

'Hunting . . . But the Erard . . .'

'Of course,' the Doctor slapped his hand on the table. 'The *Erard*. I have not forgotten it. You have been travelling for weeks to repair the Erard, I know. Don't worry, you will be tired of that piano soon enough.'

'No, it is not that. I just thought I should look at it, at least. I am hardly a hunter. Why, I haven't handled a gun since a hunt in Rangoon. A long and terrible story . . . And then on the way here—'

'On the way here you were ambushed. Khin Myo told me. You were quite a hero.'

'A hero, hardly. I fainted, I almost killed the pony, and—'

'Don't worry, Mr Drake. It is rare that I even fire a gun when I go hunting. Perhaps I will shoot a boar or two, provided we have enough riders to carry them back. But that is hardly the purpose of the trip.'

Edgar felt weary. 'I suppose, then, that I should ask what the purpose is.'

'Collection. Botanical mainly, although this often means medical as well . . . I send samples to the Royal Botanic Gardens at Kew. The amount there is to be learned is astounding. I have been here twelve years and haven't even begun to exhaust the Shan pharmacopoeia. Regardless, you should come simply because it is beautiful, because you have just arrived, because you are my guest, because it would be rude for me not to show you the wonders of your new home.'

My new home, thought Edgar, and there was another rustling in the branches across the river as a bird took flight. Carroll reached for his telescope and squinted into it. Finally he lowered it. 'A crested kingfisher. Not rare, but still lovely. We will leave inside the hour. The Erard can survive one more day out of tune.'

Edgar smiled weakly. 'Might I at least have a moment to shave? It has been days.'

The Doctor jumped to his feet. 'Of course. But don't worry about washing *too* carefully. We will be filthy within an hour.' He set his napkin on the table and spoke again to one of the boys, who ran off through the clearing. He motioned Edgar ahead. 'After you,' he said, dropping the cheroot in the sand and grinding it with his boot.

When Edgar returned to his room, he found a small basin of water on the table with a razor, shaving cream, brush and towel resting at its side. He splashed the water on his face. It relieved him briefly. He didn't know what to think of Carroll, or the postponement of his work to go looking for flowers, and he found himself troubled by vague doubts. There was something disconcerting about the Doctor's manner, about how to reconcile the legends of physician-soldier with the affable, even avuncular man who offered tea and toast and marmalade and became so excited about birds. Perhaps it is because this is all still so *English*, he thought, After all, a stroll, if that is what this was, *is* a proper way to greet a guest. Still, he was bothered and he shaved gingerly, pulling the blade over his skin and raising his palms to feel the smoothness of his cheeks.

o

They mounted a pair of Shan ponies, which had been saddled in the clearing. Someone had tied little flowers in their tails.

Soon Nok Lek trotted up on another pony. Edgar was glad to see him again and noticed that he carried himself differently from the way he had on the journey; his youthful confidence seemed more subdued around the Doctor, more deferential. He nodded to the two men and Carroll motioned for the boy to lead. He turned his pony nimbly and rode off, bouncing on its back, clearly enjoying the chance to ride alone.

They rode out of the clearing on a track paralleling the river. By the sun Edgar reckoned they were heading south-east. They passed through a small grove of willows that stretched up from the riverbed. The foliage was thick and low and Edgar had to duck his head to keep from being knocked from the saddle. The path turned uphill and slowly rose above the willows, giving way to drier brush. On the ridge that sheltered the camp, they stopped. Below, to the north-east, a wide valley stretched out covered with small bamboo settlements. To the south, a small series of hills pushed up through the slope of the land, like the vertebrae of a disinterred skeleton. In the distance, higher mountains were barely discernible for the glare of the sun.

'Siam,' said the Doctor, pointing to the mountains.

'I hadn't realized we were so close.'

'About eighty miles. This is why the War Office is so worried about keeping the Shan States. The Siamese are our only buffer against the French, who already have troops near the Mekong.'

'And these settlements?'

'Shan and Burmese villages.'

'What are they growing?'

'Opium, mostly . . . although production here is nothing like it is to the north, in Kokang, or deeper into Wa country. They say there are so many poppies in Kokang that all the bees fall into deep opium sleeps and never wake up. But the crop here is substantial enough . . . Now you understand another reason why we don't want to lose the Shan States.' He reached into his pocket and pulled out the sardine tin. He put a cheroot in his mouth, and offered the tin again to Edgar. 'Changed your mind yet?'

Edgar shook his head. 'But I read about the poppies. I thought it was forbidden by the Indian Opium Act. The reports say—'

'I know what the reports say.' He lit the cigar. 'If you read closely, you would know that the Indian Opium Act of 1878 prohibited the growing of opium in Burma *proper*; at the time we did not control the Shan States. This doesn't mean that there isn't pressure to stop. There is much more fuss about it in England than here, which is probably why so many of . . . us . . . who write the reports, are selective in what we say.'

'That makes me worry about everything else I have read.'

'I wouldn't. Most of what is written *is* true, although you will have to get used to the subtleties, to the differences between what you read in England and what you see here, especially anything to do with politics.'

'Well, I don't know much, my wife follows these issues more than I do.' Edgar paused. 'But I would be interested in what you have to say.'

'About politics, Mr Drake?'

'Everyone in London seems to have an opinion on the future of the empire. You must know much more than they do.'

The Doctor waved the cheroot. 'I actually think little about politics. I find it rather, how should I say, impractical.'

'Impractical?'

'Take opium, for instance. Before the Sepoy Rebellion, when our holdings in Burma were administered by the East India Company, opium use was even encouraged – the trade was quite lucrative. But there has always been a call to prohibit or tax it by those who object to its "corrupting influences". Last year the Society for the Suppression of the Opium Trade requested that the Viceroy ban the trade. Their request was rejected quietly. This was no surprise; it is one of our largest cash crops in India. And banning it really does nothing. The merchants just start smuggling the drug by sea. The smugglers are actually rather clever. They put the opium in bags and tie them to blocks of salt. If the ships are searched, they merely drop the cargo into the water. After a certain time the salt dissolves and the package floats back to the surface.'

'You sound as if you approve of this.'

'Approve of what? Of opium? It is one of the best medicines that I have, an antidote for pain, diarrhoea, coughing, perhaps the most common symptoms of the diseases I see here. Anyone who wishes to make policies on such subjects should come here first.'

'I never knew . . .' said Edgar. 'What do you think then about self-government? It does seem to be the most pressing question . . .'

'Mr Drake, please. It is a beautiful morning. Let's not ruin it with talk of politics. I know that after such a journey one would be interested in such matters, but I find them dreadfully dull. You will see – the longer you are here, the less such opinions matter.'

'But you wrote so much . . .'

'I wrote histories, Mr Drake, not of politics.' The Doctor pointed the smoking end of his cheroot at Edgar. 'It is not a welcome subject for me. If you have heard what some have to say about my work here, I think you can understand why.'

Edgar began to mutter an apology, but the Doctor didn't respond. Ahead, where the path narrowed, Nok Lek was waiting. The party dropped into single file and followed the path into the forest on the other side of the ridge.

o

They rode for nearly three hours. Descending from the ridge, they entered an open valley that rose slowly, south of the vertebral hills. The track was soon wide enough for two ponies, and while Nok Lek again went ahead, the Doctor rode alongside the piano tuner. It became obvious very quickly that Carroll had absolutely no interest in hunting. He spoke about the mountains in whose shadow they rode, how he had mapped the area when he first arrived, measuring altitude with boiling-point barometers. He told stories about the geology, the history, local myths about each outcrop, glen and river they crossed: Here is where the monks keep catfish, Here is where I saw my first tiger on the plateau, rare, Here is where mosquitoes breed, where I am doing experiments on the spread of disease, Here is an entrance to the world of the *nga-hlyin*, the Burmese giants, Here is where Shan sweethearts court, at times you can hear the sound of flutes. His stories seemed inexhaustible, and his tale about one hill only ended when they passed another. Edgar was astounded; the Doctor seemed to know not only every flower, but their medicinal uses, scientific classification, local names in Burmese and Shan, their stories. Several times, pointing to a flowering bush, he would exclaim that such plant was unknown to Western science, and that 'I have sent samples to the Linnean Society and the Royal Botanic Gardens at Kew, and I even have a species like it that bears my name, an orchid which they have named *Dendrobium carrollii*, and a lily named *Lilium carrollianum*, and another, *Lilium scottium*, which I named after J. George Scott, the Political Administrator of the Shan States, a friend whom I admire deeply. And there are other flowers . . .' and with this he even stopped his pony and looked directly at Edgar, his eyes bright, 'my own genus, *Carrollium trigeminum*, the species name meaning "the three roots", a reference to the Shan myth of the three princes, which I promise to tell you soon, or perhaps you should hear the Shan tell it . . . Regardless, the flower in profile looks like a prince's face and it is a monocotyledon, with three paired petals and sepals, like three princes and their brides.' He stopped occasionally to pick flowers and plants and press them into a worn leather book which he kept in a saddlebag.

They stopped by a bush covered with small yellow blooms. 'That one,' he confided, pointing, his shirtsleeve rolled up over a tanned forearm, 'has not been given an official name yet, as I hope to send samples to the Linnean Society. It has been quite a struggle to get any of my botanical work published. The army seems to be concerned that somehow my writing about flowers will reveal state secrets . . . as if the French didn't know of Mae Lwin.' He sighed. 'I suppose I will have to retire before I publish a pharmacopoeia. Sometimes I wish I were a civilian, without the rules and regimentation. But then I suppose I wouldn't be here.'

As they rode further, Edgar's nervousness and disorientation began to dissipate under the onslaught of the Doctor's enthusiasm. All of his own questions, mostly about music, about the piano, about what the Shan and the Burmese thought of Bach and Handel, about why Carroll remained, and ultimately why he himself had come, were temporarily forgotten. Oddly, nothing seemed more natural than travelling on horseback to hunt plants without names, trying to make sense of the Doctor's river of stories, Shan histories, Latin nomenclature, and literary references. Above them, a raptor circled and caught a rising current, and he imagined what the bird must see: three tiny figures winding their way along a dry track that traced the collar of the karst hills, the tiny villages, the Salween snaking languidly, the mountains to the east, the Shan

Plateau dropping to Mandalay, and then all of Burma, of Siam, of India, of the armies gathered there, grids of French and British soldiers blind to each other but visible to this bird, gathered waiting, while in between three men rode together, collecting flowers.

They passed houses on stilts, dusty roads leading to small villages, their entrances marked by wooden portals. At one a tangle of branches was strewn in front on the pathway, and a piece of tattered paper covered with swirls of writing was pinned to the portal. Doctor Carroll explained that smallpox had struck the village and the script was a magical formula to fight the disease. 'It is terrible,' he said. 'We vaccinate people in England now with cowpox – it has been mandatory for several years – yet they won't give me enough supplies to do so here. It is a horrid disease, so contagious, and so disfiguring. If one survives.' Edgar gripped his reins uneasily. When he was a boy, there had been a smallpox outbreak in the slums in east London. Sketches of victims had appeared daily in the broadsheets, young children covered with pustules, gaunt, pale cadavers.

Soon rocky outcrops began to appear, pushing out of the earth like worn molars. Edgar was mindful of the comparison, for the broad, open landscape narrowed quickly, and they followed a ravine down between high pinnacles, as if descending into the earth's intestines.

'This track would be completely flooded in the rain,' said Carroll at his side, 'but we are experiencing one of our worst droughts in history.'

'I remember reading about it in a letter you wrote, and everyone I have spoken to has mentioned it.'

'Whole villages are dying of starvation because of the meagre crops. If only the army understood how much we could accomplish with food. With food alone, we wouldn't have to worry about the war.'

'They said they can't bring in food because of the dacoits, because of the Shan Bandit Chief named Twet Nga Lu—'

'I see you have read that history too,' the Doctor said. His voice echoed off the cliffs. 'There is some truth to that, although Twet Nga Lu's legend is exaggerated in all the boisterous conversations in the officers' messes. They just want a face to put on the danger. That is not to say he isn't a danger – he is. But the situation is more complicated, and if we are to hope for peace it requires more than the defeat of one man . . . But I am philosophizing and I promised you I wouldn't. How much of the story do you know?'

'Only a little. To be honest, I am still confused by all the names.'

'We are all confused. I don't know which report you read or when it was written – I hope they gave you something I wrote. Although officially we annexed Upper Burma last year, the Shan States have been impossible to control, and thus it is almost impossible to station troops here. In our effort to pacify the region – "peaceful penetration", in the parlance of the War Office, a term I find vile – we have been engaged in fighting a federation of Shan princes calling itself the Limbin Confederacy, an alliance of Shan *sawbwas* – the Shan word for their princes – who want to overthrow British rule. Twet Nga Lu is not part of the confederacy, but an illegitimate chief operating across the Salween. We would call him a dacoit, but he has too many followers. His name is perhaps more legendary because he works alone. The Limbin Confederacy is less easily vilified because they are organized and even send their own delegations. In other words, they seem like a real government. But Twet Nga Lu refuses to cooperate with anyone.'

Edgar began to ask about the rumours of the Bandit Chief which he had heard on the river steamship, but there was a rattling from above. The men looked up to see a large bird lifting off from the crags.

'What was that?' asked Edgar.

'Raptor, although I didn't get a good look at it. What we need to beware of here are the snakes. They often come out at this time of day to get warm in the sun. Last year I had a pony bitten by a viper, leaving her with a terrible wound. The bite can cause humans to go into rapid shock.'

'Do you know much about snake bites?'

'I have made a collection of poisons and tried to study them. I have been helped by a medicine man, a hermit who lives in the hills, who, the villagers say, sells the poisons to assassins.'

'That's horrid. I—'

'Perhaps, although death by poison could be quite peaceful compared to other methods one sees . . . Don't worry, Mr Drake, he has no interest in English piano tuners.'

They continued their descent. Carroll pointed down the ravine. 'Listen,' he said, 'soon you will hear the river.' The clip-clop of hooves was answered by a distant, deeper rumbling. The track continued to drop, and the ponies struggled to keep their footing on the stones. At last Carroll stopped. 'We should dismount,' he said. 'This is too precarious for the ponies.' He swung himself off with a single, graceful movement. Nok Lek followed and then Edgar Drake, still thinking about the snakes. The sound of the river grew louder. The ravine narrowed sharply and now there was scarcely enough room for the ponies to pass. Above him, Edgar could see branches, logs, wedged into the narrow chasm, testament to past flooding. Soon the ravine took a sharp turn and the floor seemed to disappear beneath them. Carroll handed the reins of his pony to Nok Lek and walked carefully to the edge. 'Come and look, Mr Drake,' he shouted over the roar.

Edgar walked gingerly to join the Doctor where the track dropped steeply away to a river that flowed twenty feet below them. The stones were silver, polished by the flow of water. Edgar looked up. The sun winked down through a sliver of sky. He could feel spray on his face, the thunder of the rapids shaking the ground.

'In the rainy season this is a waterfall. The river is twice as high. This water comes all the way from Yunnan, in China. It is all from melted snow. There is more, come.'

'What?'

'Come here, come and look.'

Edgar picked his way uneasily over the stones, wet with the spray of the river. The Doctor was standing at the edge of the precipice, looking up the rock.

'What is it?' asked Edgar.

'Look closely,' said the Doctor. 'At the rock. Do you see them? The flowers.'

The entire face of the ravine was covered by a dull moss, sprinkled with thousands of tiny flowers, so small that he had mistaken them for beads of water.

Carroll motioned to a smooth surface on the wall. 'Now put your ear there.'

'What?'

'Go ahead. Put your ear up against the wall, listen.'

Edgar looked at him sceptically. He crouched and put his head to the stone.

From deep within the rock came a singing, strange and haunting. He pulled his head away. The sound stopped. He leaned back. Again he could hear it. It sounded familiar, thousands of soprano voices warming up to sing. 'Where is it coming from?' he shouted.

'The rock is hollow, they are vibrations from the river, a high-pitched resonance. That is one explanation. The other is Shan, that it is an oracle. Those who seek advice come here to listen. Look up there.' He pointed to a pile of rocks, on which a small wreath of flowers had been placed. 'A shrine to the spirits that sing. I thought you would like it here. Scenery fit for a man of music.'

Edgar rose and smiled and wiped off his glasses once again. While they talked, Nok Lek unpacked several baskets filled with stuffed banana leaves, which he laid out on the rocks, away from the precipice, where it was dry. They sat and ate and listened to the river. The food was different from the rich curries Edgar had eaten in the lowlands. Each banana leaf contained something different: sliced and seared pieces of chicken, fried squash, a pungent paste that smelled strongly of fish, but tasted sweet with the rice, which was different too, sticky balls of grains that were almost translucent.

When they had finished, they rose and led their ponies up the little path until it became flat enough to ride. The track climbed slowly, out of the coolness of the ravine and onto the heat of the plateau.

Carroll chose a different route back to the camp, one that took them through a burnt forest. In contrast to the first track, the land was hot and flat and the vegetation dry, but the Doctor stopped several times to show Edgar more plants, tiny orchids which were hidden in the shade, innocuous-looking pitcher plants whose carnivorousness Carroll explained in macabre detail, trees that held water, rubber, medicine.

On the lonely path they passed through a temple complex, where dozens of pagodas were aligned in rows. The structures were of various sizes and ages and shapes, some freshly painted and capped with ornaments, others pale and crumbling. On one, the body of the pagoda had been crafted into the shape of a coiled serpent. It was eerily silent. Birds flitted over the ground. The only person they saw was a monk, who looked as old as the temples themselves, his skin dark and wrinkled, his body tinted with dust. He was sweeping the path as they approached, and Edgar saw Carroll press his hands together and bow slightly to the man. The old monk said nothing, but kept sweeping, the grass broomstick swaying with the hypnotic rhythm of his chant.

The trail was long and at last Edgar grew weary. He thought how much the Doctor must have travelled on the plateau to know each stream, each hill, and how, if they were separated, he would not know how to find his way back. For a brief moment, the thought frightened him. But I have trusted him by deciding to come here, he thought, there is no reason I shouldn't now. The path narrowed and the Doctor rode ahead. Edgar watched him, his back straight, one hand on his waist, alert, watching.

They passed from the forest onto a wide ridge and back into the valley from which they had come. The sun was setting when, from the rise of one of the hills, Edgar saw the Salween. It was dark when they reached Mae Lwin.

THIRTEEN

THE FOLLOWING MORNING Edgar awoke before the children came and wandered down to the river. He expected to find the Doctor eating his breakfast or perhaps even see Khin Myo, but the bank was empty. The Salween lapped against the sand. He looked briefly across the river for birds. There was a fluttering. Another crested kingfisher, he thought, and smiled to himself, I am already beginning to learn. He walked back up to the clearing. Nok Lek was walking down from the path that led up to the houses.

'Good morning, Mr Drake,' said the boy.

'Good morning. I was looking for the Doctor. Can you kindly tell me where he is?'

'Once a week the Doctor is in his . . . how do you say?'

'The Doctor is in his surgery?'

'Yes, his surgery. He told me to get you.'

Nok Lek led Edgar up the small path to the camp's headquarters. As they were entering, an older woman passed inside carrying a crying baby in her arms, swaddled tightly in a check cloth. Nok Lek and Edgar followed.

The room was full of people, dozens of men and women in colourful coats and turbans, crouching or standing, holding children, peering over shoulders to watch the Doctor, who sat at the far end of the room. Nok Lek led the piano tuner through the crowd, speaking softly to part it.

They found the Doctor at a broad desk, listening to a baby's chest with a stethoscope. He raised his eyebrows in welcome and continued to listen. The baby lay limp and passive on the lap of a young woman Edgar guessed was its mother. She was very young, a girl of perhaps fifteen or sixteen, but her eyes looked swollen and tired. Like most of the other women's, her hair was tied up in a wide turban, which seemed to rest precariously on her head. She wore a dress tied over her bosom, a hand-woven cloth patterned with interlaced geometric designs. Though there was an elegance in the way she wore it, when Edgar looked more closely, he saw that it was tattered at the edges. He thought of the Doctor's stories of the drought.

At long last Carroll removed the stethoscope. He spoke to the woman for a moment in Shan and then turned to rummage through a cabinet behind him. Edgar peered over his shoulder at the rows of apothecary's vials.

The Doctor saw him stare. 'Much the same as any English chemist,' he said as he handed the woman a small bottle of a dark elixir. 'Warburg's tincture and arsenic for fever, Cockle's pills and chlorodyne, Goa powder for ringworm, vaseline, Holloway's ointment, Dover's powder, laudanum for dysentery. And then these.' He pointed to a row of unlabelled bottles filled with leaves and dirty liquids, crushed bugs and lizards floating in solution. 'Local medicine.'

Carroll reached back into the cabinet and took out a larger flask filled with herbs and a smoky liquid. He pulled out the stopper and the room filled with a deep, sweet scent. He dipped his fingers into the bottle and pulled out a wet mass of leaves and placed them on the baby's chest. Water pooled around the leaves and ran over the baby's sides. The Doctor began to run his fingers over its body, spreading the fluid over its throat and chest. His eyes were closed and he began to whisper something, softly. At last he opened them. He wrapped the baby's swaddling back around the leaves and spoke to the girl. She rose and bowed in thanks, and walked away through the crowd.

'What was that?' Edgar asked.

'I think the child has consumption. The little bottle is Steven's Consumption Cure,' said Carroll, 'direct from England. I somewhat doubt its efficacy, but we don't have anything better. Do you know of Koch's discoveries?'

'Only what I have read in the broadsheets. But I couldn't tell you anything. I know Steven's Cure only because we bought it for our housemaid—her mother has consumption.'

'Well, the German thinks that he found the cause of consumption in a bacterium, he calls it a "tubercle bacillus". But that was five years ago. As closely as I try to follow the advances, I am too isolated and it is difficult to know how science has changed.'

'And the plant?'

'The medicine men call it *mahaw tsi*. It is a famous Kachin cure and their medicine men guard it from foreigners. It took a long time to convince them to show it to me. I am pretty certain it is a species of *Euonymus*, although I can't be sure. They use it for many ailments, some believe that even saying the words *mahaw tsi* can cure disease. They say it is especially potent for diseases of air, and this baby has a cough. Anyway, I mix it with Holloway's ointment. For a long time I was doubtful about the herbs, but I think that I see some improvement in my patients who use them. That and prayer.'

Edgar stared at the Doctor. 'To whom?' he asked, finally. But another patient had arrived and the Doctor didn't answer.

It was a young boy, holding his left hand close to his body. Carroll motioned for Edgar to sit in a chair behind him. He reached for the boy's hand, but the boy guarded it. The boy's mother, who stood behind him, spoke to him sharply. Finally Carroll gently prised his arms open.

Three fingers on the boy's left hand were almost completely

severed, held by ragged tendons and covered with clotted blood. Carroll handled the wound carefully and the boy winced in pain. 'This is bad,' the Doctor muttered and spoke to the woman in Shan. The boy began to cry. Carroll turned and said something to Nok Lek, who removed a package from the cabinet and rolled it out on the desk. There was a cloth, and bandages, and several cutting tools. The boy started to yell.

Edgar looked uncomfortably around the waiting room. The other patients were still, unexpressive, watching.

Carroll removed another bottle from the cabinet. He took the boy's hand and stretched it over the cloth on the table. He poured the contents of the bottle over the wound. The boy jumped and screamed. Carroll poured out more, wiping the hand vigorously with the cloth. He took a smaller vial from the cabinet and poured a thick liquid onto a bandage, which he rubbed over the wound. Almost immediately the boy began to calm down.

The Doctor turned to Edgar. 'Mr Drake, I am going to need your help. The salve should numb some of the pain, but he is going to start to scream when he sees the saw. I usually have a nurse, but she is with other patients now. That is, if you don't mind helping, of course. I thought it might be interesting for you to observe our surgery at work, seeing how important such projects are for local relations.'

'Local relations?' Edgar said faintly. 'You are going to amputate?'

'I have no other choice. I have seen wounds like this turn a whole arm gangrenous. I am just going to take off the injured fingers. The wound on his hand doesn't look deep. I wish I had ether here, but my supply ran out only last week and they haven't sent me more. We could have him smoke opium, but it will still hurt. I would rather be finished with this as quickly as possible.'

'What can I do?'

'Just hold his arm. He is small, but you will be surprised how fiercely he will try to throw you off.'

Carroll rose, as did Edgar behind him. The Doctor gently took the boy's hand and laid it on the table. He tied a tourniquet above the boy's elbow and motioned for Edgar to hold his arm. He did so, but his actions felt rough and cruel. Then Carroll turned to Nok Lek and nodded and Nok Lek reached over and twisted the boy's ear. The boy shrieked and his free hand shot up to his ear, and before Edgar could turn back to the table the Doctor had cut off one, two, and then a third finger. The boy looked at them, perplexed, and then screamed again, but Carroll had already wrapped the bloody hand in the cloth.

o

The morning wore on, patient after patient filed to the examining chair before the window: a middle-aged man with a limp, a pregnant woman and a woman who could not conceive, a child whom Carroll diagnosed as deaf. There were three people with goitres, two with diarrhoea, and five with fevers, all of which Carroll attributed to malaria. From each of the feverish patients he drew a drop of blood, placed it on a slide and examined it beneath a small microscope, which reflected light from the window up through the eyepiece.

'What are you looking for?' asked Edgar, still shaken from seeing the amputation. Carroll let him look through the microscope.

'Do you see the small circles?' he asked.

'Yes, everywhere.'

'Those are red blood cells. Everyone has them. But, if you look closely, you can see that inside the cells are darker objects, like blemishes.'

'I don't see anything,' Edgar said and sat back in frustration.

'Don't worry, it is difficult at first. Until about seven years ago no one knew what they were, until a Frenchman discovered that they are the parasites which cause the disease. I have been very interested because most Europeans think the disease is caused by breathing bad air from the swamps, which is why the Italians named the disease "mala aria", "bad air". But when I was in India I had a friend, an Indian doctor who translated for me some of the Hindu Vedas, where they call malaria the "king of diseases", and attribute it to the anger of the god Shiva. As for transmission, the Vedas implicate the lowly mosquito. But no one has found this parasite in the mosquito yet, so we can't be certain. And since mosquitoes live in the swamps, it is difficult to dissociate the two. Actually, it is difficult to dissociate any of its possible sources in the jungle. The Burmese, for example, call it *hnget pyhar*. It means "bird fever".'

'And what do you think?'

'I have been collecting mosquitoes, dissecting them, grinding them up, peering at their innards through the microscope, but I haven't found anything yet.'

Carroll gave each of the malaria patients quinine tablets and an extract of a plant he said came from China, as well as a local root to ease the intensity of the fevers. For the diarrhoea he gave laudanum or ground papaya seeds, for the goitres, tablets of salt. Carroll instructed the man with a limp in how to make crutches. For the pregnant woman, he rubbed an ointment on her swollen belly. For the deaf child, he could do nothing and told Edgar how seeing such a child saddened him like almost no other disease, for the Shan had no sign language, and even if they had, the boy could never hear the songs of the night festivals. Edgar thought of another little boy, the deaf son of a client, who would push his face against the piano case when his mother played to feel the vibrations. He thought of the steamer to Aden as well, and of the Man with One Story, There are causes of deafness that perhaps even medicine cannot understand.

For the woman who could not conceive, Carroll turned to Nok Lek and spoke at length. When Edgar asked what he had recommended, Carroll said, 'This is confusing. She is barren and she walks through her village muttering to a make-believe child. I do not know how to cure her. I have told Nok Lek to take her to a monk in the north, who specializes in cures for such problems. Maybe he can help.'

Close to noon they saw their last patient, a thin man who was led to the chair by a woman who looked half his age. After talking briefly to the woman, Carroll turned to the room and announced something in Shan. Slowly those waiting rose and filed out. 'This could take some time. It is a shame I cannot see them all,' he said, 'but there are so many who are sick.'

Edgar studied the patient more closely. He wore a moth-eaten shirt and a pair of torn trousers. He was barefoot and his toes were callused and gnarled. He wasn't wearing a turban. His head was shaved, smooth, his face and eyes hollowed. As he stared at Edgar he made slow, rhythmic motions with his jaw, as if chewing his tongue or the inside of his cheeks. His hands shook slowly and rhythmically.

Caroll spoke at length with the woman, and then finally turned to Edgar. 'She says he is possessed,' he said. 'They come from the mountains, nearly a week's journey from here, from a village near Kengtung.'

'Why come here?' asked Edgar.

'The Shan say there are ninety-six diseases. This isn't one of them. She has seen all the medicine men near Kengtung and they can do nothing. Now word of this man's disease has spread, and medicine men fear him because they think that the spirit is too strong. So she came here.'

'Surely you don't believe he is possessed . . .'

'I don't know, there are things here that I have seen which I never could have believed before.' He paused. 'In some areas of the Shan States, men like this are worshipped as spirit mediums. I have been to festivals where hundreds of villagers have come to watch them dance. In England we would have called the writhing movements St Vitus's dance, for St Vitus is the patron saint of hysterical and nervous diseases. But I don't know what to call this dance, St Vitus cannot hear prayers from Mae Lwin. And I do not know what spirits cause this possession.'

He turned back to the man and this time addressed him directly, and the man stared back with empty eyes. The two remained like this for a long time until at last Carroll rose and took the man by the arm and led him outside. He gave him no medicine.

St Vitus, thought Edgar, Vitus was the name of Bach's grandfather, It is strange how all this is connected, even if only by a name.

o

When the old man had shuffled away slowly with his wife, Carroll led Edgar to another building, separate from the headquarters. Inside several patients lay on beds.

'This is our little hospital,' Carroll explained. 'I don't like to keep patients here because I think they heal better at home. But I feel as if I need to watch some of the more severe cases, usually diarrhoea or malaria. I trained Miss Ma as a nurse. He pointed to a young woman who sat wiping one of the patients with a wet cloth. 'She takes care of the patients when I am away.' Edgar nodded at her and she bowed slightly.

They walked past the patients, Carroll explaining, 'This young fellow has severe diarrhoea, which I am afraid is cholera. We had a terrible outbreak years ago, and ten villagers died. Fortunately, no one else has fallen ill, and I am keeping him here so that he doesn't infect the others . . . This next case is terribly sad and, unfortunately, terribly common. Cerebral malaria. There is little I can do for the boy. He will die soon. I want to give his family hope, so I let him stay here . . . This child has rabies. She was bitten by a mad dog, which many now think is the mode of transmission, although again I am too far from the learning centres of Europe to know the current opinion.'

They stopped by the little girl's bed. She lay twisted in tense contortions, her eyes open in frozen horror. Edgar was shocked to see that her hands had been tied behind her back.

'Why is she restrained?' he asked.

'The disease makes you mad. That is what it means; *rabere* is Latin for rage. Two days ago she tried to attack Miss Ma, so we had to restrain her.'

At the end of the room they found an old woman. 'And what is wrong with her?' Edgar asked, beginning to feel overwhelmed by the litany of diseases.

'This one?' the Doctor asked. He said something to the old woman in Shan and she sat up. 'She is fine. She is the grandmother of one of the other patients, who is currently seated in the corner over there. When she comes to visit him, he lets her rest on the bed because she says it is so comfortable.'

'Doesn't he need it?'

'He does, although he isn't in immediate danger like the other patients.'

'What's wrong?'

'Probably diabetic. I have a number of patients who come to see me because they are frightened when they notice that insects eat their urine because of the sugar in it. Some of the Shan seem particularly unnerved, they say that it is the same as having their own bodies preyed upon. Another old diagnosis, also by ancient Brahmins. He doesn't need to be in my little hospital, but it makes him feel better and gives his grandmother a place to rest.'

Carroll spoke to the man and then to Miss Ma. Finally he motioned to Edgar to follow him outside. They stood in the sunlight. It was early afternoon.

'I think we are done for today. I hope this has been worthwhile for you, Mr Drake.'

'It was. Although, I was a little taken aback at first, I must admit. It is not like an English surgery. It is not very *private*.'

'I don't have much of a choice. Although it is good that everyone can see that an English face can do more than look down a rifle.' He paused. 'You were asking me about my political opinions yesterday, no? There – an opinion.' He laughed.

'Indeed,' said Edgar slowly. 'Despite the stories, I am still amazed—'

'About what, may I ask?'

Edgar watched as the patients drifted slowly out of the clinic. 'That you have accomplished all this, that you brought music here, medicine. It is hard to believe that you have never fought a battle.'

Anthony Carroll stared at him. 'You believe that? You are quite an innocent, my dear fellow.'

'Maybe, but the men on the steamer said you have never fired a shot.'

'Then you should be happy you have seen me in my surgery and not when we question prisoners.'

A chill ran along Edgar's spine. 'Prisoners?'

The Doctor lowered his voice. 'The dacoits are known to tear tongues from mouths. I am not above their rules ... But it shouldn't bother you. As you say, you are here for music.'

Edgar felt faint. 'I ... I didn't think ...'

They stared at each other.

Suddenly Carroll's face broke into a wide grin, his eyes twinkling. 'A joke, Mr Drake, a joke. I warned you about discussing politics. You mustn't be so earnest. Don't worry, everyone leaves with their tongue intact.'

He slapped the tuner on the back. 'You came to find me this morning,' he said. 'Regarding the Erard, I imagine?'

'Regarding the Erard,' replied Edgar weakly. 'But if now is not a good time for this, I understand. This has been quite a morning already . . .'

'Nonsense, this is the perfect time. For what is tuning if not another form of cure? Let us waste not another instant. I know that you have been waiting.'

FOURTEEN

THE SUN HAD risen high above the mountain, and it was hot despite the breeze that licked up from the river. Still slightly unnerved, Edgar returned to his room to collect his tools and the Doctor led him up a narrow track to a path that ran between the buildings and the mountainside. He was surprised he had taken Carroll's jest so seriously, but the thought of finally seeing the Erard cheered him. Since arriving, he had wondered where it was kept, and would peer into open rooms as he strolled through the compound. They stopped at a door bolted with a heavy metal latch. Carroll took a small key from his pocket and fitted it into the lock.

The room was dark. The Doctor walked across the floor to the windows and opened them. The view outside spilled over the camp to the Salween, drifting past, dark and brown. The piano was covered by a blanket made of the same material Edgar had seen on many of the women, decorated with thin multi-coloured lines. The Doctor removed it with a flourish. 'Here it is, Mr Drake.' The Erard stood half in the light of the window, the smooth surface of its case almost liquid against the rough backdrop of the room.

Edgar walked forwards and put his hand on the piano. For a moment he stood silent, looking only, and then began to shake his head. 'Unbelievable,' he said. 'Really . . . this is so . . .' He took a deep breath. 'I suppose part of me still can't believe this.

I have known about this for over two months now, but I think I am as surprised as if I had just walked in from the jungle and seen it . . . I am sorry, I didn't think I would be so affected. It is . . . beautiful . . .'

He stood at the keyboard. Sometimes he was so focused on the technical aspects of piano construction that he forgot how lovely the instrument could be. Many of the Erards built during the same period were ornately decorated with inlaid wood, carved legs, even a sculpted nameboard. This one was simpler. A dark brown mahogany veneer stretched into curved, feminine legs, so smooth that they seemed almost lascivious; now he could understand why there were those in England who insisted that piano legs be covered. The nameboard was decorated with a thin, elegant line of mother-of-pearl, curling at each end into a bouquet of flowers. The case was smooth, monochrome, the only texture in the interlocking pieces of veneer.

He said at last, 'I admire your taste, Doctor. How did you know to select this one? Or an Erard, for that matter?'

'Or a piano, for that matter, you should ask.'

Edgar chuckled, 'Indeed. At times, I suppose I am a bit single-minded. It seemed so fitting . . .'

'Well, I am touched by the sentiment. You and I must think in a similar manner . . . There is something about a piano that is different from other instruments, something imposing, deserving of admiration. It is always a subject of much discussion among the Shan I know. They say it bestows honour to hear it played. It is also the most versatile of instruments, something I think anyone would enjoy.'

'And an Erard?'

'My request was actually not that specific. I did ask for an Erard, an older model. I might even have mentioned one from 1840, as I had heard somewhere that Liszt had once played one. But the War Office chose, or maybe I was just lucky and this was the only one for sale. I agree it is beautiful. I was hoping perhaps that you could educate me on its more technical aspects.'

'Of course . . . only where can I start? I don't want to bore you.'

'I appreciate your humility, Mr Drake, but I am sure you won't.'

'Very well then . . . but please stop me if I do.' Edgar ran his hand over the case. 'An 1840 Erard grand, Doctor, built by Sebastien Erard's Paris workshop, which makes it unusual, as most of the Erards you find in London are from the London workshop. Mahogany veneered. It has a double-escapement repetition action – the action is the set of levers that lift a hammer to the strings. It is designed so that after the hammer hits the strings it can fall back, "escaping". The double-escapement action was an innovation developed by Erard, but is standard on pianos now. It is very slender on Erards, hence it is common for the hammers to go out of adjustment. The heads of the hammers are made of alternating leather and felt, much more difficult to work with than those of most other pianos, which are pounded felt only. Before I even examine it, I will wager that the voicing on this one is in terrible shape. I can't imagine what the humidity has done to the felt covers on the hammers.

'Hmmm . . . What else can I tell you, Doctor? Two pedals – a sustaining pedal and an una corda. The dampers will run to the second B key above the middle octave – that is pretty typical. Erard dampers are located below the strings and held there by a spring, which is unusual, most piano dampers rest on the strings from above. I'll know when I look inside, but it should have cast-iron tension bars between the wrest plank and the rim, this was pretty standard by 1840; it served to support the tension of stronger steel wires, which were used because of their louder sound.' He touched the design that stretched above the keyboard. 'Look at the nameboard, it is mother-of-pearl.' He looked up to see a bemused look on Carroll's face, and laughed. 'Forgive me, I am getting carried away . . .'

'I am glad to see you are so pleased. I must confess, I was actually a bit concerned that you might be angry.'

'Angry? Good Lord, what would I be angry about?'

'I don't know. Part of me has felt that the piano's condition is my fault, that I put it at risk by bringing it here and that would anger a lover of musical instruments. I don't know if you remember, but I asked the War Office to give you an envelope, with instructions not to open it.' He paused. 'You may open it now. It is nothing, just a description of how I transported the piano to Mae Lwin, but I did not want you to read it until you saw that it was safe.'

'Is that what the letter was about? I *have* been quite curious. I thought perhaps it was something about the dangers here, which you might not want my wife to read . . . but the Erard's journey? Perhaps you are right, perhaps I should be angry. But I *am* a tuner. The only thing I care for more than pianos is repairing them. And regardless: it is here, and now that I am here as well . . .' he stopped and looked out of the window. 'Well, I can't think of any place more exciting and worthier of its music. Besides, the strings can stand up to incredible abuse, although perhaps not what *this* instrument has been through, and I certainly can't say the same about mother-of-pearl decoration. What I would be worried about is the sun and humidity, which can cause it to go out of tune in days.' He paused. 'Actually, Doctor, I do have one question. I have never spoken to you about this, and I couldn't find any mention of it in your letters, but I don't even know if you have played the piano yet, or what it has . . . accomplished.'

The Doctor put his hand on the Erard. 'Aah, Mr Drake. We haven't spoken about this because I don't have much to tell you. There was a celebration soon after I brought it here. An occasion notable for both sadness and rejoicing – you will read about it in my letter. The village insisted and I obliged. They made me play for hours. Of course, only then did I realize how out of tune the piano already was. If any of the Shan felt so too, they were polite, although I think that the instrument is strange enough for them; tuning was the least of their concerns. But I have great aspirations for it. You should have seen the faces of the children who came to watch.'

'You didn't play again?'

'Once or twice, but the piano was so flat—'

'Sharp probably, if it was its first time in a humid country. It will be flat now because of the dry season.'

'Terribly sharp then. And so I stopped playing. It was almost impossible for me to bear.'

'And yet, you thought you could tune it . . .' Edgar said, half to himself.

'I'm sorry, Mr Drake?'

'Well, someone who knows enough about pianos to select an 1840 Erard would know that it would go out of tune, especially in the jungle, that it would need a professional tuner. Yet, still, you thought you could do this yourself.'

The Doctor was quiet. 'That is what I told the army, but there are other reasons. I was overjoyed that they had granted my request and I was afraid to ask for more. At times my enthusiasm outruns my abilities. I have seen a piano tuned before and I thought I would try alone first. I thought that, after surgery, this would be easy.'

'I will forgive you for saying that,' said Edgar lightly. 'But I can teach you something about tuning if you like.'

Carroll nodded. 'Of course, but only for a little while. I should leave you alone. I have work to do. Besides, it has taken me a long time to become comfortable with observers in the surgery. I imagine it is even more difficult when it comes to treating sound.'

o

'These, Doctor, are my instruments.' Edgar opened his bag and spread them across the bench. 'I brought a basic set. This is a tuning hammer, these narrow-blade screwdrivers are for general use, this special thin screwdriver and drop-screw regulator are for the action. Let's see, . . . What else? Key-easing pliers and a key spacer, bending pliers, two damper-bending irons, a spring-adjusting hook, parallel pliers, a special thin capstan-screw regulator used for Erards for adjusting the hammer height – it is impossible to adjust the hammer height without this. Also: leather-covered wedges for tuning and coils of replacement piano wire of different gauges. There are other tools as well. These over here are specifically for voicing: a hammer iron, glue, and multiple extra voicing needles, as they frequently become bent.'

'Voicing? You keep using that word.'

'I am sorry, voicing means treating a piano's hammers so they produce a nice tone when they strike the strings. I am probably getting ahead of myself. You said you have seen a piano tuned?'

'Seen? Once or twice, briefly. But I have never had it explained to me.'

'Well, I'll wager that you will learn quickly. There are three basic components to tuning. Typically, tuners begin with regulating, which means aligning the action so that the hammers are at even heights and strike the strings briskly and fall back smoothly so a note can be played again. Usually that is the first step. *I* like to begin with a rough tuning, however. A piano must be tuned several times usually, as the act of tuning one string changes the dimensions of the soundboard so as to affect all the other strings. There are ways to avoid this – tuning strings sharp, for example – but, in my opinion, it is still impossible to predict the changes. Furthermore, the strings tend to settle, so it is better to leave the piano overnight before a second attempt. So I tune roughly, regulate, and then tune again – that is *my* technique, *others* do it differently. After this comes voicing, the repair of the hammer felt itself. Erard experts are usually good voicers, if I might be so immodest – the combination of the leather and felt makes the hammers more difficult to work with. There are other smaller jobs as well. For example, I need to think about whether there is a way to waterproof the soundboard. Of course, all of this depends on what is wrong.'

'And do you have any notion what will need to be repaired? Or will you not know until you play?'

'Actually, I can probably guess now. I suppose it is not unlike thinking about a patient's history before the examination. I can tell you and then I will let you go.' He turned to the piano and looked at it closely.

'To begin with, there will be a problem with the soundboard, the belly. This is certain. Whether it has cracked yet I don't know. It is very lucky it has been in Burma for only a year and thus has suffered only one year's cycle of humidity. Fortunately, as long as the cracks are minor, they can easily be repaired, or ignored even – often it is only a cosmetic concern. Bigger cracks will be more of a problem.'

He tapped his fingers on the case. 'The piano will be out of tune, of course. That goes without saying. The dry season will have resulted in the soundboard shrinking, loosening the strings and dropping the pitch. If substantial enough, I may have to raise the pitch as much as a full semitone and leave the piano for at least another twenty-four hours before fine-tuning further. Of course, the problem with doing this is that, when the rain comes again, the board will expand and the increased tension could cause terrible damage. This should have been expected, but the military didn't seem to consider it. I will have to think about this problem; perhaps I will need to teach someone here to tune . . .' Suddenly he stopped. 'My God, I forgot. In the note you sent me in Mandalay, you wrote the piano was shot. I can't believe I didn't think about this until now. It changes everything. Please, may I see the damage?'

The Doctor walked to the side of the piano and raised the lid. A pungent odour rose from the piano. It was unfamiliar, curried and heavy. 'Excuse the smell, Mr Drake. Turmeric. One of the Shan men suggested I put it into the piano to protect it from termites. You probably don't do that in London.' He laughed. 'But it seems to have worked.'

The lid opened away from the window, so it was dark inside the piano, and Edgar saw the bullet hole immediately, an oval crack in the soundboard through which the floor could be seen. Carroll's letter was right, the bullet had split all three strings of the fourth-octave A key, leaving them loose, twisting back towards the tuning and hitch pins like strands of uncombed hair. Shot through the belly, he thought, and briefly considered telling the Doctor the stories of the Reign of Terror. Instead he looked inside. There was a nick on the inside of the piano lid, in the trajectory of the bullet, but no exit hole; it probably did not have enough momentum to break through the lid. 'Did you take the bullet out?' he asked, and to answer the question himself he struck a key. There was a rattling on the soundboard. Many clients who called in London sought his services for 'a terrible racket', which turned out to be a coin or screw which had accidentally been dropped into a grand and sat rattling on the soundboard when it vibrated. He squinted into the piano, found the bullet and picked it out. 'A souvenir,' he said. 'May I keep it?'

'Of course,' said the Doctor. 'Is the damage serious?'

Edgar dropped the bullet into his pocket and peered back inside. 'Actually, not too bad. I will have to replace the strings and I need to take another look at the soundboard, but I think it will be all right.'

'Perhaps you should start. I don't want to keep you any longer.'

'I probably should. I hope I haven't bored you.'

'No, not in the slightest, Mr Drake. It has been a pleasure – most educational. I can see I have chosen my help well.' He extended his hand. 'Good luck with the patient. Shout if you need anything.' He turned and walked from the room, closing the door behind him. The force sent a tremor through the floor. There was a faint chime of the stirring of strings.

o

Edgar walked back to the bench. He didn't sit; he always told his apprentices that pianos were best tuned if the tuner was standing.

Now to begin, he thought. He hit the middle-octave C key. Too low. He tried one octave below and then C in the other octaves. Same problem: all almost a full semitone off. The treble notes were even worse. He played the first movement of the *English Suites*. Without the key with broken strings. He was always self-conscious about his skill as a pianist, but he loved the cool ivory of the keyboard, the swing and sway of playing a melody. He realized it had been months now since he had played and he stopped after several bars; the piano was so miserably out of tune that it was painful for him to listen. He could see why the Doctor had not wanted to play it.

His first tasks would be what he liked to call 'structural repairs'. On the Erard this meant mending the broken strings and the soundboard. He walked around the piano, to the hinges of the lid, removed the hinge pins and put them in his pocket. He pulled on the lid, sliding it along the top of the piano until it was balanced on the edge of the case. He bent at the knees, lifted it and set it gingerly against one of the walls. With the lid out of the way, there was enough light to work inside the piano body.

It was difficult to see all the damage to the soundboard from above, so he climbed beneath the piano and inspected its belly. The entry wound was more visible. A crack ran with the grain, but only for several inches. This is good, he thought. Although the hole would remain, he could easily repair the crack with 'shimming', which meant inserting filler wood into the holes. He only hoped the crack wouldn't affect the piano's sound. Although some tuners claimed that shimming was necessary to re-establish tension in the board, he believed that for the most part the repair was superficial, for clients who were disconcerted by long cracks in the inside of their pianos. So he hadn't anticipated shimming – it seemed superfluous given the setting – and he hadn't brought a planer to smooth out the board. But the beauty of the Erard caused him to reconsider.

There was another problem. Shimming was usually done with spruce, but Edgar hadn't brought any and he didn't know if spruce grew in the area. He looked about the room and his eyes settled on the bamboo walls. I would be the first to use bamboo to mend a piano, he thought with some pride, And it is so resonant that perhaps it will make a sound more beautiful than spruce. Besides, he had seen the Burmese peeling strips off the bamboo, which meant that the wood could probably be shaped with a penknife and he wouldn't need a planer. It wasn't without risks; using two different types of wood meant that they might respond to the humidity differently and the crack would reopen. But he welcomed the opportunity to innovate and decided to try.

First he had to file the hole, which took nearly an hour. He worked slowly; the cracks could run and damage the entire sound-board. When he had finished, he rose and sawed a piece of bamboo from the wall. This he carved and coated with glue, and worked into the hole. The broken strings allowed him to reach it from above, and he smoothed the surface. It took a long time – the blade was small – and while he worked he realized that he could have gone to ask Carroll for help, for a planer or another larger knife, perhaps for other wood. But something discouraged him. He liked the idea that he could take the wall of the fort, a product of war, and transform it into the mechanics of sound.

When he had finished shimming, he set to work on the broken strings. He removed and coiled them, and dropped them into his pocket. Another souvenir. In his bag he found string of the correct gauge and unwound it, running it from the tuning pin to the hitch pin and back. He attached the third string to its own hitch pin, and then ran it alongside its companions. When he cut it, he left a length the width of his hand, which would measure three turns around the tuning pin. The strings were bright and silver next to the dull sheen of their neighbours, and he tuned them sharp, for they would settle.

When the strings and pins were finished he walked back to the front of the piano. To raise the pitch of the entire piano, he began at the centre of the keyboard and worked outwards, striking keys and tightening strings, working quickly now. It still took nearly an hour.

It was early afternoon when he began the task of regulating. The piano's action is a complex mechanism, he would explain to clients, communicating between key and hammer, and thus the pianist and sound. Now he removed the nameboard to reach the action. He evened the hammers' heights, eased sluggish jack centres, and adjusted the set-off, where the jack kicks out from beneath the hammer. Between regulating he took breaks, easing keys, adjusting the shift of the una corda pedal. When he finally rose, dusty and tired, the piano was in workable order. He had been lucky that there were no major repairs, such as a cracked wrest plank. He knew he didn't have the tools to carry out such a repair. He had little idea how much time had passed, and realized only as he was leaving that the sun was sinking quickly over the forest.

o

It was dark when he met the Doctor in his office. A half-eaten plate of rice and vegetables was resting on the desk. The Doctor was seated before a stack of papers, reading.

'Good evening.'

The Doctor looked up. 'Well, Mr Drake, you have finished at last. The cook thought I should send for you, but I told him that you wouldn't want to be disturbed. He complained when I told him to wait until you had finished, but fortunately he is a music lover himself, and I was able to convince him that the sooner you finished the sooner he would be able to hear the piano.' He smiled. 'Please, sit.'

'Forgive me for not washing,' said Edgar, sitting on a small teak stool. 'I'm starving. I thought that I would bathe straight after dinner and then go to bed. I want to get up as early as possible tomorrow. But I wanted to ask you something.' He shifted forward on the stool, as if to speak to the Doctor in confidence. 'I mentioned this before – I do not know if the soundboard will be able to survive another rainy season. Not everyone would agree with this, but I think that we should try to waterproof it. In Rangoon and Mandalay I saw a variety of wooden instruments which must suffer from the same problems. Do you know who might know about this?'

'Certainly. There is a Burmese lute player who used to play for King Thibaw, who has a Shan wife in Mae Lwin. With the fall of the court, he has returned here to farm. Sometimes he plays when I have visitors. I will find him for you tomorrow.'

'Thank you. It will be easy to paint the bottom of the soundboard; the top is harder because one has to go beneath the strings, but there is space on the side through which I should be able to run a cloth coated with the stuff, and paint it that way. I think that will do something to protect against the humidity, although it is far from perfect . . . Oh, I have another question: when I work tomorrow, I will need something to heat the voicing iron, a little stove perhaps. Can you find that as well?'

'Certainly – much easier. I can ask Nok Lek to bring a Shan-style brazier to the room. They can get quite hot. But it is small. What is the tool like?'

'Small as well. I couldn't bring much here.'

'Excellent then,' said the Doctor. 'I am very pleased so far, Mr Drake. Tell me, when do you expect to be done?'

'Oh, it can be played by tomorrow night. But I should probably stay longer. I generally make a follow-up visit two weeks after the first tuning.'

'Take as long as you want. You are not in a hurry to return to Mandalay?'

'No, no hurry at all.' He hesitated. 'You mean to say that I must return to Mandalay once the piano is tuned?'

The Doctor smiled, 'We *are* running serious risks by allowing a civilian to come here, Mr Drake.' He saw the tuner look down at his hands, 'I think you are beginning to discover some of the reasons why I have lived here so long.'

Edgar interjected, 'Oh, I am hardly fit to *live* here! It's just that, with the condition the piano is in, I am afraid that with the onset of the rains the piano will be driven sharp and create all sorts of tuning problems, or perhaps even more serious damage, and in two weeks I will receive another letter requesting that I return to Mae Lwin to mend the piano again.'

'Of course, take your time.' The Doctor nodded politely and turned back to his papers.

o

That night Edgar couldn't sleep. He lay inside the cocoon of mosquito net, and ran his fingers back and forth over the newly-formed callus on the inside of his pointer finger, The tuner's callus, Katherine, It is the product of the constant free plucking of strings.

He thought of the Erard. Certainly, he had seen more beautiful pianos in his life. Yet he had never seen anything like the image of the Salween, framed by the window, reflected in the upturned lid. He wondered if the Doctor had planned it, or even designed the room with the piano in mind. Suddenly he recalled the sealed envelope, which the Doctor had mentioned that afternoon. He slipped out from beneath the mosquito net and he rummaged through his bags until he found it. Inside the draping, he lit a candle.

To the Piano Tuner, to be opened only upon arriving in Mae Lwin, A.C.

He began to read.

23 March, 1886

Report on the movement of an Erard piano from Mandalay to Mae Lwin, the Shan States
　　Surgeon-Major Anthony J. Carroll

Gentlemen,

I herein report the successful transport and delivery of the 1840 Erard grand piano sent from your office on 21 January, 1886 to Mandalay, and subsequently relayed to my site. The following is a detailed account of the transfer. Please excuse the informality of some of this letter, but I feel it necessary to convey the drama involved in this most demanding effort.

　　The shipment of the piano from London to Mandalay was previously reported by Colonel Fitzgerald. Briefly, the piano was carried on a P&O Line mail steamer bound for Madras and then Rangoon. The voyage was relatively uneventful: rumour has it that the piano was removed from its packing crate and played by a sergeant in a regimental band, to the delight of the crew and passengers. In Rangoon the piano was transferred to another steamship and carried north on the Irrawaddy River. This is the typical route and again the passage proceeded without incident. Thus the piano arrived in Mandalay on the morning of 22 February, where I was able to receive it personally. I am aware that there have been certain protests about my leaving my post to come to Mandalay to receive the piano, as well as, I might add, some criticisms about the effort, cost, and necessity of such an unusual shipment. To the former criticism, the Office of the Political Administrator will testify that I had been summoned to a meeting regarding recent insurgencies by the monk, U Ottama, in Chin State, and thus was already in Mandalay to receive the piano. Against the latter slander, I can only protest that such attacks are but *ad hominem* in nature and I do suspect a certain jealousy in my detractors; I continue to control the only outpost in the Shan States not to have been attacked by rebel forces, and have made the most significant progress of anyone with regard to our ultimate task of pacification and treaty-signing.

But I digress, gentlemen, for which I beg your forgiveness. To continue: we received the piano at the docks and transported it by horse cart to the town centre, where we immediately began to prepare for its transfer. The route to our site presented two general types of terrain. The first, from Mandalay to the foot of the Shan Hills, is a flat and dry plain. For this leg I commissioned a Burmese timber elephant, despite my reluctance to entrust such a delicate instrument to an animal that spends its days hurling logs. Employing Brahmin cows had been suggested, but there are times when the track grows too narrow for a pair, and it was decided that an elephant would be better. The second leg presented more daunting challenges, as the paths were too steep and narrow for such an animal. It was decided that we would have to continue on foot. Fortunately, the piano was lighter than I expected and could be lifted and carried by six men. Although I had considered travelling with a larger group, and perhaps an army escort, I did not want the locals to associate the piano with a military goal. My men would be enough; I knew the route well and there had been only rare reports of dacoit attacks. We immediately set about making a litter on which to carry the piano.

We commenced our walk on the morning of 24 February, after I had finished with official matters at army headquarters. The piano was loaded onto a large munitions cart. This in turn was attached to the elephant, a giant of a beast with sad eyes, who seemed utterly unfazed by her unusual load. She moved briskly; fortunately we had received the shipment in the dry season and we were blessed with excellent weather for our journey. Had it been raining, I think the trip would have been impossible, with inestimable damage to the piano, as well as a heavy physical toll on our men. As it was, the journey would be difficult enough.

We marched out of Mandalay, followed by a line of curious children. I rode on horseback. The ruts in the road caused the hammers to bounce against the piano strings, which made a lovely accompaniment to an arduous walk. We made our first camp at dusk. Although the elephant moved steadily, I realized that, once on foot, we would progress much more slowly. This concerned me: I had already been in Mandalay for one week. I contemplated returning to Mae Lwin ahead of the piano, but the men tended to be rough with the instrument, and despite repeatedly explaining the delicacy of its internal parts, I still had to order them to treat it gently. Considering the great effort the army has put into transporting the piano, and the important purpose it will serve, it seemed foolish to lose the instrument to impatience so close to our final goal.

Wherever we stopped we attracted a group of locals who crowded around the piano and speculated on its use. In the early days of our trek either I or one of the men would explain its function, and we would then be barraged with requests to hear it played. In such a manner, I was cajoled into playing no less than fourteen times in the first three days of our journey. The locals were delighted by the music, yet the constant playing exhausted me, as they would only disperse when I told them that the instrument had 'run out of breath', while of course really I meant the musician. On the third day I commanded my men not to tell anyone the true function of the piano. To any enquiring villager, they reported it was a terrible weapon, and subsequently our passage was given a wider berth.

The fastest route to Mae Lwin is to travel north-east to the Salween River and there descend by the river to the site. But with the drought the water has run low and, fearing for the piano, I chose to march to the bank directly across from Mae Lwin and cross there. After three days the road became steeper, rising out of the Irrawaddy basin onto the Shan Plateau. Reluctantly, we offloaded the piano from the elephant cart and transferred it to the litter, which we had constructed in the form of the palanquins used in Shan festivals – two parallel beams for the men to hold with added supporting cross-beams beneath the piano. The piano was loaded so that the keyboard was facing forward, since it was best balanced this way. The elephant's driver returned with her to Mandalay.

As the trail rose, I realized that the decision to carry the piano was well informed – the track was far too treacherous to carry it on a cart as we had across the lowlands. But my satisfaction with this decision was tempered by the sight of my men struggling beneath the load, slipping and stumbling to keep it from crashing to the ground. I truly pitied them and did my best to boost their morale, promising a festival in Mae Lwin to celebrate the arrival of the piano.

Days passed, and the routine was the same. We rose at sunrise, ate a quick breakfast and then once again raised the litter and continued our walk. It was unusually hot and the sun was merciless. I must admit that despite the discomfort I felt at making my men labour under such a burden, it was a stunning vision, the six men dripping with sweat and the piano glistening, like those new hand-coloured photographs which are now so in fashion in England and occasionally trickle into the marketplaces here – the white turbans and trousers, the dark brown bodies, the piano black.

And then about four days from camp, with some of the steepest terrain remaining, disaster struck.

On a particularly eroded jungle path, as I rode ahead chopping at the overgrowth with my sword, I heard a scream and a ringing crash. I ran back to the Erard. The first thing I saw was the piano and, after hearing the crash and thinking it destroyed, I was momentarily relieved. But then my eyes moved to the left of the piano to where the five tattooed bodies huddled around a sixth. Sensing my presence, one of the men yelled '*Ngu!*' or 'Snake!' and pointed to his fallen comrade. I understood immediately. Struggling forward, the young man had not seen the serpent, which must have been angered by my horse and struck his leg. He had dropped the piano and fallen. The remaining men had done their best to balance the Erard and keep it from crashing to the ground.

When I reached the young man his eyelids were already beginning to droop, the paralysis setting in. Somehow, he or another of his companions had managed to catch the snake and kill it; when I arrived at the scene, it lay dead and broken by the trail. The men were using a Shan word for it which I didn't know, but called it 'mahauk' in Burmese, known to us by the genus *Naja*, or the Asian cobra. But I had little stomach for scientific investigation at the time. The wound still bled from two parallel gashes. The men looked to me for medical advice, but there was little we could do. I crouched by the young man and held his hand. The only words I could say were 'I am sorry,' as he had fallen in my service. Death from cobra bite is terrible: the venom paralyses the diaphragm so the patient suffocates. It took but half an hour for him to die. In Burma few snakes other than the Asian cobra kill so fast. A Shan remedy for snake bites is to tie off the wound, which we did (although all knew that this would be to little avail), to suck on the wound (which I did), and to apply a paste of pounded spiders (but we had none and, in truth, I have always doubted the efficacy of this cure). Instead one of the Shan men said a prayer. At the side of the track, flies had already begun to gather about the snake. Some landed on the young man and one of us swatted them away.

I knew from Shan custom that we couldn't leave the body

in the forest, an act that would also have offended the respect for a fallen comrade which I believe is one of the shining principles of our armed forces. And the horse spooked when we approached her with the body. Yet simple arithmetic suggested the difficulty of carrying him out of the jungle. If six men had struggled under the piano, how would five carry the piano and their friend? Thus I realized that I too would have to bear the litter. At first the men protested, suggesting instead that one of them return to the nearest village and hire another porter. But I objected; we were already several days behind my expected arrival in Mae Lwin.

We lifted the young man and set his body on the top of the piano. I searched for rope, but we did not have enough to secure the body adequately to the Erard. Seeing this, one of the men removed the young man's turban and unravelled it. He tied it around one of the young man's wrists, passed it beneath the piano and tied it to the other wrist. Then he passed it back under and across to do the same with the opposite leg. For the young man's other leg we used the short rope. His head fell back over the keyboard, his long hair still tied in a small bundle. We were fortunate to find the means of securing the body; all were loath to think of the corpse sliding off the piano as we passed along the trail. Had not one of the Shan suggested using the turban, I do not know how we would have proceeded. Admittedly, the idea had also occurred to me, but to remove a Shan's turban in life is a mortal insult. And I did not know the customs with regard to such a death.

And so we set out. I took the young man's place at the left side of the piano and in doing so sensed a certain relief among my friends as I suspected that superstition held this to be a cursed position. By my reckoning, if we continued at our previous pace, it would be four days before we reached Mae Lwin and the body's stench would be horrific. In my mind, I made the decision that we would walk through the night, but did not tell my comrades, as I sensed their spirits were already flagging following the death of their friend. And so I joined the tri-chrome photograph, and we marched on, our friend with arms stretched over the piano, the horse now tied behind, where it walked at a leisurely pace and nibbled on the trees.

What can I share about the following hours but that they were some of the most terrible of my life? We tripped and struggled beneath the load of the piano. The litter dug into our shoulders. I tried to protect myself by removing my shirt and rolling it up to place on my shoulder, but it did little to lessen the scraping of the boards, and my skin was soon torn and bleeding. I felt pity for my friends, who had not once asked for something to soften their loads, and I saw their skin was raw. The path grew worse. One of the front bearers was forced to carry a sword in his free hand to try to clear our way. The piano caught on creepers and branches. Several times we nearly fell. On the piano's back, the young man's body had begun to stiffen with rigor mortis, so that when he shifted on the piano his arms seemed to pull at their tethers, giving the fleeting impression that he was trying to escape, until one looked once again at open, empty eyes.

Late that evening I told the men that we would walk through the night. It was a difficult decision, since I felt as if I could hardly raise my legs. But they did not protest; perhaps they were equally concerned about the body. And so, after a short break for supper, we loaded the piano back onto our shoulders. We were fortunate that it was the dry season, the sky was clear and we had a half-moon to partially light our way. But in the deeper parts of the jungle we fell into darkness, stumbling. I had one small lantern, and this I lit and hung from the cloth that bound one of the dead man's legs, illuminating the underbelly of the piano so it must have seemed as if it was floating.

We marched for two full days. Finally, one evening, the front man shouted with tired glee that he could see the bank of the Salween through the trees. The news unburdened our load and we began to walk faster. At the edge of the river we shouted to the guard on the other side, who was so surprised to see us that he took off, running up the track and into camp. We set the piano down on the muddy bank and collapsed.

It wasn't long before a group of men gathered on the other bank, piled into a dugout and rowed across. The shock over the dead body was mitigated only by their relief that all of us had not suffered the same fate. They had long feared us dead. After much discussion, two men rowed back across the river and returned with another dugout. This we lashed to the first and on top placed the piano and the young man. In this manner, the piano crossed the Salween. There was space on the raft for only two men, so I watched it from the bank. It was a strange sight indeed – the piano floating in midstream, with two men squatting below it and the body of a third stretched out above. As they lowered the piano onto the beach, the lines of the body reminded me of van der Weyden's *Descent from the Cross*, an image which will be permanently fixed in my memory.

And so our journey ended. A funeral was held for the young man and then, two days later, a festival to celebrate the arrival of the piano. There I had my first opportunity to play it for the village, but only briefly, for sadly it is already quite out of tune, a problem I will attempt to correct myself. The piano was temporarily stored in the grain room, and we made hasty arrangements to begin construction of a separate music room. But this is a story for further correspondence.

Surgeon-Major Anthony J. Carroll
Mae Lwin, the Shan States

Edgar blew out the candle and lay back. It was cool in the room. On the roof branches scratched against the thatch. He tried to sleep, but found himself thinking of the story, of his own journey to camp, of the burned fields and the steep jungles, of the dacoit attack, of how long it had been since he left. At last he opened his eyes and sat up. The room was dark, its features blurred by the mosquito net.

He lit the candle and looked back at the letter. The light of the flame cast his shadow against the inside of the net, and he began to read it again, thinking, Perhaps I will send it to Katherine with my next letter home. He promised himself this would be soon.

Somewhere in the course of the Erard's journey onto the plateau the candle flickered out.

He awoke with the letter still resting on his chest.

o

He didn't bother to shave or wash, but dressed quickly and walked straight to the piano room. At the door he reconsidered and decided it would be proper to say good morning to the Doctor, and ran back down the stairs to the river. Halfway, he met Nok Lek.

'Is the Doctor taking breakfast by the river?'

'No, sir, not this morning. This morning the Doctor is away.'

'Away? And where did he go?'

'I don't know.'

Edgar scratched his head. 'That's odd. He didn't tell you?'

'No, Mr Drake.'

'Is he often away like this?'

'Yes, he is. Very often. He is important. Like a Prince.'

'A Prince . . .' Edgar paused. 'And when do you expect him back?'

'I don't know, sir. He doesn't tell me.'

'Well, then . . . did he have any messages for me?'

'No, sir.'

'Strange . . . I would have thought—'

'He said you will tune the piano all day, Mr Drake.'

'Of course.' Edgar paused. 'Well then, I will be off to work.'

'Shall I bring breakfast to room, Mr Drake?'

'Thank you, that would be very kind.'

o

He began the day's work by voicing the hammers, repairing damaged felt so that the hammer strike would produce a good clean tone. Back in England, he often waited until fine-tuning was complete before voicing, but he had been bothered by the tone: it was either too hard and tinny or too dull and soft. He needled the harder felt to soften it and pressed the softer felt with the voicing iron to harden it, reshaping the hammer heads so that they presented an even surface to the strings. He tested the voicing by running through each octave chromatically in broken arpeggios, and finally by pounding individual keys so that the hardness deep within the felt would be noticed.

Finally he was ready to fine-tune the piano. He began an octave below the string that had been shattered by the bullet. He inserted lever wedges to mute off the side strings of each note in the octave, so that when the key was struck only the middle string would vibrate. He struck the key, reached into the body of the piano and turned the tuning pin. When the middle string was tuned he moved to the side strings, and when each note was in tune he moved one octave lower – as a builder would first lay the foundations of a house, he always told his apprentices – falling into the familiar pattern, twisting the tuning pins, testing them, key pin key, a rhythm only broken by absent-minded slaps at mosquitoes.

With the octave spanned, he then turned to the notes that lay in between, to set them in equal temperament, so that the notes were all equally spaced along the octave. It was a concept apprentices often found difficult to understand. Each note produces a sound at a particular frequency, he would explain, Strings in tune with one another can harmonize, while out-of-tune strings produce frequencies which overlap to produce a rhythmic pulse, known as a beat, a synchrony of slightly discordant sounds. On a piano tuned perfectly in a particular key, there should be no beats when correct intervals are played. But then it is impossible to play the piano in any other key. Equal temperament was an innovation that allowed for more than one key to be played on a single instrument, the sacrifice being that no key would be in perfect tune. To tune in equal temperament meant deliberately creating beats, adjusting the strings finely so that only a well-trained ear could discern that they were slightly, if necessarily, out of tune.

Edgar hummed softly as he worked. It was his habit, often to Katherine's chagrin, while he was working, to become completely absorbed in tuning. Do you *see* anything when you are working? she had asked soon after they were married, leaning over the side of the piano. See what? he had answered. You know, see anything, the piano, the strings, me. Of course I see you, and he took her hand and kissed it. Edgar, please! Please, I am asking how you work, I am being serious, Do you see anything while you work? How couldn't I, Why? It just seems that you disappear, into a different place, maybe a world of notes. Edgar laughed, What a strange world that would be, dear. And he leaned forward and kissed her. But in truth he did understand what she was trying to ask. He worked with his eyes open, but when he finished, when he thought back on the day, he could never remember a single visible image, only what he had heard, a landscape marked by tone and timbre, intervals, vibrating, They are my colours.

And so now, while he worked, he thought little of the Doctor's letter or his absence, nor did he notice that he had observers, three little boys who watched him through slats in the bamboo wall. They whispered and giggled, and had Edgar not been lost in the maze of tone and mechanics, and had he spoken Shan, he would have heard them wonder how this could be the great musician, the man who would repair their singing elephant. How peculiar these British are, they would tell their friends. Their musicians play alone and you cannot dance or sing to such strange, slow melodies. But after an hour even the novelty of espionage wore off and the little boys walked glumly back to the river to swim.

The day drew on. Shortly past noon Nok Lek brought Edgar his lunch, a large bowl of rice noodles drenched in a thick broth, which the boy said was made from a type of bean, garnished with minced meat and peppers. He also brought a jar of paste made from burnt rice husks, which Edgar painted over the bottom of the soundboard before stopping to eat. After several bites he returned to work.

In the early afternoon clouds arrived, but it didn't rain. The room grew humid. He always worked slowly, but he was surprised by his own deliberation. A thought that had begun to plague him when he first started on the piano now returned. In a matter of hours he would be done with the tuning and would no longer be needed in Mae Lwin. He would be forced to return to Mandalay and then to London. But I want this, he told himself, for it means I will be home again. Yet the immediacy of the departure became more real as he worked, his fingers raw from the strings, the monotony hypnotizing, crank, key, listen, crank, key, listen, the tuning spreading over the piano like ink spilled on paper.

Edgar had three keys left to tune when the clouds parted, and the sun shone through the window, lighting the room. He had replaced the lid on the piano overnight, and raised it while he tuned. Now he could once again see the reflection of the view in the polished mahogany. He stood and watched the Salween flow through its square of light on the piano's surface. He walked to the window and stared out at the river.

Two weeks until the piano needs to be tuned again, he had told the Doctor. What he didn't tell him was that now that the piano was tuned and regulated and voiced, to keep it in fine tune would be relatively easy, he could teach the Doctor, perhaps even one of his Shan assistants. He could tell him this, he thought, and he could leave the tuning hammer, This is only right. And then he thought, I have been away from home for a long time, Perhaps too long.

He could tell him this, and he would, eventually, but he reminded himself there was no need to rush things either.

Besides, he thought, I have only just arrived.

FIFTEEN

DOCTOR CARROLL DIDN'T return the next day as planned, nor the day after that. The camp seemed empty and Edgar saw neither Nok Lek nor Khin Myo. He was surprised that he thought of her only now, that he had been so absorbed in the excitement surrounding the piano. He had seen her only once in the few days since their arrival. Then she had passed him while he was with the Doctor, had nodded politely and stopped to whisper something to Carroll in Burmese. She stood close to the Doctor when she spoke and looked past him at Edgar, who quickly shifted his gaze out to the river. He had tried to see if there was something in their interaction, a touch or shared smile. But she only bowed slightly, and moved off gracefully down the path.

He spent the morning making minor adjustments to the Erard, fine-tuning some of the strings, touching up areas on the sound-board that had not been covered with enough resin. But he soon tired of the work. The piano was well tuned – perhaps not his finest job, he conceded to himself, as he didn't have all the tools he needed – but there were few other improvements that could further help the piano, given the circumstances.

It was noon when he left the Erard and walked down to the Salween. By the river several men stood out on jagged rocks that jutted into the water, casting fishing nets, crouching, waiting. He laid out a blanket and sat in the shade of a willow and watched two women beating clothes against a rock, naked save for their *hta mains*, which had been pulled up and tied around their chests in modesty. He wondered if this was a Shan custom or merely an English import.

His mind wandered aimlessly from the river, over the mountains, to Mandalay, further. He wondered what the army thought of his absence. Perhaps it hasn't even been noticed, he thought, for Khin Myo has also gone, and Captain Nash-Burnham is in Rangoon, and he wondered, How many days have I been away? He hoped they had not contacted Katherine, for certainly she would worry, and he could comfort himself only with the thought that she was far away and that news travelled slowly. He tried to calculate how long he had been away from home, but was surprised when he realized that he wasn't even certain how long he had been in Mae Lwin. The trip across the Shan Plateau seemed without time, a moment, a kaleidoscope of silver temples and deep jungle, and muddied rivers and swift-moving ponies.

Without time, Edgar Drake thought, and he thought of the world outside suspended, It is as if I left London only this morning. He liked the idea, Perhaps this is so, Indeed my watch stopped in Rangoon, In England Katherine is only now returning home from the docks, Our bed still holds the fading warmth of two bodies, Perhaps it will still be warm when I return. And his thoughts pushed forward, One day I will climb out of the valley of the Salween and walk back across the hills to Mandalay, and I will sit one more night and watch the *yôkthe pwè*, and this time the story will be different, a story of return, and I will take the steamer back down the river, and there I will meet soldiers and over gin I will add my tales to theirs. Forward, The trip will be faster now, for we will travel with the current, and in Rangoon I will return to the Shwedagon and I will see how the turmeric-painted woman's baby has grown, I will board another steamer, and my bags will be heavier for I will carry gifts of silver necklaces and embroidered cloth, and musical instruments for a new collection. On the steamer

I will spend my days staring at the same mountains I saw when I arrived, only this time I will stand on the starboard side, The train will speed across India as before, it will climb away from the Ganges like a prayer, the sun will rise behind us and set before us, and we will chase it, Perhaps somewhere, at some lonely station, I will hear the end of the Poet-Wallah's story. In the Red Sea I will meet a man, and I will tell him I have heard songs, but not his. In the Red Sea it will be dry, and the humidity will be drawn from my watch in invisible vapours, it will begin to work again, ticking, The time is no later than the day I departed.

He heard the sound of footsteps enter his daydream, and turned. Khin Myo stood in the shade of the willow. 'May I join you?'

'Ma Khin Myo. What a pleasant surprise,' he said, pulled from his reverie, 'Please, please sit down.' He made a space for her on the blanket. When she had sat down and smoothed her *hta main* over her legs, he said, 'I was just thinking about you earlier today. You vanished. I have hardly seen you since we arrived.'

'I left you and the Doctor alone. I know you have work to do.'

'I have been busy, I know. I regretted not seeing you, though.' His words felt somehow stilted and he added, 'I enjoyed our conversations in Mandalay, on the way here.' He wanted to say something else, but felt a sudden awkwardness about her being there. He had almost forgotten how attractive she was. Her hair was brushed back and fastened with a needle of ivory. Her blouse rustled lightly in the breeze that slipped through the willow branches. Below the damascene border of the sleeves, her arms were bare, and she held her hands folded together on her *hta main*.

'Nok Lek told me that you had finished,' she said.

'This morning, I think, although there is still some work remaining. The piano was in serious disrepair.'

'Doctor Carroll told me so. I think he feels it was his fault.' He noticed that she tilted her head slightly from side to side when she joked, a habit he had seen in many Indians. He had seen her do it before, but was particularly struck by it now. It was quite subtle, as if she was enjoying an inner joke, which was much funnier and much more profound than her words suggested.

'I know. He shouldn't, though. I am quite pleased. The piano will sound wonderful.'

'He did say that you seemed happy.' She smiled and turned to him. 'Do you know what you will do, now?'

'Now?'

'Now that you have finished. Will you return to Mandalay?' she asked.

He laughed. '*Will* I? Why, of course – I must eventually. Perhaps not straight away. I want to wait to be certain the piano has no other problems. And after that it is only fair that, after this long trip, I hear it in a performance. But then – I don't know.'

They were both silent and turned to look towards the river. Out of the corner of his eye, Edgar saw her look down suddenly, as if embarrassed by a thought, and run her finger along the iridescent silk of her skirt. He turned to her. 'Is everything all right?'

She blushed. 'Of course, I was just thinking of something else.' Silence again, and then suddenly she added, 'You are different.'

Edgar swallowed, startled. She had spoken so softly that he had to ask himself if it was her voice or just the rustling of the branches. 'I'm sorry?'

She said, 'I have been with you for many hours, in Mandalay, travelling. Most other visitors would have told me about themselves within minutes. And yet I only know that you are from England and that you have come to tune the piano.' She played with the edge of her *hta main*. Edgar wondered if it was a sign of nervousness, as an Englishman would finger his hat in his hands.

'I am sorry if I am too direct, Mr Drake,' she added when he didn't answer. 'Please don't be offended.'

'No, I don't mind,' he said. But he wasn't certain how to respond. He found himself surprised at the remark, but even more that she, who had been so reserved before, had said it. 'I am not used to being asked about myself. Especially not by . . .' he paused.

'Not by a woman?'

Edgar said nothing.

'It is fine if you were thinking that, I wouldn't blame you. I know all that is written about women of the East. I can read your magazines and I understand your conversations, remember. I know what they say, I have seen the way the sketch artists draw us in your newspapers.'

Edgar felt himself blushing, 'They are terrible.'

'Not all. Many of them are right. Besides . . . to be painted as a beautiful dancing young girl is better than being painted as a savage – as your newspapers show our men.'

'Rubbish, mainly,' insisted Edgar. 'I wouldn't pay much attention . . .'

'No, I don't mind, I only wonder, or worry, about those who come here expecting their own imaginings.'

Edgar shifted uneasily, 'I am sure once they arrive they see it isn't so,' he said.

'Or they simply change us to fit that image.'

'I . . .' Edgar paused, caught by her words. He stared at her, thinking.

'I am sorry. I did not mean to speak so strongly, Mr Drake.'

'No . . . no, not at all,' he nodded now with the resonance of a thought. 'No, I do want to talk to you, but I am somewhat shy. It is my character, really. At home in London, too.'

'I don't care. I don't mind talking. I get lonely here sometimes. I speak some Shan and many of the villagers speak some Burmese, but we are very different. Most have never left their village.'

'You have the Doctor—'. Immediately he regretted saying this.

'That is something I wish I had told you in Mandalay. If only to save you from having to ask.'

He felt the sudden and unique relief that comes when a suspicion is answered. 'He is away often,' he said.

Khin Myo looked up at him, as if surprised by his words. 'He is an important man,' she said.

'Do you know where he goes?'

'Where? No.' She tilted her head. 'Away, only. It is not my concern.'

'I might think that it is. You said you get lonely.'

She stared at him longer this time. 'It is different,' she said simply.

There was a sadness in her voice and Edgar waited for her to speak again. She was silent now. He said, 'I am sorry. I didn't intend to be inconsiderate.'

'No.' She looked down. 'You ask me many questions. That is also different.' A tremor of wind ran through the trees. 'You have someone, Mr Drake.'

'I do,' said Edgar slowly, relieved now that the conversation had moved away from the Doctor. 'Her name is Katherine.'

'It is a nice name,' said Khin Myo.

'Yes . . . yes, I suppose so. I am so used to it that I hardly think of it as a name any more. When you know someone so well it is as if they lose their names.'

She smiled at him. 'May I ask how long you have been married?'

'Eighteen years. We met when I was an apprentice tuner. I tuned her family's piano.'

'She must be beautiful,' Khin Myo said.

'Beautiful . . .' Edgar was struck by the innocence with which she asked the question. 'She is . . . although we are not young.' He continued awkwardly, if only to fill the silence. 'She was *very* beautiful, at least in my eyes . . . talking about her makes me miss her greatly.'

'I am sorry—'

'No, not at all. It is wonderful, in its way. Many men who have been married eighteen years have fallen out of love with their wives . . .'. He stopped and looked out at the river. 'I suppose I *am* different, maybe you are right, although I don't know if I mean the same thing when I say this as you mean when you say it – I love music and pianos and the mechanics of sound, perhaps that is different. And I am quiet. I daydream too much . . . But I shouldn't bother you with this.'

'You don't have to. We can talk of something else.'

'Actually, I don't mind. I am surprised only that you asked, that you noticed something about me. Many women don't like the things I just told you about; English women like men who join armies or compose poetry. Who become doctors. Who can aim pistols.' He smiled. 'I don't know if this makes sense. I have never done any of these. In England we live in a time of such accomplishment, of culture and conquest. And I tune pianos so that others may make music. I think many women would think that I am dull. But Katherine is different. Once I asked her why she chose me, if I was so quiet, and she said that when she listened to music she could hear in it *my* work . . . Silly and romantic, maybe, and we were so young . . .'

'No, not silly.'

They were quiet. Edgar said, 'It is strange, I have just met you and yet I am telling you stories I have never told friends.'

'Perhaps it is because you just met me that you are telling me.'

'Perhaps.'

They were quiet. 'I know very little about you,' he said, and the branches of the willow rustled.

o

'My story is short,' she began.

She was thirty-one years old, born in 1855 to a second cousin of King Mindon. Edgar looked surprised when she said this, and she added quickly, 'It doesn't mean much. The royal family is so large that, if anything, my ounce of royal blood meant danger when Thibaw came to the throne.'

'You cannot mean you welcome British rule?'

'I am very lucky,' she said only.

Edgar persisted. 'But many people in England strongly believe that the colonies should have their own governments. In some ways I am inclined to agree. We have done some terrible things.'

'And some good.'

'I wouldn't expect someone Burmese to say that,' he said.

'I think perhaps it is the error of the ruling to think that you can change the ruled.'

She said this slowly, a thought like water spilled, now spreading around them. Edgar waited for her to say more, but when she spoke again she told him that her father had sent her to a small private school for the Burmese elite in Mandalay, where she was one of two women in her class. There she had excelled in mathematics and English, and when she left she was hired to teach English to students only three years her junior. She had loved teaching and became good friends with other teachers, including several British women. The schoolmaster at the time, a Sergeant in the army who had lost a leg in battle, had noticed her talent, and arranged to tutor her himself in the hours after class. She spoke of him the way one tells a story with a hidden ending, but Edgar didn't ask her more. The Sergeant had fallen ill when his amputation site suddenly became gangrenous. She had left school to care for him. He died after several feverish weeks. She had been devastated, but she returned to school. The new schoolmaster also invited her to his office after hours, she said, lowering her eyes, but with different intentions.

She was dismissed two weeks later. The spurned schoolmaster accused her of stealing books and selling them in the market. There was little she could do to answer the charges and she hadn't wanted to. Two of her friends had returned to Britain with their husbands, and she shuddered at the thought of the schoolmaster's pawing hands. Captain Nash-Burnham, who had been a close friend of her father, arrived at her home two days after she was fired. He said nothing of the schoolmaster and she knew he couldn't. He offered her a position as a housekeeper in the visitors' quarters. The quarters, he told her that warm morning, are usually empty, should you choose to have friends visit, or even hold classes. That week she moved in and the following week she began to teach English at the little table beneath the papaya trees. She had been there for four years.

'And how did you meet Doctor Carroll?' asked Edgar.

'Like you, he was once a guest in Mandalay.'

o

They stayed on the riverbank for the rest of the afternoon, talking beneath the willows, and Khin Myo spoke mainly of Burma, of festivals, of stories she was told growing up. Edgar asked more questions. They spoke neither of Katherine nor of the Doctor.

As they sat together, Shan families passed on the way to the river to fish or wash or play in the shallows, and if they noticed the couple, they said nothing, It is only natural that a guest be treated with hospitality, the quiet man who has come to mend the singing elephant is shy and walks with the posture of one who is unsure of the world, we too would keep him company to make him feel welcome, but we do not speak English. He does not speak Shan, but he tries, he says *som tae-tae kwa*, when he passes us on the trail, and *kin waan*, when he likes the cook's food. *Som tae-tae kwa* means 'Thank you.' Someone should tell him this, we all know he thinks it means 'Hello.' He plays with the children: this is different from the other white men who come here; perhaps he does not have any of his own. He is quiet and the astrologers say that he is looking for something, they know this from the position of the stars on the day he arrived, and because there were three big *taukte* lizards in his bed and they all pointed east and chirped twice, the woman who cleans his room remembered this and she went to ask the astrologers what it meant. They say he is one of the kind of men who has dreams, but tells no one.

Dusk came and at last Khin Myo said, I must go, and she didn't say why. And Edgar thanked her for keeping him company, The afternoon was lovely, I hope to see you again.

I hope so, too, she said, and he thought, There is nothing wrong with this. He stayed at the river until the scent of cinnamon and coconut had drifted away.

o

Edgar awoke in the middle of the night, his teeth rattling. It is cold, he thought, This must be winter, and he pulled another blanket over himself. He shivered and slept.

He awoke again, sweating. His head was hot. He turned and sat up. He ran his hand over his face and brought it down wet with perspiration. He felt as if he couldn't breathe and gasped for air and tore off the blanket and pushed aside the mosquito net. He crawled outside, his head spinning. On the balcony he inhaled deeply, felt a wave of nausea, vomited. I am sick, finally, he thought, curled his legs up to his chest and felt his sweat dry and grow cold as the wind came up from the river. He slept again.

He awoke to the sensation of a hand on his shoulder. The Doctor crouched over him, his stethoscope hanging from his neck. 'Mr Drake, are you all right? What are you doing out here?'

The light was dim; it was dawn. Edgar rolled onto his back groaning. 'My head . . .' he moaned.

'What happened?'

'I don't know, last night was terrible, I was cold and shivering, I got a blanket, I was sweating so much.' The Doctor put his hand on Edgar's forehead.

'What do you think is wrong?' Edgar asked.

'Malaria. I can't be certain, but it definitely seems like it. I will need to look at your blood.' He turned and said something to a Shan boy who was standing behind him. 'I will get you quinine sulphate, it should make you better.' He looked concerned. 'Come.' He helped Edgar up and led him to his bed. 'Look, the blankets are still soaked. You've got quite a nasty case. Come and lie down.'

The Doctor left. Edgar slept. A boy came and woke him. He brought water and several small pills for Edgar to swallow. Edgar slept again. He awoke and it was afternoon. The Doctor was sitting by the bed. 'How are you feeling?'

'Better, I think. I am quite thirsty.'

The Doctor nodded and gave him some water. 'This is the usual course of the disease. First chills and then fever. Then you begin to sweat. And then often, as now, you suddenly feel better.'

'Will it come back?'

'It depends. Sometimes it occurs only every two days, sometimes only every three days. Sometimes it comes more often, or it is much less regular. The fever is terrible. I have had malaria uncountable times myself. I get delirious.'

Edgar tried to sit up. He felt weak. 'Go to sleep,' the Doctor said.

He slept.

o

He awoke and again it was dark. Miss Ma, the nurse, was sleeping on a bed near the door. Again he felt his chest tighten. It was hot, the air was still, stifling. He suddenly felt the need to get out of the room. He lifted the mosquito net and slid out. He stood tentatively. He felt weak, but he could walk. He tiptoed towards the door. The night was dark, the moon hidden by clouds. He took several hungry breaths and lifted his arms and stretched. I need to walk, he thought, and padded quietly down the stairs. The camp seemed empty. He was barefoot and the coolness of the ground felt good on his feet. He followed the path down to the river.

It was cool on the banks and he sat and breathed deeply. The Salween moved past silently. From somewhere came a rustling and a faint cry. He stood and walked uneasily across the beach to a small track that ran by the river through thicker brush.

The sound grew louder as he walked through the bushes. Near the end of the path he caught a glimpse of something moving on the bank. He took two more steps through the brush and then he saw them, and for a moment he stood still, shocked. A young Shan couple lay in the shallows of the river. The young man's hair was tied up above his head, the woman's hair was loose, spread out over the sand. She wore a wet *hta main* and it was pushed up her body, covering her breasts, revealing a smooth hip sprinkled with sand and the river. Her arms wrapped around the young man's back, her nails were gripping his tattoos, and they moved silently, the only sound was the shifting sand and the river as it lapped against four feet. She moaned again, more loudly now, and her back began to arch, her *hta main* pooling down against her arms, her body turning, wet sand falling from her hips. Edgar stumbled back into the bushes.

o

The fevers came again, stronger now. His body shook, his jaw clenched tight, his arms curled up against his chest, he tried to grab his shoulders, but his hands only trembled, he shook the bed and the mosquito netting. The water basin on the table rattled as he moved. Miss Ma awoke and came and covered him, but he was still cold. He tried to thank her, but he couldn't speak. The water basin on the table rattled to the edge.

He grew hot again, like the night before. He threw off the blankets. He was no longer shaking. Sweat beaded on his forehead and dripped into his eyes. He tore off his shirt, which was soaked, his thin cotton drawers stuck to his legs, and he fought the urge to tear them off too, I must be decent he thought, and his body ached and he ran his hands over his face to wipe off the sweat, over his chest, his arms. He turned, the sheets were wet and warm, he tried to breathe and tore at the mosquito net. He heard footsteps and saw Miss Ma go to the water basin to moisten a cloth. She lifted the mosquito netting and pressed the damp cloth to his head. It was cold as she ran it over his body, and the heat retreated briefly, returning once the cloth had passed. Like this she chased the fever, but it burned deeper now. He lost consciousness.

○

And now he floats above the bed; he can see himself. Water rushes from his skin, pooling, it begins to move, it is no longer sweat, but ants which crawl out of his pores and swarm. He is black with ants. He falls back into his body and he screams, slapping away at the ants, they fall on the sheets and turn to tiny fires, and as he brushes them off they are replaced by more, emerging from his pores as though from an anthill, not fast or slow, but incessant, they cover him. He screams and he hears rustling at the bedside, there are many forms now, he thinks he knows them, the Doctor and Miss Ma, and now another figure, standing behind the other two. The room is dark and red, like a fire. He sees their faces, but they blur and melt and their mouths become the muzzles of dogs, laughing mouths, and they reach for him with paws, and everywhere they touch him it is like ice, and he screams and tries to beat away their arms. One of the dogs leans towards him and presses its muzzle against his cheek, its breath stinks of heat and mice and its eyes burn clear, like glass, and in them he sees a woman, she is sitting on the bank of a river watching a pair of bodies, and he sees them too, the brown arms gripping the broad white back, pale and dirty with sand, faces close and panting. There is one boat left on the sand, and she takes it and begins to paddle away, he tries to rise, but now he lies in the grip of the brown arms and he feels a slipperiness, a heat, and feels the muzzle part his lips, a rough tongue slip into his mouth. He tries to rise, but others surround him, he tries to fight, but falls back, exhausted. He sleeps.

He awakes hours later and feels a cold moist towel on his head. Khin Myo is sitting by his bed. One hand holds the towel to his forehead. He takes the other in his. She doesn't move away. 'Khin Myo . . .' he says.

'Quiet, Mr Drake. Sleep.'

SIXTEEN

THE FEVER BROKE alongside the dawn. It was the morning of the third day since he became ill. He awoke and he was alone. An empty water basin sat on the floor next to the bed, two towels hung over its side.

His head ached. The night before was a feverish blur and he lay back and tried to remember what had happened. Images came, but they were strange and disturbing. He turned over onto his side. The sheets were moist and cool. He slept.

o

He awoke to the sound of his name, a man's voice. He turned over. Doctor Carroll sat at the bedside. 'Mr Drake, you look better this morning.'

'Yes, I think so. I feel much better.'

'I am glad. It was terrible last night. Even I was concerned . . . and I have seen many cases.'

'I don't remember it. I only remember seeing you and Khin Myo and Miss Ma.'

'Khin Myo wasn't here. It must have been the delirium.'

Edgar looked up from the bed. The Doctor peered at him, his face stern and unexpressive. 'Yes, perhaps only the delirium,' said Edgar, and he turned over and slept again.

Over the course of the next few days the fevers came again, but they were not as strong and the terrible dreams didn't return. Miss Ma left his bedside to take care of the patients in the hospital, but returned to visit him throughout the day. She brought him fruit and rice and a soup that tasted like ginger and made him sweat and his body shiver when she fanned him. One day she came with scissors to cut his hair. The Doctor explained that the Shan believed this helped to fight illness.

He began to walk. He had lost weight and his clothes hung even more loosely on his thin frame. But mostly he rested on the balcony and watched the river. The Doctor invited a man to play a Shan flute for him, and he sat in his bed beneath the mosquito net and listened.

One night, alone, he thought he could hear the sound of the piano being played. The notes drifted down through the camp. He thought it was Chopin at first, but the song changed, elusive, elegiac, a melody he had never heard.

Colour returned to his face and he began to share his meals with the Doctor once again. The Doctor asked him about Katherine and he told him how they had met. But mostly he listened. To stories of the war, of Shan customs, of men who rowed boats with their legs, of monks with mystical powers. The Doctor told him that he had sent a description of a new flower to the Linnean Society, and that he had begun to translate Homer's *Odyssey* into Shan, 'My favourite tale, Mr Drake, and one in which I find a most personal significance.' He was translating it, he said, for a Shan storyteller, who had asked for a legend of the 'kind that is told at night, around campfires'. 'I am now at the song of Demodokos. I don't know if you remember it. He sings of the sack of Troy, and Odysseus, the great warrior, cries, "as a woman weeps".'

They went at night to listen to musicians play, drums and cymbals and harps and flutes mixing in a jungle of sounds. They stayed until it was late. When they returned to their rooms, Edgar went out onto his balcony to listen once more.

After several days the Doctor asked, 'How are you feeling?'

'I am well. Why do you ask now?'

'I have to go away again. It should only be a couple of days. Khin Myo will stay. You won't have to be alone.'

o

The Doctor didn't tell Edgar where he was going, and Edgar didn't see him leave.

The following morning Edgar rose and walked to the river to watch the fishermen. He stood in the brush of blooming flowers and watched bees flit between the patches of colours. He played football with some of the children, but tired quickly and returned to his room. He sat on the balcony and looked out on the river. He watched the sun move. The cook brought him lunch, a broth with sweet noodles and crisp fried pieces of garlic. *Kin waan*, he said when he tasted it and the cook smiled.

Night came and he slept a sweet sleep in which he dreamed he was dancing at a festival. The villagers played strange instruments and he moved as if in a waltz, but alone.

o

The next day he decided to write to Katherine at last. A new thought had begun to bother him – that the army had notified her that he had left Mandalay. He had to convince himself that the military's obvious lack of interest in her before he left – which had angered him so then – meant that they were even less likely to be in contact with her now.

He took out paper and a pen and wrote her name. He began to describe Mae Lwin, but stopped after several lines. He wanted to describe to her the village above the mountain, but realized he had seen it only from a distance. It was still cool outside. A fine time for a walk, he thought, The exercise will do me good. He put on his hat and – despite the heat – a waistcoat he usually wore on summer strolls in England. He walked down to the centre of camp.

In the clearing two women were wandering up from the river carrying baskets of clothes, one against her hip, the other balancing the load on top of her turban. Edgar followed them along the small track that ducked into the forest and climbed the ridge. In the quiet of the woods, the women heard his footsteps behind them, and turned and giggled, whispering something to each other in Shan. He tipped his hat. The trees thinned, and the women climbed a steep rise, up the mountain towards the village spread over its back. Edgar followed, and as they entered the village the women again turned and giggled, and once again he tipped his hat.

At the first set of houses, perched on stilts, an older woman crouched in the doorway, the patterned fabric of her dress taut against her knees. A pair of scrawny pigs lay sleeping in the shade, snorting and twitching their tails through mysterious dreams.

She was smoking a cheroot the width of her wrist. Edgar greeted her. 'Good morning,' he said. She slowly took the cheroot from her mouth, gripping it between her gnarled and ring-laden third and fourth fingers. He half expected her to growl, goblin-like, but her face broke into a big toothless smile, her gums stained with betel and tobacco. Her face was heavily tattooed, not with solid lines like the men, but with hundreds of small points, in a pattern that reminded Edgar of a cribbage board. Later he would learn that she was not Shan but Chin, a tribe from the west, and that this was written in the details of her decoration. 'Goodbye, madam,' said Edgar, and she returned the cheroot to her lips, inhaling deeply, sucking her wrinkled cheeks into the cavern of her mouth. Edgar thought again of the ubiquitous advertisements in London: Cigars de Joy: One of these cigarettes gives immediate relief in the worst attack of Asthma, Cough, Bronchitis and Shortness of Breath.

He continued to walk. He passed small, dry fields, patterned in rising terraces. With the drought, the planting season had yet to begin, and the soil was turned up in hard, dry clods. The houses were raised at varying heights, their walls like those of the camp buildings, interlaced strips of bamboo woven to create geometrical patterns. The road was empty except for scattered bands of dusty children, and he saw that many people were gathered in the houses. It was hot, so hot that even the best soothsayers had failed to forecast that today would be the day the rains would come again to the Shan Plateau. The men and women sat and talked in the shade and couldn't understand the Englishman who took walks under such a sun.

At one house he heard a ringing and stopped to look. Two men crouched shirtless in loose blue Shan trousers, hammering metal. He had heard of the Shans' reputation as skilled blacksmiths; Nash-Burnham had pointed out knives in the Mandalay market which were forged by Shans. I wonder where they obtain the metal, he thought, and looked closer. One of the men held a railway spike between his toes, which he hammered against an anvil. Don't build a railway through a country of hungry blacksmiths, he thought, and it sounded eerily like an aphorism.

A pair of men passed him on the road. One was wearing a gigantic wide-brimmed hat like those worn in common postcard images of rice-field workers, except that the brim sloped down over the ears so the front framed the man's face like a giant duckbill. It is true, they *are* like Scottish Highlanders, thought Edgar, who had read this comparison but had never understood it until he saw the broad hat and wide, kilt-like trousers. Ahead, the women he had followed entered another house, where a girl stood, holding a baby. Edgar stopped to watch the flight of a mynah bird, and saw them peering out of the doorway at him.

Soon he came across a circle of older boys playing *chinlon*. It was the same game played by the children in the camp clearing, although it always turned to football once Edgar tried to join. Here he stopped and watched. One of the boys held up the ball to him as if inviting him to play, but he shook his head and nodded at them to continue. Thrilled by an audience, the boys returned to the game in earnest, using their feet to keep the woven rattan sphere in the air. They tapped and dived and back-kicked, and did high whirling cartwheels to send the ball soaring. Edgar stood and watched for a while, before a stray ball flew his way and he put his leg out to stop it, and the ball bounced back into the circle and one of the boys continued to play. The others cheered, and Edgar, slightly out of breath and flustered by the effort, couldn't help but smile as he bent to dust off his boots. He watched for several more kicks, but then, fearful that he wouldn't be so lucky the next time the ball flew his way, he continued his walk.

He soon passed another set of homes, where a group of women sat in the shade of the house by a loom. A naked little boy chased some chickens across the road and paused to watch Edgar as he passed, this new animal being apparently much more interesting than squawking birds. Edgar stopped by the boy. His face was completely covered with *thanaka*, making him pale like a forest sprite.

'How are you, little chap?' said Edgar, and crouched and held out his hand. The boy stood and stared impassively, his abdomen swollen and dusty. He began to urinate. 'Aaaii!' A young girl ran down the steps of a house and picked up the boy, pointing him away, trying to contain her giggling. When the boy had stopped urinating, she rotated him and placed him on her thin hips, in imitation of the older women. She wagged her finger at the child. Edgar turned to walk away and saw that more children had gathered in the road behind him.

A woman led a water buffalo up the road, and the children parted for the mud-caked beast to pass. Edgar watched the animal's thick, brush-like tail flick lazily at the flies that landed on its back.

He continued to walk, the children following at a distance. Soon the trail rose slightly, and he could see out over a small valley covered with terraced, fallow rice fields. At the side of the road, a pair of men sat and grinned the broad Shan grin he had become accustomed to. One of the men pointed to the group of children and said something, and Edgar answered, 'Yes, quite a lot of children,' and they both laughed although neither understood a word the other had said.

It was near noon and Edgar found himself sweating profusely. He stopped for a moment in the shade of a small grain store and watched a lizard do push-ups on a bare stone. He took out a handkerchief and mopped his forehead. He had spent so much time tuning the piano or sitting on his balcony that he hadn't experienced the sun, or the drought. The dead fields shook in the searing heat. He waited until he thought he was dull enough for the children to leave, but the crowd only grew in number.

He walked along a road that seemed as if it led back to the camp. Soon he passed a small shrine, where people had set out a wide assortment of offerings – flowers, stones, amulets, small cups whose contents had long evaporated, dry sticky rice, small clay figurines. The shrine itself was built like a small temple. It was similar to ones he had seen in the lowlands, built, the Doctor had explained, to please a spirit whom the Shan called 'the Lord of the Place'. Edgar, who never counted himself as a superstitious man, searched his pockets for something to leave, but found only the bullet. He looked nervously around him. There was no one there but the children and he backed away.

He continued. Far ahead on the road he saw a woman walking with a parasol. It was an image he had seen many times in the lowlands, but not yet on the plateau: the sun overhead, a lone woman hidden beneath her parasol, her dress shimmering in the mirage of the road. The air was still and he stopped to watch the thin line of dust rising from her feet. And then suddenly he realized the incongruity of the scene, that Shan women, with their wide-brimmed hats or turbans, rarely carried parasols. A hundred paces away, he recognized Khin Myo.

She approached without saying anything. She was wearing a fine red silk *hta main*, and a pressed white cotton blouse, which hung loosely and swayed in the breeze. Her face was painted with thick even lines of *thanaka* and her hair was pulled back and fastened with a pin made of polished teak, carved in a delicate filigree. Several strands had worked themselves loose and fallen over her face. She brushed them back. 'I have been looking for you,' she said. 'The cook said that he had seen you walk up to the village. I wanted to join you. One of the Shan girls said that the *nwè ni*, "ipomoea" I think you call it, have started to bloom and I thought we could walk there together. Do you feel well enough?'

'I think so. I think I am finally better.'

'I'm glad. I was worried,' she said.

'So was I . . . I think I was delirious. I dreamed a lot . . . strange, terrible dreams. I thought I saw you.'

She was silent for a moment. 'I didn't want you to be alone.' She touched his arm. 'Come, let's walk.'

As they walked, the crowd shuffled along behind them. Along the road she stopped and looked back at the children. 'Are you going to bring your . . . how do you say it?'

'Entourage?'

'A French word, no?'

'I suppose so. I didn't know you speak French.'

'I don't. A couple of words only. Doctor Carroll likes teaching me the meanings of words.'

'Well, I would love to learn how to say "Go home" to my entourage. They are charming, but I am not used to such attention.'

Khin Myo turned and said something to them. They squealed and ran back several paces before stopping to watch again. Khin Myo and Edgar continued to walk. The children didn't follow.

'What did you tell them?' asked Edgar.

'I said that Englishmen eat Shan children,' she answered.

Edgar smiled. 'Probably not the type of propaganda we want,' he said.

'Oh, quite the opposite. A number of the most famous Shan spirits eat children. And they have been worshipped since long before you arrived.'

They walked and followed a trail that rose over a small hill. They passed a house that Khin Myo said belonged to an old woman with an evil eye, and she warned Edgar to be careful. She said even this with a playfulness, a lightness, and the sense of sadness he felt from the memory of their talk by the river seemed distant. They entered a small grove of trees and began to climb the hill. The trees thinned and the ground became spotted with flowers.

'Are these the ones you are looking for?' asked Edgar.

'No, there is a meadow on the other side of the ridge. Come.'

They reached the top of the hill and looked out over a field of tall shrubs, covered with dark red and salmon-coloured flowers.

'Oh, how lovely!' exclaimed Khin Myo, and she ran down the track with a childlike gait. Edgar smiled and followed, walking, but then, reflexively, his legs began to run as well. A little. Khin Myo stopped and turned, and she started to say something, and Edgar tried to stop, but the downward momentum of the hill prevented him, and he skipped, once, twice, before finally stopping before her. He was out of breath, his face red and flushed.

Khin Myo looked at him and raised an eyebrow. 'Were you just skipping?' she asked.

'Skipping?'

'I think I just saw you skipping.'

'No, never. I just was running too fast and couldn't stop.'

Khin Myo laughed. 'I think that I saw you skipping! Mr Drake . . .' She smiled. 'And now look, you are blushing.'

'I am not blushing!'

'You are indeed. Look, you are turning red this very instant!'

'It is sunburn; that is what happens to Englishmen when they go out into the sun.'

'Mr Drake, I hardly think even *English* skin will burn so quickly beneath a hat.'

'Exertion then. I am not a young man.'

'Exertion then, Mr Drake.' And once again she touched his arm. 'Come, let's look at the flowers.'

It was not the type of meadow to which Edgar was accustomed, not the soft dew-coated fields he knew from the English countryside. This was dry, and the stalks and brushes exploded through the hard soil with hundreds of flowers, in hues he couldn't imagine, for a man trained to tell the difference in notes may not recognize the subtlety of vision. 'If only it would rain,' said Khin Myo, 'there would be even more flowers.'

'Do you know the names?' he asked.

'Only a couple. I know more of the lowland flowers. But Doctor Carroll has taught me some. That one is honeysuckle. And that one is a type of primrose, also found in China. And that one is St John's Wort, those will be wild roses.' She picked some as she walked.

From over the hill they heard singing, and a young Shan girl emerged, first her head, as if disembodied, then her torso, and then her legs and feet, which pattered along the path. She walked quickly, and lowered her head in respect. Ten paces along the track, she turned back to look at them again, quickened her pace, and disappeared behind a rise.

Neither Edgar nor Khin Myo spoke, and Edgar wondered if Khin Myo had noticed what had been implied in the young girl's stare, what it meant for the two of them to be alone in the meadow of flowers. Finally he cleared his throat. 'Perhaps they will get the wrong idea, if we are alone here together,' he said, and immediately wished he hadn't spoken.

'What do you mean?'

'I am sorry, never mind,' he looked at her. She was standing very close to him, and a wind from across the meadow mixed the scent of flowers with that of her perfume.

Perhaps she sensed his discomfort, for she didn't ask again, but raised the flowers to her nose and said to him, 'Come, smell, there is nothing like it.' And slowly he lowered his head close to hers, only the scent of the flowers hanging in the air between their lips. He had never seen her so close to, the details of her irises, the cleft of her lips, the delicate powder of *thanaka* that ran across her cheeks.

Finally she looked up and said, 'It is getting late, Mr Drake. You have just been sick. We should go back. Perhaps Doctor Carroll is here already.' And she didn't wait for him to answer, but pulled an ipomoea from the bouquet and reached behind her head to fasten the flower in her hair. She began to walk back towards the camp.

Edgar stood only long enough to watch her walk away and then set off down the trail to follow her.

o

Doctor Carroll didn't return that afternoon but, after six months of drought on the Shan Plateau, the rain did. It caught the two of them as they made their way down the track, and they began to run together, laughing, big warm drops spinning down through the air with the force of hailstones. Within minutes they were soaked. Khin Myo ran ahead of him with her parasol at her side, her hair swinging with the weight of the water. The ipomoea stayed briefly, held by the tension of droplets, and then, carried off by them, drifted to the ground. With a nimbleness that surprised him, and without breaking the mad, muddy rush, Edgar reached down and picked it up.

At the edge of the village they ran through crowds charging up from the river to escape the sudden downpour, everyone laughing, covering their heads, shouting. For each woman who ran for shelter to protect her carefully tied turban, two children rushed out into the rain to dance in a swelling puddle in the clearing. Edgar and Khin Myo finally reached shelter, in front of her room. Water rushed over the lip of the roof and fell curtain-like, separating them from the shouts that filled the camp.

'You are soaked,' laughed Khin Myo. 'Look at you.' 'And you too,' said Edgar. He watched her, her long black hair plastered against her neck, her light blouse to her body. Her skin could be seen through the translucent cloth, the outline of her breast pressing at the cotton. She looked up at him and brushed wet hair from her face.

He stood and watched her and for a moment she held his gaze, and in the deep recesses of his chest he felt something stir, a longing that she would invite him to her room, to dry off only, of course, he would never ask more. To dry off only, and then in the darkness of the room, scented with coconut and cinnamon, a wish that perhaps their hands would brush, first accidentally, then again, perhaps, bolder, deliberate, that their fingers would meet and entwine and they would stand like that for a moment before she looked up and he looked down. And he wondered if she thought the same as they stood outside and felt the coolness of the water on their skin.

And perhaps it could have been had Edgar acted with the spontaneity of the rain, had he moved towards her with the same boldness with which water falls. But not now. This expects too much of a man whose life is defined by creating order so that others may make beauty. It is expecting too much of one who makes rules to ask that he break them. And so, after a long silence, as they both stand and listen to the rain, his voice cracks and he says, 'We'd better change then. I must find dry clothes.' Fleeting words that mean little and much.

o

It rained all afternoon and through the night. In the morning, when the sky cleared, Doctor Anthony Carroll returned to Mae Lwin, having ridden all night through the rain, racing through the storm with the emissary of the Shan Prince of Mongnai.

SEVENTEEN

Edgar was sitting on the balcony, watching the frothy waters of the Salween pass, when he heard hoof beats. The riders broke into camp: Doctor Carroll, followed by Nok Lek and a third man he didn't recognize.

A group of boys ran out to help the men dismount. Even from a distance Edgar could see that they were soaked. The Doctor removed his pith helmet and tucked it under his arm. He looked up and saw the piano tuner outside his room. 'Good morning, Mr Drake,' he shouted. 'Please come down. I would like to introduce you to someone.'

Edgar pushed himself out of his chair and descended to the clearing. When he reached the group, the boys had taken the ponies away and Carroll was wiping off his gloves. He wore a riding jacket and puttees spattered with mud. A damp cheroot hung smouldering between his lips. His face was ruddy and tired. 'I trust you have survived in my absence?'

'Yes, Doctor, thank you. The rains came. I worked on the piano a bit more. I think it is finally tuned.'

'Excellent, excellent, Mr Drake. That is exactly what I wanted to hear, and I will explain why in a moment. First, let me introduce you to Yawng Shwe.' He turned to his companion, who bowed slightly before offering his hand. Edgar shook it.

'You can see he is familiar with our customs,' Carroll said of the visitor.

'A pleasure to meet you, sir,' said Edgar.

'He doesn't speak English. Handshaking only,' said Carroll wryly. 'Yawng Shwe is here as an emissary from the *sawbwa* of Mongnai. You must have heard of it. It is to the north. The Shan Prince – the *sawbwa* – of the state of Mongnai has traditionally been one of the most powerful in the cis-Salween states. We raced to get here because tomorrow the *sawbwa* will visit Mae Lwin, and I have extended an invitation to him to stay at the camp. It is his first visit here.' The Doctor stopped. 'Come,' he said, wiping his wet hair back from his face. 'Let's find something to drink before we talk further. We are completely parched from a night of riding. And this despite all the rain.'

The four men turned up the slope and began walking towards the headquarters. At Edgar's side, Carroll spoke again. 'I am very pleased the piano is ready. It seems that it will be needed sooner than we thought.'

'Sorry?'

'I would like you to play for the *sawbwa*, Mr Drake.' He saw Edgar begin to speak and interrupted. 'I will explain more later. The *sawbwa* is an accomplished musician and I've told him much about the piano.'

Edgar stopped walking. 'Doctor,' he protested, 'I am not a pianist. I have told you this many times.'

'Nonsense, Mr Drake. I have heard you play while you are tuning. Perhaps you are not ready for a London concert hall, but you are more than fit to perform in the jungles of Burma. And besides, we have no other choice. I told him that you came especially for him, and I must sit with the *sawbwa* to explain the music.' He put his hand on the tuner's shoulder and fixed his gaze on him. 'There is much at stake, Mr Drake.'

Edgar shook his head again, but the Doctor didn't give him another chance to speak. 'Now, let me make our guest comfortable.

I will meet you in your room.' He called out in Shan to a boy who stood at the door of the headquarters. The emissary of the *sawbwa* laughed and the men disappeared inside.

o

Edgar returned to his room to wait for the Doctor. He paced nervously, This is ridiculous, I don't need to be part of his games, This is not what I came for, I have told him many times I don't play, He is like Katherine, they don't understand this.

He waited. An hour passed, and then perhaps two, although he couldn't be certain, and couldn't even indulge the habit of looking at the broken watch, as he had recently left it in his bag.

Another hour. Slowly his anxiety began to lift. Perhaps the Doctor has changed his mind, he decided, He has thought about this more carefully and now knows that it is a misbegotten idea, that I am not ready for such performances. He waited, increasingly convinced that this was true. He went out on the balcony but could see only the women at the river.

At last he heard footsteps on the stairs. It was one of the servant boys. 'Doctor Carroll give this to you,' the boy said, handing him a note, bowing.

Edgar opened the letter. It was written on Shan paper like all others he had seen, but the handwriting was scrawled, hasty.

Mr Drake,

I apologize for not meeting with you as promised. The *sawbwa*'s emissary requires more attention than anticipated, and unfortunately I will be unable to speak to you about your performance. My only request is this: as you know, the *sawbwa* of Mongnai is one of the leaders of the Limbin Confederacy, with whom British forces under Colonel Stedman have been at war for the last two months. I hope to propose a preliminary treaty with the *sawbwa* while he is in Mae Lwin, and, more importantly, to request that he arrange a meeting with the Confederacy. All I ask of you is to select and play a piece that will move the Prince with emotions of friendship, to convince him of the good intentions of our proposals. I have the *utmost confidence and faith* in your ability to select and perform a piece appropriate for this occasion.

A.C.

Edgar looked up, to protest, to someone, but the boy was gone. When he looked out over the camp, it was empty. He cursed.

He spent the night in the piano room, at the bench, thinking, beginning pieces and stopping, No that is not right, I cannot play that, thinking, beginning again. Thoughts of what he should play alternated with questions of what the visit meant, who the *sawbwa* was, and what the Doctor intended by the music, by the meeting. He stopped sometime in the early hours of dawn, when he rested his arms on the keyboard and his head on his arms and fell asleep.

o

It was afternoon when he woke with the impression that he had fallen asleep in his shop back in England. As he walked back to his room, he was amazed at how the camp had transformed itself overnight. The pathway had been swept of the detritus left by the rains and fresh pieces of timber laid out to make dry steps. Banners were strung from the houses and fluttered in the light of dusk. The only sign of the British presence was the flag hanging outside the headquarters, which had been converted into a dining hall. It seemed oddly out of place, he thought, he had never seen it in the camp before, which now seemed peculiar – after all, it was a British fort.

He returned to his room and waited until the evening, when a boy came and knocked on the door. He washed and dressed, and the boy led him up the steps to the headquarters, where a guard instructed him to remove his shoes before entering. Inside, the tables and chairs had been replaced by cushions laid out over the floor before low wicker tables. The hall was quiet; the *sawbwa* and his retinue had yet to arrive. He was led across the room to where Doctor Carroll and Khin Myo were seated. The Doctor was wearing Shan clothing, an elegantly tailored white cotton jacket hanging to the top of a *paso* of iridescent purple. It looked quite regal, and Edgar was reminded of the day he arrived, and how Carroll had stood by the river, dressed like his men. Since then, Edgar had only seen him in European clothes or army khakis.

There was an empty cushion between the two of them. The Doctor was engaged in deep conversation with an older Shan man seated several cushions away and motioned to Edgar to sit. Khin Myo was speaking to a boy who crouched at her side, and Edgar watched her as she spoke. Her blouse was of silk and her hair looked darker, as if she had just bathed. In it she wore the same teak pin she had worn on their walk. At last, when the boy had left, she leaned over to Edgar and whispered, 'Have you prepared what you will play?'

Edgar smiled weakly. 'We will see.' He looked about the room. He could barely recognize it as the drab clinic or office he was accustomed to. Torches burned in each corner, filling it with light and the aroma of incense. The walls had been draped with carpets and skins. Around the room stood servants, many of whom Edgar recognized, others he didn't. They were all dressed in fine flowing trousers and blue shirts, their turbans clean and impeccably tied.

There was a sound at the door and a hush fell over the room. A large man in glittering regalia entered. 'Is that him?' Edgar asked.

'No, wait. He is smaller.' And as she said this, a short, plump man in an extravagantly sequinned robe entered the room. The

Shan servants at the door dropped to the floor and kowtowed before him. Even Carroll bowed, and Khin Myo, and – glancing to his side to imitate the doctor – Edgar bowed as well. The *sawbwa* and his retinue crossed the room until he reached the empty cushion beside Carroll. They sat. They were all dressed in matching uniforms, pleated shirts with sashes, their heads tied with clean white turbans. All save one man, a monk, who sat back from his table, which Edgar understood as a refusal of food, as monks should not eat after noon. There was something different about the way the man looked, and as Edgar continued to stare he realized that what he had first thought was unusually dark skin was a blue tattoo, which covered his entire face and hands. When a servant came and lit a bright torch in the centre of the room, the blue skin stood out sharply against the saffron robes.

Carroll spoke to the *sawbwa* in Shan, and although Edgar couldn't understand their words, he sensed murmurings of approval around the room. The hierarchy of the seating surprised him, that he should sit so close to the *sawbwa*, closer than the village representatives, and closer to Carroll than Khin Myo. Servants brought out fermented rice wine in carved metal cups, and when all had been served Doctor Carroll raised his cup and spoke again in Shan. The room cheered, and the *sawbwa* looked especially pleased. 'To your health,' whispered Carroll.

'Who is the monk?'

'The Shan call him the Blue Monk, I think you can see why. He is the *sawbwa*'s personal adviser. He doesn't travel anywhere without him. When you play tonight, play to win the heart of the monk as well.'

And the meal was served, a feast unlike anything Edgar had seen since he had arrived in the Shan States, dish after dish of sauces, curries, bowls of noodles served with thick broth, water snails cooked with young bamboo shoots, pumpkin fried with onion and chili, seared pork and mango, shredded water buffalo mixed with sweet green aubergines, salads with minced chicken and mint.

They ate much and spoke little. Occasionally, the Doctor would turn to say something to the *sawbwa*, but for the most part they remained silent, and the Prince grunted his approval at the food. Finally, after countless dishes, each of which could have ended the meal, a plate of betel nuts was set before them and the Shan began to chew vigorously, expectorating into the spittoons the party had brought with them. At last the *sawbwa* leaned back and, with one hand draped over his stomach, spoke to the Doctor. Carroll turned to the piano tuner. 'Our Prince is ready for music. You may go to the room before us, to prepare. Please bow to him when you stand and keep your head low as you walk out of the room.'

Outside the sky had cleared, and the path was lit by the moon and rows of burning torches. Edgar climbed the path, his chest tight with apprehension. There was a guard outside the piano room, a Shan boy he recognized from the mornings on the Salween. Edgar nodded to him and the boy bowed deeply, an unnecessary action, as the tuner had come alone.

In the torchlight the room looked much larger than before. The piano stood on one side and someone had laid a number of pillows over the floor. It feels like a true salon, he thought. At the far side of the room the windows which faced towards the river had been propped open, flooding the room with the serpentine course of the Salween. Edgar walked to the piano. The blanket had already been removed from the case, and he sat down at the bench. He knew he shouldn't touch the keys – he did not want to reveal the song or let the others think that he had begun without them. So he sat with his eyes closed and thought about how his fingers would move and how the music would sound.

Soon he heard voices on the path below and footsteps. Carroll and the Prince and the Blue Monk entered, and then Khin Myo, and then others. Edgar stood and bowed low, like the Burmese, like a concert pianist, for in this respect the pianist has more in common with cultures of the East than those of the West, he thought, who choose to greet by taking the hand of their visitor.

He stood until they had reclined on the pillows and then seated himself again on the piano bench. He would begin without introduction, without words. The name of the composer would mean nothing to the Prince of Mongnai. And surely Carroll knew the piece; he could explain what it meant, or what he needed it to mean.

He began with Bach's prelude and fugue in C sharp minor, the fourth piece of Bach's collections of preludes and fugues known as *The Well-Tempered Clavier*, or as simply *The Forty-Eight* after the number of prelude variations, which are arranged into two books, each of twenty-four chapters. It was a tuner's piece, an exploration of the possibilities of sound, and a series that Edgar knew from testing the tuning of professional pianos. He had always called it a testament to the art of tuning. Before the development of equal temperament, the even spacing of notes, it was impossible to play the entire piece on the same instrument. But with equally spaced notes the possibilities suddenly seemed endless.

He played through the prelude, the sound rose and fell, and he felt himself sway as he played. There is much I could tell the Doctor, he thought, about why I have chosen it. That it is a piece bound by strict rules of counterpoint, as all fugues are, the song is but an elaboration of one simple melody, the remainder of the piece destined to follow the rules established in the first few lines. To me this means beauty is found in order, in rules – he may make what he wishes from this in terms of law and treaty signing. I could tell him that it is a piece without a commanding melody, that in England many people dismiss it as too mathematical, as lacking a tune which can be held or hummed. Perhaps he knows this already. But if a Shan does not know the same songs, then just as I have been confused by their melodies, so might the Prince be confused by ours. So I chose something mathematical, for this is universal, all can appreciate complexity, the trance found in patterns of sound.

There are other things he could say, of why he began with the fourth prelude and not the first, for the fourth is a song of ambiguity and the first a melody of accomplishment, and it is best to begin courtships with modesty. Or that he chose it simply because he often felt deeply moved when he heard it. There *is* emotion in the notes, If it is less accessible than other pieces, perhaps this is why it is so much stronger.

The piece began low, in the bass strings, and as it increased in complexity soprano voices entered, and Edgar felt his whole body move towards the right and remain there, a journey across the keyboard, I am like the puppets moving on their stage in Mandalay. More confident now, he played and the song slowed, and when at last he finished he had almost forgotten that others were watching. He raised his head and looked across the room to the *sawbwa*, who said something to the Blue Monk and then motioned for Edgar to continue. Beside the *sawbwa*, he thought he could see the Doctor smile. And so he began again, now D major, now D minor, and forward through each scale, moving up, each tune a variation on its beginnings, structure giving rise to possibilities. He played into the remoter scales, as his old master had called them, and Edgar thought how fitting a name this was for a piece played into the night of the jungle, I can never again believe that Bach did not leave Germany.

He played for nearly two hours, to a place where, halfway in the piece, there is a break, like a rest house on a lonely road, which settles in the wake of the prelude and fugue in B minor. On the last note his fingers stopped and rested on the keyboard and he turned his head and looked out over the room.

EIGHTEEN

Dear Katherine,

It is March, although I am not certain of the date. I write to you from the fort and village of Mae Lwin, on the banks of the Salween River, in the Southern Shan States in Burma. I arrived long ago, and yet this is my first letter home from here, and I apologize for not having written to you sooner. Indeed, I am afraid that such silence must worry you greatly, as by now you must have come to expect my letters, which I wrote so often before leaving for the Shan Hills. Unfortunately, I don't think you will read this letter for a long time, as there is no way to get mail to Mandalay. Perhaps it is for this reason that I have been hesitant to write, but I think that there are others as well, some that I understand and others I do not. When I have written to you before, it has always been about some idea, or event, or thought, which makes me wonder why I haven't written since arriving here, since much *has* happened. Weeks ago I wrote to you that what saddened me most about coming here was the feeling that I would leave incomplete. Strangely, since I left Mandalay, I have seen more than I could have imagined and I have understood more of what I have seen, but at the same time this incompleteness grows more acute. Each day I am here I await an answer, like a salve, or water which satisfies thirst. I think this is why

I have postponed writing, but I have found few answers. So now I write because it has been too long since I wrote last. I know that when I see you the events I describe in this letter will be old events, the impressions long past. So perhaps I also write simply because I have a deep need to put words on a page, even though I may be the only one who will read this.

I am sitting beneath a willow tree on the sandy banks of the Salween River. It is one of my favourite spots. It is quiet and hidden, and yet I can still see the river and listen to the sounds of people around me. It is early evening. The sun has begun its descent, and the sky is purple with the gathering of clouds; perhaps we will have more storms. Four days have passed since the rains first began. I will remember that day better than I will remember the day I left Mandalay, for it marked such a change on the plateau. Indeed, I have never seen anything like the rain here. The drizzle that we call rain in England is nothing compared to the pounding of a monsoon. At once, the sky opens and soaks everything, everyone runs for shelter, the footpaths turn to mud, to rivers, the trees shake, and water pours off leaves as if out of a jug, there is nothing dry. Oh, Katherine, it is so strange: I could write for pages only about the rain, the way it falls, the different sizes of the drops and how they feel on your face, its taste and smell, and its sound. Indeed, I could write for pages only on its sound, on thatch, on leaves, on tin, on willow.

My dear, it is so beautiful here. The rains have arrived early this year and the forest has undergone a most incredible change. In only a matter of days the dry brush has transformed itself into explosions of colours. When I took the steamer from Rangoon to Mandalay, I met young soldiers who shared with me stories of Mae Lwin, and at the time I couldn't believe that what they were saying was true, yet now I know that it was. The sun is bright and strong. Cool breezes drift up from the river. The air is filled with the incense of nectar, the scent of spices cooking, and sounds, what incredible sounds! I sit beneath the willow now, and the branches hang low, so I can see little of the river. But I can hear laughter. Oh, if only I could capture the laughter of children in the vibrations of string, or put them on paper. But here words fail us. I think of the language we use to describe music, and how we are unequipped for the infinity of tones. Still, we do have ways to record it; in music our inadequacies are confined only to words, for we can always resort to signatures and scales. And yet we still haven't found words for all the other sounds, nor can we record them in signature and script. How can I describe what I mean? To my left three boys are playing with a ball in the shallows, and it keeps drifting out to deeper waters, and a young Shan woman washing clothes – perhaps she is their mother, or maybe their sister – scolds them when they swim out to retrieve it. And yet they keep losing the ball and keep swimming after it, and between the losing and the swimming there is a particular laughter like none I have ever heard. These are sounds forbidden to the piano, to bars and notations.

Katherine, I wish you could hear it too; no, I wish that I could take it home, remember it all. As I write, I feel both a tremendous sadness and a joy, a wanting, a welling from within me, something ecstatic. I choose my words carefully; this is truly what I feel, for it rises in my chest like water from a well, and I swallow and my eyes brim with tears as if I will overflow. I don't know what this is or where it came from, or when it began. I never thought I could find so much in the falling of water or in the sounds of children playing.

I realize what an odd letter this must be for you, for I have written so much, and yet still I have described so little of what I have done or seen. Instead I babble like a child to the paper. Something *has* changed – you must know this already by the way I write. Last night I played the piano for an audience, and quite a distinguished one at that, and part of me wants to mark this as the moment of change, although I know that it isn't – the change is something that has come more slowly, perhaps it even began at home. What this change means I don't know, just as I don't know if I am happier or sadder than I have ever been. At times I wonder if the reason I have lost track of time is that I will know when to return, not by a date, but when an emptiness is filled. I will come home, of course, for you remain my greatest love. But only now am I realizing the reason *you* wanted me to go, what *you* told me before I left. There is a purpose in all of this – you were right, although I do not know yet what it is, let alone if I have even accomplished it. But I must wait now, must stay now. Of course, I *will* return, soon, perhaps tomorrow. Now I write because I feel you must know why I am still here. You will understand, dear, I hope.

Katherine, it is growing dark, and even cold, for it is winter here, strange as that may sound. I wonder what others would think if they read this letter. For, by all superficial appearances, I look the same, I don't know if anyone else has noticed a change in me. Perhaps this is why I miss you so, you always said you heard me even when I was silent.

I will write more, for there are other things that remain unsaid, if only for the limits of space and ink and sunlight.

I remain,

Your loving husband,

Edgar

It is still light. There are other things that remain unsaid – he knows this, but his pen trembles when he brings it close to the page.

Khin Myo stood at the edge of the willow tree. Her face was drawn. 'Mr Drake,' she said. He looked up. 'Doctor Carroll sent me to find you. Please, come. And hurry. He says it is important.'

NINETEEN

Edgar folded the letter and followed Khin Myo up from
the river. She said nothing, but left him at the headquarters
and walked quickly back down the track.

Inside, he found the Doctor at the window, staring out over
the camp. When he entered, the Doctor turned. 'Mr Drake,' he
said, 'please, sit down.' He motioned to a chair, and sat on the
other side of the broad desk he had used for the amputation.
'Sorry to disturb you, you seemed so peaceful by the river. You
more than anyone deserve a moment of repose. You played
beautifully.'

'It was a technical piece.'

'That was far more than a technical piece.'

'And the *sawbwa*?' Edgar asked. 'One can only hope that he
felt the same.' The Prince had left that morning on a throne
mounted on an elephant's back, the flash of his sequins disappearing into the greenery of the jungle. He was flanked on
either side by horsemen, their ponies' tails dyed red.

'Charmed. He wanted to hear you play again, but I insisted
that there would be better times for that.'

'Did you get the treaty you were asking for?'

'I don't know. I haven't asked for it yet. Directness rarely works
with the princes. I merely told him of our position and asked
nothing, we shared a meal, and you played. The, let us say,

"consummation" of our courtship will have to await the approval of the other princes. But with the *sawbwa*'s support, our chances of a treaty are better.' He leaned forward. 'I brought you to my office to ask your further assistance.'

'Doctor, I can't play again.'

'No, Mr Drake, this time it has nothing to do with pianos and all to do with war, regardless of my poetics on the meeting of the two. Tomorrow night there will be a meeting of Shan Princes in Mong Pu, north of here. I want you to accompany me there.'

'Accompany you? In what capacity?'

'Company, only. It is half a day's journey, and the meeting should only last a day or a night, depending on when they begin. We will travel on horseback. You should at least join us for the journey – it is one of the most scenic in the Shan States.'

Edgar began to speak, but the Doctor gave him no time to refuse. 'We will leave tomorrow.' It was only when Edgar was outside that he realized Carroll hadn't invited him out of camp since their trip to the ravine that sang.

He spent the remainder of the evening by the river thinking, bothered by the suddenness of the trip, by the urgency he sensed in the Doctor's voice. He thought of Khin Myo and their walk in the rain, Perhaps he doesn't want us together. But he dismissed this, There is something else, I have done nothing wrong, nothing improper.

Clouds came. In the Salween, women beat the clothes against the rocks.

o

They left the following afternoon. For the first time since Edgar arrived the Doctor wore his officer's uniform: a scarlet patrol jacket with black braid and his gold rank badge. It gave him a regal and imposing air; his hair was combed, dark and oiled. Khin Myo came out to say goodbye, and Edgar watched her closely as she talked to the Doctor in a mixture of Burmese and English. Carroll listened, and took the sardine tin from his breast pocket and selected a cheroot. When Khin Myo turned at last to Edgar, she didn't smile, but only stared as if she seemed not to see him. The ponies were washed and groomed, but the flowers had been taken from their manes.

o

They rode out of camp, accompanied by Nok Lek and four other Shan on ponies, all holding rifles. They followed the main trail up the ridge, and then turned north. It was a beautiful day, cool with echoes of the rain. The Doctor carried his helmet on the saddle before him and smoked pensively as he rode.

Edgar said nothing, but thought of the letter he had written to Katherine, folded in the confines of his bag.

'You are unusually quiet today, Mr Drake,' said the Doctor.

'Me? No. Daydreaming only. I wrote to my wife for the first time since I arrived in Mae Lwin. About the performance, the piano . . .'

They rode. 'It's strange,' the Doctor said at last.

'What's strange.'

'Your love of the Erard. You are the first Englishman who has not asked me why I want a piano in Mae Lwin.'

Edgar turned. 'Why? Oh, it has never been a mystery to *me*. I have never seen a place more worthy.' He drifted off into silence again. 'No,' he said. 'I wonder more why *I* am here.'

The Doctor looked at him askance. 'And I thought you and that piano were inseparable.' He laughed.

Edgar joined him. 'No, no . . . It must seem that way at times. But I am serious now. I must have been here weeks since I completed my commission. I should have left long ago, shouldn't I?'

'I think that is a question for you to answer.' The Doctor

tapped dark ashes from the end of the cheroot. 'I have not held you here.'

'No,' Edgar persisted, 'but you haven't encouraged me to go either. I expected to be asked to leave as soon as the piano was tuned. Remember, I am "quite a risk" – those were your words, I believe.'

'I enjoy your company, our conversations. It is well worth the risk.'

'To talk about music? I am flattered, but really there must be more than that. Besides, there are those who know music much better than I, men in India, in Calcutta, in Burma even. Or if you merely wanted conversation, naturalists, anthropologists. Why would you make such an effort for me to stay? There could be others.'

'There *have* been others.'

Edgar turned to face the Doctor. 'Visitors, you mean?'

'I have been here for twelve years. Others have come, naturalists, anthropologists, as you say. They came and stayed, never for a long time, only long enough to collect samples, or make sketches, and expostulate on some theory or another on how the biology, the culture, the history of the Shan States fitted into their opinions. Then they returned home.'

'I find that hard to believe. It is so enchanting here . . .'

'I think you are answering your own question, Mr Drake.'

They stopped at the top of a rise to watch a flock of birds take flight.

'There is a piano tuner in Rangoon,' said Carroll when they began to move again. 'I knew that long before I sent for you. He is a missionary. The army doesn't know he tunes pianos, but I met him once long ago. He would have come, had I asked.'

'I imagine that would have saved everyone a lot of effort.'

'It would have. And he would have come and stayed briefly. And left. I wanted someone for whom this would be new. I don't mean to mislead you, of course: that was not my primary intention in bringing you here.' He waved the cigar. 'No, I wanted to have my piano tuned by the best tuner of Erard pianos in London, and I knew this request would force the army to acknowledge how much they depend on me, that they know my methods work, that music, like force, can bring peace. But I also knew that if someone did make the journey all the way here to answer my request, it would be someone who believed in music as I did.'

'And if I hadn't come?' asked Edgar. 'You didn't know me, you couldn't have been certain.'

'Someone else, more visitors, perhaps the missionary from Rangoon. And they would have gone home after several days.'

Edgar saw the Doctor stare into the distance.

'Have you ever thought of returning home?' he asked.

'Of course. I remember England very fondly.'

'You do?'

'It's my home.'

'And yet you continue to stay, why then?'

'I have too much to do here, projects, experiments, too many plans. I hadn't intended to stay. I first came for work. There was only a glimmer that it was for something different. Or maybe it is simpler than that, perhaps I won't leave because I am afraid to hand over my command to someone else. They would not do this . . . peacefully.' He paused, and took the cigar from his mouth. He stared at the smoke seeping from its end. 'There are times when I have doubts.'

'About the war?'

'No, perhaps I am expressing myself poorly. I don't doubt what I have done here. I know it is right. I doubt only what I have missed in doing it.' He rolled the cheroot back and forth between his fingers. 'I listen to you, and how you speak of your wife – I had a wife once. And a daughter – a tiny baby who was mine for one day. There is a Shan saying that when people die it is because they have done what they needed to, because they are too good for this world. I think of her when I hear them say this.'

'I am sorry,' Edgar said. 'The Colonel told me. But I didn't feel it was my position to ask . . .'

'No, you are too considerate . . . But I should apologize, Mr Drake: these are sad, distant thoughts.' He straightened his back in the saddle. 'Besides, you asked me why I stay. That is a difficult enough question. Perhaps everything I just told you about not wanting to give up the camp is wrong. Perhaps I stay simply because I cannot leave.' He put his cigar back in his mouth. 'Once I tried. Not long after I began to work at the hospital in Rangoon another surgeon arrived with his battalion, to remain in Rangoon for a year before moving upcountry. It had been years since I visited England and I was given the option to return home for a few months. I booked a berth on a steamer and travelled from Rangoon, where I was stationed at the time, to Calcutta, and there boarded the train to Bombay.'

'It is the same route that I followed.'

'Then you know how stunning it is. Well, that trip was even more stunning. We were not thirty miles from Delhi when the train stopped at a small supply depot, and I saw a cloud of dust rise up over the desert. It was a group of riders, and as they drew closer I recognized them as Rajasthani herders. The women were dressed in exquisitely coloured veils, which still glowed a deep red despite the dust that had settled over them. I think they had seen the train from a distance and had come to inspect it out of curiosity. They moved back and forth beside us, pointed at the wheels, the engine, the passengers, all the time talking in a language I couldn't understand. I watched them, the passing colour, still thinking, and I boarded the steamer to England. But when the boat reached Aden, I disembarked and took the next steamer back to Bombay, the next train back to Calcutta. One week later I was back at my post in Pegu. I still don't know exactly why seeing the herders made me turn back. But the thought of returning to London's dark streets while those images continued to dance in my head seemed impossible. The last thing I wanted to become was one of those sad veterans who bores any listening ear with disjointed tales of unfamiliar places.' He inhaled deeply on the cheroot. 'You know, I told you how I have been translating the *Odyssey*. I always read it as a tragic tale of Odysseus's struggle to find his way home. Now I understand more and more what Dante and Tennyson wrote about it, that he wasn't lost, but that after the wonders he had seen Odysseus couldn't, perhaps didn't want to, return home.'

There was silence. 'That reminds me of a story I once heard,' said Edgar.

'Yes?'

'It was not long ago – three months, maybe – when I first left England. I met a man on the ship in the Red Sea. An old Arab.'

'The Man with One Story.'

'You know him?'

'Of course. I met him long ago when I was in Aden. I have heard many speak of his story. A story of war is never lost on a soldier.'

'A story of war?'

'I have heard soldiers tell me the same story for years. I can almost recite it now; the images of Greece are so vivid. It turns out the story is true, both he and his brother were just boys, whose families had been killed by the Ottomans, and worked as spies during the War for Independence. I once met an old veteran from the war who said that he had heard of the brothers, their valour. Everyone wants to hear the story. They feel that it is auspicious, that those who hear it perform bravely in battle.'

Edgar stared at the Doctor. 'Greece?'

'Yes?' asked the Doctor.

'You are certain it was about the Greek War for Independence?'

'The story? Of course. Why? Are you surprised that after so many years I still remember it?'

'No . . . I am not surprised at all. I too remember as if I heard it yesterday. I *too* can almost recite it now.'

'Is there something wrong then?'

'No, nothing wrong, I suppose,' said Edgar, slowly. 'Just thinking of the story.' Thinking, Was it different only for me? I could not have imagined it all, this all.

They rode on and passed through a grove of trees with long twisted seed pods that made rattling sounds as they shook. The Doctor said, 'You wished to say something. That the Man with One Story reminded you of something I said.'

'Oh . . .' Edgar reached up and picked one of the pods. He broke it open, the dried seeds spilling out over his hands. 'It doesn't matter. It is just a story, I suppose.'

'Yes, Mr Drake.' Carroll looked quizzically at the piano tuner. 'They are all just stories.'

o

The sun was low in the sky as they passed over a small rise to look down on a collection of huts in the distance. 'Mong Pu,' said the Doctor. They stopped by a dusty shrine. Edgar watched Carroll dismount and lay a coin at the base of a small house that held a spirit icon.

They began their descent, the ponies' feet splashing in the mud of the trail. It grew darker. Mosquitoes came out, great clouds, breaking and coalescing like dancing fragments of shade.

'Foul creatures,' said the Doctor, swatting at them. His cheroot had burned to a short stub and he took the sardine tin once again from his pocket. 'I recommend that you smoke, Mr Drake. It will keep the insects away.'

Edgar remembered the malaria attack and conceded. The Doctor lit a cigar and passed it to him. Its taste was liquid, intoxicating.

'I should probably explain a little about the meeting,' said the Doctor, as they began to ride again. 'As you have read, since the annexation of Mandalay there has been active resistance from a union of forces called the Limbin Confederacy.'

'We spoke of this when the *sawbwa* of Mongnai came.'

'We did,' said the Doctor. 'But there is something I didn't tell you. For the past two years I have been in close negotiation with the *sawbwa*s of the Limbin Confederacy.'

Edgar took the cigar awkwardly from his mouth, 'You wrote that no one had met the Confederacy . . .'

'I know what I wrote and what I told you. But I had reasons for that. As you probably know, at the time that your boat was somewhere in the Indian Ocean a force was established at Hlaingdet under Colonel Stedman: companies from the Hampshire Regiment, a Gurkha company, Bombay sappers, with George Scott as political officer, which gave me hope this wouldn't turn into a full war; he is a close friend, and I don't know anyone as sensitive to local issues as he is. But since January our forces have been engaged in active battle near Yawnghwe. Now, the Commissioner feels that the only way to control the Shan States is through force. But, because of the overtures by the Mongnai *sawbwa*, I think we can negotiate peace.'

'Does the army know about this meeting?'

'No, Mr Drake, and this is what I need you to understand. They would oppose it. They don't trust the Princes. I will put it bluntly – I, and now you, are acting in direct defiance of military orders.' He let the words sink in. 'Before you speak, there is something else. We have also spoken briefly about a Shan dacoit Prince named Twet Nga Lu, known as the Bandit Chief, who once seized the state of Mongnai, but who has since retreated to terrorize the villages ruled by the true Mongnai *sawbwa*. They say that few people have ever seen him. What they haven't told you is what they don't know. I have met the Bandit Chief many times.'

He waved away a swarm of mosquitoes. 'Several years ago, before the rebellion, Twet Nga Lu was bitten by a snake near the Salween. One of his brothers, who sometimes trades in Mae Lwin, knew that we were only several hours' downstream. He brought the sick man to me, and I administered a poultice of local herbs that I had learnt from a Mae Lwin medicine man. He was nearly unconscious when he arrived, and when he awoke he saw my face and thought he had been captured. He grew so angry that his brother had to restrain him and explain that I had saved his life. Finally, he calmed down and his eyes settled on the microscope, and he asked what it was. He didn't believe me when I tried to explain it, so I took a sample of pond water I had been examining, placed it on the slide and asked him to look. At first he had trouble with the microscope – opening the wrong eye and so forth – and looked ready to throw the instrument to the ground, when the light, reflected from the sun through the canted mirror, met his eye, bringing images of the tiny little beasts familiar to any English schoolboy. The effect could not have been more profound. He staggered back to his bed, muttering that indeed I must have magical powers to summon monsters from pond water. What would happen, he exclaimed, if I decided to set them loose from the machine! He now seems to believe I have a form of magical vision which the Shan believe can be found only in amulets. Of course, I won't protest, and since then he has returned to me several times, asking to see the microscope. He is very bright and is learning English quickly, as if he knows who his new enemy is. Although I still cannot trust him, he seems now to accept that I personally have no designs against Kengtawng. In August last year he seemed increasingly distracted and asked me if there was anything I could do to block the signing of a treaty with the Limbin Confederacy. Then he disappeared for three months. The next time I heard his name was in a Mandalay intelligence briefing on an attack on a fort near Lake Inle.'

'And then he attacked Mae Lwin,' said Edgar. 'They told me this in Mandalay.'

There was a long pause. 'No, no, he didn't attack Mae Lwin,' Carroll said slowly. 'I was with Twet Nga Lu the day Mae Lwin was attacked. Mandalay doesn't know this. The villagers say that the attack was by the Karenni, another tribe. I haven't reported this because the army will certainly send troops, the last thing we need here. But it wasn't Twet Nga Lu.' Carroll spoke more quickly now. 'I have spoken to you in confidence and now I need to ask your assistance. We will be in Mong Pu soon. This is the first time in a long while that Twet Nga Lu has met the *sawbwa* of Mongnai. If they cannot settle their differences, they will not stop fighting until one of them is dead, and we will be forced to intercede with our armies. Of course, there are many in the War Office, bored by the peace since the annexation, who are anxious for war. If there is any chance of peace, they will destroy it. Until the treaty is signed, no one can know that I am here.'

'I have never heard you speak so candidly of the war.'

'I know, but there are reasons. The Limbin Confederacy thinks that I have orders from superiors within the British command. If they know I am alone, they won't fear me. So today, if anyone asks, you are Lieutenant-Colonel Daly, civil officer of the Northern Shan Column, stationed at Maymyo, representative of Mr Hildebrand, Superintendent of the Shan States.'

'But the *sawbwa* of Mongnai has seen me play.'

'He already knows and has agreed to keep this a secret. It is the others whom I need to convince.'

'You didn't tell me this when we left,' said Edgar. He felt an anger growing.

'You wouldn't have come.'

'I am sorry, Doctor. I cannot do this.'

'Mr Drake.'

'Doctor, I can't do this. Mr Hildebrand is—'

'Mr Hildebrand will never know. You will need to do nothing, to say nothing.'

'But I can't. It's seditious . . . It is—'

'Mr Drake, I had hoped that, after almost three months in

Mae Lwin, you would understand, that you could help me. That you were not like the others.'

'Doctor, there is a difference between believing that a piano can help bring peace and signing treaties without orders, impersonating others, defying one's Queen. There are rules and laws—'

The Doctor spoke harshly. 'Mr Drake, your defiance began when you came to Mae Lwin against orders. You are now considered missing, perhaps already under suspicion.'

'Under suspicion! For what—'

'What do you think, now that you have disappeared for so long?'

'I do not need to participate in any charades. I am due to return to Mandalay any time now.' He gripped the reins tightly.

'From here, Mr Drake? You can't turn back now. And I know as well as you that you do not want to return to Mandalay.'

Edgar shook his head angrily. 'Is this why you called me to Mae Lwin?' It was dark now, and he stared into the Doctor's face, illuminated by the dull glow of his cigar.

The end of the cheroot flickered light. 'No, Mr Drake, I brought you to tune a piano. But situations change. We are, after all, at war.'

'And I am walking into battle unarmed.'

'Unarmed? Hardly, Mr Drake. You are with me. Don't under-estimate my importance.'

Edgar's pony twitched her ears at the mosquitoes that buzzed around her head, the only sound. Her mane shivered.

o

There was a shout from the road ahead. A man rode up on horseback.

'Bo Naw, my good friend!' Carroll exclaimed.

The man bowed slightly from his mount. 'Doctor Carroll, the

Princes are all here, with their armies. We are waiting only for you.'

Carroll looked to the piano tuner, who returned his stare. A faint smile ran across the Doctor's lips. Edgar wrapped his fingers once again in the reins. His face was still.

Carroll took his helmet and fitted it over his head, fastening the strap over his chin like a soldier. He took his cigar from his mouth and flicked it into the air, where it traced a golden trajectory. He hissed.

For a moment Edgar waited alone. Then, sighing heavily, he took the cheroot from his mouth and threw it to the ground.

o

It was nearly dark as they galloped down a track that passed between stone outcrops. In the distance, Edgar could see the glow of torchlight. They rode through a rough barricade, past vague silhouettes of guards. Soon the track rose and they approached a fort, hidden in a dark grove of trees.

The fort was long and low, surrounded on all sides by a stockade of sharpened bamboo. A group of elephants was tethered to the wall. Armed guards saluted the riders. They stopped at the entrance to the stockade, where a sentry emerged into the torchlight. He eyed the men suspiciously. Edgar stared into the fort. The path that led up to the building was lined with more men, and in the flickering light of torches he could see the glint of spears, cutlasses, rifles. 'Who are they?' he whispered.

'Armies. Each *sawbwa* has brought his own troops.'

Beside them, Bo Naw spoke in Shan. The guard walked forward and took the reins of their ponies. The Englishmen dismounted and entered the stockade.

As they stepped inside the ramparts, Edgar sensed a movement of bodies, and for a brief second he thought that it was a trap. But the men were not advancing. They were kowtowing, bowing before the Doctor like a wave, their backs glistening with sweat, weapons clanging.

The Doctor walked swiftly, and Edgar caught up with him by the door. As they ascended the steps to the fort, he looked behind him. At the vision of the backs of the warriors, the fierce stockade and the forest beyond. Crickets screamed, and in his mind now echoed a single word. The man at the entrance had called Carroll not 'Doctor', or 'Major', but 'Bo', the Shan word that Edgar knew was reserved for a warrior chief. Anthony Carroll took off his helmet and tucked it beneath his arm. They stepped inside.

o

For several long breaths, they stood and stared into a deep darkness, until shapes shifted slowly out of the dim light. There were several Princes seated in a semi-circle, each dressed in some of the finest clothes Edgar had seen in Burma, bejewelled costumes like those of the puppets which had danced at the *yôkthe-pwè*: sequinned jackets with brocaded wings on the shoulders, crowns shaped like pagodas. The men had been talking when they had entered, but the room was now silent. Carroll led Edgar around the circle to two open cushions. Behind each Prince other men stood in the darkness, barely licked by the dancing lights of tiny fires.

They sat, still silent. Then one of the Princes, an older man with a finely combed moustache, spoke at length. When he finished, Carroll answered. At one point he motioned to the piano tuner, who heard, 'Daly, Lieutenant-Colonel, Hildebrand,' but he understood nothing else.

When Carroll's introduction was complete, another Prince began to speak. The Doctor turned to Edgar. 'All is fine, Lieutenant-Colonel. You are welcome here.'

The meeting began and soon the night was lost, a blur of jewelled gowns and candlelight, a canto of strange tongues. Soon

Edgar felt himself doze off, so that it all took on the quality of a dream. A dream within a dream, he told himself, as his eyelids fell slowly, For perhaps I have been dreaming since Aden. Around him, the Princes seemed to float; the upturned candleholders hid the floor from the flames. Only at occasional breaks in the conversation did Carroll speak to him, 'That man who is speaking is Chao Weng, *sawbwa* of Lawksawk, next to him is Chao Khun Kyi, the *sawbwa* of Mongnai – whom you must recognize. Then that is Chao Kawng Tai of Kengtung, who has travelled a great distance to be here. At his side is Chao Khun Ti of Mongpawn. Next to him is Twet Nga Lu.'

And Edgar asked, 'Twet Nga Lu?' But Carroll had returned to the conversation, leaving Edgar to stare at the man whom he had heard about since the steamer voyage, whom some said didn't exist, who had escaped hundreds of British raids, who perhaps was one of the last figures standing between Britain and the consolidation of the empire. Edgar stared at the Shan Bandit Chief. There was something familiar about him which he couldn't place. He was a small man, with a face that was soft even in the angular shadows cast by the candlelight. Edgar could see none of his fabled tattoos or talismans, but he noticed that he spoke with an eerie self-assurance, a half-grin cast into the smoke-filled air like a threat. And although he rarely said anything, when he did the room grew quickly quiet. Edgar then realized why he recognized the man, or if not the man, why he recognized the confidence, the elusiveness. He had seen the same in Anthony Carroll.

So to this dream of the Shan Princes entered a new character, a man whom Edgar thought he knew, but who now seemed as inscrutable as the *sawbwa*s who sat before him, who spoke a strange tongue, who held the respect and fear of foreign tribes. Edgar turned to watch the Doctor, to look for the man who played the piano, who collected flowers and read Homer, but heard only a language of strange tones, words that even a man who controlled the intricacy of notes couldn't understand. And for one brief, terrifying moment, as the glow of candles flickered upward across his face, Edgar thought that he recognized the high cheekbones, the long brow, and the intensity of stare and speech that the other tribes say make a Shan.

But this only lasted briefly and, as swiftly as it arrived, the haunting left him. And Anthony Carroll was still Anthony Carroll and he turned and his eyes flashed, 'You holding up, old man? Is something wrong?' It was late, and it would be many hours before the meeting finished.

'Yes, I am holding up,' Edgar answered. 'No . . . there is nothing wrong at all.'

o

The meeting lasted until dawn, when sunlight finally began to trickle through the rafters. Edgar didn't know if he had been sleeping when he sensed a shuffling around him, and one of the Shan Princes, and then another, rose and walked out, bowing to the Englishmen as they left. As the others stood there were more formalities, and Edgar remarked how gaudy and caricatured the costumes seemed in the daylight, extravagance beyond the pomp and posture of their wearers. Soon they rose too, to follow the Princes. At the door Edgar heard a voice at his back and turned to find himself face to face with Twet Nga Lu.

'I know who you are, Mr Drake,' said the Shan Bandit Chief in a deliberate English, a smile slinking along his lips. He said something in Shan and raised his hands before him. Edgar stepped back, suddenly frightened, and Twet Nga Lu, now laughing, turned his palms down and began to move his fingers before him in the mocking mime of a pianist.

Edgar looked to see if Carroll had seen this, but the Doctor was engaged in conversation with another Prince. Twet Nga Lu passed, Edgar saw Carroll turn, and the two men stared at each other. It was a brief exchange and then Twet Nga Lu walked out of the room, and a group of Shan warriors fell into formation behind him.

o

On the road back to Mae Lwin they spoke little. The Doctor stared out into the mist that covered the track. Edgar's thoughts were thick with fatigue and confusion. He wanted to ask about the meeting, but the Doctor seemed lost in contemplation. At one point the Doctor stopped to point out a group of red flowers by the side of the track, but for the remainder of the trip he was silent. The sky was heavy and the wind picked up, whipping along the lonely crags and open road. Only when they were climbing the hill above Mae Lwin, did Carroll turn to the piano tuner.

'You haven't asked what happened at the meeting.'

'I am sorry,' Edgar said warily, 'I am tired, that's all.'

Anthony Carroll shifted his gaze down the track. 'Last night,' he said, 'I received a conditional surrender from both the Limbin Confederacy and from Twet Nga Lu, to end their resistance to British rule in one month's time, in exchange for limited autonomy guaranteed by Her Majesty. The revolt is over.'

TWENTY

THEY ARRIVED IN camp shortly after noon. In the clearing, a group of boys came out to meet them, taking away the men's ponies. The camp seemed eerily silent. Edgar expected announcement, movement, something to acknowledge the accomplishment. He had the unsettling feeling that he had just witnessed history. But there was nothing, only the customary greetings. The Doctor disappeared, and Edgar returned to his room. He fell asleep still dressed in his riding clothes.

○

He awoke at midnight, sweating, disorientated, having dreamed that he was still on horseback, on the long ride from Mong Pu. Only as he recognized the features of his room, the mosquito net, his bag, the stack of papers, and the tuning tools, did his heart slow.

He tried again to sleep but couldn't. Perhaps it was his thoughts of the Doctor, or his dream of a journey without end, or perhaps it was only because he had been sleeping since the early afternoon. He was hot and dirty and parched and he found himself breathing fast, Maybe I am sick again. He pushed aside the mosquito net and rushed to the door. Outside the air was fresh and cool, and he took deep breaths and tried to calm himself.

It was a still night and a sliver of moon passed between indecisive rain clouds. Below his room the Salween was dark. He slipped down the stairs and out across the clearing. The camp was silent. Even the guard at the watch post slept, seated outside the hut, his head rolled back and resting on the wall.

As Edgar walked, the soil curled up against his toes. He passed through the thicket of flowers and onto the beach. He was moving faster now, tearing off his shirt and throwing it onto the sand. He stepped out of his riding breeches. His toes touched the water and he dived.

The river was cool and smooth with suspended silt. He rose to the surface and rested, floating. Upriver, the rocks jutted into the river, breaking the current into eddies which curled along the shore. He felt himself move slowly upstream.

He finally climbed out of the water and stood on the bank. Pulling his clothes back over his wet body, he walked barefoot to the northern edge of the beach and picked his way over the rocks until he reached the large boulder where the fishermen stood to cast their nets. He lay on his back. The stone was still warm from the day's sun.

He must have fallen asleep because he didn't hear anyone walk down to the beach, only the sound of splashing. He opened his eyes slowly, puzzled at who also might have made the night-time pilgrimage to the river, Perhaps the young couple have returned. Slowly, carefully, so as not to reveal his presence, he turned on his side and looked down the beach.

It was a woman and she was kneeling, crouched away from him, her long hair tied above her head. She was washing her arms, lifting water in cupped hands and letting it run down her skin. She was wearing her *hta main*; even in solitude, she bathed with modesty, as if she knew well of the lecherous eyes of owls. The *hta main* soaked up the water from the river and clung to her torso and to the swell of her hips.

Perhaps he knew who she was before she turned towards him

and saw him, and the two of them froze, each aware of their mutual violation, the shared sensuality of the river, of the sliver of moon. Then she moved hastily, gathering up her other clothes, her soap. Without looking back, she ran up the path.

The clouds shifted. The moon returned. He walked onto the beach. On the sand there was a comb, ivory, incandescent.

o

The Doctor left again on another 'diplomatic mission' and Edgar returned to work on the piano. With the arrival of the rains, the soundboard had swollen, a nearly imperceptible change, perhaps noticeable only to those who wish to tune.

For two days he kept the comb.

In moments of privacy he would take it out and examine it, running his fingers over the orphaned strands of black hair that wove themselves through the ivory prongs. He knew he should return it to her, but he waited, out of indecision or expectation, out of a sense of intimacy which grew along with the waiting and the silence, which became more acute with each brief, awkward conversation they shared in the unavoidable moments when they passed each other on the paths. And so he kept the comb. Convincing himself he must work, he delayed returning it during the day, while at night he told himself he must wait again until morning, I cannot go to her when it is dark. The first night he stayed late at the piano, tuning and retuning. On the second night, while he played alone, he heard a knock on the door.

He knew who it was before the door drifted open and she stepped inside tentatively. Perhaps it was the delicate, patient sound of the knocking, distinct from the Doctor's confident pounding or the servants' hesitancy. Perhaps the wind had shifted, bringing the scent of wet earth down from the mountain, and, on its route, lifted her perfume. Or perhaps he recognized the direction, the inevitability, that they moved in age-worn patterns, destined repetitions.

From the doorway, came the voice, the accent liquid. 'Hello.'

'Ma Khin Myo,' he said.

'May I come in?'

'Of . . . course.'

She closed the door lightly. 'Am I interrupting you?'

'No, not at all . . . Why would you think that?'

She tilted her head slightly. 'You seem preoccupied. Is something the matter?'

'No, no.' His voice trembled, and he forced a smile. 'I am only passing the time.'

She stayed by the door and held her hands together. She wore the same light blouse she had worn the day she had met him by the river. He could see she had painted her face recently and thought of the incongruity, *There is no sun now, no reason to wear thanaka* but that it is beautiful.

'You know,' she said, 'in all the time that I have had English friends I have heard the piano played often. I love its sound. I . . . I thought maybe you could show me how you work.'

'Of course. But isn't it late? Shouldn't you be with . . .' he hesitated.

'With Doctor Carroll? He is not in Mae Lwin.' She was still standing. Behind her, her shadow reclined against the wall, curves against the lines of bamboo.

'Of course, of course. I knew, didn't I?' He took his glasses and polished them on his shirt. He took a deep breath. 'I have been here all day. So many hours at the piano can drive one a bit . . . mad. I am sorry. I should have sought your company.'

'You still haven't even offered me a place to sit.'

Edgar started at her directness. He moved over to clear a place on the bench. 'Please.'

She moved slowly across the room, towards the piano, her shadow on the wall growing longer. She gathered her *hta main* together and sat beside him. For a moment he only looked at her as she stared down at the keys. The flower she wore was fragrant, freshly picked; he could see where tiny grains of pollen had dusted her hair. She turned towards him.

'I am sorry if I seem distracted,' he said. 'I'm always slow to come out of the trance that I enter when I tune. It is another world. It's always a bit startling to be interrupted by . . . visitors . . . It is hard to explain.'

'Perhaps like being awakened from a dream.'

'Perhaps. Perhaps . . . But I am awake in a world of sounds. It is as if I have begun to dream again . . .'. When she said nothing, he added, 'That must seem strange.'

'No.' She shook her head. 'At times we confuse what is real with what we are dreaming.'

There was silence. Khin Myo lifted her hands and placed them on the keyboard.

'Have you ever played before?' he asked.

'No, but I have always wanted to since I was a little girl.'

'You can play now, it is much more interesting than watching me tune.'

'Oh, I shouldn't, really. I don't know how.'

'That's all right. Just try. Press the keys.'

'Any key?'

'Try where your finger is now. That is the first note of the prelude and fugue in F minor. It's part of *The Well-Tempered Clavier*, which I played for the *sawbwa*.'

She pressed the key. The note rang out in the room, echoing back to them.

'See,' said Edgar. 'Now you have played Bach.'

Khin Myo didn't turn from the piano. He saw the corner of her eyes wrinkle, the hints of a smile. 'It sounds so different, sitting here.'

'It does. There is nothing quite like it. Please, perhaps I can teach you more of the piece.'

'Oh, I wouldn't want to bother you. Actually, you are right: maybe it is late. I didn't want to interrupt your work.'

'Nonsense. You are here now.'

'But I can't play.'

'I insist. It is a short motif, but one of great meaning. Please, now that we have started, I couldn't let you leave. The next note is that one: hit that with your forefinger.'

She turned to him.

'Go on, play,' he said and pointed to the key. She pressed it. Deep in the piano, the hammer leaped towards its string.

'Now, next key to the left, now the key above that. Now back to the first. Yes, that one, the first key that you played. Now the second one again, that one. And above. There, that's it. Now play it again, faster now.' Khin Myo struggled through it.

'It doesn't sound like much,' she said.

'It sounds like everything. Try it again.'

'I don't know . . . Maybe you should.'

'No, you are playing wonderfully. It will be much easier if you use your left hand for the lower notes.'

'I don't think I can. Can you show me?' She turned, her face close to his.

Edgar's heart pounded suddenly and for a brief moment he was afraid she would hear it. But the sound of the music emboldened him. He stood, and he moved behind her and lowered his arms over hers. 'Put your hands on mine,' he said.

Slowly, she lifted her hands. For a moment they waited, floating, and then she let them settle gently. Neither moved, each feeling only the other's hands, the rest of their bodies but pale outlines. He could see their reflections in the lacquered mahogany of the nameboard. Her fingers only reached halfway along his.

The piece began slowly, tentatively. The fugue in F sharp minor from Book Two of *The Well-Tempered Clavier* always reminded him of an opening of flowers, a meeting of lovers, a song of beginnings. He hadn't played it on the night of the *sawbwa*'s visit because it is the thirty-eighth piece and he had stopped at the twenty-fourth. So at first his hands moved slowly, uncertain, but with the soft weight of her fingers he moved through each bar steadily, and within the piano actions glided up with the touch of the keys, leaping and falling back from the jacks, leaving strings trembling, rows and rows of tiny intricate pieces of metal and wood and sound. On the case the candles trembled.

As they played, a strand of her hair broke loose from where it had been tucked beneath the flower. It tickled his lip. He didn't pull back, but closed his eyes, and moved his face closer so that it traced itself over his cheek as he played, over his lips again, now over the lashes of his eyes.

The music rose faster, then dipped sweetly, softer, and then it ended.

Their hands rested together on the piano. She turned her head slightly, her eyes closed. She said his name, her voice composed only of breath.

He asked, 'Is this why you came here tonight?'

There was silence and she answered, 'No, Mr Drake.' She whispered it now. 'I have been here for ever.'

And Edgar lowered his lips to her skin, cool and moist with perspiration. He let himself breathe in the scent of her hair, taste the sweet salt of her neck. Slowly she moved her hands, and her fingers entwined themselves within his.

And for that moment everything stopped. The warmth of her fingers, the smoothness of her skin on his calluses. The light of the candle dancing over the soft surface of her cheek, catching only the shadows of the flower.

It was she who broke their embrace, softly untangling her hands from his, which still rested on the keyboard. She traced her fingers along his arm. I must leave. And he closed his eyes again, inhaled one last time and let her go.

TWENTY-ONE

EDGAR SPENT THE night at the piano, drifting in and out of sleep. It was still dark when he awoke to the sound of the door creaking, footsteps. He opened his eyes, expecting to see the children, but found himself staring into the eyes of an old woman. 'Doctor need you. Hurry,' she said, her breath rank with the smell of fermented fish.

'Sorry?' He sat up, still lost in sleep.

'Doctor Carroll need you. Hurry.'

He stood and straightened his shirt. Only then did he associate the Doctor's call with last night, with Khin Myo.

The old woman led him from the room. It was still early dawn and cold, the sun was far from breaking over the mountain. At the door to the headquarters she grinned, her mouth full of betel-stained teeth, and hobbled away down the path. Edgar found the Doctor inside, standing over maps spread out on his desk. 'You sent for me,' he said.

The Doctor stared at the maps for a moment before looking up, 'Yes. Hello, Mr Drake, please sit down.' He motioned to a chair.

Edgar sat and watched the Doctor flip earnestly through the maps, one hand tracing lines on the paper, the other raised and massaging the back of his neck. Suddenly he looked up and pulled the pince-nez from his nose. 'Mr Drake, my apologies for waking you so early.'

'It is all right . . .'

'This is rather urgent,' the Doctor interrupted. 'I returned several hours ago from Mongpan. We raced to get here.' His voice seemed different, distracted, formal, the timbre of confidence now gone. Only then did Edgar notice that he was still dressed in riding clothes, still splashed with mud. He wore a pistol in his belt. Edgar felt a sudden sense of guilt, This is not about Khin Myo.

'Mr Drake, it is best that I approach this bluntly.'

'Of course, but . . .'

'Mae Lwin is going to be attacked.'

Edgar leaned forward, as if to hear him better, 'I am sorry, I don't understand. Attacked?'

'Perhaps tonight.'

There was silence. For a moment Edgar thought it was a jest or one of Carroll's projects, that there was more which the Doctor would explain. He looked again at the pistol, the muddy shirt, Carroll's eyes, lined and exhausted. 'You are serious,' he said, as if to himself. 'But I thought we signed a treaty. You told me—'

'The treaty still stands. It is not the Limbin Confederacy.'

'Who then?'

'Others. I have enemies. Perhaps shifting alliances, men I once thought were friends, but whose loyalty I now question.' He stared back down at the map. 'I wish I could tell you more, but we must prepare . . .' He paused before looking up again. 'I can tell you only this. A month before you arrived we were attacked – you know this, you were detained in Mandalay. Several of the attackers were later captured, but they refused to reveal who had employed them, even under the pain of torture. Some say they were petty thieves, but I have never seen petty thieves armed so well. What's more, some of the rifles they carried were British, which meant they had been stolen. Or that the men were former allies turned traitors.'

'And now?'

'Two days ago I travelled to Mongpan, to discuss building a road to Mae Lwin. Only hours after I had arrived, a Shan boy ran into the Prince's quarters. He had been fishing on one of the small Salween tributaries, where he saw a group of men camped in the forest, crept up on them and listened to their conversation. He couldn't understand everything, but heard the men talking of a plan to attack Mongpan and then Mae Lwin. Again they carried British rifles, and this time the group was much larger. If the boy is correct, I am confused about why any dacoits would venture this far onto the plateau to attack us. There are many possibilities, but I don't have time to discuss them with you now. If they are in Mongpan already, they may be here as soon as tonight.'

Edgar waited for the Doctor to say more, but he was still. 'And now what will you do?' he ventured.

'From what was described to me, the group is too large for us to defend the site. I have called for reinforcements. I have sent riders out on horseback. Tribes loyal to me will send men if they can get here soon enough. From Mongpan, from Monghang, from . . .' He turned again to the map, listing villages, but Edgar was not listening. He thought only of the image of riders descending on Mae Lwin from the hills. He saw the men riding swiftly through the karst, across the open plateau, the banners flying, the ponies' tails dyed red, the armies gathering in camp, the women seeking shelter, Khin Myo. He thought now of the meeting of the Confederacy of Princes. Now the Doctor wore the same uniform, the same distant stare. 'And I . . .'

'I need your help, Mr Drake.'

'How? I will do anything. I am not good with a rifle, but—'

'No, more important. Even with reinforcements Mae Lwin may fall, and even if we are able to repel an attack, it will be with much damage. It is only a small village'

'But with more men—'

'Perhaps, or perhaps they will burn the camp. I must think about this. I cannot risk everything I have spent twelve years working for. The army will rebuild Mae Lwin, but I cannot expect any more. I have already arranged for my medical equipment, my microscopes, my plant collections, to be moved and hidden. But then—'

'The Erard.'

'I don't trust my men to carry it out alone. They don't understand its fragility.'

'But where?'

'Downriver. You will float out this morning. It is only several days to British forts in Karen country. There you will be met by troops who can escort you back to Rangoon.'

'Rangoon?'

'Until we know what is happening. But Mae Lwin is no longer safe for a civilian. The time for that is past.'

Edgar shook his head. 'This is all happening too fast, Doctor. Perhaps I can stay . . . or I can take the piano into the mountains. I cannot bear this . . .' his voice drifted off. 'What about Khin Myo?' he asked, suddenly. I can ask this now, she is part of this, inextricably so, She is no longer in my thoughts only.

The Doctor looked up and his voice grew suddenly stern. 'She will stay with me.'

'I only asked because—'

'She is safer here, Mr Drake.'

'But, Doctor—'

'I am sorry, Mr Drake, but I cannot talk longer. We must make preparations to leave.'

'There must be a way I can stay, now.' Edgar tried to control the panic in his voice.

'Mr Drake,' said the Doctor slowly, 'I do not have time for this. I am not giving you a choice.'

Edgar stared at him, 'And I am not one of your soldiers.'

There was a long silence. The Doctor massaged the back of his neck again and stared down at the maps. When he looked up again, his face had softened. 'Mr Drake,' he said. 'I am sorry that this had to happen. I know what this means to you, I know more than you think I know. But I have no choice now. I think one day you will understand.'

o

Edgar stumbled out into the sun.

He stood still and tried to calm himself. Around him, the camp spun with dizzying activity. Men arranged sandbags or ran to the river with rifles and ammunition. Others cut and tied bamboo into sharp ramparts. A line of women and children worked as a fire brigade, filling buckets, clay vessels, cooking pots with water.

'Mr Drake.' These words from behind him. A small boy holding his bag. 'I am taking this to the river, sir.' The piano tuner only nodded.

His eyes followed a line of activity up the mountain to where the front wall of the piano room had been completely removed. He could see men working inside, shirtless bodies toiling at a bamboo and rope pulley. A crowd had gathered below to watch, buckets of water and rifles still in their hands. Above he heard shouting. Further up the track a group of men strained at a rope. He saw the piano lurch into the air, uneasy at first, but in the room the men steadied it, pushing it onto a slide made of long pieces of bamboo which had been lashed together. The men at the rope groaned, the piano swung out on the pulley, flying now, slowly, down, and Edgar heard a ringing as they let it drop, the rope burning their hands. For a long time the piano remained suspended, inching slowly down the bamboo, until at last it touched the ground, and another group of men rushed to catch it, and Edgar took his first breath since he had looked up.

The piano stood on a dry patch of earth. It seemed very small in the light, against the backdrop of the camp.

More shouts and running, bodies moved about him in a blur. He remembered the afternoon he had left London on the steamer, how the fog swirled, how all became silent and he was left alone. He felt a presence beside him.

'You are leaving,' she said.

'Yes,' he looked at her. 'You know?'

'He told me.'

'I want to stay, but—'

'You should go. It isn't safe.' She looked at the ground. She was standing so close to him that he could see the top of her head, the stem of a single purple flower twisting itself into the darkness of her hair.

'Come with me,' he said suddenly.

'You know I can't.'

'By this evening I will be miles downstream, by morning you and Doctor Carroll may be dead, and I will never know—'

'Don't say those things.'

'I . . . hadn't planned for this. There is so much left that I want to say. I may never see you again, I don't want to say this, but it could be—'

'Mr Drake . . .' she began to speak and stopped. Her eyes were moist. 'I am sorry.'

'Please, come with me.'

'I must stay with Anthony,' she said.

Anthony, he thought, I have never heard his name. 'I came here because of you,' he said, but already his words sounded empty.

'You came here for something else,' she said, and from the river came a call.

TWENTY-TWO

T HEY CARRIED THE piano through the flowering brush at the
edge of the camp and down to the river. There a raft was
waiting, a rough contraption of logs three times the length of the
piano. The men splashed into the shallows and set the piano on
the raft. They lashed its legs down through spaces between the
logs. They worked quickly, as if familiar with the task. When
the piano was secured, a large chest was placed on the other end
of the raft and similarly fastened. 'Your belongings are inside,' said
Carroll.

It was still unclear who among the many men wading through
the water, twisting rope, tying, adjusting, would accompany him,
until at last the piano and the chest were secured and the raft
balanced. Then two boys walked up to the bank, picked up two
rifles each and walked back to the raft.

'This is Seing To and Tint Naing,' said the Doctor. 'They are
brothers. They are very skilled boatmen and they speak Burmese.
They will accompany you down the river. Nok Lek will go as well,
but in a dugout, to scout the rapids ahead. You will float to Karen
country, or perhaps as far as Moulmein, which should take five or
six days. There you will be deep into British territory and safe.'

'And then what should I do? When should I return?'

'Return? I don't know, Mr Drake . . .' The Doctor was silent, and then held out a small piece of paper, folded and sealed with wax. 'There is one last thing as well. I want you to have this.'

'What is it?' Edgar was surprised by the offer.

The Doctor thought for a moment. 'That is for you to decide. You must wait to read it.' Behind him one of the boys said, 'We are ready, Mr Drake. We need to go.'

Edgar extended his hand and took the paper, and folded it once more and slipped it into his shirt pocket. 'Thank you,' he said quietly and he stepped onto the raft. They pushed off from the shore. Only looking back at the bank did he see her, standing in the flowers, her body half-hidden in the brush. Behind her Mae Lwin rose to the mountain, layers of bamboo homes, one without a wall, open and naked to the river.

The raft was caught by the current and swept downstream.

o

The rains had swollen the river considerably since Edgar had first floated down months before. He thought of the night they had arrived, descending silently through the darkness. How different a world it seemed from the one in which he now travelled, the wooded banks drenched in heavy sunlight, the garish scintillation of the leaves. Sensing their approach, a pair of birds took off from the shore, flapping under the weight of the light until they caught a current of air and banked downstream. Hoopoe, *Upupa epops*, Perhaps they are the same ones I saw the day I arrived, he thought, surprised that he knew their name. The boat followed the birds, sunlight flashing off the case of the piano.

No one spoke. Nok Lek paddled ahead, singing a soft song. One of the brothers sat on the chest at the back of the raft, a paddle in his hand, his lithe muscles flexed against the current. The other stood at the bow, staring downstream. From the centre of the raft Edgar watched the bank reel past. It was an unworldly feeling, the smooth descent past hills and streams that tumbled down to join the Salween. The raft rode low in the river, and at times water washed up over the logs and touched his feet. When it did this, the sunlight flashed on the waves, hiding the raft beneath a thinness, a fluttering of light. He felt as if he and the piano and the boys were standing on the river.

As they floated, he watched the birds diving and rising on the currents of air, coursing in flight with the river. He wished he was with the Doctor, to tell him that he had seen them, so that the Doctor could add them to his collection of sightings. He wondered what the Doctor was doing now, how they were preparing, if he too would bear arms against the attack. He imagined the Doctor turning back and seeing Khin Myo standing in the flowers. He wondered how much he knew and how much she would tell. No more than twelve hours had passed since he had touched his lips to the warmth of her neck.

And from Khin Myo his thoughts drifted to a memory of the old tuner he had once been apprenticed to, who used to sneak a bottle of wine from a wooden cabinet after they finished work in the afternoons. What a distant memory, he thought, and he wondered where it had come from, and what it meant that now was the moment of its remembering. He thought of the room where he had learned to tune, and the cold afternoons when the old man would wax poetical about the role of a tuner, and Edgar would listen with amusement. As a young apprentice, his master's words had seemed maudlin. Why do *you* want to tune pianos? asked the old man. Because I have good hands and I like music, the boy had answered, and his teacher laughed. Is that it? What more? replied the boy. More? And the man raised a glass and smiled. Don't you know, he asked, that in every piano there lies a song, hidden? The boy shook his head. Just the mumblings of an old man, perhaps, But you see, the movement of a pianist's fingers are purely mechanical, an ordinary collection of muscles and tendons that know only a few simple rules of rate and rhythm. We must tune pianos, he said, so that things as mundane as muscles and tendons and keys and wire and wood can become song. And what is the name of the song that lies in this old piano? the boy had asked, pointing to a dusty upright. Song, said the man, It doesn't have a name, Only song. And the boy had laughed because he hadn't heard of a song without a name, and the old man had laughed because he was drunk and happy.

The keys and hammers trembled with the sway of the current, and in the faint ringing that rose up Edgar again heard a song with no name, a song made only of notes but no melody, a song that repeated itself, each echo a ripple of the first, a song that came from the piano itself, for there was no musician but the river. He thought back to the night in Mae Lwin, to *The Well-Tempered Clavier*, It is a piece bound by strict rules of counterpoint, as all fugues are, the song is but an elaboration of one simple melody, we are destined to follow the rules established in the first few lines.

It makes you wonder, said the old man, lifting his wine glass, why a man who composed such melodies of worship, of faith, named his greatest fugue after the act of tuning a piano.

o

They floated downstream. In the afternoon their progress was slowed by a steep drop through rapids, around which they were forced to portage.

The river widened. Nok Lek tied his dugout to their raft.

In the early evening they stopped at a small deserted village by the edge of the river. Nok Lek paddled the canoe to shore and the two other boys jumped into the shallows, splashing while they pulled the raft. At first it resisted, like a recalcitrant animal, but slowly they pulled it out of the current and into an eddy. They fastened it to a log that lay on the beach. Edgar helped them to untie the piano and lift and carry it to the bank, where they rested it on the sand. The sky was heavy and they made a shelter of woven mats and covered the piano.

At the edge of the buildings the boys found a discarded *chinlon* ball, and began to kick it about in the shallows. Their playfulness seemed incongruous to Edgar, whose thoughts raced one upon the other, Where now are the Doctor and Khin Myo? Has the fighting begun? Perhaps the battle is already over. Only hours ago he had been there, but now he could see no smoke, nor hear gunfire, nor screams. The river was calm, and the sky clear save for the gathering mist.

He left the boys and walked up the bank. It had begun to drizzle lightly, and his feet punched out dry footprints in the moist sand. Curious as to why it had been deserted, he followed a track that ran up from the shore and towards the village. It was a short climb; like Mae Lwin, it had been built close to the river. At the top of the path he stopped.

It was, or had been, a typical Shan village, a collection of huts gathered in disarray, crowded on the bank like a flock of birds. Jungle swelled behind it, flowing down between the huts in tangles of vines and climbing plants. Edgar sensed the burning before he saw it, a mistiness in excess of the rain, a stench of soot that sifted up from the charred bamboo and mud. He wondered immediately how long ago it had been abandoned, if the stench of burning was fresh or but a reincarnation in the rain. Moisture destroys sound, he thought, but enhances smell.

He walked slowly. Details emerged from soot stains and ashes.

Most of the huts were badly burnt, leaving many of the structures standing bare and roofless. In others, walls had collapsed, and roofs of intertwined leaves undulated in half-suspension. Burnt fragments of bamboo lay scattered on the ground. At the base of the lowest houses, a rat ran through the debris, the pattering of its feet violating the silence. There were no other signs of life. Like Mae Lwin, he thought again, but absent were the chickens that pecked at fallen grain on the path. Absent the children.

He walked slowly through the village, passed burnt and abandoned rooms, looted, empty. At the edge of the jungle creepers had already begun to sneak through the interlacings in the walls, the slats in the floorboards. Perhaps it has been abandoned long ago, he thought, but plants come quickly here, as does decay.

It was nearly dark, and mist from the river sifted through the burnt structures. Suddenly Edgar felt afraid. It was too silent. He had not wandered far, but now could not tell the direction back to the river. He walked swiftly through the mass of homes, which seemed to loom, doors like burnt mouths, skeletal, leering, mist collecting on the rooftops and coalescing into droplets, rivulets, running now. The houses weep, Edgar thought, and through the slats of a hut he saw the flames of a fire, lighting the mist, and darkened shadows that swelled against the hillside and danced.

The boys were sitting around the fire when he approached.

'Mr Drake,' said Nok Lek, 'we thought you were lost.'

'Yes, I was, in a way,' said Edgar, pushing his hair from his eyes. 'This village, how long has it been abandoned?'

'This village?' asked Nok Lek and turned to the other boys, who crouched by the opened baskets and rolled small bits of food in their fingers. He spoke to them, and they answered in alternation.

'I don't know. They also don't know. Months maybe. Look how the jungle has come back.'

'Do you know who lived here?'

'They are Shan houses.'

'Do you know why they left?'

Nok Lek shook his head and turned to ask the brothers. They shook their heads in turn and one of them spoke longer.

'We don't know,' said Nok Lek.

'And what did he say?' asked Edgar, motioning to the boy who had spoken.

'He asked why you want to know about this village,' said Nok Lek.

Edgar sat in the sand beside the boys. 'No reason. Only curiosity. It is very empty.'

'There are many abandoned villages like this. Maybe the dacoits did it, maybe British soldiers. It doesn't matter, the people move somewhere else and build again. It has been this way for a long time.' He passed Edgar a small basket of rice and curried fish. 'I hope you can eat with your fingers.'

They sat and ate in silence. One of the brothers began to speak again. Nok Lek turned to Edgar, 'Seing To asked me to ask you where you will go when we reach British territory.'

'Where?' said Edgar, surprised by the question. 'Well, I don't know, really.'

Nok Lek answered the boy, who began to laugh. 'He says that is very strange. He says you are going home, of course, that is what you should answer, unless you forgot the way. He thinks this is very funny.' The two boys were giggling in starts, covering their teeth. One reached over and held the other's arm and whispered something. The second nodded and placed another ball of rice in his mouth.

'Maybe I *have* forgotten the way,' said Edgar, laughing now himself. 'And Mr Seing To, where will he go?'

'Back to Mae Lwin, of course. We will all go back to Mae Lwin.'

'And I'll wager *you* will not get lost.'

'Lost, of course not.' Nok Lek said something in Shan and the three boys began to titter again. 'Seing To says he will get home by the scent of his sweetheart's hair. He says he can smell it even now. He asked if you too have a sweetheart. And Tint Naing said you do. It is Khin Myo, so you will come back to Mae Lwin.'

Edgar protested, thinking, There are terrible truths in the taunts of children, 'No, no . . . I mean, yes I do have a sweetheart, I have a wife, she is in London, in England. Khin Myo is not my sweetheart, you should tell Tint Naing that he should get rid of this silly thought right now.'

The brothers were giggling. One put his arm around the other and whispered to him. 'Stop that,' said Edgar weakly, and felt himself beginning to laugh again as well.

'Seing To says that he wants an English wife. If he goes to England with you, can you find him a wife?'

'I am certain that there are many nice girls who would like him,' said Edgar, playing along with the joke now.

'He asked if you have to be a piano man to have a beautiful wife in England.'

'He asked that? If you have to be a *piano* man?'

Nok Lek nodded, 'You may ignore his questions. He is young, you know.'

'No, that is fine. I rather like that question. Nok Lek, you may tell him that, no, you do not need to mend pianos to have a beautiful wife. Although it doesn't hurt, I imagine.' He smiled, amused. 'Other men, even soldiers, find beautiful wives.'

Nok Lek translated. 'He says it is too bad he must return to his sweetheart in Mae Lwin.'

'It is a pity indeed. My wife has many friends.'

'He said that since he can't meet her, he wants you to describe her. He wants to know if she has yellow hair and if her friends have yellow hair.'

This is getting somewhat silly, thought Edgar, but as his thoughts returned to her, he found himself speaking earnestly. 'Yes, she . . . Katherine – that is her name – she does have yellow hair, it has streaks of brown now, but it is still very pretty. She has blue eyes, and she doesn't wear spectacles, like me, so you can see how lovely they are. She plays music too, much better than I do, you would like very much to listen to her play, I think. None of her friends are as beautiful as she is, but you would still be happy.'

Nok Lek translated for the other two boys, who stopped laughing and stared, enthralled by the description. Seing To nodded sagely and spoke, this time in a sober tone.

'What did he say?' asked Edgar. 'More questions about my wife, I suppose?'

'No. He asked if you wanted to hear a story, but I told him not to bother you.'

Edgar was surprised, 'No, I would be interested. What is the story?'

'Nothing really, I don't know why he is so insistent that I tell you.'

'Do tell me. I am rather curious now.'

'Maybe you have heard it before. It is famous. It is about the *leip-bya* – a Burmese word. It is a Burmese story, so I don't know it well like Seing To. His mother is Burmese. The *leip-bya*, it is a kind of spirit, with wings like a butterfly, but it flies at night.'

'A moth, perhaps.' There was something about these words which bothered him, as if he had heard them before. 'I am unfamiliar with this story,' he said.

'Actually, maybe it is not a story. Maybe just a belief. Some Burmese say that the life of a man lies in a spirit that is like a . . . moth. The spirit stays in his body, a man cannot live without it. The Burmese also say that the *leip-bya* is the reason for dreams. When a man sleeps, the *leip-bya* flies from his mouth and goes about here and there, and sees things on its journey, and these are dreams. The *leip-bya* must always return to a man by morning. This is why the Burmese don't want to wake sleeping people. Perhaps the *leip-bya* is very far away and it cannot return home fast enough.'

'And then?'

'If the *leip-bya* is lost, or if in its journey it is caught and eaten by a *bilu* – how do you say . . . an evil spirit – then this is a man's final sleep.'

The boy reached forward and prodded the fire, sending up sparks.

'And that is the story?'

'I told you – a belief only, but he wanted me to tell you. I don't know why. He is strange sometimes.'

It was warm by the fire, but Edgar felt a chill. From his memory, images of India, of a train ride, a boy falling, a baton flashing in the night.

'A Poet-Wallah,' said the piano tuner softly.

'Sorry, Mr Drake?'

'Oh . . . nothing, nothing. Tell him that it gives me much to think about. Perhaps one day he should be a storyteller.'

As Nok Lek spoke, Edgar stared across the fire at the small boy, who sat in the embrace of his brother. He only smiled, his body lost in the smoke of the fire.

o

The flames grew low and Nok Lek left, disappearing into the darkness and returning with more wood. Across the fire, the brothers had fallen asleep in each other's arms. It began to drizzle, and Nok Lek and Edgar rose and put out the fire. They woke the boys, who mumbled and followed them up to the shelter. It rained several times during the night, and Edgar could hear the drumming of the raindrops on the mats covering the piano's case.

In the morning they struck camp beneath overcast skies. As they floated on, they left the woven mat over the piano. The rain clouds broke in the late morning, the sky cleared. The river, swollen with tributaries, flowed more swiftly. By early afternoon Nok Lek told Edgar that they had passed into land controlled by the principality of Mawkmai, that within two days they would enter Karen country. There the British had border posts on the river, across from northern Siam; there they could stop, they did not need to travel all the way to Moulmein.

It will all be over soon, thought Edgar, It all becomes but a memory. And without being asked by the boys, he removed the woven mat from the piano and stood at it once again, deciding what to play. A finale, for if tomorrow we leave the river, tomorrow the dream ends, and the pianist will become a tuner once again. The raft floated lightly with the current, and the strings rang with the wave of hammers. Ahead, on the bows of the raft, one of the brothers turned to watch.

He did not know what to play, only that he must begin and the song would follow. He thought perhaps he should play Bach again, and tried to think of a piece, but it didn't seem right now. So he closed his eyes and listened for something. And in the vibration of strings, he heard a song that had risen to the sky weeks ago, one night on the Irrawaddy, and then that moonlit evening in Mandalay, when he had stopped to watch the *yôkthe pwè*. The song of loss, the *ngo-gyin*. And he thought, Perhaps this is fitting now. He put his fingers to the keyboard and, as he began to play, the song descended from where it had risen once, sounds that no tuner could have created, sounds that are foreign, new, neither flat nor sharp, for Erards are not constructed to be played on a river, nor to play the *ngo-gyin*.

Edgar Drake played and there was a crack of gunfire and a splash, and another, and another. And only then did he open his eyes, to see two of his companions floating in the water and the third, face up, silent on the deck of the raft.

o

He stood at the piano, the raft spinning lazily from the force of the fallen bodies. The river was quiet; he did not know from where the shots had been fired. Trees on the bank rustled slightly in the wind. Rain clouds drifted slowly through the sky. A parrot called and flew off from the opposite bank. Edgar's fingers remained still, suspended above the keys.

And then, from the right bank, a rustling, and a pair of dugouts pushed off from the shore, making their way steadily downstream to the raft. The piano tuner, who did not know how to control the raft, could do nothing but wait, stunned, as if he too had been shot.

The current was slow and the dugouts gained on him. Each dugout held two men. When they were about a hundred yards away, Edgar saw they were Burman and that they wore Indian army uniforms.

The men said nothing as their dugouts pulled alongside him. One man from each dugout climbed out onto the logs. The arrest was swift, Edgar didn't protest, but only lowered the nameboard over the keys. A rope was tied from the dugouts to the raft, and they paddled to shore.

They were met on the bank by a Burman and two Indians, who escorted Edgar up a long path to a small clearing of guard-houses, above which flew a British flag. They walked to a small bamboo hut and opened the door. There was a chair in the centre of the room 'Sit,' said one of the Indians. Edgar sat. The men left, closing the door. Light shone through the slats in the bamboo. Outside two men stood guard. There were footsteps, the door opened and in walked a British lieutenant.

o

Edgar rose to his feet. 'Lieutenant, what is happening?'

'Sit down, Mr Drake,' the man's voice was severe. He wore a freshly pressed uniform, its angles sharp and starched.

'Lieutenant, those boys were shot. What . . .'

'I said sit *down*, Mr Drake.'

'You don't understand – there has been some dreadful error.'

'This is the last time I will ask you.'

'I—'

'Mr Drake.' The Lieutenant took a step forward.

Edgar stared him in the eyes. 'I demand to know what is going on.' He felt anger rising, replacing shock.

'I am asking you to sit *down*.'

'And I won't. Until you tell me why I am here. You have no right to command me.'

'*Mr Drake.*'

The blow was swift, and Edgar could hear the crack of the man's hand as it crashed across his face. He fell back in his chair. His hands rose to his throbbing temple, sticky with blood.

The Lieutenant said nothing, but only eyed Edgar warily. The tuner nursed his cheek and stared back. The Lieutenant pulled a chair out of the shadows. He sat facing Edgar and waited.

Finally he spoke. 'Edgar Drake, you are under military arrest by order of army headquarters in Mandalay. These papers record the nature of your crimes.' He lifted a stack of folders from his lap. 'You will be held here until an escort arrives from Yawnghwe. From there you will be taken to Mandalay and then to Rangoon for trial.'

Edgar shook his head. 'This must be a mistake.'

'Mr Drake, I have not given you permission to speak.'

'I need no permission.' He rose again from his chair and the Lieutenant rose as well. They faced each other.

'I . . .' Edgar was cut short by another blow. His glasses fell. He stumbled back, almost knocking over the chair. He held onto it for support.

'Mr Drake, this will be much easier if you cooperate.'

Shaking, Edgar reached down and picked up his glasses and put them back on. He stared through them with incredulity. 'You have just murdered my friends. You strike me and you request cooperation? I am in the service of Her Majesty.'

'No longer, Mr Drake. Traitors are not accorded such respect.'

'Traitor?' He felt his head spinning. Now he sat, stunned. 'This is mad.'

'Mr Drake, these charades will get you nowhere.'

'I know nothing. Traitor! On what charges?'

'The charges? Aiding and abetting Surgeon-Major Anthony Carroll, a spy and himself a traitor to the Crown.'

'Anthony Carroll?'

The Lieutenant didn't respond.

Edgar thought he saw a faint sneer on the man's face. 'Doctor Anthony Carroll? Anthony Carroll is Britain's finest soldier in Burma. I have no idea what you are talking about.'

They stared at each other.

There was a knock at the door. 'Come in,' said the Lieutenant.

The door opened and in walked Captain Nash-Burnham. At first, Edgar barely recognized the stout, jovial man he had spent an evening with at the *pwè* in Mandalay. His uniform was dirty and rumpled. His cheeks were unshaven. Deep bags underlined his eyes.

'Captain!' said Edgar, rising once again. 'What is happening?'

The Captain looked at Edgar and then back to the Lieutenant. 'Lieutenant, have you informed Mr Drake of the charges?'

'Only briefly, sir.'

'Captain, tell me. What is going on?'

Nash-Burnham turned to Edgar. 'Sit down, Mr Drake.'

'Captain, I demand to know what is happening!'

'Damn it, Mr Drake! Sit down!'

The Captain's harsh words stung more than the Lieutenant's hand. Edgar lowered himself onto his chair.

The Lieutenant rose and gave Nash-Burnham his seat. He stood behind him.

The Captain spoke slowly. 'Mr Drake, there exist very serious charges against you and Surgeon-Major Carroll. I can advise you that it is in your best interest to cooperate. This is as difficult for me as it is for you.'

The piano tuner said nothing.

'Lieutenant.' The Captain turned to the man behind him, who began to speak.

'We will make this brief, Mr Drake. Three months ago, in a routine review of files at the Home Office in London, a short note written in Russian was found appended to the back of a classified document. The document was traced to Colonel Fitzgerald, the officer in England in charge of Carroll's correspondence, and the man who first contacted you. His desk was searched and other correspondence found. He was arrested as a spy.'

'Russian? I can't see how this has to do with—'

'Please, Mr Drake. You will be well aware that we have been involved in a fierce struggle with Russia for holdings in central Asia for decades. It has always seemed unlikely that Russia would be interested in a territory as distant from its borders as Burma. Yet in 1878, in Paris, there was a meeting between the Honorary Consul of Burma and a seemingly unlikely diplomat, the great Russian chemist Dmitri Mendeleev. The event was noted by British intelligence in Paris, but its implications were poorly understood. The case was soon forgotten, one of many diplomatic courtships that failed to bear fruit.'

'I can't see how this has anything to do with Doctor Carroll, or me, or—'

'Mr Drake,' the Lieutenant growled.

'This is nonsense. You just killed—'

'Mr Drake,' said Nash-Burnham, 'we do not need to tell you any of this. If you don't wish to cooperate, we can send you directly to Rangoon.'

Edgar closed his eyes and clenched his jaw. He sat back, his head pounding.

The Lieutenant continued. 'The arrest of the Colonel led us to investigate others associated with his command. Our results turned up little, except a letter dated 1879 from Surgeon-Major Carroll to Dmitri Mendeleev, entitled "On the astringent properties of the extract of *Dendrobium* of Upper Burma". Although there was nothing in the letter directly to suggest espionage, suspicions were raised, and the presence of copious chemical formulae in the letter suggested code, as of course did the numerous music sheets sent from our office to Surgeon-Major Carroll in Mae Lwin. The very same music sheets which you, Mr Drake, carried there. When we re-examined the music sheets sent *from* Carroll, we found most of the notes unintelligible, suggesting that they contained not song, but some covert communication.'

'This is ridiculous,' Edgar protested. 'I heard that music played. It is Shan music; the scale is completely different. Of course it sounds different on European instruments, but it isn't any sort of code—'

'Naturally, we were loath to level accusations at one of our most successful commanders in Burma. We needed more proof. Then, days ago, we received intelligence reports that Carroll and yourself had met at Mong Pu with both representatives of the Limbin Confederacy and the Bandit Prince, Twet Nga Lu.'

'This much is true. I was there. But—'

'There, Mr Drake, Carroll formed an alliance with the Limbin Confederacy to repel British forces from Yawnghwe and re-establish Shan autonomy.'

'Nonsense!' Edgar sat forward in his chair. 'I was there. Carroll acted without orders, but he had to. He convinced the Confederacy to submit to a peace treaty.'

'Is this what he told you?' Nash-Burnham looked up at the Lieutenant.

'Yes, but I was there. I saw it.'

'Tell me, how much Shan do you speak, Mr Drake?'

For a moment Edgar was silent. Then he shook his head. 'This is ludicrous. I have been in Mae Lwin for nearly three months, and not once has the Doctor shown any indication of insubordination to the Crown. He is a man of principle, a scholar, a lover of art and culture . . .'

'Let's talk about art and culture,' the Lieutenant sneered.

'What do you mean?'

'Why did you go to Mae Lwin, Mr Drake?'

'You know very well why I went to Mae Lwin. I was commissioned by the army to tune an Erard grand.'

'The piano that now floats at the shore of our camp.'

'That is right.'

'And how did you get to Mae Lwin, Mr Drake? Were you escorted there as outlined in your commission?'

Edgar said nothing.

'Mr Drake, I will ask you again. How did you get to Mae Lwin?'

'Doctor Carroll sent for me.'

'So you went against orders?'

'I had come to Burma to tune a piano. Those were my orders. I could not return to Rangoon. When I received Carroll's letter I went. I am a civilian. It was not insubordination.'

'So you went to Mae Lwin.'

'Yes.'

'What type of piano did you go to tune, Mr Drake?'

'An Erard grand. You know that. I don't see what this has to do with this matter.'

'Erard . . . that's an unusual name. What kind of name is that?'

'French. Sebastien Erard was actually German, but he moved to France. I—'

'French? You mean the same French who are building forts in Indo-China?'

'This is ridiculous . . . you are not suggesting that . . .'

'Only a coincidence, or maybe a matter of taste? There are many fine British pianos.'

Edgar looked at Nash-Burnham. 'Captain, I can't believe I am hearing this. Pianos don't make alliances . . .'

'Answer the questions,' said Nash-Burnham flatly.

'How long does it take to tune a piano, Mr Drake?' asked the Lieutenant.

'It depends.'

'All right then, just give me an approximation. In England, what is the most time you have ever spent tuning a piano?'

'Tuning only?'

'Tuning only.'

'Two days, but . . .'

'Two days. Really? Yet you yourself said that you have been in Mae Lwin for nearly three months. If a piano can be tuned in two days, why have you not returned home?'

Edgar was silent. He felt a spinning, a coming apart.

Minutes passed and still he said nothing.

At last Captain Nash-Burnham cleared his throat. 'Will you be able to answer the charges and testify against Surgeon-Major Carroll?'

The piano tuner answered him slowly. 'Captain, what you are saying cannot be true. I was at Mong Pu, I saw them meet. I spoke to Twet Nga Lu. Doctor Carroll was negotiating peace. You will see. I believe him. He is eccentric, but he is a genius, a man who can win hearts with music and science. Only wait, and when the Limbin Confederacy presents its proposal to the Crown, you will believe me.'

'Mr Drake,' the Lieutenant said, 'two days after the meeting in Mong Pu, the Limbin forces, led by the *sawbwa* of Lawksawk, with the support of troops we believe were sent by Carroll, attacked our positions in one of the strongest offensives of their campaign yet. Only by the grace of God were we able to drive them back to Lawksawk and there burn the city.'

Edgar was stunned. 'You destroyed Lawksawk?'

'Mr Drake, we destroyed Mae Lwin.'

TWENTY-THREE

IT WAS DARK. Since the Captain's words, Edgar had not spoken. He sat on the chair in the centre of the room, and the Lieutenant and Captain Nash-Burnham left, the door clattering shut behind them. He heard the hollow resonance of a chain being drawn over the bamboo frame and the scrapings of a key. He heard the men walk away, silent, and he watched the sunlight fade and listened to the sounds of the camp growing dim beneath a swell of insects singing. He touched the inside of his palm, and ran his fingers over the calluses, They are from the tuning hammer itself, Katherine, This is what happens when we hold onto something too tightly.

It was dark and the voices of insects rose up, and through the slats in the wall sifted a heavy air, laden with mist and murmurs of rain. His mind wandered. He thought of the movement of the river, of the shaded banks, and he followed them back, against the current, Thoughts do not obey the laws of falling water. He stood on the banks of Mae Lwin before the bamboo huts and they were burning, flames dancing over them, consuming, leaping to trees, branches dripping fire. He heard screaming, and looked up, thinking, It is only the sound of the jungle, the cries of beetles. He heard the chain running over the bamboo.

The door opened and a figure entered, floating, a shadow as dark as the lightless night. Edgar, hello.

335

The piano tuner said nothing. May I come in, the shadow asked. The door swung softly. I am not supposed to be here, it said, and the tuner answered, Neither am I, Captain.

For a long moment there was silence, before the voice floated once again out of the darkness, I need to talk to you.

I think we have spoken enough.

Please, I am already under suspicion myself, If they know I am here, they will arrest me as well, I have been interrogated. Is that meant to comfort me? This is not easy, Edgar, None of this is easy, I only want to talk. Talk then. Edgar, I want to speak as we spoke before today. As we spoke before you killed the boys. Edgar, I killed no one. Is that so? Three of my companions are dead. I shot no one, I asked them not to kill anyone, but I have been suspended from my command. Nok Lek was fifteen, said Edgar Drake, The others were only boys.

They were silent, and the insects entered again in chorus, and Edgar listened to the trill, The sound is so strong yet it comes only from the scraping of tiny wings.

Edgar, I am risking everything to come here to talk to you.

He heard a deeper rising falling from the insects' call, Those are beats, sound built from the interaction of unequal tones, Sound made from discord, I am surprised I have not heard this before.

I need you to talk to me, think of your wife.

Sound of discord, he thought, and he answered, You have not asked me a question.

We need you to help us find him, said the shadow.

The sound of the insects seemed to cease, the piano tuner lifted his head. I thought you said you captured Mae Lwin. We did, But not Carroll. And Khin Myo? Both escaped, we do not know where they are.

Silence.

Edgar, we only want to know the truth.

It seems in short supply.

Then perhaps you can talk to me and this can end without

more bloodshed, and you can go home. I have told you what I know, Doctor Carroll was a great man.

Those are empty words at times like this. For you, perhaps, certain that is the difference. I only want to know facts, After that we can decide what he was. You mean *you* can decide, It should be clear I have decided already. I don't think that is true, There are many reasons to disappear into the mountains, to bring pianos into the jungle, to negotiate treaties, There are many possibilities.

He loved music.

That is one possibility, There are others, Is it too much to admit that? Admit, perhaps, but not doubt, I have not doubted him. That is not true, We have your letters, You shouldn't lie, It helps no one.

My letters?

Anything you wrote since you left Mandalay.

Those were for my wife, They are my thoughts, I didn't—

You didn't think that we would wonder about a man who disappeared?

She never read them.

Tell me about Carroll, Edgar.

Silence.

Edgar.

Captain, I have questioned *intentions* only, I have not doubted his loyalty. You admit this. Yes I do, but intentions and loyalty are not the same, There is nothing wrong with questions, We mustn't destroy everything we don't understand. Tell me those questions then. My questions. Your questions, Edgar.

Perhaps I wonder why he asked for a piano.

You wonder. Of course, I have asked myself this every day since I left Britain. And have you answered it yet? No, Must I, What does it matter why he requested it, why he requested me, Perhaps it was central to his strategy, Perhaps he only missed music and was alone.

And which do you believe?

I don't think it matters, I have my own thoughts.

As do I.

Tell me your thoughts, Captain.

The shadow shifted, Anthony Carroll is an agent working for Russia, He is a Shan nationalist, He is a French spy, Anthony Carroll wants to build his own kingdom in the jungles of Burma, Possibilities, Edgar, only admit that they are possibilities.

We signed a treaty.

You don't speak Shan.

I saw it, I saw dozens, no hundreds, of Shan warriors bow down before him. And you were not surprised? No. I don't think that is true.

I wondered, perhaps.

And now?

He gave me his word.

And then the Limbin Confederacy attacked our troops.

Perhaps they were traitors to him.

The two were silent, and in the vacuum of their words once again came the sound of the forest.

I believed in him once too, Edgar, Perhaps more than you. In this bloody war of dark intentions, I thought he stood for the best of England. He remained the reason I stayed here.

I don't know if I can believe you now.

I am not asking you to, I am asking you only to dissociate what he was with what we wanted him to be, from what *she* was, from what you wanted *her* to be.

You do not know about her.

Nor do you, Edgar, Was that smile only the hospitality due a guest?

I don't believe that.

Then do you believe her affections were his request, a seduction only to make you stay, Do you believe he didn't know?

There was nothing to know, there was no transgression.

Or he had faith in her. Faith in what? Possibilities only, Think,

Edgar, beyond your fleeting glances, you did not even know what she was to him.

You know nothing about this.

I warned you once, Do not fall in love.

I did not.

No, Perhaps not, Yet she remains entangled in everything.

I don't understand you.

We come and go, armies and pianos and grand intentions, and she remains, and you think that if you can understand her, the rest will come, Think, Was she also your creation, Is the reason you couldn't understand her because you couldn't understand your own imaginings, what you wanted to be, It is not too much to suppose that even our own dreams elude us?

Silence again.

You don't even know what this has meant to *her*, what it is like to be someone else's creation. Why are you telling me that? Because you are different now from when I met you last. What does it matter? We are not talking about me, Captain. When I met you last, you said that you couldn't play the piano. I still cannot. Yet you played for the Shan *sawbwa*.

You don't know that.

You played for the Shan *sawbwa* of Mongnai, and you played *The Well-Tempered Clavier*, but only to the twenty-fourth fugue.

I told you, you cannot know that, I have not told you that.

You began at prelude and fugue no. 4, that is sad, No. 2 is so beautiful, You think that your song would have brought peace, You cannot admit Anthony Carroll is a traitor because it denies everything you have done here.

You don't know that.

I know a lot more about you than you think.

You aren't here.

Edgar, don't destroy that which you cannot understand, Those are your words.

You aren't here, I hear nothing, you are only the crickets' shrill, you are my imagination.

Perhaps, or perhaps only a dream. Perhaps I am only the night playing tricks. Perhaps you picked the lock on the door yourself. Possibilities, no? Perhaps four shots were fired from the bank instead of three. Perhaps I came here not to ask questions for anyone but myself.

And now.

The door is open. Go, I won't stop you, You are escaping alone.

Is this why you came?

I didn't know until now.

I wish to embrace you, but that will answer a question I do not yet want to answer.

You wish to ask if I am real, or but a ghost.

And you wish to answer.

We have been ghosts since this all began, said the shadow.

Goodbye, said Edgar Drake and walked through the open door and into the night.

o

The camp was empty, the guards were all asleep. He moved silently and left the door open behind him. He began heading north, thinking only of putting distance between himself and the camp. Heavy storm clouds covered the moon and the sky was black. He walked.

He ran.

TWENTY-FOUR

ONLY MINUTES AWAY and rain began to fall. He was running, already breathless, when the first drops hit him, one two three points of moisture on warm skin. And then, without hesitation, the sky opened. Like a dam breaking, clouds cracking as if sundered. Water drops falling like spools of unravelling thread.

As he ran, Edgar tried to picture a map of the river, but his memory was blurred. Although they had been travelling for almost two days, they had been slowed by the piano and could not have travelled more than twenty miles. And the wide bends in the river meant that perhaps Mae Lwin was even closer by land. Perhaps. He tried to recall the terrain, but distance suddenly seemed less important than direction. He ran faster through the falling water, his feet kicking up soft mud.

And then, suddenly, he stopped.

The piano. He stood in a small clearing. The rain pounded on his body, stronger now, washing over his hair, running down his cheeks in rivulets. He closed his eyes. He could see the Erard, floating at the shore as the soldiers had left it, shaking in the current. He could see them coming down to take it, pulling it in, grabbing it, pawing it with hands dirty with rifle grease. He could see it sitting in a powdered parlour, revarnished, retuned, and deep inside a piece of bamboo removed and replaced with spruce. He stood still. Each breath brought the warm spray of rain. He opened his eyes and turned. Back to the river.

The bank was heavily forested, making walking almost impossible. At the river, he slipped into the water, its surface shaking with the drumming of the storm. He let the current move him downstream. It wasn't far, and he pulled himself into the shore with the willow branches. Water laced his face. He struggled onto the bank.

Around him the rain crashed through the trees in massive sheets, carried on lashes of wind that whipped through the willows. Tied to a tree on the bank, the raft tugged wildly, the river foaming over its edge, threatening to tear it downstream. The piano was still tied to the deck. They had forgotten to cover it, and the rain beat at the mahogany.

For a moment Edgar stood and felt the current build up against his legs, the sting of water through his shirt. He watched the piano. There was no moon, and in the shifting curtains of rain the Erard trembled in and out of perception, its shape outlined by the droplets that shattered against the dark wood, its legs tensing as it swung with the cant of the raft.

They would realize his absence soon, he thought with rising panic, perhaps they already had and all that was keeping them from finding him was the rain. He waded through the water to where the raft was tied to the tree and dropped to his knees. The rope had already begun to rub the bark from the trunk, the raw pulp out-turned where the fibres had torn it. He fumbled at the knot with his hands, but the raft had pulled it tight and his numb fingers couldn't loosen it.

The raft tugged against its ropes, water gurgled up over the logs, it could capsize at any moment. The wail of the Erard seemed to say this, the shaking of the raft was throwing the hammers back against the strings, the notes crescendoing with the roar of the river. He then remembered the bag he had packed. He led himself along the rope towards the raft and found the large chest. Struggling, he opened it, and reached his arm inside. His fingers touched dry leather and he pulled the bag out.

Fumbling with the ties, he opened it and frantically tore through its contents until he found the penknife. The piano's song was getting louder, all strings at once, all arpeggios. He threw the bag into the water, where it floated briefly in the eddy formed by the current against the raft, and he turned back to the bank. The river caught him off balance, and he fell to his knees, catching himself on the rope. His glasses were knocked from his face, and he caught them in the water and shoved them back on his nose. He reached for the rope, opened the penknife and began to saw, the twine of the rope peeling apart under the tension as each strand was cut, until he reached the final fibres and the rope broke on its own. The raft shook, the piano sang as the hammers were slung up with the energy of the release. The raft paused briefly in the current, turning, then caught in willow branches, their leaves stroking the piano's surface. And then a curtain of rain and the piano was gone.

o

With difficulty, he pulled himself to the bank. He thrust the penknife into his pocket and began again to run. Through the underbrush, slapping branches from his face, hurtling through clearings drenched with walls of rain. In his mind he saw the piano floating, waves of rain pounding its case, the wind tugging the lid open, the two playing a duet on its keys. He saw foam and current pushing it downriver, past other villages. He saw children pointing, fishermen paddling out with their nets.

When lightning struck again, it illuminated a spectacled man, clothes torn, hair plastered to his forehead, running north through the forest, a black mahogany grand piano bobbing south in the current of the river, inlaid with mother-of-pearl, which caught the light. They spun out as if released from a locus, where a guard dog tore forward at its leash, and a reconnaissance team of soldiers frantically gathered their lanterns.

o

His feet pounded the track, splashing mud against his body. The path cut through a dense grove of trees and he followed, riding it into the dark, crashing through branches. He stumbled, fell spinning into the mud. He pulled himself up, pushed forward. Panting.

After an hour he turned towards the river. He wanted to wait until he was closer to Mae Lwin to cross, but he was afraid that the dogs would catch his scent.

The river moved swiftly, swollen with rain. Through the darkness and the downpour he could not see the other side. He hesitated at the edge of the water, trying to discern the far bank. His glasses fogged with rain, blurring his vision even more. He removed them and thrust them into his pocket. For a moment he stood at the edge of the flowing river, seeing nothing but blackness, listening to the current. And then, far in the distance, he heard the bark of a dog. He closed his eyes and dived.

It was calm and quiet beneath the surface of the river, and he swam through the darkness, the current swift but smooth. For a few short seconds he felt safe, the cold water running over his body, his clothes fanning out with each stroke. And then his lungs began to burn. He pushed forward, fighting the need to rise, swimming until he could not endure the burning any longer and shot to the surface, exploding into the rain and wind. For a moment he rested, catching his breath, feeling the river carrying him away, and briefly he thought how peaceful it would be just to give up and let the river carry him. But then lightning flashed again and the whole river seemed to burn, and once again he was swimming with fast wild strokes, and when he felt he couldn't lift his arm again, his knee brushed against rocks, and he opened his eyes to see the shore and a sandy bank. He pulled himself forward onto the bank, and collapsed in the sand.

The rain beat down on his body. He took deep rapid breaths, coughing, spitting up river water. Lightning struck again. He knew he could be seen. He struggled to his feet and began to run.

Through the forest, struggling over fallen logs, crashing arms first, blindly, through the lianas, he pushed forward, panic growing, for he had thought he would hit a trail which followed the left bank south from Mae Lwin, a route which he had never travelled but which he had heard of from the Doctor. But nothing, only forest. He ran down a slope, dodging trees, to a small river, a tributary of the Salween. He tripped and skidded down through the mud, falling instead of running, until the slope evened and he was back on his feet, and across the stream on a fallen tree trunk, up the other side of the bank, scampering, pulling himself up through falling clods of dirt, and at the top of the slope stumbling, falling, back up again running, and then suddenly his feet caught in the brambles of a thicket and he fell again, crashing into the brush. The rain beat down. When he tried to rise, he heard a growl.

He turned slowly, expecting to see the leggings of the British soldiers. But instead, inches from his face, a dog stood, alone, a mangy animal, soaked, its mouth full of broken teeth. Edgar tried to move back, but his leg was caught in the bushes. The animal growled again and lurched forward, its teeth snapping. A hand shot out of the darkness, grabbing the animal by the skin of its neck, pulling it back, barking, angry. Edgar looked up.

There was a man and he was naked except for a pair of Shan trousers, rolled up to reveal sinewy, muscled legs, streaming with water. He didn't speak, and slowly Edgar reached down and untangled his foot from the brush and rose to his feet. For a brief second the two men stood, staring at each other. To each other, we are phantoms, Edgar thought, and lightning flashed again, and the man materialized out of darkness, his body glistening, tattoos winding over his torso, fantastic shapes of jungle beasts, alive, moving, shifting with the rain. And then it was dark again, and Edgar was running through the brush, the forest getting thicker and thicker, until he burst into the open, a road. He wiped the mud from his eyes and turned north running, slowing tired, running again. The rain came down in sheets, washing him.

o

In the east it began to get lighter. Dawn broke. The rain relented and soon stopped. Exhausted, Edgar slowed, walked. The road was an old ox-cart road, overgrown with weeds. Two narrow tracks ran in uneven parallel, slashes cut by the worn edges of cartwheels. He looked for people, but the land was still. Further along, the trees dropped away from the side of the road, becoming scrub-brush, scattered grasses. It began to grow warm.

As he walked, he thought of little, but looked only for signs that could lead him to Mae Lwin. It became hot and he felt beads of sweat mix with the drops of rain in his hair. He began to feel dizzy. He rolled up his sleeves and opened his shirt and in doing so, felt something in his pocket. It was a folded piece of paper, and for a moment he tried to remember what it could be, until he recalled his last moments on the shore with the Doctor and the letter he had given him. He unfolded it as he walked, peeling the wet sheet open. He held it out before him, and stopped.

It was a page torn from Anthony Carroll's copy of *The Odyssey*, a printed text annotated with Indian ink swirls of Shan script, and lines underlined:

My men went on and presently met the Lotus-Eaters,
nor did these Lotus-Eaters have any thoughts of destroying
our companions, but they only gave them lotus to taste of.
But any of them who ate the honey-sweet fruit of lotus
was unwilling to take any message back, or to go

away, but they wanted to stay there with the lotus-eating people, feeding on lotus, and forget the way home.

Through the translucence of the wet page, Edgar saw more writing and turned the paper. In dark strokes the Doctor had scrawled, 'For Edgar Drake, who has tasted'. Edgar read the words again and slowly lowered his hand, so that the page flapped at his side in the breeze. And again he began to walk, now with less urgency, slowly, perhaps it was only because he was tired. In the distance the land rose to become the sky, blurring together in watercolour strokes of distant rainstorms. He looked up and saw the clouds, and it was as if they were burning, the pillows of cotton turning to ash. He felt the water from his clothes evaporate, steaming, leaving him as a spirit does the body.

He passed over a rise, expecting to see the river, or perhaps Mae Lwin, but there was only a long road stretching forward to the horizon, and he followed it. In the distance he saw a single blemish on the open stretch of land and, as he approached, he saw that it was a small shrine. He stopped in front of it. This is an odd place to leave offerings, he thought, There are no mountains or homes, There is no one here, and he stopped and looked over the bowls of rice, the wilted flowers, joss sticks, the now-decaying fruit. There was a statue in the spirit house, a faded wooden sprite with a sad smile and a broken hand. Edgar stopped in the road and took the paper from his pocket, and read it once again. He folded it and tucked it next to the little statue, I leave you a story, he said.

He walked and the sky was light but he saw no sun.

o

In the afternoon he saw a woman in the distance. She carried a parasol.

She moved slowly along the road, and he couldn't tell if she was approaching him or walking away. All was very still, and then from a distant memory came the echoes of a single summer day in England, when he had first taken Katherine's hand in his and they had walked through Regent's Park. They had said little, but watched the crowds and carriages and other young couples. She had departed with only a whisper, My parents are waiting, I will meet you soon, and disappeared across the green beneath a white parasol, which caught the sunlight and danced slightly in the breeze.

He thought now of this moment, the sound of her voice growing clearer, and he found himself walking fast, now a half-run, until from behind him he thought he heard hoofbeats and then a voice, a calling to halt, but he did not turn.

Again, the shout, Halt, and he heard mechanical sounds, clink-ings of metal, but they were distant. There was another shout, and then a shot and then Edgar Drake fell.

o

He lay on the ground, a warmth spreading beneath him, and he turned and stared at the sun, which had come back, for in 1887, as the histories say, there was a terrible drought on the Shan Plateau. And if they don't tell of the rains, or of Mae Lwin, or a piano tuner, it is for the same reason, for they came and vanished, the earth turning dry once more.

The woman walks into a mirage, the ghost of light and water that the Burmese call '*than hlat*'. Around her, the air wavers, splitting her body, separating, spinning. And then she too dis-appears. Now only the sun and the parasol remain.

Author's Note

An old Shan monk sat deep in argument with the Hindu ascetic.

The monk explained that all Shans believe that, when a man dies, his soul goes to the River of Death, where a boat waits to take him across, and this is why, when a Shan dies, his friends place a coin in his mouth, it is to pay the ferryman who takes him to the other side.

There is another river, said the Hindu, which must be crossed before the highest heaven is reached. Everyone sooner or later reaches its shore, and has to search out his own way across. To some it is an easy and quick crossing, to others it is a slow and painful struggle to reach the other side, but everyone gets home at last.

Adapted from Mrs Leslie Milne, *Shans at Home* (1910)

Edgar Drake, Anthony Carroll and Khin Myo, the site of Mae Lwin, and the delivery of an Erard piano to the Salween River are fictional.

Nevertheless, I have attempted to place my story within a true historical context, a task facilitated by the fact that the history and characters of the Shan Revolt are more colourful than any imagination can conjure. All historical briefs in the story, from Burmese history to the Erard piano, contain true information. The pacification of the Shan States represented a critical period in British imperial expansion. The Limbin Confederacy was real and their resistance determined. My story ends in approximately April 1887, when the principality of Lawksawk was occupied by British forces. Following this military victory, British domination of the Southern Shan States was swift. The Limbin Prince surrendered on 13 May and by 22 June A. H. Hildebrand, the Superintendent of the Shan States reported that 'the Southern Shan States have now all given in their submission'.

True historical figures referred to in this work of fiction include the Political Officer to the Shan States, Sir James George Scott, who introduced football to Burma while Principal of St John's School in Rangoon, and Burma to me with his scholarly and sympathetic work, *The Burman*, the first academic piece I read on the country and the inspiration for much of the cultural background to my story. His books, from meticulous descriptions of the *yôkthe pwè* in *The Burman*, to the encyclopedic compendium of local histories in *The Gazetteer of Upper Burma and the Shan States*, to the collection of his letters, *Scott of the Shan Hills*, were an invaluable source of information, as well as an endless pleasure to read.

Dmitri Mendeleev, the father of the periodic table, did meet the Burmese consul in Paris. What they discussed is still unknown.

Maung Tha Zan was a star of Burmese *pwè*. He was not as skilled as Maung Tha Byaw.

Belaidour, which Berbers call *adil-ououchchn*, is known to Western science as *Atropa belladonna*, and is used primarily for hearts that beat too slowly. It earned its species name because its berries also make women's eyes wide and dark.

Anthony Carroll's suspicions about the spread of malaria were correct. That the mosquito carries the disease would be proven ten years later by another Englishman, Dr Ronald Ross, also in the Indian Medical Service, but at a different hospital, in the city of Secunderabad. His use of 'a plant that came from China' was also prescient. Qinghaosu is now used to make artemisinin, a potent antimalarial drug, whose efficacy was 'rediscovered' in 1971.

All the *sawbwa*s are real and are still local heroes in the Shan States. The meeting in Mong Pu is invented.

As for Twet Nga Lu, the Bandit Prince was captured at last by the British forces, and the description of his death by Sir Charles Crosthwaite, in *The Pacification of Burma* (1912), is worth quoting here:

> Mr. Hildebrand was instructed therefore to send Twet Nga Lu back to Mongnai to be tried by the Sawbwa. On the way he attempted to escape and was shot by the Beluchi guard escorting him. The men returned to Fort Stedman and reported what had happened, saying that they had buried him on the spot . . .
>
> All doubt on this point was removed afterwards. The scene of the brigand's death was in the wooded hills which border Mongpawn. The day after he was shot, a party of Shans from Mongpawn disinterred, or rather lifted, the corpse from its shallow grave, and shook off the loose earth. The head was cut off, shaved, and sent to Mongnai, and exhibited there at the north, south, east, and west gates of the town during the absence of the Assistant Superintendent at Fort Stedman. The various talismans were removed from the trunk and limbs. Such charms are generally small coins or pieces of metal, which are inserted under the skin. These would be doubly prized as having been enshrined in the flesh of so noted a leader, and no doubt were eagerly bought up. The body was then boiled down, and a concoction known to the Shans as *mahe si* was obtained, which is an unfailing charm against all kinds of wounds. So valuable a 'medicine' did not

long remain in the hands of the poor, and soon found its way into some princely medicine-chest . . . Such was the end of Twet Nga Lu. It was certainly, so far as the body is concerned, most complete.

Or, as Lady Scott, who edited *Scott of the Shan Hills* (1936), wrote of the Bandit Prince, 'This was the wholesale end of this remarkable man.'

Details of Shan myths and culture, local medicine and natural history I collected in Burma and Thailand and from the literature of the period. While I believe most of the literature I encountered to be well intentioned and well researched, I fear that many of the sources contain prejudices or simple misinterpretations common to Victorian England. For this novel, however, what Victorians thought to be fact before the turn of the century is more important to me than what is known to be fact now. Thus I apologize for any factual inconsistencies that have resulted from this decision, an example of which looms in the paragraph cited above: the relationship of the Kachin *mahaw tsi* used by Doctor Carroll, which according to the great plant hunter, Frank Kingdon-Ward, was made from a species of *Euonymus*, and Crosthwaite's etymologically similar *mahe si* is still a mystery to me, yet clearly intriguing.

I am indebted to countless sources. Among the books I found indispensable, in addition to those by Scott, Kingdon-Ward, and Crosthwaite were: Ni Ni Myint, *Burma's Struggle Against British Imperialism (1885-1895)* (1985) for its discussion of the Shan Revolt from a Burmese perspective; Mrs Leslie Milne, *Shans at Home* (1910), a wonderful ethnography of the Shan; and Ma Thanegi, *The Illusion of Life: Burmese Marionettes* (1994) for its details of the *yôkthe pwè*. Thant Myint-U, *The Making of Modern Burma* (2001) is worth noting for its discussion of the Anglo-Burmese wars, a refreshing analysis of many opinions long held by historians, as well as by characters in my book. Finally, I am indebted to William Braid White, *Piano*

Tuning and Allied Arts (1946) for rounding out Edgar Drake's technical skills.

○

On a final note, after a year studying malaria along the southern Thai-Myanmar border, when I was well into writing this story, I journeyed north to the small town of Mae Sam Laep, where the swollen waters of the Salween River etch the border, far downstream from the imaginary site of Mae Lwin. There I travelled on a long-tailed trading boat through the wooded, silent shores, where we stopped at Karen villages hidden in the forest. It was hot that afternoon and the air was still and silent, but at a muddy trading post on the banks of a small river a strange sound rose up from the thick brush. It was melody, and before the motor kicked in and we moved away from the shore, I recognized it as the sound of a piano.

Perhaps it was only a recording, creaking out on one of the dusty old phonographs that can still be found in some of the more remote markets. Perhaps. It was, however, terribly out of tune.

Acknowledgements

The research for this book would have been impossible without the help of the staff at the following organizations: in Thailand, the Mahidol University Faculty of Tropical Medicine and Ranong Provincial Hospital; in the United Kingdom, the British Library, the Guildhall Library, the National Gallery and the Museum of London; in the United States, the Henry Luce Foundation, the Strybing Arboretum and Botanical Gardens in San Francisco, and the libraries at Stanford University, the University of California at Berkeley and the University of California at San Francisco. The names of the many locations in Myanmar (Burma) that inspired this story are too numerous to mention, but without the warmth extended to me by the people throughout that country, this book would have never been written.

I wish to acknowledge individually the support of Aet Nwe, Guha Bala, Nicholas Blake, Liza Bolitzer, Mary Lee Bossert, William Bossert, Riley Bove, Charles Burnham, Michael Carlisle, Liz Cowen, Lauren Doctoroff, Ellen Feldman, Jeremy Fields, Tinker Green, David Grewal, Emma Grunebaum, Fumihiko Kawamoto, Elizabeth Kellogg, Khin Toe, Peter Kunstadter, Whitney Lee, Josh Lehrer-Graiwer, Jafi Lipson, Helen Loeser, Sornchai Looareesuwan, Gene McAfee, Jill McCorkle, Kevin McGrath, Ellis McKenzie, Mimi Margaretten, Feyza Marouf, Maureen Mitchell, Joshua Mooney, Karthik Muralidharan, Myo,

Acknowledgements

Gregory Nagy, Naing, Keeratiya Nontabutra, Jintana Patarapo-
tikul, Maninthorn Phanumaphorn, Wanpen Puangsudrug, Derek
Purcell, Maxine Rodburg, Debbie Rosenberg, Nader Sanai,
Sidhorn Sangdhano, Bonnie Schiff-Glenn, Pawan Singh, Gavin
Steckler, Suvanee Supavej, Parnpen Viriyavejakul, Meredith
Warren, Suthera Watcharacup, Nicholas White, Chansuda Wongs-
richanalai, Annie Zatlin, and the countless others in Myanmar and
Thailand who told me their stories, but whose names I never
learned.

For advice on Burma, I am especially indebted to Wendy
Law-Yone, Thant Myint-U, and Tint Lwin. Two piano tuners
helped to train Edgar Drake: David Skolnik and Ben Treuhaft.
Ben's experience tuning pianos in Cuba, and time spent repairing
an 1840 Erard grand once played by Liszt, made him a perfect
adviser for another grand in another tropic. Of course, all errors
with regard to Myanmar, piano tuning, or any other matters are
entirely my own.

Finally, several people have been particularly devoted to this
book. My deepest gratitude and affection go to Christy Fletcher
and Don Lamm for their advice and guidance on all matters, and
to Maria Rejt at Picador, in the UK, for helping to make Edgar
Drake a truer Londoner. Robin Desser at Knopf has been a
wonderful editor; her insightful and incisive comments, support,
and sense of humour leave me, after so many days spent discussing
nothing but words, with a profound loss of them to express my
true appreciation.

From the day I first told them about a piano by a river my
parents, Robert and Naomi, and sister Ariana have welcomed
Edgar Drake into the family and encouraged my imagination to
leave home. My greatest love and thanks go to them.